Dear Reader,

I'm beyond thrille
of the Sweetblood
a group of vampire
Northwest. The wo
one, where Guardia   protect humans from
Darkbloods—vicious members of their race who
still kill humans like their ancestors did and sell their
blood on the vampire black market. The rarest, called
Sweet, is very addictive and commands the highest
price.

It's hard to believe that just last year the series began
with *Bonded by Blood*. Don't worry if you haven't read
the other books, though. I wrote each one to stand
alone.

When I first met Tristan Santiago, the region
commander, he stormed onto the pages of *Bonded*
and stole the show. He's hotheaded and very hard to
ignore.

Because I own horses, I was reminded of the dynamics
of herd behavior as I wrote Santiago's story. In a
nutshell, the horse that persuades the other horses to
move their feet and get out of his way is the dominant
one. I had a horse like this once. He was sweet to
my daughter and me, but when he was around other
horses, he expected them to move out of his space.
And if they didn't, he bit or kicked them.

That's Santiago. If he gives you an order, he expects
you to obey, and if you don't… Well, let's just say it's
not going to be pretty.

Once, my horse encountered another who seemed immune to his authority, who didn't care that my horse thought he was in charge. It really threw the poor guy for a loop. He was confused and wasn't himself for a while.

Guess what? Roxy Reynolds has that same effect on Santiago. Unlike everyone else around him, she isn't impressed with his authority and does things her way. She doesn't jump when he tells her to jump. She gets under his skin like no one else has ever done, which upsets his entire world and sense of self. And then, of course, he falls madly in love with her.

As you can imagine, I had a great time torturing Santiago with Roxy. I hope you enjoy reading their story as much as I enjoyed writing it.

All my best,

Laurie

LAURIE LONDON

SEDUCED by BLOOD

HARLEQUIN®

entertain, enrich, inspire™

If you purchased this book without a cover you should be aware that this book is stolen property. It was reported as "unsold and destroyed" to the publisher, and neither the author nor the publisher has received any payment for this "stripped book."

Recycling programs
for this product may
not exist in your area.

ISBN-13: 978-0-373-77669-6

SEDUCED BY BLOOD

Copyright © 2012 by Laurie Thompson

All rights reserved. Except for use in any review, the reproduction or utilization of this work in whole or in part in any form by any electronic, mechanical or other means, now known or hereafter invented, including xerography, photocopying and recording, or in any information storage or retrieval system, is forbidden without the written permission of the publisher, Harlequin HQN, 225 Duncan Mill Road, Don Mills, Ontario M3B 3K9, Canada.

This is a work of fiction. Names, characters, places and incidents are either the product of the author's imagination or are used fictitiously, and any resemblance to actual persons, living or dead, business establishments, events or locales is entirely coincidental.

This edition published by arrangement with Harlequin Books S.A.

For questions and comments about the quality of this book, please contact us at Customer_eCare@Harlequin.ca.

® and TM are trademarks of Harlequin Enterprises Limited or its corporate affiliates. Trademarks indicated with ® are registered in the United States Patent and Trademark Office, the Canadian Trade Marks Office and in other countries.

www.Harlequin.com

Printed in U.S.A.

To Tyler. I'm very proud of you!

Acknowledgments

First, I'd like to thank you, the readers of the Sweetblood series. Without your enthusiasm, *this* would not be possible.

Thanks to my critique partner, my sister Becky, who lovingly and gently tells me when I suck. And my beta readers, Janna, Mandy, Kathy, Shelley and Kandis, whose shrewd and thoughtful assessments have saved me a lot of heartache down the road. I love you guys!

To my wonderful editor, Margo Lipschultz, who seems to "get" me even when I don't "get" myself. To all the people behind the scenes at Harlequin HQN, thanks for all that you do. And to the talented folks in the art department who make the awesome Sweetblood covers: you rock!

Much thanks to Cherry Adair, Delilah Marvelle, Larissa Ione and Alexis Morgan for your friendship and your words of wisdom. I am so very grateful.

To the Cherryplotters, thanks for your creativity and inspiration.

To my GIAM buddies, my friends at Romance University, my GWRWA chapter mates and the Bookinville ladies, thanks for all your support.

And finally, to my husband, Ted, and two children: I love the three of you very much.

**Also available from
LAURIE LONDON
and Harlequin HQN**

Bonded by Blood
Embraced by Blood
"Enchanted by Blood"
in *A Vampire for Christmas*
Tempted by Blood

**Don't miss an ebook exclusive Sweetblood novella,
available now:**

Hidden by Blood

SEDUCED
by BLOOD

CHAPTER ONE

WHEN ROXANNE REYNOLDS rounded the corner in her rental car, the last thing she expected to see in the headlights was a half-naked man stumbling on the side of the road.

She slammed on her brakes, pulled the car to the shoulder and fumbled to find the emergency flasher switch. Not only was this section of the Sea to Sky highway a terrible place to stop, but it wasn't exactly somewhere a sane person would be taking a walk, especially after midnight.

With his shirt ripped down the front and one of the sleeves missing, the man held up a hand to shield his face from the glare.

Her first thought was that he'd been involved in a car accident. But when she noticed he wasn't wearing shoes, she nixed that conclusion. Maybe a wild animal had attacked him. Given how remote this area was—the last town she passed had to be ten miles back—it wouldn't be too hard to imagine. She wasn't certain what sorts of predators lived in this part of British Columbia, but surely a bear or a mountain lion would be capable of taking down a full-grown man.

She found the switch and jumped from the car. But

when she got her first big whiff of the cool night air, she knew instantly that it wasn't an animal.

Although some would argue that a vampire *was* an animal.

The sweet smell of the man's blood assaulted her senses, making her gums ache as her fangs prepared to drop. Running toward him, she automatically shut down her body's natural instincts to his very rare and highly addictive blood-type and the sensation dissipated. Given her work as a scent tracker, she'd followed the trail of many sweetbloods, but unlike most vampires, she could control how they affected her without much difficulty.

The guy stumbled and fell to his knees just as she got to him, his legs clearly unable to support his weight any longer. He must have been running on pure adrenaline.

"Are you okay?" she asked, pulling him back to his feet. "What happened to you?" She'd come all the way from Florida to help out a friend, but this seriously wasn't how she'd expected her stint in the Northwest to begin.

Blood splatters covered what was left of his long-sleeved shirt, scratches crisscrossed his exposed skin—including his scruffy, somewhat pimply face—and an IV line dangled from a piece of tape on his arm. The fact that he was young, barely out of his teenage years, didn't surprise her. Sweetbloods rarely made it past the age of twenty, thirty at the outside, before a vampire somewhere came across them. The Darkblood Alliance made buckets of money selling vials of Sweet on the vampire black market. With just one taste, even those who had never killed a human before were likely to get carried away. A fact she knew firsthand but wished she didn't.

"They tried…to kill me," he choked, leaning heavily on her arm.

She didn't need to ask who—she had a pretty damn good idea who'd do something like this. "Where were you being held? How far away?"

"I don't know. It feels like…I've been…running forever." He put his hands on his knees, trying to catch his breath. "A few kilometers on the other…side of the creek…just past those trees." Without looking, he stabbed a thumb over his shoulder.

Thick, old-growth forest pressed in on them from both sides of the highway. Unaccustomed to trees this tall and roads this twisty, she felt claustrophobic not being able to see long distances around her.

"I'm so dizzy…they took a lot…of blood." He pressed a fist to his forehead and his body swayed slightly. She held his arm tighter to steady him. "I know this is going to sound crazy but they…they were vampires." His gaze darted around wildly as if he expected them to pop out from the woods or drop from the trees.

That didn't surprise her in the slightest. She was half-tempted to track his captors herself, but that would mean the young man would have to stay here by himself. After what he'd just been through, she couldn't in good conscience do that to him, even if his memory would get wiped later.

"Okay, in the car. Let's get you out of here."

Other than the residual smell on the man's clothes, she didn't detect any active Darkblood odor in the immediate vicinity, but that could change in the blink of an eye. Maybe they hadn't discovered their prisoner was gone yet. If they had, they'd have quickly shadow-moved in the darkness, easily following the sweetblood scent, and retrieved him. Best to get out of here now.

"I'm serious," he said forcefully, as if she didn't believe him. His teeth chattered and his hands shook. "They kidnapped m-m-me in Vancouver…and brought me up here. They had fangs…black eyes…even their whites were black."

Darkbloods for sure, then, and not some random rogue who got carried away when he ran into a sweetblood. A vampire's eyes would turn black over time when they only consumed blood. She put her arm around him, trying to comfort him as she steered him to the car. He was going into shock and he needed medical attention. If only there was a blanket in the car to keep him warm, but all she had were a few light jackets in her suitcase. She took off her hoodie and wrapped it around his shoulders, trying not to think about how insanely cold she was. "What's your name?"

"M-Mason."

"Well, Mason, I believe you."

His eyes widened. "You…you do? You're not just saying that?"

"Nope." And then, because she didn't want to sound patronizing, she added, "I know it's a fact because I've seen this before." She wasn't about to tell him she was a vampire and that she'd rescued lots of sweetbloods, including one an old lover had almost killed. The truth was necessary only up to a point. "Now come on."

Unarmed and most likely outnumbered because Darkbloods worked in pairs, she wasn't eager to confront the enemy if they stepped out of the darkness right now.

She helped Mason into the passenger seat, careful not to touch or focus on the bruises and scratches that ran up and down his arms. It was best to avoid contact with any of his blood, whether she trusted herself or not. "You're going to be just fine. I promise."

The medical staff at region headquarters would see that he was healthy before returning him to his normal life, the memory of his ordeal wiped from his head, and their agents could deal with the Darkblood situation themselves.

A pair of headlights pierced the darkness. Just her luck. They had company. Positioning herself between the young man and the roadway, she tried to block him from view. The last thing she needed was more human witnesses.

A red pickup slowed down and a man with a ball cap stared out at her. When she noticed the circular insignia on the side, her breath caught in her throat.

Cascade Search and Rescue.

Great. What were the chances that they'd simply drive past if they thought someone needed help? And what if they were actually out looking for this guy?

On the drive up here, she vaguely remembered hearing a radio bulletin about two hikers who'd failed to report back to their Whistler hotel, prompting authorities to organize a search. Maybe these guys were headed up there.

She smiled and gave a cheery wave to signify everything was okay. Manipulating the memory of one human who'd had an encounter with vampires was one thing, but multiple humans? Not only was she not skilled enough to perform a group mind wipe, but given that she hadn't taken any blood in days, most likely she didn't have the energy needed to perform one.

"Thank God, the authorities," Mason said. "Someone needs to…go after those monsters…who tried to…kill me before they do this…to someone else."

"I agree." The authorities, yes, but not the human variety.

Darkbloods often brought human prey back to their dens, where they drained their blood and disposed of the bodies. Given the IV line, that clearly was what they'd been doing to Mason. He was lucky to have gotten out of there, especially considering he was a sweetblood. But it was odd they'd locate their den in this remote area and in the same vicinity as the region office. This wasn't exactly a good place for an illegal blood siphoning operation and it was far from their clientele, who tended to stick close to larger cities where there were more humans to feed from.

Also, Darkbloods in northern areas weren't normally as brash or bold as they were down South. Because ultraviolet light in the Pacific Northwest was low for most of the year, the energy in the human blood supply wasn't as volatile. This in turn led to a less aggressive nature in the small vampire population who fed from them, including Darkbloods.

At least, that's how it worked in theory. She'd never been far north enough to experience it for herself.

Mason's hands couldn't fasten the seat belt, so she snapped it for him. But before she could jog around to the driver's side, she noticed that the red truck had eased off the road in front of them and turned around.

Damn. Her stomach sank like a pair of concrete shoes. They were coming to help.

Whatever happened to humans who didn't want to get involved? The kind of people who could watch a mugging from a balcony and not call the police. The kind who would hide behind a Dumpster, either too scared or too indifferent to come to the aid of a dying man who had helped them. It was just her luck that the truck was *not* being driven by that kind of person. An image of a similar situation many years ago stirred in her mind, but that one didn't involve humans. Cowardliness and apathy were common traits in both races.

But then she considered the flip side. The problem with being too concerned was that you could get sucked into doing something you hadn't planned, which, ironically, was what had brought her here in the first place.

Her friend and former student, Lily DeGraff, had told her about a pre-wedding trip she was going to take with her fiancé and daughter—a trip that would have to be postponed because of her work with the Agency, the enforcement arm of the Governing Council.

Alfonso, her future groom, was excited to show them his ancestral home in the Hill Country of Spain as well as reconnect with his sister to invite her to the wedding this summer. Lily had dreaded telling Alfonso they'd need to change their plans.

As she listened to Lily's predicament, Roxy had recalled the last time she'd been in Spain. She'd also gone with a man she loved, but she didn't mention anything about it to Lily at the time. Some memories were best left in the past. No one had known the truth about Ian. Not their coworkers in the Agency, not his friends. Only his mother knew, and Roxy had vowed not to tell another soul. If the truth got out, it would've destroyed his family.

"He's going to be so disappointed," Lily had confided. "He's been looking forward to this trip for a long time. I'm not sure how I'm going to make it up to him."

Though Roxy had never met Lily's region commander before, Tristan Santiago had a reputation for being a hard-ass and totally inflexible. Maybe that was the issue. He wouldn't give Lily the time off. Roxy had worked with men like him, men who enjoyed their authority and weren't afraid to use it. Lily's commander needed to understand that he couldn't keep treating his people this way. Technically, Lily didn't actually work for him—she provided tracking services to his region. He couldn't expect to—

"No, it's not that," Lily had said when Roxy voiced

her opinion. "Santiago would probably let me go if I asked. I mistakenly scheduled myself to teach a Tracker Academy prep-class and my students are counting on me."

Hearing the unhappiness in her friend's voice, Roxy had thought once more about her own long-ago trip. The beautiful countryside. The gracious people. The food. The vibrant energy.

So she'd offered to teach the class in Lily's place.

Getting involved did have its price, she thought now, and she sure as hell was paying for it. A dog barked inside the red truck as a man climbed out. Must be a canine search and rescue team. Good. She related better to people who liked animals.

She rubbed the onyx pendant around her neck, a habit she had when she needed a little luck. God, it was arctic-cold up here, especially without that thin sweatshirt. When had she last seen her breath fog in front of her face like this? If she had known she'd be outside, she'd have worn something warmer…like a heavy parka, ten pairs of wool socks, sheepskin boots, fuzzy mittens—

"What seems to be the trouble?" the man called, adjusting his ball cap as he approached. Mr. Search and Rescue wore jeans, cowboy boots and one of those quilted flannel shirts that acted like a coat. Clearly, a local who was used to the weather.

"Just picking up a guy who…ran out of gas." She rubbed her bare arms, trying to get warm.

"Out of gas? From what we could see when we drove

past, we thought a bear had mauled him. You know, they have a serious black bear problem up here."

"Yes, I've heard that." Not really, but she didn't want him to go into a lengthy explanation about animal/human interactions. She just wanted to be on her way with as little conversation as possible.

"So, he's okay?"

"Yeah, he's—" Something pricked the veil of her awareness and she jerked her head to the left. Something way off in the distance through the trees. A slight breeze ruffled her hair as her tracker senses stretched into the night like an arrow shot from a bow. Although the scents here were much different from those back home, there was no mistaking this stench.

Darkbloods. Two of them. Somewhere deep in the forest.

From the strength of the smell, she estimated they were a mile or two away. If they were shadow-moving, she wouldn't have much time.

"He's fine," she said hastily.

The man scowled, his eyes narrowing to slits. "What's wrong? Are you sure you're okay?"

"Yeah, but we've got to get out of here."

One eyebrow shot up. "I'm getting the feeling there's more to this story than just a guy running out of gas."

She didn't have the luxury of time to come up with a reasonable explanation as to why they needed to hightail it out of here. Things wouldn't be pretty if they stayed.

She started to reach for him, intending to give him a mental push to get back into his rig and drive away—if she could even manage it right now—when someone called out from the truck.

"What's going on? Do you need me to call an aid car?"

Damn. The other guy with him.

She'd have to come up with another plan. If Darkbloods showed up while they were all still here, she'd have to take care of them herself and wipe the minds of the witnesses before they could alert the human authorities. At one point in her life, she'd have easily been able to take down a couple of Darkblood losers, but she was out of practice. She was a teacher now. She hadn't been a field agent in years.

And if the DBs were high on Sweet... Shit.

So she did the only other thing she could think of.

Grabbing her cell phone, she called the one person who'd be able to help out right now, who happened to be the last one she wanted to ask.

THE GUY STARING up at Tristan Santiago was pleading for his life, but that wasn't the reason he decided not to kill him.

Instead, Santiago yanked him to his feet and slammed him against the wall. The Darkblood clutched at his hands, trying to break the hold, but it was no use. Santiago outweighed him by at least forty pounds and was a helluva lot stronger.

"How did you know where to find us?" Santiago hissed through his bared fangs.

"What?"

"My men. How did you know we were waiting for you?"

"I don't know what you're talking about."

Had it been two weeks, two days, even two hours ago, he'd be handling things differently right now. He'd have unsheathed Misery, plunged the silver blade into the guy's heart muscle, and watched him turn to ash. But as it turned out, he needed a few answers first.

"Oh, really." It was a statement, not a question. The guy was bullshitting him and they both knew it.

There was no way DBs should've known Guardians would be coming. Their intel about the location of this den came through only yesterday. Now, one of his men had been injured on a job that should have been routine.

Misery hung heavily beneath his coat. He pulled out the blade, placing the point just inches away from the guy's eye. Most Darkbloods wore sunglasses to hide the fact that the whites of their eyes were black, but this one didn't. Either that or he'd lost his during the chase.

"Don't kill me. I swear to God, I don't know."

"I'm not planning to kill you." The guy relaxed ever so slightly and Santiago smiled, flashing his own set of fangs again. "But don't think I'm being nice. I don't do nice."

His phone vibrated in his pocket but he ignored it. Instead, he let Misery's razor-sharp point prick the skin and a small bead of blood teardropped down the guy's cheek.

"Please, no," the bastard pleaded.

The blade wanted to go deeper and Santiago considered letting it. No one fucked with his people. No one.

The lone overhead light snapped and fizzled as its filament started to fail, creating grotesque shadows on the curved cement walls. Soon they'd be enveloped in total darkness, which would make shadow-moving much easier. Footsteps pounded in the tunnel behind him as one of his men approached.

"What's wrong?" Kip Castile glanced at the two of them, confused. Guardians didn't show mercy when it came to their enemies. Justice was swift and unforgiving. "Why didn't you charcoal him? Wait. You're saving him for me, aren't you?" With a cold smile, the young Guardian-in-training withdrew his stiletto and advanced on the prisoner.

What a sadistic son of a bitch. *I knew I liked the kid.*

The Darkblood cringed, tried to take a step sideways, but Santiago held him tight. "No," he told Kip. "He is not to be injured."

At least, not right now and not any more than he had been already. Let the guy be relieved for a while, get him to drop his guard, then they'd threaten him again, but with more force. This untrained Darkblood lackey would soon be singing like a canary.

Kip dropped his hand and tapped the flat part of the knife impatiently against his black cargo pants. The kid was like a runner in the starting blocks, itching to move, to do something. Luckily, he wouldn't have to wait for long.

A quick pat down revealed the Darkblood's black

trench coat was filled with a shitload of syringes and vials. Santiago yanked it off and tossed it aside. "Planning on a little door-to-door selling, huh? 'Ding dong, Darkblood calling.'"

"I don't know what you're talking about." The guy sneered, making Santiago reconsider his decision to keep him alive. He should be pleading for his life, not acting cocky.

Maybe he should let Kip waste him. Or better yet, he'd do it himself and show the kid how it was done. Misery suddenly felt a little lighter in his hand, as if urging him to continue on with this way of thinking.

"Jet's gonna be okay," Kip said, looking at his mobile device. "Says it's a surface injury. The blade didn't go deep."

Damn. That's right. He couldn't charcoal the guy. Santiago needed him alive to figure out what he knew about the operation that could've killed one of his men.

"Didn't your mama ever teach you to tell the truth?" He shoved the DB face-first against the wall again, spread-eagling his legs using the oh-so-gentle toe of his boot. With a hand on his back, he searched him for weapons.

Kip piped up. "Shouldn't you—"

Santiago shot him a cold look that said "Shut your piehole."

Sure, regulation stipulated he put on a pair of latex gloves to protect him from the effects of any silver he may find, but his way was faster.

That was the problem with having a new guy shadow

him. They knew all the rules and were puppydog-eager to demonstrate their knowledge. Like they were being tested. Which, of course, they were, but fieldwork was more flexible than that. You did things by instinct, by what felt right. Not by some rulebook you memorized in a classroom setting for a test you were about to take on a computer. Santiago had never let himself get caught up in bullshit created by the so-called experts, and his wariness had served him well over the years. Street smarts won out over book smarts when lives were at stake.

Kip mumbled something under his breath that Santiago didn't quite catch and didn't care to either.

He started to turn his attention back to the DB, when the guy jolted sideways away from the wall and made a move for the weapon at his feet. Before he could pick it up, Santiago stomped on his fingers and kicked the knife away. It spun against the cement floor, hitting the wall with a metallic *ting* that echoed down the corridor. The guy howled, tried to pull free, but trapped beneath Santiago's foot, he wasn't getting anywhere. His efforts got noticeably weaker as he squirmed on the pavement.

"See the metal strip on the toe of my boot there?" Santiago twisted it as if he was grinding out a cigarette butt. The man groaned. "Answer me."

"Y-yes."

"It's on the heel, too. But it's not steel. It's silver."

"What…what do you want from me?"

"The boots get 'em every time," Santiago said over his shoulder to Kip. With hands on his hips, he turned his attention back to the DB loser. "So you lost the attitude, have you? Ready to talk now?"

"Yes," the guy groaned. "Just get off my hand."

Santiago pretended not to hear and kept his foot firmly planted. "Tell me how you knew we would be at the landing."

"I told you, I don't know. We were just there." His gaze darted furtively to the left a few times as he bit the inside of his cheek.

You didn't need to be a shrink to figure out that this guy knew something and was trying to cover it up. "Well, you'd better pray you remember something. Next time, I'm not going to be as forgiving as I am right now." He quickly cuffed the asshole with silver-lined cuffs, hauled him to his feet and shoved him at Kip. "Take him to one of the holding cells." Maybe after a little persuasion, the guy's memory would improve.

"Me? You want *me* to take him?"

A flash of anger heated Santiago's veins. "Are you questioning me, boy?"

A muscle in Kip's jaw ticked and his nostrils flared slightly. For a split second, he thought the kid was going to argue with him. Tell him it wasn't his job. That it was for the capture team to bring in a prisoner, not a Guardian. Jesus Christ. Did youngsters these days have no respect for their elders? Not that Santiago was all that old, but he might have to show the kid a thing or two about respect.

An old friend's words rang in his head. *Respect is earned, Santiago, not demanded.*

Ha. You respected what you feared.

Then, just like that, Kip's brain started functioning again. He turned away and grabbed the DB's arm. "No, sir."

Smart kid. Santiago wasn't known to react kindly to those who didn't do exactly what he ordered. He expected people to do what he told them to do without asking any questions. And to do it with a damn smile on their faces. He didn't lead by committee or a show of hands. In these parts, his orders were as good as the laws written in the old edicts. You did what you were told or you were out. It didn't get any simpler than that.

As Kip led the loser away, Santiago stooped to pick up the DB's weapon, careful not to touch the business end. He was about to tuck it into his weapons belt then check his phone to see who'd been trying to get ahold of him, when something about the blade drew his attention. From the uneven marks, it appeared to be hand-forged, not machine made, and the hilt was obviously carved by a talented artisan.

How strange. DBs were not known for their high-quality weaponry, but this thing was gorgeous. A piece of friggin' art. He turned it over in his hands. When the overhead light caught on the metal, it flashed in his eyes like a powerful mirror, making his pupils contract.

Holy shit. He blinked a few times, wondering if it was just his imagination, but he angled the blade just so, the light flashed and his pupils tightened again.

Just as a real pearl could be distinguished from the fakes by the gritty feel of it against your teeth, only a few blades were so finely made that they'd cause an ocular reaction like this. Misery was one of them.

This was a Guardian's weapon—Santiago was sure of it.

CHAPTER TWO

Santiago was surprised. And that didn't happen often.

After listening to the voice mail Roxanne had left on his cell, he assumed he'd arrive on the scene to find chaos and a boatload of collateral damage: Darkbloods, screaming humans who'd need their memories wiped, maybe a few dead bodies. Instead, things looked relatively calm. Just two vehicles pulled off to the side of the road and Roxanne near the edge of the forest, standing over a pile of what probably used to be a Darkblood. From the looks of it, Misery wouldn't be needed.

Although he'd heard of Roxanne Reynolds—Lily couldn't say enough complimentary things about her— he'd never actually met her in person. What he did know, though, was that she was into some weird spiritual crap—meditation, mind-over-matter kind of shit. Sure, the touchy-feely stuff was popular with her students. Lily, for instance, gushed about her at every opportunity, but as far as he was concerned, anyone who practiced nonsense like that had to have a screw loose somewhere.

He exited his vintage Corvette and jogged toward the red Search and Rescue truck. Oddly enough, two men were slumped over, sleeping in the front, while their dog barked its head off in the back. How could they not wake up with that racket? His acute hearing picked up the regular sound of their heartbeats, so he didn't bother to open the door. It was obvious they were both healthy and alive.

"It's okay, boy," Santiago said to the German shepherd as he passed the vehicle.

Before he got to Roxanne, the Capture Team's panel van pulled up alongside him and a tinted window slid down.

"Where do you want us?" one of the capture team agents asked.

"I've got things handled here." He motioned for them to continue. "But I want temporary roadblocks set up ahead and behind us. If anyone asks, say there's been a rock slide." This remote part of the highway wasn't well traveled at night, but he didn't want to take any chances.

"Yes, sir." The vehicle drove away and the sound of its engine was soon swallowed by the night.

He quickly assessed the scene as he crossed the road, his boots crunching loudly on the pavement. Crickets chirped in the nearby bushes, apparently undisturbed by what had just happened. He didn't detect any live Darkblood scent, just the scent of the sweetblood who was stowed safely in what he assumed to be Roxanne's car about twenty feet away.

"Hola," he said as he approached. "Roxanne, I presume?"

She straightened her spine at the sound of his voice

and turned to face him. And for just a moment, he forgot entirely why he was here.

Since joining the Agency over a century ago, he'd been stationed in various parts of the world that most people only experienced by reading books and magazines, seeing pictures online or news clips on television. And he'd witnessed many astounding things. Tattooed pleasure workers in Thailand, secret Incan mating rituals, French courtesans well versed in the sexual arts. In short, he'd seen a lot, experienced a lot. There wasn't much that could take his breath away.

Until now.

"And you must be Santiago."

God, he even liked the sound of her voice.

She picked at a twig nestled in her dark blond hair, which fell past her shoulders in messy, tangled curls, but she wasn't having much luck.

"Here, let me get that." Without thinking, he reached over and had to use two hands to keep from pulling her hair too much. "There, got it."

It was only after he was done that he realized how intimate an action it had been. He stepped away and folded his arms over his chest as he studied her.

Despite the frigid night air, she wore a cream-colored tank top with a surf shop logo that sported a few blood stains, dark brown yoga pants—the kind that felt different depending on whether you ran your hand up or down the fabric—and slip-on, once-turquoise tennis shoes that were now covered in mud. The juxtaposition between feminine perfection and scrappy street fighter was so utterly arresting that the world fell away for one brief moment.

Although none of her individual features stood out on their own—straight nose, golden eyes framed by dark lashes, and lips that were neither thin nor generous—when they were put together, she was striking. Her face was oval, her skin smooth and unblemished except for a smudge on one cheek. He had the sudden urge to brush his fingertips against her skin to see if it was dirt or blood. She wasn't old, but the confidence reflected in her eyes indicated that her Time of Change, when a vampire youthling's blood cravings began, was decades behind her.

"So what do we have here?" he asked, glancing at the charred remains. His tone was purposely sharp and businesslike as he attempted to shake off his lingering reaction to her. He didn't like losing control of his thoughts like this.

She fingered her necklace. "Turned out I was able to handle the situation on my own."

"And the human witnesses?"

"They'll need to be dealt with. I didn't have the energy to wipe their minds, only to insert a sleep suggestion."

Very clever, he thought, noticing for the first time the weariness in her eyes. "What about the other Darkblood? You said there were two."

"I took care of them both. Here—" she toed her sneaker against the pile of ash at her feet "—and over there about twelve to fifteen feet beyond that downed tree."

"I don't understand. You said on the phone you didn't have any weapons."

"I didn't."

"Then how—?"

"I used theirs," she said matter-of-factly, as if disarming two Darkbloods who were probably high on Sweet was something a teacher dealt with every day.

It still didn't make sense. His confusion must've been apparent because she continued.

"I pretended I was trying to get away from the sweet-blood human, that I was concerned I might kill him, and needed their help."

"So they knew you were a fellow vampire."

"Yes, but they had no idea I knew they were Darkbloods. As soon as they didn't consider me a threat and dropped their guard, it was a simple matter to strip their weapons and use them to my advantage."

Jesus, Mary and Joseph.

This woman performed under pressure as well as any Guardian he'd worked with, and yet she was just a teacher at Tracker Academy. What happened to the adage, "those who can't do, teach"?

"Good work," he said begrudgingly.

She shot him a faint smile, like all of this was no big deal, that she could've done it in her sleep.

There was nothing hotter than an attractive woman who could handle her own, especially when the odds were stacked against her. As his gaze roamed unintentionally over her curves, the heat of desire rushed head-long through his veins, muddling all rational thought for a moment. He was acutely aware of the thin fabric of her shirt stretched tightly over her breasts, molding to her narrow waist, and how her yoga pants hung low on her hips.

Since vampires' sexual needs were much stronger than humans', it wasn't uncommon for friends or co-workers to sleep together. It was a safer, much more ac-cepted way to expend extra energy than infighting or feeding on the blood of a host. But there was something different about this woman. Something unpredictable and unknown making him feel as if he had to tread carefully around her. That a roll in the sack would be a mistake. But for the life of him, he couldn't quite figure out why, because, damn, she was attractive.

Reading beneath the surface of people was a skill that had served him well as region commander and he'd learned to trust his gut instincts. He had the vague sense that the two of them would clash. And that it wouldn't be pleasant. No, he needed to keep the gorgeous Rox-anne Reynolds at arms' length and nix any thoughts of bedding her. She might be capable and loyal, but that didn't mean she wasn't trouble.

Determined not to be drawn in by her beauty, he did his best to ignore it. He preferred dealing with finite things that were within his control. Besides, he didn't do women with baggage. His counterpart down in her region had hinted that she had some.

"Where did you say you charcoaled that other DB?"

She turned and pointed into the woods. "Over there."

And that's when he saw it. The tattoo on her shoulder. A small infinity symbol over a red rose. He took a half-step backward.

Damn. That explained the woo-woo shit and why he had such a strange feeling about her. He hadn't known she was *dakai,* a member of the same blood-worshipping cult as his sister. Like Roxanne, Rosa had been a capable woman, with her whole life in front of her, until she'd gotten involved.

The *dakai* worshipped blood goddesses and required members to contribute their wealth in order to purify their lifeblood. Once their blood was "purified," it was extracted and combined with other "clean" blood into the *Chalice la Sangre* from which they would all drink. Pure blood led to acceptance by the Great Mother, so that when they died, they'd ascend and become blood goddesses, as well. Or so they believed. It was all a bunch of horseshit as far as Santiago was concerned.

Roxanne stood with her arms hanging loosely at her sides. "Want me to show you where he is?"

"No, we'll handle things now." Sidestepping away, he texted the capture team and told them to get back here. He didn't want this woman any more involved in agent enforcement issues than she already was.

"Need help tracking the scent back to their den?" she asked him when he finished. "I'd be happy to do that. It's odd that they'd locate one so close to the region office."

Her words were a rusty barb under his skin. He didn't

need a stranger—a *dakai,* no less—reminding him that this Darkblood operation was right under his goddamn nose.

"We don't require your assistance any longer."

Her eyes darkened with an emotion he couldn't quite read. Was she pissed to be taking orders from him? Well, this was his jurisdiction and his decision. And this was his problem, not hers. He'd take care of the whole damn situation himself without further involvement from her.

"Will you be taking the young man, the sweetblood, back to region for a debriefing and a health check?"

"Yes," he snapped. Just because a couple of DBs brazenly set up shop nearby didn't mean things were out of control or that protocols weren't followed. Those were standard procedures when a Darkblood prisoner was found. "We do things up here just like the big boys do down in Florida."

He half expected her to argue with him, but the earlier fire in her eyes had been replaced by a flat nothingness, as if this sort of thing had happened to her before. He ignored the tiny voice inside his head that said he could be such a prick sometimes. Being a good leader meant that not everyone was going to agree with you or want to be your Scrabble buddy.

"Very well." She rubbed her hands over her bare arms.

Good. She knew where he stood and what her role in Guardian affairs was while she was here—nada.

"I'll wait by my car for you to collect him, then I'll be on my way."

Which, unfortunately, was to the same place he was headed.

A SOFT KNOCK on the door interrupted Roxy's concentration. She looked up from the student files spread on her desk to see a flaxen-haired woman in hospital scrubs enter the classroom. She smelled faintly of sweetbloods—several of them.

"You must be Roxanne." The woman held two coffee mugs emblazoned with the Guardian logo, but from the scent permeating the air, Roxy could tell they contained tea. "I'm Brenna Stewart. I work here at the medical center."

Roxy smiled stiffly. She wasn't exactly the best audience for a welcoming committee, preferring instead to keep to herself most of the time. Not that she didn't like people, but she'd learned to be wary.

"Please, call me Roxy." When people said her full name, it reminded her of her mother, who used it to get her attention. As a pre-change youthling, Roxy had had a habit of getting so engrossed in what she was working on that she'd forget the outside world existed. Although her mother had been gone for years now, she still got that ache around her heart whenever she thought of her.

The woman—Brenna—set one of the mugs on the desk then pulled up a chair. "Roasted green tea. Lily said it's your favorite. Careful though. It's hot."

Roxy liked the woman's comfortable, easy vibe. "You know Lily?"

"Yeah, she's a good friend of mine. Sorry I didn't come earlier. I meant to stop in and say hello as soon as you arrived, but we were treating several injured Guardians yesterday and then a sweetblood human came in needing to be rehabilitated. Things were pretty crazy in the clinic for a while."

"No problem. I went straight to bed as soon as I got in anyway." As she'd been bone-tired from the long trip and then that business with the Darkbloods, Roxy was glad the woman hadn't popped in. She wasn't used to idle chitchat anyway—most of her friends from her Guardian days had distanced themselves after what had happened with Ian and she'd never bothered to cultivate new ones at the Academy. Instead, she'd immersed herself in her work, reminding herself that if you didn't let people in, you were less likely to get hurt. "How's Mason doing? The sweetblood."

Brenna looked confused. "You know him?"

"I was the one who found him walking on the side of the road yesterday."

"That was you?" Her green eyes went wide. "I heard that someone took down the Darkbloods who were after him, but you're not even an agent." She didn't say it maliciously or with condescension, so Roxy didn't take offense.

"Yep. That was yours truly."

"Well, I am superimpressed. No wonder you were exhausted when you got here."

It had to have been someone on the capture team who'd told Brenna what had happened, not Santiago. She recalled how he'd arrived on the scene and taken charge, as if he was the one who took those guys down and not her. He was a typical domineering male who worked on the Agency side of things. It had come as no surprise that he didn't take her up on her offer to help track the DB den. Men like him preferred to do things themselves and get all the glory, which was fine with her. She preferred to work on her own as well, though she'd just as soon stay out of the limelight.

From what she'd heard about Santiago, she figured he'd have a forceful personality, but she hadn't been prepared for how formidable he looked. With short dark hair, a square jaw peppered with stubble, and a rigid, soldierlike posture, he was six and a half feet of pure dangerous male. And then there was that strange tattoo on the side of his neck, which stretched into his hairline. She hadn't been able to see where it began or ended and even now, she found herself wondering how far it went. To his shoulder? His arm? Maybe down his torso?

And that voice of his. Oh, God, that voice. Rough around the edges like the gravel that had worked its way into her shoes during the Darkblood scuffle, and just as hard to ignore. She wondered what her name would sound like on his tongue. But then she remembered those eyes—hard and unforgiving—framed by equally dark thick lashes. It was as if he had the ability to look straight into her soul and didn't like what he saw.

He was definitely a man to be avoided. She shoved

him from her thoughts and turned her attention back to Brenna.

"Lily wanted me to tell you about Finn, my husband-to-be. He's human and a sweetblood, which…ah… explains the smell on me. Most don't notice it, but Lily said you definitely would, considering that you basically trained all the trackers working in the Agency today."

Roxy had noticed the scent but assumed it was because Brenna worked in the clinic. "I don't know about *all* of them."

"Most then. How's that?"

It was somewhat unusual for a vampire to be in a relationship with a human, much less a human who was a sweetblood and knew that he was in love with someone who could kill him.

Brenna continued, "Finn's a helicopter pilot for the Seattle field but doesn't come to region much. Not all of us can be trusted being around a sweetblood. I still worry about myself sometimes, although he has been trying to talk his way into becoming a changeling."

Although changelings were relatively rare, Roxy had met a few of them over the years. Except for those who'd been illegally turned against their will, most went through the transformation because they fell in love with a vampire. A painful process that required the blood of two vampires, it had to be approved by the Council after a long waiting period, but it was possible.

"There must be something really special between you then. Sounds like he's totally in love with you."

"Yeah," Brenna said, staring into her cup. "And I'm crazy about him, too."

Roxy detected some reluctance. "You don't want him to become a changeling?" Some vampires thought of themselves as monsters, was that it? Brenna didn't want the love of her life to become like her?

"Oh, God, I want nothing more than to live out our long lives together without worrying about my friends and coworkers being around him. And he wants to be just one of the guys in the Seattle office. It's just that I'm worried about the actual process, you know? It's not without risk. He could die. Given my line of work, I see the worst of the worst. Motorcycle accidents, gunshot wounds, regeneration problems, head traumas, silvies that miss the heart by inches. To knowingly put my man in danger like that is not something I'm prepared to do. I like him the way he is. Alive. But believe me, he's trying to wear me down."

Roxy wrapped her hands around the mug and found it to be just a notch below scorching now, so she took a sip. "Roasted green tea. Lily knows me too well."

Brenna smiled, the trace of worry gone from her eyes. "Speaking of Lily, have you heard how she's doing?"

"No, and I'm not really expecting to either."

"You're not?"

Roxy shook her head. "I told her if she so much as checks in with anyone here, I'll know about it."

"Sounds like she listens to you. I could've told her that but she never—" Brenna's pager vibrated. She glanced at it then stood up. "Gotta go. Hey, do you run? I could show you some great trails around here."

"That'd be nice, but isn't it too cold to be outside?" She remembered just how chilly it was when she found Mason. Would her warm-weather body be able to withstand the frigid elements well enough to go running? She certainly didn't have the right workout clothes. Hell, when she got to her room after yesterday's adventure, she'd never been more thankful in her entire life to see an electric blanket on her bed. "I'm kind of a wimp when it comes to cold weather."

"It's actually been mild for this time of the year," Brenna said, her hand on the door, "but I forgot you're from Florida. Do you swim? We've got a great pool."

The two women made plans to meet later so that Roxy could get a tour of the region's pool and gym facility located on the far end of the complex.

Besides, she had a lead—albeit a slim one—about Ian's death that pointed to the Seattle area, so she wanted to ask the woman a few more questions about Agency operations here. Although she didn't hold out much hope—all her previous leads had gone nowhere—she couldn't *not* investigate.

CHAPTER THREE

SANTIAGO AWOKE EARLY. His sheets were sandpaper against his skin, his pillow a contoured brick under his head.

He threw back the covers, his feet hitting the cold tile floor with a thump, and stumbled to the small refrigerator he kept in his sleeping quarters. He ate a piece of leftover pizza and chugged orange juice directly from the carton.

With the sun still high in the late-September sky and his delivery not coming till later, he couldn't leave for the Ridge yet, though he was antsy to get up there. Only a handful of his top people knew he had a home located in a remote part of the mountains but even they didn't know what he did there. Frankly, it was no one's business but his own.

He hadn't been expecting to go again so soon, but running into Ms. Reynolds had changed his plans. When she'd pointed out the fact that Darkbloods had located a den so close to region HQ, he didn't need to see the disdain for his leadership in her expression—he could hear it in her voice. But then, as always, he needed to be realistic. She'd identified his weaknesses and, as much as he hated to admit it, things had to be dealt with.

Although he could've used her help in tracking down the den, he'd managed to find it on his own. Given that Darkbloods were notoriously sloppy and the tiny house had been clean, almost barren, it was obvious that the place hadn't been in operation for long. Even their coffins—which most DBs were sleeping in nowadays as a nod to their violent ancestors—weren't there yet. He and the capture team had lit the place on fire and watched it burn to the ground.

But her subtle criticism remained, ringing in his ears long after he got back and taunting his nightmares. Sure, she hadn't come right out and said anything specific, but he could tell she was thinking it. Thing was, she was right. No way should a den have been located that close to region. It reflected badly on him and his leadership ability and could hurt his reputation among his kind. Despite his best efforts, somehow he'd let himself get lackadaisical and careless and that just wasn't acceptable. Winners didn't allow their enemies to take advantage of them and make them look like fuckups. Only losers did.

After quickly showering and dressing, he made his way from his chambers to his office before anyone else was up. Normally he liked the quiet, but after last night, he was on edge. His hands and feet began to tingle, but it had nothing to do with the chill. By the time he sat down at his desk and began working, the numbness had snaked its way through his gut, making it hard to concentrate.

His errors could not go unpunished. He would do

what he needed to do in order to get rid of this deadlike sensation. These feelings of nothingness threatened to overtake him whenever he made a mistake and caved to weakness.

On virtual autopilot, he worked throughout the late afternoon and into night. He took a few calls, had a few meetings, talked to one of his counterparts down South who was having trouble with a particularly aggressive den of Darkbloods, and reviewed all the sweetblood reports that the field offices had recently turned in. Then he approved a few big-ticket expenditures from both the region's medical director and from Jackson Foss's fiancée, Arianna, who was starting a sweetblood refuge home just over the border in Washington State.

Fortunately, the delivery came shortly before dawn, so rather than wasting time until night fell again when he could comfortably get to the Ridge, he'd be able to leave now.

He pulled back the heavy damask drapes in his corner office. The early-morning sky had lightened to an inky purple. Given the cloud cover, the UV light wouldn't be too strong yet, and although he'd still feel the pull of the energy drain as he headed out, after today he wouldn't be able to tell the difference anyway.

He gathered up a few files from his massive mahogany desk and put them into his briefcase next to the laptop. Although he wasn't sure why he bothered. He never looked at work when he got to the Ridge. It was more a formality and, he had to admit, for appearance's sake, as well.

"Jenella, I'm taking the next few days off, so I'll need you to handle my calls and inquiries." He stepped out of his office and pulled the door shut behind him.

His assistant tucked a pencil behind her ear as she placed a notebook on the shelf behind her desk and selected another. "Yes, I know, sir."

She did? How? He hadn't said anything to her yet.

He must've had a confused look on his face because she added, "You had me move tomorrow's staff meeting to next week, you blocked off the next few days on your calendar and you tidied up your office. That's what you always do when you leave."

God, was he that predictable?

But then, not much got past Jenella, which was why he liked her. That, and because she was the only one who would put up with him. She was efficient and knew what needed to happen whether he was there to give her the specifics or not. She didn't need to be babysat. But there still were a few things she didn't know about him. No one would. He preferred to keep some details all to himself.

"Very good. If Eddie calls, tell him I haven't forgotten our plans. I'm still flying out next week to visit."

He thought about his good friend, who'd been badly injured several years ago while on assignment in Mexico and was left with a horrible disfigurement. A vampire's natural ability to regenerate damaged tissue and bone only went so far. Although the guy was lucky to be alive, he didn't always believe he was. Even though he would never admit it, he thrived on Santiago's pep talks.

"Text me if one of the field offices needs something and I'll get back to them."

When he'd appointed the field office team leaders, he'd been careful to select individuals who could make wise decisions independently from him. He let them think he was breathing down their necks, but it was partially the specter of his potential wrath that drove them to make the right decisions in the first place.

The What-Would-Santiago-Do mentality kept the Horseshoe Bay Region and all its field offices running efficiently.

When each individual was strong, the whole team was strong. He didn't need or want his people checking in with him for every little thing. He wanted the region to run efficiently and the field offices to feel as though they had the authority to make many of their own decisions without needing his input.

Oh, sure, he knew they chuckled behind his back whenever he'd give one of his infamous motivational talks, but it didn't bother him. They could laugh as much as they wanted, but his methods worked. He was driven, a hard charger who expected a lot from his people, but they respected him for it and got things accomplished. A good leader knew when to press his people and when to back off. Yin and yang, give and take, dickhead and best friend.

"And if Ms. Reynolds needs anything, I trust you can handle it." He hoped that wouldn't come back to bite him. The last thing he needed was his staff deciding they should burn incense and start meditating like she did. He'd walked past the classrooms earlier and the scent of eucalyptus had been heavy in the air.

"Yes, of course."

An hour later, he was unlocking the front door of the Ridge—keys in one hand and the small delivery box in the other. The sky had lightened to the point when he could feel a slight drain from the sun. But he didn't pay much attention. Things were about to get much worse.

After changing into a T-shirt and shorts, he pulled a box cutter from the top drawer in the tiny kitchen. Carefully, he slit the tape around the cardboard and lifted out the red plastic box inside. Unsnapping the metal latch, he opened the lid. There, arranged in neat little rows, were two dozen vials of human blood. AB negative, his personal favorite. He stuffed three into the pocket of his shorts and refrigerated the rest. Although he was tempted to grab a fourth, he had enough to get by. Besides, he'd be desperate for the rest of them later.

With a glass of water in one hand and a small hand towel tucked under his arm, he climbed the narrow ladder in the living room and pushed open the trap door in the roof. Early-morning sunlight streamed into his eyes, burning his retinas. He pinched them shut to block out the sting then squinted and climbed the rest of the way through. Like water in a leaky bucket, energy began to trickle from his body. Slowly but surely, he became weaker and weaker.

A mattress covered in plastic lay between two iron stakes bolted to the roof. At least it wasn't raining this time, he thought as he glanced at the sky.

An eagle soared high overhead and several smaller birds followed close behind. Dive-bombing and squawking, the weaker birds tried to chase the eagle away, but he didn't alter his course. Strong and majestic, he kept circling until finally landing in the top of a nearby Douglas fir. He perched like a beacon and surveyed the terrain, unperturbed by the voices around him.

After setting the water glass on the roof next to the mattress, Santiago double-checked that the key was still hanging from a hook near the trap door. He knelt down, grabbed the chains and snapped the cuffs around his ankles. He pulled to make sure they were tight. Yep. He wasn't going anywhere.

Then, as the sun rose higher in the sky, he lay back on the mattress, stretched out his arms and closed his eyes.

SOMETHING STRANGE IS *going on with Santiago.*

Even though she didn't know him well, she couldn't quite put her finger on it. He seemed…different.

Earlier this week, he'd left for a few days and when he returned, Roxy noticed an odd intensity in his demeanor that hadn't been there before. Although he walked through the region offices as confidently as he always had, there was a numbness behind his eyes, a weariness, as if a tiny part of him had died.

When she'd mentioned it to Brenna, the woman shrugged and said he would get that way sometimes and they'd all learned to watch their step around him.

Was something bothering him? Roxy wondered.

Since she'd arrived, she'd done a good job of staying out of his way, but every time she did interact with him, he made her feel vulnerable, stripped bare. She didn't let many people past her defenses, but there was something about him that weakened them, that demanded she let him in.

And she didn't like it.

Now, in an empty exercise studio in the gym, she was doing a few yoga poses when something outside the window caught her attention. She looked up to see Santiago arriving via a seldom used outside entrance rather than the main lobby. He stopped, reached his hand in his pocket then stooped down. What was he doing?

She walked closer to the glass for a better look. With the lights off inside, he wouldn't be able to see her.

His arm was stretched out and he had something in his hand. Was that a—

It looked like a peanut in a shell.

Just then a squirrel ran out from a nearby bush and stopped about three feet away from him. His lips moved as if he were talking to it. She wondered what he was saying. Though he wiggled the peanut, the animal didn't advance any closer, so he tossed it. The squirrel quickly grabbed it with his little paws and ran away. Santiago mounded a few more peanuts near his feet then stood and entered the gym.

What was a man like that doing keeping treats in his pockets for the squirrels?

Twenty minutes later he was lifting weights, heavy ones, over and over like a machine, not making eye contact with the two other agents in the room. All traces of what she'd just witnessed—the gentleness, the kindness—were gone.

Who knew this fierce warrior had a soft spot in his heart for animals? She had a feeling he wouldn't be happy to know she'd seen that. She thought about her own dog back home. Was Ginger missing her right now? Roxy sure missed her. As she continued her own workout in the privacy of the darkened studio, she found herself drawn to this powerful and fascinating man.

In between sets, he headed to the water fountain and opened up the cabinet underneath, searching for something. A towel? She glanced at hers sitting next to her water bottle. She'd taken the last one. Yeah, that must've been what he was looking for because, not finding one, he stripped off his collegiate gray T-shirt and mopped his forehead.

Good thing she was in an enclosed space because she almost lost her balance and most certainly gasped.

His chest and stomach rippled with corded muscle, the skin stretched tautly over them. To call them washboard abs wouldn't have been accurate because that implied a flat plane. Twin ridges of muscles on his hips angled inward, drawing her attention down, down, down…to a thin line of dark hair on his lower belly that disappeared beneath his waistband. Even though she wasn't into hot yoga, beads of sweat trickled between her breasts. She grabbed her towel and dabbed her chest then her forehead. Try as she might, she couldn't wrench her gaze away.

She'd always wondered how far his tattoo went and now she had her answer. Well, almost. The strange barbed curlicues stretched from his hairline, along the left side of his neck, to his shoulder blade and heavily muscled back, then disappeared somewhere beneath those shorts.

Good God, he'd have been the perfect model for the original Grey's Anatomy drawings. She shook her head. She didn't need to be thinking this way. He was egotistical and insensitive and totally not her type. She turned up her music and resumed a different pose. One that wouldn't allow her to watch him.

But little good that did. Soon, her attention was drawn to him again.

Facing away from her now, he straddled a bench and lifted two sets of huge dumbbells. The muscles in his back glistened and flexed with every movement. She found herself wondering if he'd be able to bench-press her. If she did a plank pose, how many reps would he be able to do? Would he lift her with ease? And what would it feel like to have his hands on her? She imagined how hard his magnificent, powerful body would feel beneath hers. He was strong, of course, but could he be gentle?

Then she remembered the squirrel.

CHAPTER FOUR

VENTRA CAPELLI KNEW that her days were numbered—
not just as the Seattle area sector mistress, but in gen-
eral. The Darkblood brass wasn't pleased that one of
their most profitable companies had been destroyed and
that two sector masters had been killed because of her.

The man across the table from her lifted the wineglass, swirled the contents for a moment, then brought
it to his lips. "I'm sure you can understand my position."

"Yes, of course." Ventra twisted one of her priceless
sapphire earrings, a gift to herself when she'd been appointed sector mistress. It was a tangible reminder of
her success.

The whole thing was not her fault and yet she was
being blamed for it. Consequently, her superiors felt
she was a weak and ineffective leader. And that pissed
her off.

How was she to know that the Guardians had an in-
sider working for the company? As a result, one of them
had sneaked onto the yacht and killed the two sector
masters just as she was presenting a business idea to
them. If she hadn't held that sweetblood girl for leverage, she'd have been charcoaled, too. It was the only
thing that had saved her.

Although she'd love to get her hands on the Guardian who did the killing—she'd never encountered a living vampire who had the powers he did—the real enemy was his superior, who'd orchestrated and approved the whole thing. He was the one she wanted, because once that thorn in her side was out of the picture, the rest of them would be easy pickings.

She resisted the urge to nervously touch her earring again. Instead, she folded her hands carefully in her lap and watched her guest.

"This really is quite lovely," he said after taking a sip. "Thank you."

Ventra was completely aware that Loric Rayne, second in command under the new Overlord, held her fate in his hands. These next few moments were crucial.

Even though her two loyal bodyguards were stationed just behind the dining room doors, she didn't want to have to use them, for if she did and Rayne was killed, she'd forever be on the run from the Alliance. Her future in the organization was teetering on the edge of a blade right now and it was because of those goddamned Guardians. All she'd ever wanted was respect and they'd taken that from her. Those self-appointed protectors of their people had no real authority anyway. Centuries ago, they'd usurped the power from the old ones, convincing their people that humans and vampires could exist peacefully, yet secretly, side by side. Well, that was bullshit. There was a reason vampires had fangs and a craving for blood. Because they were meant to feed from humans, not make friends with them.

Rage erupted inside her, but she didn't let it show on her face. On the outside, she was as calm and cool as a glass of ice water—sparkling, with two twists of lime and a fancy little umbrella—but inside, she was a boiling caldron of oil. "I'd be happy to show you how I prepare it."

"You didn't import it?" He swirled his glass again and watched how the blood clung to the sides like a fine wine. "It's got quite a zip to it. More than I'd have expected from the supply up here."

"No, sir. Harvested from a local human under a technique I came up with."

Because the UV levels in the Northwest were fairly low, the energy in the indigenous population was low as well—a big reason most vampires hated living too far north. But if the host was exposed to several hours of UV light—either a full spectrum tanning bed or a sunny day—their blood was infused with more energy than what was typical here. Not quite to the levels you'd find in humans down South, but much better than one pulled directly off the street and drained. A little patience and prep work always paid off in the end. Other vampires were willing to pay more for the fortified stuff and although it wasn't as good as Sweet—hell, nothing was as good as Sweet—the supply was much more plentiful, which meant a lot more money in her, and the Darkbloods', coffers.

"Yes, I'm very curious. I'd like to see how you do it sometime."

Her tightly knotted shoulders relaxed just a touch.

The fact that he referenced a *sometime* meant that there was hope for her within the organization. Maybe he didn't come to Seattle to kill her after all and she would be given a chance to make things right. She had a few things in place already, and if given the chance by her superiors, she'd strike the Guardians when they least expected it.

After I get through with them, they'll wish they had the agreement some of their other field offices have with the Alliance.

"As I was saying," Rayne said, his gaze wandering to the center of the table, "you've put me in a precarious spot. I went to bat for you in Prague, believing you had what it took to exploit the Seattle area to its fullest. Blood raves, blood clubs, pinpointing our target market through that video game, and Sweet addictions on the rise. I had high hopes for you, Ventra, but I'm afraid you've greatly disappointed me. Your failures don't sit well with the Overlord. And when he's not happy, I'm not happy."

Setting down his now empty glass, he reached for the centerpiece, which was laid out on a plastic sheet covering the table. "But I'm willing to give you another chance." With the pads of his fingers, he caressed the skin of the donor host's belly with great care.

When the female whimpered, Ventra shot her a withering look that said "Move a muscle and I kill you *and* your sister."

The look in Rayne's eyes was almost trancelike as he continued to gaze at the living centerpiece, which gave the concept of body shots a whole new meaning. With her golden skin and the smell of sun in her hair, she was a beautiful girl, giving him every reason to stare. But then again, he was probably trying to decide which vein to start with first. Drinking from a live sweetblood could be pretty intoxicating. Who the hell cared what they looked like, although Ventra was a firm believer in the power of eye candy.

"But only if," he said, pushing his chair from the table and standing up, "you can do something to prove you haven't lost total control here."

He leaned over the female and the greyed-out whites of his eyes darkened further.

"Oh, God, please. No." Black mascara tracked down both sides of the human's face.

Rayne tilted her head to the side, and without any more preamble than that, sank his teeth into her neck. She screamed and arched her body as best she could, but the bindings on her ankles and wrists kept her firmly affixed to the tabletop.

Ventra had debated whether to gag her or not but at the last minute decided to keep her au naturel. And she was glad she did. Many vampires liked the thrill of hearing their victims scream in terror—the fear added a special zing to the energy—and Rayne seemed no different. With his lips seared to her neck, he swallowed mouthful after mouthful of her sweet blood.

After a few moments, when the girl's screams had died down to a weak whimper, he lifted his head, his lips stained deep crimson.

"Magnificent."

"Glad you like her. I kept her outside all day to maximize the ultraviolet energy in the blood."

His gaze roamed the female's body. "Ah, that explains the bikini then. And the smell of the sun on her tanned skin." He removed his expensive Italian suit jacket and set it carefully over the back of his chair. "I have faith in you, Ventra. You're able to think outside the box. This—" he swept his hand along the woman's thigh and rested it just inside her knee "—is evidence of that. I believe you have what it takes to make even the most dismal city a success."

She beamed with pride that such a powerful player in the Darkblood organization felt so strongly about her. She vowed not to fuck it up this time.

He loosened his tie and rolled up the sleeves of his handmade dress shirt. Indicating the female's right arm, he said, "Remove the binding. I'd like to try that vein next."

DOMINIC SERRANO FLATTENED his back against the dingy brick wall and waited for his team to get into position. Peering through the darkness, past a torn blue awning outside an import/export company in south Seattle, he had a clear view of the target location.

Knee-high weeds grew in the cracks around the entrance and a few fast-food wrappers had gathered in the shallow door well. A basket with long-dead plants hung from a hook to the left of the roll-up doors. Situated in a run-down portion of the industrial district, the warehouse appeared to be vacant, but according to their intel, it was anything but empty.

He glanced at his watch. A few more minutes till they went in. Several days ago, they'd learned that Darkbloods were expecting a large shipment of illegal weapons and Guardians weren't about to let them get distributed.

Had it really been almost three years since he'd last been to this part of town? It was where he'd charcoaled one of the DB bastards chasing Mackenzie. He flexed his fists and felt her blood coursing through his veins.

Fighting their enemies always cranked up his energy level. Given their blood bond, she knew it and sensed it from him. He didn't care where she was or what she was doing when he got home after being out on a mission like this. He needed sex. And he needed it badly.

Once, after a crazy pursuit of several DBs that took all night, he'd found her in the field office computer lab. She'd known he was coming for her and was wriggling off her panties as he stormed into the room. Thinking the place was empty, he shoved her up against the wall, unzipped his fly and plunged himself into her heat.

"Nice ass," Jackson had said to him the next night when they were shooting hoops in the gym.

"Huh?"

"A couple of us guys were playing poker over at Cordell's."

"Yeah, and?"

"You apparently forgot that he set up a live feed to the computer lab to answer questions while he was home helping Shannon after her surgery. We enjoyed the show last night, although all we could see of it was your cute little bum."

"Glad you liked it," he'd said, throwing the basketball hard at Jackson's chest. "Hope you picked up a few pointers."

"We were glued to the monitors."

Electronic static crackled in his ear and jerked him back to the present. When he got home tonight, he'd make sure to check for wayward camera equipment first.

He touched his earpiece. "Everyone in place?"

Jonah and Sadie answered first. "Affirmative." Positioned on the north end of the warehouse, they'd enter the building at the loading docks.

The line crackled again then Jackson said, "Mitchie and I are ready to kick some Darkblood ass." A grunt and scuffling could be heard through the connection. "Hey. Ouch."

Mitch didn't like that nickname, which only gave Jackson more ammunition to harass him with.

"Ladies, no catfights."

One more team to report, then they'd go in.

Based on intel Santiago had obtained from a DB captured near Region, they surmised that the shipment contained very deadly weapons—blades and bullets—made from high quality Mexican silver. Merely touching *Santa Muerte* silver would weaken a vampire, which was why the Agency used it in handcuffs and other restraints. One nick from a blade caused very severe silver poisoning, more than a lesser-quality silver would. If this shit got out on the streets and into the hands of DBs and other reverts, it could cause all sorts of problems. While most Agency-forged blades were made with the stuff, Darkbloods' weapons weren't. Having been shot by such a bullet once, Dom knew only too well how devastating an injury from it could be and absently rubbed his shoulder. If Mackenzie hadn't stumbled across him when she had, he surely would have died.

It wasn't often this kind of silver was found in non-Agency weapons. Many years ago, the *Santa Muerte* mines had been shut down and sealed. Darkbloods conducted raids from time to time, trying to get their hands on the raw material, but as far as anyone knew, they never succeeded. The weapons they did find were ones they'd plucked from charcoaled Guardians.

"Team three? You there?"

No answer.

"Gibson?" With Lily gone, he'd requested Jackson's friend Val Gibson come up from the San Diego office to help them out here in Seattle. They often traded personnel when either of the two offices needed more agents. He'd arrived yesterday and had been fully briefed on the situation.

Where the hell was he? His team should've checked in by now.

For a moment Dom wondered if they did things differently down there. With the relatively small vampire population up here compared to Southern California, there were apt to be variations in protocol. But they went over everything back at the field office and Gibson assured him he understood procedure. His team was to get into position near the west entrance and wait for the signal from Dom. Wasn't the guy right behind them when they got out of the van back at the staging point a mile up the road?

"Gibby," Jackson said, the strain in his voice obvious. "Where the hell are you?"

Dom was seriously considering aborting the mission when the guy finally answered.

"Yeah, sorry." He sounded out of breath. "Tambra and I are here and in place."

Jackson cursed through the line. "What the hell were you doing? Getting a blow job?"

"Ha, I wish. Maybe later."

A woman coughed. "Don't you be giving me the hairy eyeball, Gibby, because it's not happening."

Joking aside, Dom was proud of his team, how everyone worked together. They poked fun and harassed each other, but they were some of the finest Guardians in North America—highly trained and very loyal. "Now, does everyone know what we're doing when we get in there?"

Yeses and uh-huhs echoed through the line.

"None of you better be lying to me about wearing your protective gear either. If this shipment is what we think it is, they're going to be armed with *Santa Muerte* silver."

He tugged at the neckline of his vest. Even though it was standard procedure, he'd always been averse to wearing them, but now that he was a husband and father, he was living for more than just himself. The snug fit and added bulk wasn't the pain in the ass it used to be.

They all confirmed they were wearing their gear.

Knowing they had this mission tonight, he'd taken Mackenzie's blood so that he was fully energized and able to use his special powers if he needed to. Because they were *Enlazado por la Sangre*—bonded by blood— her lifeblood did all sorts of things to him, including infusing him with the ancient power to *vapor.* By turning himself into smoke, he could seep through the smallest of cracks.

The ability had come in handy several times, including last week when his son accidentally locked himself in the bathroom. Miguel was crying and couldn't figure out how to unlock the door from the inside. When Dom *vapored* under the door and materialized on the other side, Miguel stared at him a moment then burst out laughing. With thick tears still streaming down his face, he held out his fat little arms for Dom to pick him up and comfort him. His heart swelled just thinking about how much he loved his son and loved being a father.

The scent of Darkbloods was thick in the air. Dom considered having his Guardians go in stealthily, but they needed to get in fast and prevent anyone from leaving or destroying anything. The Agency needed to find out how they were getting the weapons, who was supplying them.

"Okay, then. We go in on three…two…one. Go." Dom spun away from the wall and sprinted across the small expanse of pavement to the east entrance. A well-placed kick and the door flew open. Once inside, he morphed into the darkness and shadow-moved quickly past a row of stacked pallets.

Jonah and Sadie emerged from the left. Jackson and Mitch came through the double doors at the far end. Gibby and Tambra ran in from the right. They all met in the middle.

Dom stood with his hands on his hips and surveyed the place. Where were the DBs? Though he was no tracker, he distinctly picked up the scent of several of them and yet the place seemed empty. Something must've alerted them to the Guardians' presence. With rows of boxes and shelving that stretched to the ceiling and several offices along the back wall, it was possible they were hiding.

"They've got to be in here," he said through clenched teeth. "I can smell them."

"Me, too," someone said.

"Let's fan out." As everyone scattered, he followed the scent to several palettes of flattened cardboard in front of a Dumpster. They must be inside.

Dom kicked the Dumpster and the sound echoed throughout the warehouse. Nothing stirred inside. As he reached for the warped lid, the scent hit him. It was old blood without an energy signature.

Carefully, he lifted the black cover and peered inside. There, on a big heap of garbage, were the mangled bodies of three Darkbloods. Regeneration could grow back limbs, but not severed heads.

He didn't understand. His team was the only Guardian unit with authority here. He'd even pulled a few agents off other assignments. But if not Guardians, who else would've killed them? And why wouldn't they have been staked? That was the typical way his people dispensed with their enemies, not by dismemberment.

Something wasn't right. He backed away from the Dumpster, noticed a few of his agents slipping between the rows of shelving. It occurred to him that maybe it hadn't been Guardians who had done this, but other Darkbloods. It was vicious, not clean and fast.

Why would DBs kill their own people? A turf war? Maybe another group not affiliated with them were after the weapons and—

"What the hell is that?" Sadie came up behind him and pointed to a series of wires on the ground leading from the nearest pallet and disappearing behind one of the shelves.

Craning his neck, he noticed similar wires wrapped around the metal support beams, but he couldn't tell where they originated. The tiny hairs on the back of his neck prickled.

And then a goddamn freight train sounded in his ears.

"It's a trap!" he yelled at his team. Darkbloods had dismembered their own people in order for Guardians to think they were inside. "Get your asses out of here."

Boots pounded and echoed through the building as everyone bolted for the doors. Everyone, that is, except Sadie.

Goddamn it. He spun around and, spotting her back by the Dumpster, he shadow-moved to her as quickly as he could. "I gave an order, Agent. Let's go."

"Hold on. I've been trained in render safe procedures. I can disarm it." She started to follow a set of wires down one of the aisles, but he grabbed her arm.

"There's no time. It's too risky."

"But—"

He didn't wait for her to finish. Instead, he hauled her toward the nearest exit, ignoring her protests.

As he shoved her through the door, he heard a faint clicking noise behind him and threw a quick glance over his shoulder. Was another member of his team still left inside? He could've sworn he'd made an accurate head count. Goddamn it, why didn't any—

And then the building exploded.

CHAPTER FIVE

THE HELICOPTER LANDED just before dawn. Many of the people who worked at Region stood near the landing pad or just inside the doors, waiting for the injured to be taken off the aircraft. From what Roxy understood, there'd been an explosion in Seattle and several Guardians had been severely injured.

Santiago rushed the helicopter as the rotors spun loudly above him.

The doors opened and the medics wasted no time whisking a dark-haired man wrapped in bandages into the region's medical facility. A young woman followed closely behind them, her face ashen, a squirming toddler wrapped in her arms. Brenna waved to the pilot as she fell into step behind the group.

"Jesus Christ, what the hell happened?" Santiago asked the man on the gurney.

This was obviously someone of importance, as he didn't address his question to the two other people who had climbed out of the aircraft under their own power. The attendants who were pushing the patient down the sterile hallway didn't slow down, so Santiago had to jog after them to keep up.

"Our location…compromised," the man called out,

his voice strained and laced with pain. "They knew… we were going…to be there."

The gurney burst through the doors of the surgical wing and Brenna had to stop Santiago and the woman from following.

"Please tell me he's going to be all right," the woman sobbed. "That man…is my life."

Brenna gave her a quick hug. "We'll do everything we can to save him, Mackenzie. I promise."

The double doors had hardly swung shut before Santiago erupted in a volley of cursing and punched his fist through the wall. Clutching the boy like a lifeline, the woman slid to the ground.

EVER SINCE THE injured had been brought in, the offices had been strangely quiet. No loud talking or laughing by anyone anywhere, just hushed whispers. Although the tragedy had happened down in Seattle, it clearly had a profound impact on everyone. The gym was empty, the cafeteria subdued. When someone passed in the hallway, instead of a "Hi, how are you," no one gave more than a thin-lipped smile of acknowledgment. Having gotten used to everyone's friendly and welcoming natures, the change was obvious to Roxy.

Her students filed into the classroom one by one, their gazes fixed to the ground. As usual when Roxy pressed the button on the remote control for the interactive whiteboard showing today's topics, nothing happened. The screen should've dropped from the ceiling and the Powerpoint slides, which were displayed on her monitor, should've been displayed there, as well. She pressed another button. Still nothing.

She glanced around the room. Her go-to guy hadn't arrived yet. No matter. She was an intelligent woman and this was just a simple piece of technology. Hell, she used such teaching equipment down at the Academy, just not this brand.

Pushing a chair directly under the ceiling-mounted control panel, she kicked off her heels and stepped onto the seat, careful not to let her skirt ride up too much. Just inches away from it now, she aimed the remote right at the thing and stabbed at a few more buttons. Again, nothing.

Exasperated, she stepped down. "Is Raymond coming?" She could've sworn that she was pressing the same buttons he did, but he was the only one who could get the thing to work.

"I'm not sure, Ms. Reynolds. He knows one of the guys who was hurt, so I'll bet he's pretty shaken up."

Without putting her shoes back on, she sat down on the edge of the desk, thinking. Given that three other students weren't here either, Raymond wasn't the only one too upset to come to class. And of those who did come, she could see in their eyes how distracted they were. If only there was a chalkboard or something else to write on, but that fancy whiteboard was it.

"Tell you what. I can see that everyone's heart isn't into this. And to tell you the truth, neither is mine. How about we cancel class for today and I'll email you the assignment?"

The students murmured their agreement.

"Let's hope we hear good news soon."

After everyone gathered their things and exited the classroom, she tucked her laptop under her arm and left, as well. She considered heading back and getting lost in a book for the rest of the day, but the thought of sitting by herself wasn't very appealing. Normally, she enjoyed being by herself, but with everything that had happened, she found herself dreading being alone.

Seeing Mackenzie's husband laid out on the stretcher reminded her of the night when Ian was killed. Only Ian wasn't brought in on a gurney, but in a plastic bag. She only hoped that Mackenzie wouldn't experience what she had all those years ago, when the man she once loved had died.

No, she definitely didn't want to be alone in her room in a strange place. It brought up too many terrible memories she'd just as soon forget.

She planned to head back to drop off her things and change, then go find the sanctuary Brenna had told her about. She'd light some candles and say a few prayers for the injured. She was deep in thought when she realized she was in a part of the labyrinth of offices she hadn't been before. Nothing looked familiar. And then she heard the soft sounds of a woman crying.

She peered around the corner into a small waiting area and realized she must be in the medical clinic part of the offices.

There in the corner on a sofa sat Mackenzie. Her son was wrapped in a blanket on her lap, his thumb in his mouth, sleeping. It was apparent she was trying not to cry and wake him.

Roxy hesitated at first. Maybe Mackenzie wanted to be alone in her sorrow. But then she remembered the horrible emptiness she'd felt while she waited for news from the doctors. She had hoped they'd come in and tell her that the charcoaled remains weren't Ian's. That he'd just been injured and it was one of the other agents who'd been killed. She'd longed for someone to sit with her quietly and be her rock, but she'd had no one.

She grabbed a box of tissues from a nearby side table and set them next to Mackenzie. "Can I get you some water?"

Mackenzie looked up at her with tear-filled eyes and nodded.

Roxy wanted to wrap her arms around her and tell her that everything was going to be okay. That her husband was not only going to live but that he'd make a full recovery so the two of them would have a long life together, filled with happiness and many more babies. Instead, she returned a moment later with a bottle of water from the small refrigerator near the door.

"Want me to hold him for you?" Roxy whispered, handing her the bottle and sitting down next to her.

Mackenzie smiled gratefully and took a small sip. "That's okay. He'd probably just wake up anyway."

The woman drank almost the whole bottle and Roxy wondered when was the last time she'd had anything to eat. "They're good up here, you know. The clinic." Lily's mom was one of the finest doctors in all of North

America and if Roxy ever got hurt, she'd want to be
treated by Dr. DeGraff.

"I hope to God it's enough."

"WE'RE COMING back."

Even through the secure video feed into the region's
conference room, the stress on Alfonso's face was as
obvious as if it had been etched with black sharpie. Normally an expert at hiding his emotion, he was having a
hard time controlling it today. Santiago had to bite his
tongue to keep from ordering him to stay put. He knew
the man needed the time away, but Dom was Alfonso's
brother. The two had been estranged for years and just
recently had been able to put the past behind them.

"They're doing all they can to save him. There's not
much you can do at this point except pray."

"Not much we can do?" Alfonso looked as though
he might lunge through the monitor and strangle him.
"We can be there for my sister-in-law and nephew."

"How's Mackenzie doing?" Lily asked, her hand on
Alfonso's arm. "I've been trying to call her but it keeps
going straight to voice mail."

Her pained expression was a stark contrast to the
bright colored headband she wore, which she'd probably picked up in one of the Hill Country's local mar-
kets. Santiago could hear Spanish guitar music floating
in through the open window behind them.

"She's pretty shaken up," he replied. "But Roxanne
has been staying with her. Hasn't left her side."

That morning, he'd walked past the clinic waiting

room and had seen Mackenzie crying into her shoulder while Roxanne rubbed her back. Why did everyone else seem to find her presence so calming when she had just the opposite effect on him? She drove him crazy with her incense and candles, and for some reason, he became acutely aware of his faults, his every imperfection when she was around. It made it hard for him to think clearly.

Alfonso scrubbed a hand over his face. "From what you've said, I can't help thinking there's a traitor in the Seattle field office."

"Impossible." Jackson put his boots on the conference room table and leaned back in his chair. He'd been quiet up till now. "I know everybody there. We're a tight-knit group. None of the Guardians would do something like this."

"I agree," Lily said.

"Was there anyone on the outside who knew about the bust?" Santiago asked. "Any support staff? Warehouse worker?"

Jackson scowled, thinking. "Not that I know of. Just the Guardians who were there. Could it have been a setup? You got the intel from a DB up here, right?"

Santiago nodded, remembering the guy with the Guardian blade. "I've thought about that already, but we had to torture him for the information. He wasn't forthcoming."

"Then it's got to be a traitor," Alfonso said. "Having been a double agent for years, I know how these things work. You build up trust and loyalty with your peers and when they think you're one of them, you can get lots of information."

"I don't know, love," Lily said. "I have to agree with Jackson. I can't imagine anyone in the Seattle office who would be capable of that."

Alfonso shook his head. "Would you think I was capable of such deception when I worked inside the Alliance?"

The silence in the conference room was heavy. No one could picture how Alfonso had lasted all those years inside without his cover being blown.

"How else do you explain it?" he continued. "Dark-bloods knew that Dom and his team would show up. Sounds like an inside job to me."

A traitor under his command? Santiago pounded his fist on the table, making the video monitor jump. "Then I'm going down there and talking to every goddamn person in that office. And when I find out who it is, I'm going to stake the bastard myself."

"It could be a woman," Lily said.

"Then I'll stake the bitch."

"Or a human," Alfonso said. "I ran across several who worked for the Alliance who'd have done any-thing to be changed. Evil sycophants. That's what my friend N—" He coughed, looking uncomfortable for a moment. Santiago knew the Agency had others work-ing on the inside, doing just what Alfonso had done for decades. "That's what I called them. They could be more cutthroat and brutal than Darkbloods themselves."

Santiago gripped the edge of the table so hard that a

piece of it broke off. He hurled it against the wall and heard the sound of glass breaking. "Then I'll rip his... or her throat out."

"An equal opportunity killing," Jackson mumbled from across the table.

Alfonso leaned in close to the monitor. "If the person truly is a good enough liar to have fooled everyone, what makes you think you'll be able to root him or her out? They'll spook. They'll see you coming a mile away and either take off or have their guard locked up so tight you'll think they're as trustworthy as your father."

Bad analogy, Santiago thought. His father was as far from trustworthy as they got.

Lily cleared her throat. "Santiago, I'm afraid I have to agree with Alfonso. You're not exactly subtle. Have you tried picking up the scent track from the warehouse? Maybe the trail will lead you back to the traitor."

"Kip tried but came up with nothing." Santiago picked at a wood splinter in his finger with his teeth. "It's been raining solid since the explosion and all trace of any scent has been washed away."

"What about Roxy?" Lily asked. "Have you asked her?"

Santiago froze. He didn't need or want an outsider involved in an issue that should be handled as quietly as possible from within. Especially a critical outsider. "No."

"Why not? She's *the* best tracker in the Agency. I learned everything I know from her. Besides, she's really good at reading people. If the scent trail is gone,

she might be able to figure out who in the office is behind this."

"Take it from me," Alfonso said, "having worked
undercover for years, you get a nose for when people
are poking around. If Roxy goes down there and starts
asking questions, they'll totally be onto her."

"Yeah, that won't work," Lily said, shaking her head.

"Hell," Jackson said, "what if you and Roxy pretend
you're lovers?"

Santiago's head snapped up. "What the hell for?"
It didn't surprise him that Jackson would bring up the
topic of sex. Before Arianna, there hadn't been an attractive woman within miles of him that he hadn't
bedded or thought about bedding. At the clubs, they
practically threw themselves at his feet. Sex was all
the guy thought about.

"You know, Santiago," Alfonso said, slowly, as if
Jackson's dumbass comment was for real, "that's not
a half-bad idea."

Jesus, Mary and Joseph.

He rubbed his temples. He was seriously on the verge
on one giant motherfucking headache.

Jackson jumped from his chair and rubbed his hands
together gleefully, like a youthling preparing to do
something naughty. "Think about it. The two of you
could masquerade as a couple so that no one realizes
she's down there to scope things out. You could attend
the regional awards gala and be all over each other.
Dancing, kissing, slipping into one of the private sa-

lons for a little—" he made a kissing sound "—and no one would think anything of it."

Clenching his jaw so hard that his molars ached, he did his best to ignore Jackson's asinine idea. "That reminds me. I'm cancelling the ceremony. It doesn't seem right to celebrate Guardians' achievements when several of our own are suffering. I'll postpone the event and give out the awards another time."

A few of them murmured in agreement.

"Plus," Lily said, "it may not be safe. This attack was orchestrated, premeditated. Guardians are clearly a target and until we find out who's responsible, Darkbloods could strike again and injure innocent members of the vampire community."

"I disagree," Alfonso said, shaking his head. "Cancelling the ceremony would be a big mistake."

Santiago scowled. He didn't like to be challenged.

"In my personal opinion," Alfonso added benignly.

"A mistake?" The more he thought about it, the more his pupils dilated with anger. Trying to keep his people safe wasn't a strong enough reason to cancel the damn party?

It was Santiago's responsibility to keep the region as free from Darkblood scourge as possible, not Alfonso's. He needed to ensure the safety of the small vampire community who lived peacefully among the humans here in the Northwest. Thanks to Dom's contact in the Seattle Police Department—a man he knew through some military training they'd done together—a meth lab explosion was what the papers had reported. Damage control when humans died or disappeared was difficult enough. But an entire building?

He stood, kicking the chair out from behind him and paced around the room. He'd root out these bastards once and for all. Wearing a daysuit, he'd find where they slept in those coffins of theirs and let Misery carve them into little pieces. They'd find justice all right. At the point of his knife. He sure as hell didn't have time for a damn party.

"Listen," Alfonso said. Santiago spun around to see him holding up his palms. "I'm not trying to challenge your authority on this, but in my opinion, the ceremony shouldn't be cancelled. Darkbloods may not know the extent of the collateral damage. If you cancel it, they'll know they succeeded. They'll scurry around like a bunch of rats when the cat dies and you'll have more problems on your hands. On the outside, I say it should be business as usual. Don't let them know how deeply they affected us. And then behind the scenes, when they're least expecting it, we nail their asses."

Jackson pulled out a half sandwich from somewhere and took a bite. "He does make a good p—"

"Stop. Just shut the hell up. Everyone." Santiago fired off a string of expletives in several languages, ignoring that they all were lifting their eyebrows and rolling their eyes at his outburst. Let them. It was no skin off his nose. They could bellyache all they wanted, but in the end, it was his decision to make.

The room was uncomfortably silent as he absently scraped at another splinter in this thumb. Last thing

Santiago wanted was for Darkbloods to think they had the upper hand. Leave it to a guy who spent years inside Darkblood operations feeding intel to the Agency, to know how the bastards thought and operated. He had to admit, Alfonso did make some good points.

"We'd have to step up security," Santiago said finally. "Eliminate all possible breaches."

For the next few minutes, they hashed out exactly what needed to be done if the ceremony wasn't cancelled.

"That doesn't solve the original problem," Lily said quietly when everyone was done talking. "We don't know the source of the leaks."

"I still think you and Roxy should pretend to be lovers," Jackson said bluntly, wiping the back of a hand over his mouth. "What a fun way to find the traitor."

"I don't care about *fun*." Santiago pinched the bridge of his nose as his head began to pound. The lingering effects of UV exposure weren't something he needed right now. If he had known all this was going to happen, he would have fought the urge to go to the Ridge. "Some might know she's the head tracker at the Academy."

Jackson shrugged. "So what? We have various trackers there all the time. She could be your new hot girlfriend who's in town because she's going to the ceremony with you. She could poke around, ask a few innocent questions, and no one would be the wiser."

Alfonso turned to Lily. "Do you think she'd go for it?"

"I could ask," she said.

"I don't see why it has to be her, why we have to involve an outsider." Santiago was well aware that his argument was getting flimsier, but this couldn't be the only solution. "I'm perfectly capable of reading people. I'll go down there myself."

Lily laughed. "And you're about as subtle as my fist to Jackson's nose. Seriously, Santiago, Roxy's amazing at analyzing people and their underlying motivations."

"Hey," Jackson protested. "Leave my nose out of this."

Lily recounted an event that happened when Roxanne was mentoring her out in the field when she was a trainee at Tracker Academy. "We were following Darkblood scent in New Orleans, which led to a small voodoo shop in the French Quarter. With all the smells permeating the small space—herbs, potions, gris-gris— I was having a hard time distinguishing the one I'd been tracking. The shop owner, an elderly human woman whose face was as weathered as a dried apple, was arguing with a customer. It was obvious she didn't want him to leave. I assumed she wanted him to buy one of her concoctions, but Roxy said it had nothing to do with making a sale. She could tell that the woman's motives for keeping him in her shop were pure, not selfish. But the man didn't listen. Ten minutes later, he was killed in the middle of Canal Street by a runaway carriage."

Jackson sat forward in his chair. "So the old woman was a psychic."

"Yes, and Roxy knew she was telling the truth simply by listening to her."

"Remind me not to invite her to play poker," Jackson said.

Alfonso was nodding his head. "That's pretty compelling, Santiago. She didn't have to talk to the woman to get a good read on her intentions. All she did was listen. I say you should do this thing. What would it hurt?"

Santiago was fighting a losing battle and started to protest again.

"Guess you could always send her down there on her own," Lily said.

"Kind of defeats the purpose though," Alfonso countered. "People would wonder why she was there. Sure, you could invent something, but this is the simplest solution of all. She's Santiago's girlfriend, in town to attend the gala. Doesn't get much simpler than that."

With every beat of his heart, this headache grew stronger. Santiago did not want to pretend to be Roxanne Reynolds's lover. That would mean she'd have to share his room at the field office, that they'd have to put on a show and act like they cared about each other. She was too different from him to make a charade like that work.

Besides, he didn't let affairs of the heart control him in real life, so he sure as hell didn't want to pretend they did. Hell, he wouldn't even know how to act in a fake relationship. He rarely let himself carry on with a woman longer than a few days and he always kept his heart out of it. His father's philandering ways had destroyed their family and Santiago had vowed long ago that he'd never repeat his mistakes. A night or two with the same woman was one thing, but several weeks?

He could almost smell his father's cigar now as he thought about one of the last conversations they'd had.

"The sins of the father are passed down to the son," his father had said, tilting his head back and blowing out a thick stream of smoke. "You have to realize that the men in our family were not meant to be monogamous. This nature of ours—it is in our genes and there is nothing we can do about it. Our seed does not belong inside just one woman."

As far as Santiago knew, his father hadn't produced any children outside his marriage, but it wasn't from a lack of trying. His parents had been pressured to get married and have more offspring after his mother had gotten pregnant. Given the low birth rates among their people, when a pairing turned out to be fruitful, their society urged them to have more.

Having seen what his father's actions had done to his mother, Santiago swore he'd never do the same to any woman. If promiscuity truly was in their genes, then he didn't want to destroy a woman like his father had done. Because when the mother suffered, so did the children. And he sure as hell didn't want to produce sons who'd do the same thing. As far as he was concerned, the sins of the father stopped with him.

Besides, there was something about Roxanne that unsettled him, caused him to think about things he'd rather not. And he happened to like himself just the way he was.

"You two could play house," Jackson said. "Who knows? You might actually like it."

For the second time tonight, Santiago pounded his fist on the conference room table. "Absolutely not."

THERE HAD TO be a crib here at region headquarters somewhere, Roxy thought. Mackenzie said there wasn't, which seemed crazy. Miguel couldn't be the only child to ever stay here, no matter how uncommon vampire children were. But if there really wasn't a crib here, then Roxy planned to head into town and buy one. And Santiago would just have to run it through as an expense.

She pushed open the door to his outer office, but it was empty. His assistant's chair was tucked into her desk and the few personal things on the top were arranged neatly. Had the woman even been in today? It sure didn't look like it. Either that or she was extremely neat and tidy. Glancing around at how orderly the colored files were behind her desk, Roxy figured the latter was true.

She stared at the closed double doors, wondering what she should do. If she knocked, would he even answer? Her tracker senses told her he was there. Maybe she should come back another time when Jenella was around. As she debated what to do, she heard a series of crashes behind the doors. Without thinking, she grabbed the handles and pushed them open.

The office was an absolute mess—chairs overturned, papers scattered everywhere, chunks of plaster and dust covered much of the floor. He'd thrown something—a chair, maybe?—at the ceiling at some point. With his back to her, Santiago said something in a language she didn't recognize—no doubt a curse—and swiped a hand over the remaining items on his desk. Everything on top of it went flying, including his computer monitor.

"Whoa," she said, ducking. It landed with a crash on the wall about three feet away from her and shattered.

He spun to face her, an angry fire blazing in his eyes. "What the hell do you want?"

This was madness. What had gotten into him that he'd want to completely destroy his office like this? It wouldn't be a matter of just righting a few desks and chairs and straightening papers. This would take a whole crew of repairmen to fix the damage.

Breathing heavily, he stared at her, his nostrils flared, his mouth slightly ajar, exposing the tips of his fangs. His tattoo seemed darker all of a sudden, more ominous than it had before.

At first, she thought about turning on her heel and coming back another time. Clearly, she was not meant to have witnessed this, but she wasn't going to let him scare her off. Where was the in-control man she was used to seeing around the offices? The man who confidently fired off orders that people eagerly followed through on? Even though a part of her wanted to leave, she knew she needed to stay strong and continue.

"I came to ask a question but I can see that the commanding officer has been possessed by a madman."

"Where's Jenella?" His voice sounded as if he'd just straight-shot a glass of gravel. "Why did she let you in?"

Roxy shrugged. "She wasn't there."

He kicked at what she thought was a part of his printer. "You shouldn't be here either. Leave."

She bristled. Not before she got what she came for.

"Are you through yet?" She could see him stiffen, but she wasn't dissuaded from continuing. Miguel needed a crib. Mackenzie needed him to sleep in one, in order for her to get some decent rest. Something told Roxy to keep pushing. "What's gotten into you? Why have you destroyed your office?"

"You weren't supposed to see this," he said. "No one was."

"Well, the noise was hard to miss." Several books were balanced precariously on the edge of the shelf so she pushed them all the way in and stooped to pick up one from the floor.

"Don't."

"Don't what?" She slid it back onto the bookshelf. Judging by the leather spines, there were some old ones here. It'd be a shame if any of them got bent or torn.

"I don't want you coming in here and...cleaning up."

Yeah, he probably expected his assistant to do it. Maybe that was why she was gone in the first place. She wanted her boss to clean up his own damn mess for once.

His chest continued to rise and fall, the muscles in his arms bulging, reminding her of a bull in an arena ready to charge. Only she wasn't scared. She'd always felt sorry for the bulls.

"This wasn't the reason I came." She spotted another

book on the floor behind the broken computer monitor. Oh, for goddsake. It was a first edition of The Call of the Wild. "What is the matter with you?"

He exhaled, his shoulders slumping slightly in defeat. "What do you want?"

She flung her hand around. "I want to know what this is about."

"There's nothing for you to understand. I already told you to leave. This is none of your concern."

But she couldn't just leave. She wanted to know more. Why the tantrum? He seemed like the most controlled and in-charge man she'd ever met. And this, she thought, looking at all the broken computer equipment and upended furniture, was far from that.

She narrowed her eyes and studied him. He seemed to have calmed down a little; his pupils weren't quite so dilated, his breathing had slowed. Maybe the problem was that he was cool on the outside while torment raged on the inside. She had no idea why, but for some reason, it was important for her to keep pushing in order to better understand him.

"What if I don't want to leave? What if I...care why you've done this?"

His head snapped up as if he'd been slapped, his eyes dark and menacing. "Why would you care about me? I've not exactly been warm and welcoming to you."

He made it sound as if he'd been consciously trying to act like a jerk. She'd done nothing to warrant being treated like that on purpose. Then it dawned on her.

Maybe her past had followed her. Maybe he'd heard the accusations from long ago and didn't want her here.

She stood a little taller and put a wall of iron around her heart. "Well, for one thing, I need to know how to get a crib set up in Mackenzie's room. She's exhausted and the only way she's going to get any rest is if Miguel sleeps in his own bed. Which means the region needs a damn crib. If you don't have one, then I'm driving to the nearest town right now and buying one. And you're going to reimburse me."

His expression seemed to soften just a little and he leaned on the edge of his desk. "And what was the other reason?"

"I…I…don't know. Guess I just wanted to see if I could help."

His gaze darted around the room. He seemed to see the destruction for the first time through the eyes of a reasonable man because he actually looked a little sheepish. He strode over to the wet bar and grabbed a bottle of scotch. "Want one?"

Was that supposed to be a peace offering of some sort? She crossed her arms over her chest. "Not if I'm going to have to drive to the store and buy a crib."

He smiled then, not one of those big, movie-star smiles with the gleaming eyes and the perfect teeth that made you want to strip off your panties, but a quiet, almost diminutive smile that said he knew she was right, he was wrong, and that maybe her past was still in the past after all.

He picked up his phone, barked a few orders and

hung up. "Okay, Roxanne. Miguel will have a crib within the hour."

"Thank you. That's going to make it so much better for Mackenzie." She ran her hands along the spines of the books and smiled. "Please, I'd like it if you called me Roxy."

He studied her face for a moment before his gaze traveled slowly down her body all the way to her feet then back up again as if he were seeing her for the first time, as well. A ball of warmth concentrated in her belly and radiated outward, making her cheeks feel as if they were on fire. She resisted the urge to cool them with her palms.

He held up the bottle again. "Are you sure?"

"Um, thanks, but no. I'm a frou-frou drink person all the way." At the amused expression on his face she added, "You know, daiquiris, cosmos, anything that comes with an umbrella."

He poured himself a drink and knocked it back in one swallow. Twisting the glass around in his hand, he seemed to be inordinately interested in the tiny amount of scotch that was left at the bottom. A tiny muscle in his jaw ticked as if he was chewing on his thoughts.

"Positive?" He set the glass down and looked at her pointedly. "Because you might want one after what I'm about to ask you."

A dozen red flags flapped in her head and her mouth went dry. First he wanted her out of his office and now he wanted to chat? Why the turnaround? She had a really bad feeling about this. Maybe she should take him up on his offer because she was suddenly very thirsty. Too bad she hated scotch.

She supposed it wouldn't hurt to hear him out. Trying to maintain her composure, she opened the small refrigerator and spotted a small can of grapefruit juice. "Got any vodka?"

"Right here."

"Then I'll have a greyhound. And don't add too much juice. I want to be able to taste the alcohol."

Grabbing a glass that hadn't been broken, he made the drink, poured himself another scotch and pointed to the couch, the only piece of furniture unaffected by his tirade. "Take this and sit down," he said in that gravelly voice of his. "But I'm afraid I'm fresh out of umbrellas."

CHAPTER SIX

THE CHAMBER WAS lit only by candles. Hundreds of them. Encased in identical frosted-glass votive holders, they sat on almost every flat surface, casting a warm, flickering light on the stone walls.

People came here for answers, comfort or guidance, which Santiago had never understood. He didn't feel he should have to look beyond the borders of his own skin for validation or support. He was a firm believer in being the driver of your own life. If you wanted something, you took it. If you worried about something, you figured it out. If you needed someone to do something, you told them. You didn't stew or fret or ask for opinions. He sure as hell didn't live his life by committee—earthly or divine. A savvy combination of fists and brainpower was the only formula for success he subscribed to and it had served him well the past two hundred years.

So, when he stepped inside the sanctuary, it wasn't answers he sought.

Roxy was bent over the small altar on the dais, lighting candles with a long match that reminded him of the cigarette holders used by old Hollywood starlets. And like those women, there was something timelessly beautiful about her look, something that would never go out of fashion.

Nothing about her was hurried. She was agonizingly slow in everything she did and it drove him mad. Deliberate and methodical, she spent way too much time thinking about shit. Introspection and Santiago were like oil and water. They didn't mix no matter how hard you shook them. He was a shoot-now-ask-questions-later kind of guy, but without the questions.

Her off-white gauzy dress skimmed her ankles and because her movements were slow and fluid, it gave her the appearance of floating on the stage. She was barefoot, and the light from behind silhouetted her long legs through the thin fabric. Her arms were ballet-dancer graceful and something sparkled in the soft, loose curls that fell past her shoulders. Whether it was now or a hundred years ago, men would find her classically beautiful and elegant.

If she thought she could avoid dealing with "his proposition," as she'd called it, by running and hiding out here, she was sadly mistaken. Not much happened around region headquarters without him knowing about it. A snap of a finger or a terse phone call and his people told him everything he wanted to know. Which included reports that she'd gone into the sanctuary.

But it wasn't a proposition he'd given her back in his office. It was a goddamn order.

She still hadn't acknowledged him with so much as a glance in his direction or a nod of her head, so he shut the heavy, hand-carved doors behind him with a bang.

She didn't jump or act surprised. She simply turned around and those golden eyes burned right through him, as if she'd known the whole time that he was here.

Undaunted, he strode up the center aisle between the rows of pews, the sound of his boots echoing irreverently throughout the chamber. "Are you trying to hide from me, Ms. Reynolds?" Going back to formalities emphasized who was in charge—him.

"Hide? Try *ignore*."

"Because if you are, it's a waste of time. My people tell me everything. You cannot—"

Wait. Did she say she was ignoring him? He came to a screeching halt. The woman came here because she was…snubbing him? Impossible. No one gave the region commander the brush-off. When he gave an order, people did what they were told.

"No one ignores me, Ms. Reynolds."

"Am I supposed to be thrilled for you?" She turned back around and continued lighting those damn candles, dismissing him.

His blood boiled up like an active volcano and he spat out the toothpick he kept clenched between his teeth.

She was belittling him, discounting his authority. No one dared defy him like that.

No one.

He wanted to pound his fists through the walls and rip the sanctuary apart. Yank out a bench, lift it over his head, and throw it across the room. Instead, he stormed between the last set of pews and kicked at a hymnal that someone left lying on the floor. When he stomped onto the dais, the whole thing shook and a dozen tiny flames flickered.

She turned to face him, hands on her hips. From the defiant tilt of her chin, it was clear he didn't intimidate her in the slightest. "What is your problem?"

Eucalyptus from either her shampoo or lotion faintly filled the air around him, while the fire in her eyes stirred up his insides. Both sensations were pleasing and he started to relax until he remembered the *dakai* thing. His sister had smelled of weird scented oils, too, because of that cult.

He moved in close until he towered over her, but she didn't back away. Even with her head cranked back, she seemed to be able to level a stare at him. This vexed him even more. "I gave you a direct order."

"Yes, I know you did." She wasn't at all impressed. "Too bad you have no authority over me." There was a gleeful tone to her voice. It was subtle, but it was there.

Rather than stare her down, he stormed off the dais and stalked around the room.

"And don't think you can go and have another one of your juvenile tantrums to make me cave," she called after him.

"Juvenile? Where do you get off thinking you can call me that?"

"Oh, I'm sorry. You're right. You're not juvenile."

He started to relax. She was right to be apologizing because—

"You're more infantile than anything."

What? His head was seriously going to explode. No

one spoke to him this way. Back in his office, he'd told her she was going to accompany him to Seattle and masquerade as his lover in order to root out the traitor. End of story. He didn't expect her to like the plan, but he damn well expected her to go along with it.

With an expression devoid of all emotion, she'd listened quietly to the rationale of posing as lovers in order to throw people in the Seattle field office off guard. When she didn't react, he continued. He told her what Lily had said, that she had an uncanny ability to tell if someone's motivations were good or not. Figuring he was stroking her ego, he assumed she'd jump at the chance to work on such an assignment with someone of his stature. When he was done, however, she'd stood from the couch, calmly placed the glass on his desk and walked out of the room without a word or a backward glance. He'd been so stunned by this it took him a moment to go after her. But by then, she was gone.

He gripped the back of one of the pews and glared at her. There she was on the dais looking like a damn angel. A pissed off but gorgeous angel. Even the light from behind framed her like a halo.

It wasn't him, was it? No, it couldn't be. Most women would jump at the chance to be his lover, so what was her problem?

The overturned hymnal at his feet, its pages curled under and bent, reminded him of the book she'd rescued from his office. He grabbed it, smoothed out the pages then set it back in on the seat.

Maybe she was fighting him because he was going

about it the wrong way. He slumped down on the bench and rested his elbows on the seat in front of him. "The crib and bedding arrived and were put in Mackenzie's room. Miguel fell asleep promptly, so…ah…thanks for bringing that to my attention."

"Glad to hear it. Now, are you finished? I'm busy." With her hands on her hips, she didn't look the slightest bit intimidated by his gruff manner. In fact, if he wasn't mistaken, she actually seemed to welcome it. Her eyes were livelier than he'd ever seen them before. There was a fire behind them now.

God, this woman was infuriatingly frustrating. He jumped to his feet.

What she needed was… He stormed around the room and cast around for good ideas. Hell, what she needed was a good paddling. And he'd enjoy giving her one, too, he thought. His hand to her bare butt. He wouldn't do it hard—he'd make it sting just enough to hurt, to let her know who was boss.

Oh, for fuck's sake. He wasn't that much of a Neanderthal, was he? Rubbing the tattoos on this neck, he had to admit it did sound a little exciting. Actually, more than just a little. He stiffened just thinking about it.

He gave her a sidelong look. The flickering candlelight brought out the golden highlights in her hair. It looked like spun gold, making him ache to run his fingers through it to discover if it was as luxurious as he remembered when he pulled that twig from her hair on the side of the road. She had the kind of hair that a real caveman would hold on to for leverage as he thrust inside her every night.

"This is not a request, Ms. Reynolds. You will share my quarters when we get to the field office and we'll act the part of lovers in order to get to the bottom of what's going on. I will not have another Guardian in this region hurt because of some goddamned traitor." He couldn't care less that she didn't want to or that he'd spoiled her little meditation party. His needs and the needs of the region were more important right now. They superseded everything. He waved his hand in the air and the nearby candles flickered again. "Pack your things. We depart for Seattle at dusk."

She gave a little laugh and lit another one of those long matches. "You think you can just waltz in and bully me into something that I want no part of? Whatever is going on here is the Horseshoe Bay Region's problem, not mine."

"I'm not a bully," he said gruffly.

"I don't know what else to call it. You're trying to force me into doing something that I don't want to do. I mean, I sympathize that you want to get to the bottom of this, but I…I'm not the one to help you do that." The flame she held shook slightly, belying her calm exterior. There was something more to her reluctance to help him out, he thought. Something she was hiding.

An unexpected sensation tugged at his insides, one he wasn't familiar with. He suddenly didn't want to scare or intimidate her. He wanted her to choose to do this with him, not be forced into it. Why couldn't she just do what he wanted her to do? Life would be so much easier that way.

Given what Lily had said, Roxy may be the only one with the finesse to help him out. "No one else has the skills you do."

"This is your fight. Not mine."

There had to be more to it than that. She'd seen what Mackenzie was going through. He'd have thought that would be motivation enough for her to get on board.

Was it the whole posing as lovers thing? It couldn't be that…could it? Normally, women found him very desirable and he couldn't ever remember having this much trouble talking a woman into sharing his bed. And he didn't even have plans to have sex with her.

What was it then? He racked his brain for an answer, but came up empty. He discreetly checked his breath. No, it was fine, but he popped in a breath mint anyway.

Maybe it was as simple as her not liking him. For some reason, this possible explanation bothered him more the most.

"I'd like it…if you could help me." The words felt unfamiliar as they formed on his tongue, the tone awkward and clunky. It reminded him how it felt to write and eat with his right hand. As a boy, his mother told him that the left hand was the hand of the devil, so she'd tie it behind his back to force him to use his right hand instead. Fortunately (or unfortunately, depending on who you asked), it didn't work and he grew up as left-handed as they came. "I need to find out who's doing this to my people so that no other family has to go through what Dom's family is going through right now."

Her hard expression cracked and a range of emotion played out on her face. It was as if a part of her wanted to help, but something was holding her back. "I'm not a Guardian any longer. Haven't been one for decades. I'm just a trainer." She turned away from him and continued lighting candles.

Just? She was the premiere trainer of all the Agency's best scent trackers and a highly respected educator around North America. She single-handedly took down two Darkbloods without being armed. Surely, she didn't doubt her own abilities. He frowned, not understanding her reaction. Could her refusal to help out have nothing to do with him? The realization hit him like a hammer over the head. He hadn't considered that possibility before. He wasn't used to not having things revolve around him.

Was she was afraid to get involved in an Agency mission again?

He recalled the latest tidbit of intel he'd received but hadn't shared with anyone yet. "I know what happened to Ian."

The chamber was so quiet, he could hear the faint sizzle of all those burning candle wicks. Slowly, she turned around and when her gaze met his, her expression had changed.

Gone was the mask of serenity he'd become accustomed to seeing. The calm eyes, the sensible tone in her conversations with students. She had an unshakable steadiness about her. Until now. In its place was a smoldering fire.

He continued. "I know that he was killed by Darkbloods."

Her eyes narrowed to slits. "And why do you believe that? There are many within the Agency who think I was responsible for his death."

"Well, they're idiots." He had the sudden urge to find out everyone who thought she was guilty and pound his fist into their faces. "For one thing, I don't believe you're capable of doing something like that."

"They talked about bringing me before a tribunal, you know."

"Yes, I do." And he knew just who was responsible for that—the prick of a CO down there.

"Then you'll also know that they believed that I'd left my post, which in turn left Ian vulnerable."

"Bullshit lies." He eyed another hymnal but refrained from kicking it. "I know Dax Sturgeon and how he operates. He was new to the region at the time, eager to establish his influence and power. You were a means to that end. I've had many run-ins with him myself."

Gripping the table, she eyed the candles in front of her and for a moment, Santiago thought she might send them flying with a flick of her hand. At least he would, if he were her.

"I don't know why I'm even telling you this," she mumbled under her breath. "I don't talk about what happened with anyone. It's in the past and best forgotten."

A strange sensation welled up inside him that he

couldn't quite identify. He felt suddenly protective of her and had the urge to make things right in her world. "You're telling me because you can sense that I care and that I truly believe you."

"Ha. *You* care about *me?* You've got a funny way of showing it. Why should I take you seriously? You've probably got an agenda just like Sturgeon did."

Santiago did have an agenda, but she knew exactly what it was. "For one thing," he said quietly, "I knew Ian."

Her head jerked up. "And you didn't say anything to me?"

He shrugged, tried to brush off her prickly stare. "I didn't think it was important. We met when we were both part of the Madrid Seven, a private mercenary group."

The fact was, they were very different people. Whereas Santiago was not afraid of hard work, Ian was always looking for the easy way out. But the guy had a big heart and had been very generous. He had a much larger stipend from his family and would often cover Santiago's expenses when they went out to the inns for a tankard of ale and to dally under a few skirts.

"He and I hung out back in the day. We caroused together and commiserated about our lot in life. I suppose it's because we came from very similar family backgrounds—our fathers were both assholes—and intuitively we understood what it was like to be in each other's shoes. I'd have to imagine that he loved you very much."

He paused, expecting her to agree quietly. It wouldn't surprise him to see a tear trickle down her face.

Instead, she quickly blew out the candles in front of her, sending thin spirals of smoke drifting up to the ceiling. Walking around the perimeter, she blew out the rest of the candles, saving the ones nearest to him for last.

He rubbed a hand over his close-cropped hair and searched for something to say to make her change her mind. If she didn't agree, he wasn't sure what other options he had. This was the best one—he didn't want to settle for anything less. A seed of desperation crept into his gut.

"Look, Roxy. I honestly think you're the best person for this job. My people are suffering and as much as it kills me to admit this, I…I may not have the ability to help them." God, he hated admitting he was weak, but what other choice did he have? "My style is too confrontational. The traitor would see my motives a mile away. You…you're subtle, smart, and people instantly gravitate toward you. I know it's not the ideal situation—masquerading as lovers—but it sets up your cover beautifully. You may be our only hope to get to the bottom of this as quickly and as quietly as possible without risking more lives."

She turned to face him, her gauzy dress swirling around her. "Okay," she said, her golden eyes blazing, "when do we leave?"

CHAPTER SEVEN

ROXY HADN'T REALIZED she'd dozed off until Santiago pulled out one of her earbuds. She rubbed her eyes and looked around. They were sitting at a red light, the city streets deserted. Straight ahead of them, on the other side of the intersection, was a nondescript building. "Where are we?"

"Fresno," he said without skipping a beat.

Smart-ass. "Okay, dumb question. I guess I wasn't expecting to get to Seattle so soon." She should've known the relaxation music would knock her out. Santiago had taken several calls during the drive, so rather than listen to him chew out yet another person, she put on her headphones and promptly fell asleep.

"What can I say, I'm an efficient driver."

She'd been expecting the drive from the Canadian border to Seattle to take at least three hours. How the hell had he made it in two? "Either that or an insane one." On second thought, maybe she didn't want to know.

He revved the Corvette's engine, twice, and it roared loudly as if answering. Either that or it was announcing, "We're here."

Subtlety clearly wasn't one of his strong points. What

was it with men and their cars? A guy who drove a vintage sports car like this must like the attention he got from people. The looks. The admiration. The jealousy. Looking at the retro instrument panel and hearing the powerful drone of the engine, she had to admit it was a pretty sweet ride.

"You ready?"

She looked at him, confused.

"The cloaking device. It's set to maximum."

"Oh, thanks for the heads-up." Most Guardian offices were kept cloaked, especially ones located in the cities. She gathered the length of her hair back with a hand. "Okay. Ready."

Santiago punched the accelerator and the sports car jumped forward, thrusting Roxy deep into the leather seat. The tiny hairs on her arms tingled when they hit the invisible shield surrounding the building. A split second later, bolts of electricity snapped around them, lighting up the outside of the car with a rainbow of colors. The brick of the building's facade morphed into a parking garage entrance and the car plunged inside.

"Whew. You weren't kidding about that being set high," she said as he pulled into an empty parking space next to a jacked-up pickup truck. Her hair still felt slightly lifted from her scalp. She did her best to smooth down the errant locks and rubbed her hands over her arms.

"They had some problems here a while back so we beefed up everything, implemented a lot of changes."

She grabbed the bag near her feet. Good thing she

packed lightly. The storage in this car was roughly the size of a dog. A small one.

"Roxanne, you'll need to—"

"Hold on," she said, her hand on the door. "If you want the charade to be as realistic as possible, you'd better start calling me Roxy like my friends do."

"We're not friends though, we're lovers."

The way he said it, as if it were a fact and not a charade, sent shivers up and down her spine. The good kind of shivers. The kind that made you want to take off your clothes and wrap your body around his. "Same difference."

Lovers. A vision of a naked Santiago flashed in her mind, sparking a warmth in her belly that quickly heated her insides. She had to admit, taking him as a lover would be pretty spectacular. To stroke her hands over his powerful muscles as he moved inside her. To press her nose to his flesh and drag his scent into her lungs. Would he be as commanding in bed as he was out of it? Despite her years at the Academy surrounded by the kinds of men she wanted to be attracted to— thoughtful and intelligent men, those who weighed their decisions carefully and were driven by logic, not their emotion—she was still hopelessly drawn to these rough, brash, military types. Was he one of those men who would take what he needed from a woman, assuming it was the same thing she needed? Would her teeth sink easily into his vein or would she have to bite down a little harder and force her way in? She had a feeling that anything involving Santiago wouldn't be easy. No doubt, he tasted as good as he looked. Her gums tingled imagining it.

Hell, what was she thinking? She took a deep breath to clear out these crazy thoughts. Blood sharing wasn't all that common during sex and it usually happened between committed couples, not casual acquaintances. Except for that botched tryst with another instructor at the Academy, Ian was the only man she'd shared blood with. So why she was thinking of it with Santiago was beyond her comprehension. Too bad she couldn't blame it on being in a drunken stupor, but she was as sober as a preacher's wife on Sunday morning.

They exited the car and the shock of cold thankfully jolted her out of la-la land, chilling her libido. She did not need to be thinking of the man this way. He'd already made it clear that he was not interested in her.

"Here." Santiago must've noticed her shivering because he took off his leather jacket and held it out to her.

"I'm fine."

"No, you're not. You're from Florida."

A laugh bubbled from her throat at his unintended slight.

"You know what I mean." Amusement danced in his eyes. "Take it."

When she didn't immediately grab it from him, he draped the coat over her shoulders anyway. The warmth was heavenly. The smell, too. Sandalwood and cedar and a touch of something else that she couldn't quite identify. It was nice though. She pulled the lapel tightly around her.

As they went through the series of security checkpoints where several guards were standing duty, Santiago kept his hand on the small of her back, like a lover would. When he removed it to stand before the optical scanners right before the main doors to the field office opened, she felt cold again. His hand was like a comforting heater, warming her from the outside in.

The reinforced steel door slid open and as they stepped through, it closed with a heavy thud behind them. All the field offices she'd visited had fairly tight security, but this had to be the tightest. She hummed a few bars of the *Get Smart* theme song.

Santiago headed for the conveyor belt to pick up his scanned weapons. She, on the other hand, had none. He didn't think it would play well into their scheme of things if she had weapons on her. When she'd called him on it, his only reply was that she was just a girlfriend, not an agent, and girlfriends didn't carry weapons.

Ha. We'll see about that.

A young man wearing a freshly starched uniform stood at attention near a bank of closed circuit monitors showing various locations throughout the complex. A woman walking down a hall. A dark-haired man in a kitchen. Two people leaning against a doorway with white workout towels tossed over their shoulders.

Santiago leaned casually on the receptionist desk and smiled. "Kato, thanks for the tip last week. I won a couple hundred bucks on that horse."

The young man beamed. "You're welcome, sir. I told you Hot Cha Cha was looking good."

"Who you picking for the Mile?"

"I haven't decided yet. Pee Diddly has been running well lately, but then so has Make Me A Winner, but it'll depend on the track conditions. If it's muddy, then I'm looking at Slew Or Don't. His daddy was a mudder and those other two are girlie-men when it comes to a sloppy, wet track. Sir."

"Pee Diddly, Make Me A Winner and…what's the last one? Yes Or No?"

"Slew Or Don't." Kato tried to hide a smile, but that one dimple on the left side of his mouth gave him away. "How about if I email it to you like I did last time?"

"That'd be perfect."

Santiago turned toward her and lifted a brow in an unasked question.

She wasn't picking up any strange vibes from Kato other than nervousness at being around the CO, so she subtly shook her head. One down. How many dozens more to go? And that was only counting those who worked at the field office. It didn't count the people who'd be attending the awards banquet.

Santiago motioned her toward the open elevator. Once inside, he pushed an unmarked button on the panel, but she couldn't tell if they were going up or down. She assumed down because she knew the Seattle field office was located in a portion of Underground Seattle, but she couldn't be sure.

Santiago leaned down close to her ear. She started to take a half step backward but his arm shot out and held her close. Her hips were practically grinding against his. "Security cameras," he explained. If she turned her head slightly right now, her lips would meet his. "Have you decided on a last name yet?"

"I still think that's unnecessary. Who cares that you're 'dating' Roxanne Reynolds?"

"I know you haven't met anyone here, but who knows if someone looks into your background once they meet you?" His breath was hot against her cheek. "Your storied reputation at Tracker Academy might put the traitor on edge. I want you to simply be a pretty face. Someone who asks wide-eyed, innocent questions. Can you do that?"

She bristled at his patronizing tone, but she was here now, so what choice did she have? "I don't agree with you. I think it's ridiculous, but this is your mission, so whatever you say goes."

When he pulled away from her slightly, she detected a satisfied look in his eye. As though he knew she'd eventually cave to his demands if he pushed her hard enough. What a sore winner. If only agreeing with him wasn't so painful.

"Just make it easy, a name that we can both remember."

"Why? Do you have a bad memory?"

"I don't want some damned complicated Eastern European or Polish name. If it's hard to pronounce, it'll be hard to remember, so keep it vanilla. Something like Smith or Jones."

She ground her teeth together and could feel her nostrils flare. Her mother was Polish. "I'll make sure it's easy enough that your simple mind can retain it."

He chuckled and gave her a kiss on the cheek as if he truly enjoyed her put-down. Sure, it was just for the cameras but a tiny part inside—a lonely, stupid, achy part—wished it were real. That they were so familiar with each other that good-natured teasing and a peck on the cheek were as common as holding hands.

"That's my girl."

She stared at him, unblinking for a moment as his words sank in. Had he really seriously just called her a girl? Her nails dug into the palms of her hands and those feelings fled like Harrison Ford in *The Fugitive*. So much for fantasizing about Santiago in bed. Right now, all she wanted was to turn that infuriating smile of his into a look of shock.

Just you wait. Next time I'll be doing the smiling.

"Me and my pea brain thank you."

The elevator stopped soundlessly and the doors opened with a whoosh. She bent to pick up her luggage, but he beat her to it and hefted the strap over his shoulder. Okay fine. It was the whole chivalrous boyfriend thing, so she folded her arms and let him.

He gave her a strange look, one of confusion or possibly disbelief.

"What?" she asked. Did he expect her to protest? Think she wouldn't want to accept his help after being insulted like that?

"It's so lightweight."

"Yeah, and your point is?"

"You don't have much inside." Then, lowering his voice he said, "We could be here for several weeks."

"I travel lightly, what can I say?"

"And did you think to bring something to wear to the banquet? It's formal attire, you know."

She hadn't thought about that. Clothes weren't a huge priority for her. She liked looking good but it didn't dawn on her to spend a lot of time worrying about it. She was as low maintenance as they came, preferring very little makeup and her yoga attire over tight clothes and skyscraper heels. Besides, what appropriate clothes she had were down in Florida. She hadn't planned on attending any fancy affairs while she was here. "I...ah..."

"Just as I suspected. I'll arrange to take you shopping at nightfall tomorrow."

Arrange? As in have someone take her so that he can foot the bill? Nope. Not happening. Even for the purposes of this charade, she was not a kept woman. She took her independence seriously and she didn't wanted to feel indebted to this man for anything, whether he held it over her head or not. Carrying her bag was one thing. Buying her clothes was another.

A large table with a huge bouquet of fresh flowers stood straight ahead of them in the foyer. The corridor stretched out on both sides and Santiago hesitated.

"Lost?"

"No, just deciding whether to head to my suite of rooms first or whether I should take you into the offices."

"What would a romantic couple do?"

He looked at her and smiled. "Good point."

They walked down the empty corridor in silence, the lights clicking on and off as they passed various motion sensors. How far down were his rooms anyway? she wondered after a few minutes. It felt as if they'd walked ten miles already. After climbing a half-flight of stairs and rounding another corner, he stopped. Finally. Just like the outside of the building, the door was unremarkable.

His rooms were done in a masculine forest-green with old-fashioned English paintings of horses and dogs on the walls. God, the guy really did love animals. In one corner was a comfortable reading nook with two leather wing chairs you could sink into, a brass-bound chest that served as a coffee table and a shelf of books— collectors' editions given the fancy bindings—behind them. Santiago really was a reader? For some reason, he didn't strike her as having the patience to actually sit down and open a book, let alone read one from cover to cover. He seemed the type who would read a few pages—maybe a chapter or two—then give up to go do something he felt was more important. Unlike her colleague at the Academy who read anything he could get his hands on and could quote just about anything ever written, Santiago possessed none of these characteristics. She figured the books in his region office were just for show.

A huge, dark hardwood bed, covered in sumptuous green linens and pillows, stood proudly on the far side of the room. Not far from it stood a door.

Was her room through there? Santiago had referred to his suite of rooms—plural. She didn't care about sleeping in his office on a rollaway cot or fold-out couch. They'd have to coordinate the use of the bathroom, however. Even if there was another one nearby, it'd look very out of character if she stumbled out of bed and down the hall to use it.

She walked over and opened the door only to find that it led to a large walk-in closet. A chuckle sounded behind her. She ignored it, instead focusing on the sudden pounding of blood behind her temples. The only other door had to be the bathroom, but she tried it anyway. Sure enough. It was luxuriously tiled with a huge soaking tub, freestanding glass shower with two showerheads, and a mile-long marble counter with two sinks and elegant faucets curved like a swan's neck. She spun back around. Santiago stood in the center of the room, his hands on his hips. One thing was glaringly missing.

"Looking for something?"

She glanced around the room. "I… A…"

"If you need to use the facilities, I can assure you I won't be able to hear a thing out here. All the rooms at the field office, even interior ones, are very private." He chuckled as if he were remembering something.

"I assumed we'd have adjoining rooms or at the very least, a pullout bed."

"You assumed wrong." He brushed past her and stepped into the bathroom as casual as could be. She could hear the water in the shower turn on. He even started whistling.

This was just not acceptable. She hadn't agreed to this. At all. "But what about—"

He popped his head out. At some point, he'd pulled off his shirt. Did he have any idea what the sight of him like this did to her? His well-muscled chest and abs were like candy under a glass case.

Beautiful. Tempting. Unreachable.

She tried not to stare at him, but she had a feeling she was doing a lousy job. Her eyes seemed to want to take him all in whether she wanted them to or not.

"Lovers would not use separate beds." Even his voice sounded deeper, sexier than it had five minutes ago. "Maybe chaste religious types would, but I can assure you, I'm neither chaste nor religious."

There was that warm feeling in her stomach again. She glanced at the bed and suddenly it didn't look as big as it did when they first walked in. It was entirely too small. Postage-stamp small, if you asked her. "Then I'll find a sleeping bag."

He opened the bathroom door wider and she could see that the top button of his pants was unfastened. "You'll do no such thing. That will tip off everyone if you go around asking for a sleeping bag to be brought to my room. No. You're sleeping in my bed. With me. And that's final."

CHAPTER EIGHT

SANTIAGO STOPPED AT the first conference-room door and turned around when he realized Roxy wasn't keeping up with him. She had stopped with one hand resting on the wall and the other hand on her chest. All the color had drained from her face and it looked as if she was having a hard time breathing. He rushed to her side and grabbed her elbow to steady her.

Jesus, was she going to pass out? "What's wrong? Are you okay?"

"Yeah, I'm fine." She sounded out of breath.

"Don't bullshit me. No, you're not."

Leaning heavily on his arm, she shook her head. "It's probably nothing. Just give me a minute." She took a deep breath, held it a moment, then pursed her lips and blew it out slowly. He watched her do it three more times.

Despite his better judgment, he found her impossibly attractive. In direct contrast to the storm brewing inside him, she had a peaceful calm about her that drew him in like a magnet. With her eyes closed like this, he could really study her face close up. Her skin was creamy smooth and her dark lashes lay against her cheeks like tiny brushes. For a moment, he forgot who they both were and wondered how her lips would feel against his. Would she be yielding or demanding? Would she be the type of lover who would wait for his lead or would she be the one in charge? In the time she'd been here, he'd seen instances where he could imagine both scenarios.

He wanted to stroke his thumbs along her cheekbones and pull her mouth to his just to see what she would do. To mess up this calming routine of hers. To see how she'd react to something completely out of the blue. But it would be purely an experiment and not because he felt any sort of attraction to her either. Hookups between vampires routinely occurred with no romantic intentions by either party. That was all this was.

It felt as if he were watching a demonstration on yoga breathing techniques before she finally opened her eyes. They were a little brighter but none of the color returned to her face.

"Better?"

"A little." She didn't sound very convincing.

"So are you going to tell me what's going on?"

She shrugged her shoulders. "I'm fine now. This… this happens to me sometimes."

"*What* just happened? Tell me, Roxy."

She glanced down the corridor both ways then lowered her voice. "I'm getting a really strange feeling that I can't seem to shake. It's kind of like a panic attack. It's happened before. Sometimes it strikes without warning and for no reason, but at other times, there's something going on."

A pang of guilt jabbed him in the gut and he instantly

regretted what he'd said about her earlier. His mouth had a habit of working before his brain did. "What do you mean *something?*"

"I've always been good at reading people and situations. When something is, well, off, it affects my—" she waved her hands around "—my space. Maybe it's just the atmosphere down here. The air. I do tend to get claustrophobic."

"Even though the field office is located in a secret part of Underground Seattle, fresh air from above is circulated regularly through air cleaners."

"No, it's not that."

He was confused. She said it was the air and now it wasn't?

"Something's not right with the energy of this place. I can't help feeling that some*thing* or some*one* is not who they say they are."

"The field office isn't known to any humans walking above us on the streets. Our very office is a deception."

"That's not it. The *prana* of this space, the vital energy, has been disrupted somehow, but I'm not gifted in that area so I can't be for sure. I'm just feeling a disturbance, that's all."

It sounded far-fetched and if he hadn't gotten to know Roxy lately, he'd still be thinking that. "How so? What does it feel like?"

"Here, take my hand."

As soon as he did, he felt a strange jolt of energy. "What the—" He tried to pull away from her but she held him steady.

"It's very unusual to connect to another person's energy like I can with you, but let me push some of what I'm feeling to you and see if you can feel what I'm experiencing."

The tingling in his hand and arm intensified. At first, it was a very pleasant sensation. He'd never shared energies with another vampire before. It wasn't unheard of, sure, but it was highly unusual. But then, just as quickly, his gut began to churn and he seriously thought he might be getting sick.

"Jesus Christ, what the hell is going on?"

She smiled, practically beaming. "You can really feel it?"

"Yes."

"Oh, wow, that's fantastic. I was hoping you would."

"You wanted me to feel sick?" She must have a warped sense of humor. If he wasn't mistaken, she looked very proud of herself.

"What is going on?"

"I've never done it before. You know, projected onto another person like this, but I had a feeling it might work with you."

He didn't know what she was talking about but he was tired of asking questions. A good leader asked questions, absorbed the information, then formulated a response. He didn't want to admit that he had no idea what the hell she was talking about.

"I've extracted the negative energy from the atmosphere and I'm pushing it to you for you to experience, as well."

"That's insane," he said with amazement.

For an instant, he thought she looked embarrassed but then, just as quickly, it was gone. "You gotta watch us tracker types. We've got a lot of tricks up our sleeves."

He watched as she took a deep breath again and exhaled. All of a sudden the nausea was gone, as if she'd expelled it from him. What remained, however, was her warm, calming energy. When he told her this, her nostrils flared slightly and she wouldn't meet his gaze. Was she embarrassed about this for some reason?

"So what do you think is going on?"

She chewed on her lower lip a moment. "I'm not sure. I can't even tell if the person is male or female. Or for that matter, vampire or human. But it's strong enough that I wonder if it's more than just my imagination."

How much more of an idiot could she be?

Why had she felt the need to open up to Santiago? What good did it do to have him know that she suffered from panic attacks sometimes? She preferred to keep personal stuff to herself as much as she could, especially stuff like this. She didn't like to be vulnerable and show her soft underbelly to anyone.

"Is there a main area where everyone here hangs out?" she asked in an effort to forget what had just happened.

"Yeah, the kitchen. Xian, the office manager who is also the cook, makes homemade pastries every Friday. His family used to own a bakery so anything he makes

is crazy good. Anyone who's around will be there waiting for samples."

Now that he mentioned it, she did smell something
delicious. "Sounds like he does a little of everything
around here. Is he a Guardian, too?"

"No, he's human."

As they walked, he had his arm draped casually
around her in order to convey to everyone that they were
a couple. Trouble was, it felt so authentic. The way he
absently rubbed his thumb along the top of her shoulder
blade. How he shortened his long stride to match hers.
She wasn't sure if it was her imagination or not, but it
was as if her little bout back there made him act more
concerned. Even a little protective. Maybe it was the
energy sharing that had changed things between them.

Well, she didn't need or want his protection, she
thought, stiffening. She was capable of looking out for
herself. Despite that, a ball of warmth formed in the
center of her body again, making not only her cheeks
heat up but her fingers tingle, as well.

God, how she missed companionship like this. Nothing sexual, just the routine habits you had with someone you cared about. She could really get used to this
again. Not that she hadn't been with anyone since Ian
had passed away, but she had never let them get very
close, holding them out at arm's length, afraid to let
them in too much. But since she was forced to let Santiago into her little circle because of their sham, it was
like a part of her thought it was real. The whole "smile

and you'll soon be happy" philosophy. Act like you want
to be treated. The power of positive thinking.

Crap. Her inner thoughts were starting to sound like
one of Santiago's motivational talks he gave his people.

But it wasn't real. Not the concern in his eyes, the
protective way he hooked his arm around her shoulder, and not the domineering attitude he had with her
back in his bedchambers. Well, that part was real, but
it was all based on a lie. A well-crafted one they had
to construct. But as much as she hated to admit it, that
show of his back in the bedroom had really turned her
on. Although he was rough, insensitive and domineering, he was also exciting, gorgeous and one hundred
percent male.

Hell. Maybe that's why she'd had a panic attack. She
wasn't used to his commanding presence nor was she
used to being so deceptive. It made complete sense that
her energy would be disrupted. As soon as she could,
she'd slip out of the office and pay a visit to an unsus-
pecting human. No doubt they had vials of blood here,
but she felt the need for the real thing. Even though it
had only been a week or so, she could feel her energy
stores slipping. She might as well make plans to replenish what she'd lost. She'd have to figure out a good place
to go since she wasn't familiar with Seattle. Besides,
it'd give her an excuse to follow up on that lead about
Ian, no matter how far-fetched it was.

"Well, what do we have here?" A dark-haired man in
jeans and a muscle shirt came around the corner. Santiago's grip on her shoulder tightened. The man held a

couple of beer bottles in one hand and let his gaze linger slowly over her body, making her hackles go up.

I'm not an object, dickhead.

"Santiago, you devil. I didn't know you were with someone new. Whatever happened to that chick you met—"

"Roxy," Santiago said, cutting him off, "this is Val Gibson. He's on loan from the San Diego office. Up here in the Northwest, we're a little more civilized than that ragtag outfit down there, so don't pay attention to his poor manners."

On loan. It made him sound like a library book. Bummer. She liked libraries.

"Gibson, this is Roxy. She's…my fiancée." The last word fell from his mouth like a bomb.

She jerked her head up. Fiancée? Since when were they getting fake married? She sure as hell didn't remember agreeing to that. Santiago had an impish glimmer in his eye as if he was enjoying torturing her. Well, two could play at this game.

"Holy shit, Santiago. When did this happen? You horny dog, you." Gibson grinned exactly like a hyena, she decided. If hyenas could grin, that is. No, wait. She changed her mind. An alligator. She liked mammals a lot more than she like reptiles.

"We've known each other for a while but recently got reconnected and…well…one thing led to another and here we are." Santiago patted her bottom.

She gritted her teeth while trying to keep a smile plastered to her face. This was absolutely ridiculous.

Girlfriend was one thing, but fiancée? How far-fetched and unbelievable was that?

Gibson looked her up and down again with this new information. "So the CO doesn't need to be chasing skirt night after night now that he's got it waiting for him back home. Were you getting tired and decided you needed a sure thing?"

God, she hated both of them right now.

She wrapped her arms around Santiago's waist and rested her head on his chest, ignoring the amazing way he smelled. Turning slightly so that she could see Gibson, she gave him her sweetest smile. "Aw, baby," she said to Santiago, "we really can't be lying to folks like this. Go on, tell him. He doesn't look like he'll be too upset." She poked him playfully in the stomach.

"Upset?" Santiago looked down at her, confused.

She held out her hand to the alligator, half-expecting to get some strange energy vibe from him when they touched, but there was nothing. "It's so lovely to meet you, Mr. Gibson. I'm Roxy. Mrs. Roxy Santiago."

"You're…you're married?"

"Yeah, isn't it great?" She looked up at Santiago with the best adoring, new-bride expression she could muster.

He stood there, rigid, shocked. Good.

Gibson's eyes went as wide as dinner plates and his gaze ping-ponged between them.

"I kept trying to tell Pookie here that we needed to have a big wedding and invite all of our family and friends, but he insisted on eloping. Said he couldn't wait that long until everything was official. He was eager to start our lives together as husband and wife, isn't that right, sweetie?"

The murderous look on Santiago's face was priceless. It was all she could do to keep from laughing. Her stomach hurt from holding back.

"I…ah…"

"So we flew to Vegas and got married by Elvis."

CHAPTER NINE

THE MINUTE THE door to his bedroom chamber slammed shut behind him, Santiago erupted with every swear word he could think of. "What the hell was that back there?"

He stalked over to where Roxy was standing next to the closet. She didn't back away from him as he would have expected, which made him all the more frustrated. He wanted people to move, to be affected by him, and she wasn't. Balling his hands into fists, he had half a mind to sweep off all the items from a nearby credenza and listen as they crashed to the floor. Then maybe she'd react.

She stood with her feet shoulder-width apart and crossed her arms over her chest. That little move pushed her breasts up, creating visible cleavage where there had been none, and it shot straight to his groin.

"I could ask you the same thing," she said, her eyes fiery and determined, like she wasn't about to back down.

"Now everyone thinks we're fucking married."

As soon as they got to the kitchen, Gibson had opened his big mouth. People were surprised, of course. The women flocked around Roxy with smiles and hugs, while the men congratulated Santiago with hearty handshakes and promises of celebratory cigar smoking. Xian, who had been making donuts, made what he called a "wedding donut" iced with hastily colored red frosting, and had them feed pieces to each other. Claimed it was some Chinese good luck thing. But Santiago had his doubts—donuts didn't seem very Chinese to him.

She calmly brushed a strand of hair from her face. "Guess you should've thought through the ramifications of your brilliant announcement to Gibson."

"Me? You were the one who told him we got married in Vegas."

The smudge of powdered sugar on her lower lip made him long to lick it off. Given the donuts she'd eaten, her mouth would be sticky and sweet. He wanted to kiss her just to find out. To push his tongue past the seam of her lips, press his body against hers. Maybe even slip his hand up her shirt and fondle one of her breasts. No doubt the sweetness would transfer to him when he pulled away. Licking his lips now, he could almost taste it.

"Sorry to break the news to you, but that's what usually comes after you get engaged, so it's your own damn fault. You did tell me to pick out a last name that was easy to remember. I figured you wouldn't forget your own. I just hope you didn't blow it."

"What are you talking about?"

"Last time they saw you, you didn't even have a girlfriend other than the bimbos—wait, the skirts that you chased. How credible is it that you're now married?"

She did have a point. "Well, they know I'm an impulsive person sometimes."

The whole engagement thing had come out of the blue. When he saw how Gibson was looking at Roxy with those dark, lascivious eyes of his, Santiago lost his mind for a moment. "She's mine," he wanted to hiss at Gibson, "so keep your goddamn hands off of her." He almost grabbed her and kissed her right then, making a public show of it. Or better yet, drag her into one of the alcoves designed for little trysts between casual acquaintances and make love to her in order for his scent to be mixed with hers. Then there'd be no question that she was his. Announcing their engagement to Gibson was mild compared to what he'd been thinking.

She examined her nails as if the state of her cuticles was more important than him. "You know what this means, don't you?"

No, he didn't know. Why was he always so thick-headed around her? It was as if he lost all ability to make rational, well-thought-out decisions. The engagement thing being just one example, because that clearly was a huge mistake. "I'm not sure I want to know."

"You'll need to buy me a ring."

He almost choked. "What? A ring?"

"Yep. What woman—engaged or married—doesn't have a ring? The women I met in the kitchen asked to see it, so I had to make up an excuse, how we really hadn't planned this, that it just sort of happened. If you want this new little plan of yours to be authentic, I'll need one."

Could this day possibly get any worse? What kind of a trench did he dig himself into? "Okay fine. We'll get you a wedding band."

"No, I want a diamond. A big one." One corner of her mouth quirked up. She was really enjoying this.

"Oh, for godsake." Running a hand over his close-cropped hair, he was at his wit's end with this woman. He was hanging off the edge of a cliff with just his pinkie finger, and even that was slipping.

"Tell me about it."

He stormed around the room, cursing. The vibration of his pounding boots rattled the items on his desk. This woman was impossible. Simply impossible. She was a five-foot-seven-inch pain in his ass and he was supposed to pretend they were married?

She continued standing right where he'd left her, watching him like you'd watch a dancing bear with a tutu—slightly amused, slightly incredulous and slightly perturbed that someone would put a skirt on an animal.

But the more he thought about it, the more he realized she was—he sighed heavily—right. It killed him to even admit that to himself, let alone her, but there was no getting around it. "Fine," he grumbled. "We go ring shopping tomorrow."

"Good. That's the first logical thing I've heard you say since we got here." With her chin jutted out, she tossed her hair behind her shoulder and headed toward the bathroom. Despite being angry with her, he loved how she walked away from him, the little spring in her step, the slight sway in her hips. He was pretty sure she knew he was watching.

Well, two could play at this game. "Engaged, married. Guess we'd better get on with things then."

"Excuse me?" she said, turning.

He proceeded to strip off his T-shirt, tossing it onto a nearby chair. Then he kicked off his boots and started unbuttoning his pants.

"Now hold on there." Her eyes widened and suddenly that bravado of hers was gone. She was staring at his hands on his zipper. He rather liked it and he could feel himself growing harder under her scrutiny. "What are you talking about?"

"A newly married couple would be having a lot of sex, so why don't you slip into some sexy lingerie and meet me under the covers in, oh, say, twenty minutes?" He stepped out of his jeans, aware that his black boxer briefs did little to hide things.

She froze for a moment and two bright spots of color appeared on her cheeks. But then she seemed to catch herself and reloaded her indignation.

"Screw you."

He grinned. "Exactly what I had in mind."

SLIP INTO SOME *sexy lingerie? Ha.*

The only thing Roxy was slipping into was this sensible swim suit in her gym bag. She'd do a few laps in the field-office pool and Santiago could chill out back in the room. Alone.

What in the hell had she gotten herself into, she thought as she entered the women's locker room and changed in one of the private stalls.

If she wasn't so attracted to him, none of this would be a big deal. They'd have had a civil conversation about what to do then each would've retired to their respective sides of the bed.

But a relationship with Santiago could never be casual—it was too volatile for that.

With his domineering, bossy ways, he'd worked his way into every little nook and cranny of her being, whether she wanted him there or not. She tried not to think about him now, but when she breathed, she could still smell him. One of the stripes on a towel someone left behind perfectly matched his eye color. As she exited the locker room and headed for the pool, the *drip drip drip* of a faucet reminded her that time was running out and that she'd soon be sharing a bed with him.

Maybe if she swam enough laps, he'd be asleep when she got back. And if not...

Hell, what would be so bad about caving in to his demands? He was without a doubt the most gorgeous man she'd ever met. Sex with him would be off the charts. When he'd undressed in front of her, it was all she could do to keep upright. She wanted to grip the wall or the edge of the desk, but she was determined not to show the effect he was having on her. Seeing him like that—his trim stomach, his flexing muscles, the large mound barely concealed beneath his boxer briefs, and, yes, she had to admit, the verbal sparring—made her desire him all the more. She thought she might die from sheer pleasure, right then and there.

Most women would be thrilled and excited at the prospect of sleeping with a man like Santiago and jump at the chance. Normally, she was able to control her emotions and feelings better than that, but with him, the dam broke, the rope was cut and the rubber band snapped, all at the same time.

Setting her towel on a nearby bench, she dived into the deep end and began methodically slicing through the water. As she swam, her thoughts clarified.

If she gave in, if she let him into the most vulnerable part of herself, she might never get it back. Instinctively, she knew that Santiago would not be just a casual hookup, that things with him would be so much more. He affected her in ways that she hadn't experienced in a long time. Maybe ever.

Besides, a relationship with him would never make sense. They lived too far apart, he was too hotheaded, and her first priority was the promise she'd made to Ian's mother, Mary Alice. If she let herself get distracted by affairs of the heart, she may never find out who killed Ian and that simply wasn't acceptable. She needed to remain focused and committed to her original goal and letting Santiago in would change her priorities.

She was so distracted that she lost count of her laps. Instead, she swam until thirty minutes had elapsed and hoped she'd done at least sixty. After a quick shower, she headed back to Santiago's rooms. Fully expecting him to be propped up like a king in that bed of his with his hands clasped behind his head, waiting for her, she was surprised to see him at his desk. With a phone to his ear, he wore a black silk robe and didn't turn around when she shut the door behind her.

Good. Maybe he was too busy to come to bed just yet. She changed into a T-shirt and an old pair of yoga pants, the furthest thing from sexy lingerie she had. Her hair was still damp, so she tied it into a loose ponytail on the top of her head and climbed under the covers.

The sheets were warm. He'd turned on the electric blanket for her. She grabbed two of the pillows and laid them down the center of the bed as a sort of barrier, akin to old Scottish courtship traditions. She'd stay on her side and he'd stay on his. Rolling over, she listened to the richly textured tone of his voice. It was clear that he was talking to Mackenzie about Dom's condition. Not wanting to eavesdrop, she grabbed her iPod and played some relaxation music.

She closed her eyes just to rest them. She wanted to stay awake so that she could ask him how Dom was doing and how Mackenzie was holding up.

She awoke with a start, not realizing she'd fallen asleep. Pulling out her earbuds, she glanced at the clock and noted it wasn't time to get up yet. Without looking, she knew he wasn't on his half of the bed. His scent was strong enough that she knew he was nearby, but when she stilled her breathing, she couldn't hear him.

She slowly rolled over and looked across the room. He wasn't at his desk and— How strange, his chair was gone. In fact, his side of the bed was still made up, as if he hadn't been in it at all. Something near the closet drew her attention. She pushed up on her elbows and saw what looked to be a skinny beam of sunlight streaming out from under the closet door. What the hell? These rooms were far underground, weren't they? She had been in the closet earlier and hadn't noticed a window.

She flung the sheets back and padded across the room in her bare feet. Careful to stay out of the tiny patch of light, she slowly opened the door.

The light hit her exposed skin and she felt the drain immediately. She jerked back in alarm. It was a UV light.

Shading her eyes, she peered cautiously around the corner and almost choked. Santiago sat in the middle of the closet right underneath that blasted light. His eyes were closed and his expression was twisted into one of extreme pain. He was purposely sitting under a UV light.

"What are you doing?"

His head jerked in her direction, the contortions in his face a mixture of anger and pain. "Leave me alone," he roared. He didn't make a move to leave.

"Not till you turn that light off and tell me what's going on."

"This is private. Get back to bed."

She leaned on the wall outside the closet, just out of the beam of light jutting into the room. "No."

He exhaled heavily and she could almost hear the gears of his thoughts making all sorts of mental calculations. "I'll be…out in…a sec."

Folding her arms, she counted to ten. Why would he do such a thing to himself? There was no benefit to bathing in UV light. Unless you deemed weakness and a craving for blood to be a benefit. She heard no rustling to indicate he was coming out.

Screw it. If he wasn't going to come out on his own, then she was going in after him. It was madness to wait any longer. Shading her eyes with her hand, she plunged into the closet, found the electrical cord, and pulled it out of the socket. The room went full dark, the pull on her energy stopped, and she spun to face him.

"What are…you doing? I said to leave me alone." His face was drawn, the tiny lines around his eyes more pronounced.

"It's too bad I don't follow direction well." Now, to get him out of here and into bed. Although sleeping would help replenish what he'd lost, what he really needed was blood.

She looped his arm around her shoulder and forced him to stand. Despite his protests, he leaned heavily on her and walked out of the closet.

"How long were you in there? And why would you purposely do such a thing? That's just—"

"Crazy?"

"Well…yeah."

Depending on how long he'd been in there like that, it could take him several days or a healthy ration of blood to replenish what he'd lost.

He mumbled something she couldn't quite make out as she got him into the bed. His fingers and toes were little bricks of ice. She pulled the covers up around him and stooped down to see him eye to eye.

Little good that did. He turned away from her, obviously not wanting to talk about it. Without thinking, she reached out and gently massaged his shoulder.

"Ouch."

"No wonder it hurts. You've got knots on top of knots. Now roll over." He tried to protest, but she'd have none of that. "I'm going to work on these kinks and you're going to tell me what you were doing with the UV light. Hold on. I'll be right back."

She rummaged around in her suitcase, grabbed a few things, and returned to the bedside. She was going to ask him to remove his robe, but he looked totally wiped, so she'd do it for him as soon as she plugged the little speaker into her iPod. Relaxation music poured into the room and she turned back to the bed.

"Here, let's take your robe off."

This time he didn't protest, just kind of lifted his arms for her to remove it. As he lay facedown on the bed, she tried not to think about how it would feel to put her hands all over him. She would try to make this as clinical as possible.

Pouring out a small amount of eucalyptus oil into her hand, she rubbed her palms together and began working on his shoulders. His skin was pulled tight across bunched muscles as her hands slid over them, kneading as she went. She tried her best to get at a knot just under his left shoulder blade but she couldn't quite get it from this angle. So she climbed onto the bed and strad-

dled his torso. Yes, much better. Although he groaned
as she worked, she kept going and slowly his muscles
began to loosen.

"So why were you under that light? Are you trying
to torture yourself or what?"

"You weren't supposed to see that."

"Well, I did."

"I thought you were sleeping. I figured I had plenty
of time."

"I woke up." She located a particularly hard area
under his shoulder blade. "Breathe in. Yes, good. Now
hold it." She pressed her thumb onto the knot and leaned
all her weight on it. "Breathe out slowly."

"Oh, God," he groaned, exhaling. "That hurts like
a motherf—"

"Yeah, but let's do it once more and I'll bet it'll be
just about gone." They repeated the steps, and sure
enough, that took care of it. Neither one of them said
anything for a while. She continued to work on him,
knot by knot, and he continued to groan with each one.
Placing the heels of her hands on either side of his spine,
she pressed down and heard it crack.

"Oh, my God, that felt good," he mumbled when
she was done.

"Okay, so tell me why you do that to yourself."

He shifted and she quickly moved off of him to sit
cross-legged on her side of the bed. Though he still
looked tired, he was much more relaxed now.

"Only if you tell me why you joined the *dakai*."

CHAPTER TEN

"YOU MUST BE referring to my tattoo." She rubbed her right shoulder, leaving a slight mark on her T-shirt from the massage oils still on her hand. "I'm surprised you recognized it. Not many do."

"I'm familiar with it. My sister was a member."

She furrowed her brows. "Yours, too? I mean, not that I have a sister. It was a coworker's sister who got involved. I was asked to infiltrate the group in order to get her out."

"What?" He jerked his head up too fast and the room began to spin. Despite that awesome massage, he was still weak. Pinching the bridge of his nose, he asked, "So you're not a *dakai*?"

"Nope. They're a freaky bunch, let me tell you, but I knew they wouldn't accept me without the tattoo. What happened to your sister?"

He sank back in the pillows, feeling as though a rug had been pulled out from under him, but not in a bad way. He'd been keeping a healthy distance from Roxy because he thought she practiced the ways of the *dakai*. Finding out she wasn't was like finding out she was a completely different person. She was the same, of course, but it was his perception of her that radically changed. "She's gone. The cult left her penniless and she died in Prague many years ago."

"I'm so sorry." She reached out and touched his arm, emphasizing her sincerity.

He didn't understand. What about the aromatherapy? The meditation? The yoga? The bizarre chanting music that was still playing in the background. "Why do you practice all this—" he waved his hand in front of him "—mumbo-jumbo shit then, if you're not in the cult?"

She scowled and he realized that he'd offended her, which hadn't been his intention. "Sorry to break it to you, but some of these techniques happen to work. Case in point—I'll bet you feel better right now than you normally do after you do that UV *mumbo-jumbo* shit of yours."

Okay, so he deserved that.

He stretched his neck first one way then the other. The tightness was gone and his muscles did feel much looser. He'd had massages before, but there was something about the way she did it that was different. Maybe some of these bizarre practices did have a place after all. "You're right. I do feel much better." She still looked pissed. "Sorry," he added. "I didn't mean to come across so—"

"Ignorant? Condescending?"

"Yeah, I guess so," he said, feeling pretty sheepish. She'd just spent thirty minutes giving him a pretty killer massage. He didn't need to insult her.

"Apology accepted. Okay, it's my turn to ask a question."

"Fine. Ask away."

"I want to know why you sit under a UV light? I get the impression this isn't the first time."

As if he didn't know that was coming. "You won't understand."

"Try me."

He thought about lying, making up some crazy-assed story, but he realized he didn't want to. He felt like telling her the truth. There was a sincerity in her voice that made him want to open up and have her understand how he ticked. But this was uncharted territory. He was used to keeping things to himself. Not knowing where to start, he chose the blunt route.

"Because it's the only thing that makes me feel in control again. After a royal fuck-up, my inner voice tells me what a loser I am and only through punishment will I learn to be stronger."

She looked pissed again. "What kind of self-talk is that?"

"The brutally honest kind."

"No, it's toxic and destructive, that's what it is. You seem very capable to me. When your people were hurt, you jumped to action and quickly formulated a plan. How is that screwing up and warranting *that* kind of mumbo-jumbo shit in the closet?"

"Do you need a list?"

"It's just that you're so wrong about yourself, Santiago. I wish I could make you see that. You're one of the most take-charge leaders I've ever met."

"Do I need to remind you that several of my agents have been badly injured and one is fighting for his life?"

"And you blame yourself? That occurred down here in Seattle. You were up at the Region offices. How could you possibly be to blame?"

"All Guardians in the region are my responsibility. When something like this happens under my watch, it's because I didn't do enough. Didn't prepare them enough. Didn't recognize a dangerous situation when I saw it. Hell, I was the one who gave them the intel about the arms shipment. I should've seen something like this coming."

"I'll bet you anything Dom would be pissed off to hear you say that."

He didn't want to look at her face. She was right, of course. Dom would be livid. He could almost hear him now, saying how Santiago didn't trust him. But he didn't want to let her know that she was right. Being miserable took effort and he wasn't quite ready to let go yet. For her to poke holes in his logic wasn't helping.

"By taking the blame like that, it says you don't have faith in your own people. That you don't think they can make their own decisions. You're the wise, know-it-all father and they're just a bunch of children who don't know any better."

"I'm not saying that."

"Then what is it that you're saying by torturing yourself like that? They knew the risks going in. You can't possibly be in all places, Santiago. You hired good people. You need to let them do their jobs. Being a Guardian is dangerous sometimes. It was Darkbloods who caused it. Not you."

"But—"

"Bad things happen to good people. It's not your fault, so you need to stop telling yourself that it is. The world isn't a perfect place," she said, her voice getting a little softer, "despite the fact that you're in it."

He wasn't sure whether to take that as a compliment or an insult.

"Aren't you wiped out for days at a time after you do this?"

"Yes, but just like this massage, you have to go through some pain and discomfort to get to your goal."

"And what is your goal, Santiago? To make yourself sick? To weaken yourself to the point that you're incapacitated? There's a reason they tell you to put on your oxygen mask before helping the person next to you. It's because you'll be no good to anyone if you don't think of yourself first."

When she put it that way, it made sense, but he couldn't just discard decades of doing this to himself that easily. "I need to find out who's betraying my people."

"And you think self-torture is going to help you achieve that?"

"It reminds me what happens to losers, to those who are weak. I don't want to be weak. It'll make me stronger in the long run."

"So it's a punishment of sorts? As a way you cope with the stress?"

He nodded.

At some point she'd reached out and was stroking his arm. He liked the gentle, nonthreatening way she touched him. It wasn't demanding or judgmental. It was just…Roxy trying to get through to him.

"Well, I can show you some other, less destructive ways to handle stress. Believe me, I know a thing or two about stress. But first of all, you really need to keep your energy up. If not, you're giving negativity a foothold. If you're dragging, you're more likely to let things affect you in a less than positive manner."

Still sitting cross-legged, she shifted to face him squarely. He liked that he was the object of her undivided attention. Excitement simmered in her eyes and tone, and she touched him occasionally to emphasize a point. She really believed this mind-over-body stuff and he rather enjoyed how she was drawing him in. He couldn't help but be affected by her enthusiasm. Okay, so maybe some of this stuff did have merit. That massage certainly was incredible.

"What I'm saying," she continued, "is that it's a vicious circle. You feel shitty, so you do this to yourself and then you feel even worse. I would imagine it becomes harder and harder to pull yourself out of it."

He'd been doing it for so long that he didn't really have anything else to compare it to. It was a habit. It was part of who he was.

"Unless you have vials of blood in your little refrigerator over there, I want you to drink from me." She held out her wrist.

Just the mention of her blood had his gums aching. "No, this is my problem. I will not make it yours."

"Fine." She made a move to climb off the bed.

"There's no blood in the refrigerator."

"No big deal. I'll go to the kitchen then. Surely, the field office keeps a supply on hand for emergencies."

Her hair was messy, her face was fresh from her bedtime routine, and her T-shirt was stretched a little too tightly across her breasts. It looked like she was ready for bed or had just climbed out, which she had. And Gibson was just the one to try to take advantage of that if he saw her padding to the field-office kitchen looking like that.

"No, you're staying here."

"Well, you don't look like you're in any shape to stumble down there right now."

"I'm not. Usually I just—"

She thrust her wrist under his nose and his fangs stretched from his gums whether he wanted them to or not. So much for mind over body.

"I know it's not a perfect substitute for human blood, but it's better than nothing."

Tiny blue veins crisscrossed just under the surface of her delicate skin. His teeth would easily sink in if he bit her. The visible flicker of her pulse caught his attention—the *thump, thump, thump* showing exactly where he should place his fangs. How would she taste? Given how good she smelled, he imagined it'd be exquisite. He found himself supporting her forearm in his hands as he closed his eyes and breathed deeply.

"Yes, that's it. There you go."

And because he was too weak to fight it any longer, he held her wrist to his mouth and with as much gentleness a starving man could muster, he let his fangs puncture her skin.

She inhaled sharply at first then caressed his shoulder encouragingly as her blood began to flow and fill his mouth.

He couldn't remember the last time he'd had another vampire's blood. Or maybe it was the fact this was so amazing that it drowned out any memories of having had it before. He only allowed himself a few swallows before he released his hold on her and sealed the puncture wounds with a lick.

"You can take more than that." Her voice was husky and her eyes had darkened.

"No, that's enough. I'll feed from a live host tomorrow."

"No vials?"

"Nah, I prefer to live life on the edge."

They both laughed.

"Thank you." Then, without thinking whether it was a good decision or not, he pulled her close and kissed her.

Her lips were hot against his, eager, inviting, demanding. She smelled of eucalyptus oil, which, he decided, was his new favorite scent. Without breaking the kiss, he pulled her on top of him again, only this time he was facing her rather than having his back to her during the massage. She smoothed her strong but elegant hands over him as if she enjoyed feeling the muscles of his chest and shoulders. His erection was painfully hard as it pressed against her bottom, feeling every little movement she made. He held her hips down to increase the incredible friction between their two bodies. And from the way she moved, she was just as interested in feeling him, as well.

"Your clothes," he managed to say against her lips. "Take them off."

She pushed away then and sat up, leaving her hands splayed on his chest. A few strands of hair fell haphazardly across her face, her mouth slightly swollen from his kisses. "N-no. This probably isn't a good idea."

"But I thought… You don't want this?"

She wouldn't make eye contact with him. "I'm just not sure we should take things—us—any further. Maybe things need to remain platonic."

At first he wondered if she was uncomfortable with him, but given that she was still straddling him and her hands were still touching him, he doubted that was the issue. Could she be worried that *this* could lead to an *us?* He searched her face, looking for an answer, but she was so hard to read that he couldn't be sure of anything. All he knew was that she was uncomfortable.

He thought about reminding her that many of their kind hooked up for casual sex and that it rarely led to anything more personal. But for some reason, he didn't.

"I want you, Roxy," he whispered. "I want…*this*. You…your hands feel so good on me."

Say yes, he urged her with his thoughts. *Let me make love to you.*

He held his breath, his erection pressed hard against her, but still, she said nothing.

She absently stroked the tips of her fingers against his skin, her touch so light it left a tingling sensation in its wake. Clearly, she was torn.

"If you don't want to, I can respect that. It's just that…" God, this was so awkward. He looked past her, up to the ceiling as he searched for the right words. He wasn't used to baring his soul like this, but for some reason, he felt compelled to open up to her. "Your nonjudgmental concern about my…problem makes me feel… well, closer. To you. And I want more. Of that."

Her hands stopped moving, the faraway look in her eyes gone. "Another disadvantage of that UV business," she said, grabbing the hem of her T-shirt, "is you're too weak to properly undress a woman you plan to make love to."

Yes! His heart banged against his rib cage. He was dimly aware that his words—truthful, secret ones, spoken from a place deep inside—not barked demands, were what had swayed her.

In one graceful movement, the shirt was gone. And there, almost within reach of his mouth, were her breasts. God, they were perfect. He wanted to run his tongue over her dusty pink nipples and see if he could get them to peak even more than they already were.

As if reading his mind, she arched her back and with just a slight lift of his head, one was in his mouth. His fangs hadn't fully retracted yet, so he took great care not to score her tender skin. He brushed his tongue over the tip of one nipple and softly twisted the other one.

She moaned and pressed her bottom harder against him.

While he suckled and licked, she somehow managed to slip out of her yoga pants and strip off his boxer briefs. Cool fingers gripped the base of his erection and stood his shaft up. Her body wriggled above his as she positioned herself just so, and before he knew it, he was plunged straight into heaven.

It was hot in there, so slick and tight. If he weren't careful, he'd finish inside her before they really got started.

"Oh, God, Santiago," she gasped. "You feel so amazing."

Hearing her say his name like that filled him with an incredible amount of masculine pride. He wanted to roll over on top of her, cover her body with his, and get her to scream it the next time as she came. But even with her blood circulating in his veins, he still was fairly weak, so he let her ride him instead.

She shoved his hands above his head and held him there as she slid up and down his length, making tiny adjustments so that he rubbed her just where she needed it. Fortunately for him, everything she did rocked his world, so he could sit back and enjoy it.

Her breasts teased him, just out of reach. He tried to lift his head, to pull a nipple into his mouth again, but the way she held him prevented him from moving much.

"Can you release my hands?" He could pull free, but he decided he'd rather have her do it. It was strangely erotic having her control him like this.

"Only if you tell me why." Her eyes were dark, heavy with lust. "What will you do if I let you go?"

"I want to rub my hands along your buttocks and thighs, feel your muscles working just under the softness and I can't do that with you holding me immobile like this."

A mixture of amusement and satisfaction flitted over her expression. They both knew he could escape her if he tried. "You do?"

"Yes." He liked that she had some womanly curves, that his fingers would be able to grip her slightly before they encountered the hardness. In his opinion, women needed curves. They didn't need to be smaller versions of men. Just because they were softer, didn't mean they weren't every bit as capable.

"What else?"

"I want to reach around and feel where we are joined together, where I fit into you. To get a little of your silkiness on my fingers since I didn't get a chance to do that before we started."

"Are you saying you feel deprived that there was no foreplay?"

"I do enjoy it, yes. I would've loved seeing if I could pleasure you that way, but I don't feel deprived."

He was pretty sure her inner muscles tightened around him just then. And things definitely felt slicker as the friction between them changed ever so slightly.

Was she turned on by the sex talk? One thing was certain, he definitely was—the pressure in his balls was almost to the breaking point now.

She released his hands then and kissed him hard, her mouth fervent and demanding. He did what he told her he was going to do. His fingers found the union of their bodies, where she was stretched tightly around him.

"Ah, that's what I'm talking about." She was slick and hot. "I like that. Very much." She'd better be about ready, for if she wasn't, at this rate, he wouldn't last much longer.

Again, the tightness increased around him. Was she—

"I'm coming, Santiago," she said breathlessly against his lips. "Oh, my God. Oh, my God."

That was just what he needed to hear. All the nerve endings along his shaft became hypersensitive as she shattered around him. Holding her hips down to keep himself seated as deeply into her heat as he could, the last thread of his control snapped. One powerful thrust was all it took and he released himself into her body.

And in those few glorious seconds, when everything faded into the background while their pleasure intertwined, his world came unglued and sharply into focus, all at the same time.

CHAPTER ELEVEN

WHEN THE MAN walked through the front door of Big Daddy's Brew Pub and weaved his way around the crowded tables, everyone looked up and glanced in his direction. With broad shoulders, a rugged face and ass-hugging jeans that fit tightly around his thick thighs, his commanding presence filled the entire space. Someone dropped a glass, a guy at one of the pool tables missed his shot, and three women in a nearby booth stopped their conversation to stare. Instinctively, they sensed there was something different about him. Maybe even dangerous.

Cosette was the only human in the place who knew why.

"That's him?" she said, trying to swallow past the lump in her throat. Although he appeared to be a normal human male—albeit a tall, very powerful-looking one—he was a Guardian, whatever that was. If they were even half as evil as Darkbloods, she was in a lot of trouble. Not that she had much of a choice.

"Yes, Cosette, it is." The sound of that deceptively sweet female voice saying her name sent shivers down her spine.

She wasn't sure whether to be more nervous about

the vampire in front of her or the one behind her. Either way, she was caught between a rock and a very hard, unforgiving place. But family came first, which was why she agreed to do this.

"He's the target you're to contact."

Target? Contact? It sounded so James Bond-ish. So clinical. The woman should've just said, "Yes, that's the man you need to seduce in order to save your sister." That would've been more appropriate.

"Okay, then. Here goes." She grabbed her order pad and made a move toward him, but the woman stopped her.

"Hold on." She reached for Cosette, quickly unbuttoning the top two buttons of her shirt and untucking it from her jeans.

"Hey, what are you doing?" she said, trying to pull away from her. It gave her the willies for this woman to touch any part of her even though she wore latex gloves. Cosette had wanted to know why she had them on, but she was afraid she wouldn't like the answer.

A few patrons glanced over at them. The woman sank deeper into the shadows, pulling Cosette with her and pinning her against the wall. Cosette turned her head away so she wouldn't have to look at her.

"You are not to draw attention to me or this little plan of ours, do you understand? Look at me when I'm talking to you."

Cosette reluctantly complied, noticing immediately that the woman's eyes were even darker than before and the tips of her fangs were now indenting her lower lip.

"You'd better pray he didn't hear your outburst just now. If he even suspects that your seduction is a setup, your sister dies. In fact, I'll see to it that she becomes my next meal. Have I mentioned how utterly famished I am?"

Although the woman had a benign, totally unremarkable appearance, Cosette had a feeling it was carefully orchestrated. She wanted to blend into the background and not stand out for someone to remember later. Even Cosette, who'd seen her a few times now, would be hard-pressed to single out anything distinctive about her. Shoulder-length blond hair, average height, jeans, sneakers and a plain navy sweatshirt. Except for the freaky grayed-out whites of her eyes, half the women in Seattle matched that description.

But those eyes—

They were the eyes of a shark. Unemotional and deadly.

"I'm…I'm sorry."

The tension in the woman's face relaxed. "That's a good girl. I'm simply making you more appealing to him, which increases the odds he'll take you up on your offer. Males, whether human or vampire, are goal-oriented, lazy creatures. The slutty look tells them they'll get what they want without expending too much effort to get it." She tied the ends of the shirttails above Cosette's midriff, exposing some skin. "You need some lipstick. Your face is too pale."

Yeah, because you took some of my blood.

She shivered. Even her fingers and toes had gone cold.

The woman gave her a hard appraising look from heat to toe, appearing not to miss a single detail. Flyaway hair? A stain on her shirt? Lint on her shoulder? Shoes on the wrong feet? She acted like a stage mom, an evil one…or a madam.

As Cosette hurriedly applied some lip gloss she found in her pocket, she vowed to do whatever it took to get her sister back. And when she did, she'd pack up their things before the woman changed her mind and they'd get the hell away from this god-awful city.

Moving to Seattle was supposed to be an exciting adventure for the two girls from Montana. Their French mother who had fallen in love with their rancher father and moved to the States told them that having an adventurous spirit ran in the family. Though she'd have preferred the girls move to New York or Paris "to see what the world has to offer," Seattle was the next best thing for two girls who weren't quite as adventurous as their mother. But this nightmare was more than either sister had bargained for.

There were no guarantees this woman would follow through with her promise, but Cosette had no other options. She couldn't go to the police. Not only would they think she was nuts when she told them that she and her sister had been kidnapped by vampires, but if the woman found out, she'd kill Yvonne. She didn't want to think about the place where they were holding her. The gothic house was old, damp and creepy. The woman had taken them on a tour of what she called the Extraction Room, which was basically a torture chamber, where dozens of human skulls stared out at them from the walls, their dark eye sockets and grisly smiles a portent of the girls' possible fate. Unless Cosette agreed to do this, she and her sister would be added to the woman's grisly collection. But first, they'd strap her sister down and extract every last ounce of her blood because of how special it supposedly was.

The process would take about an hour from start to finish, the woman had said. "First, we'll strap her to that gurney over there and immobilize her. Then my extraction expert—" she pointed to a squat, evil-looking man smiling a little too eagerly from the other side of the room "—will insert a needle into one of her arteries. Not a vein, as we want the blood to be as oxygen-rich as possible." Yvonne began trembling and Cosette held her close. "She'll get weaker and weaker," the woman had explained, "then very thirsty, and that's when the headaches will start. I'm told it's a deep, throbbing kind of ache—a migraine of epic proportions as the body's fluids are diminished. Then she'll become unconscious and slip into a coma. Before you know it, I'll have eight pints of blood and your sister will be dead. Why do I know all this, you ask? Because I'm there for as many of these as possible and ask a lot of questions. Death fascinates me. Knowledge is power, don't you think? So what do you say? Are you in or out?"

Knowing what would happen to Yvonne, refusing these demands had not been an option. The woman told Cosette to apply for jobs at various bars Guardians were known to frequent. Big Daddy's had been the first to call back. Tonight was only her third night on the job. Her hands still felt weak from when she read the woman's text message, saying a Guardian had been spotted heading in this direction.

She peered around the pillar. An empty glass sat in front of him and he was doing something on his phone. Given the way he was biting his tongue in Michael Jordan fashion, he must be playing a game of some sort. A twinge gnawed at her stomach. He looked so human, so normal. Just like any other guy. But whatever this woman had in store for him, Cosette had to remember that at least he was a vampire. He stood a much better chance of surviving than Yvonne.

Yvonne. She couldn't let her sympathies for a stranger get in the way of what she needed to do. "You promise not to hurt him?"

"He won't even know we were there."

She hoped to God that the woman was telling the truth. If she wasn't… Cosette was willing to do just about anything to get her sister back. Steal. Lie. Sleep with a stranger who was actually a vampire. But she drew the line at murder and being an accessory to one. Or at least she thought she did. If faced with that decision, could she actually kill someone if it meant her sister would live? Could she betray someone, knowing he would die, if it meant she and her sister would see another day? Until all this, she'd never felt that the ends justified the means in any situation, but then she and Yvonne hadn't been staring death in the face either.

When the woman was done fussing over her, Cosette

gladly moved away and headed toward the man. For the first time in her life, she was grateful for all the acting lessons her flamboyant mother had put her through. Everything was riding on how well she played this part.

Stretching her arms out on the brass railing, she leaned forward suggestively. Surely, he'd be able to see straight down her shirt all the way to her belly button. Although her heart was thundering behind her rib cage, she flashed her best I Want You To Take Me Home To-night smile. Which wasn't much of a stretch if she forgot the fact that he was a vampire. The guy was hot. He had the kind of eyes that could melt a girl's panties with just a glance. "What can I get you?"

His head snapped up from the phone in his hands. With narrowed eyes, he studied her for a moment. It was as if he knew that something was wrong.

Vampires didn't read minds, did they? Was he trying to glamour her? She didn't know what myths about them were true or not. The garlic thing wasn't. And neither was not being able to come into a home without an invitation. She and Yvonne wouldn't have been kidnapped if that was the case. She shivered, remembering how the woman had been sitting on their sofa when they came home after a midnight run to the store for snacks.

Cosette knew they could wipe minds—it was a big reason she was so eager to do whatever the woman demanded of her. If she didn't, the woman could wipe her memory and she'd have no way of knowing where Yvonne was or what had happened to her. All she would know was that her sister, whom they said was a sweetblood, was gone. But surely, the woman would have told her that vampires could read minds since Cosette was about to deceive one.

This strange expression of his had to be from something else. He didn't find her distasteful, did he? Despite what the woman had said, maybe he wasn't into the slutty look.

"What do you have on tap?"

Was that the trace of an Australian accent? "Well, we have Fosters."

He looked vaguely amused. "I'm not Australian, if that's what you're getting at."

Oh, crap, he wasn't British, was he? That had to be a major faux pas to confuse the two. She could've sworn—

"I recently spent some time there, but I didn't know I'd picked up much of an accent. You're very perceptive."

"Oh, good," she said, relieved. "For a moment there, I was thinking I'd really offended you, not being able to tell the difference."

"Even if I were British, I wouldn't have been offended. At least, not by you."

Her cheeks heated at the compliment. "So is it a Fosters or do you want to go with a local microbrew instead?"

"Fosters, it is, mate," he said, drumming up a heavy accent.

She let herself laugh.

It was good he'd warmed up to her so quickly. Things

would be so much easier than if she'd been forced to throw herself at him. Though she hadn't really expected that either. Most guys found her and her sister fairly attractive. "Okay, then. I'd say something clever right now, but the only Aussie slang I know is about throwing shrimps on the barbie."

"Works for me."

"I do speak a little French, however."

"Really?" His eyes gleamed. "Did you ever see *A Fish Called Wanda?* I'm like Jamie Lee Curtis's character, but in reverse. I'm turned on by women talking in other languages to me."

"Je parle français. Vous avez un beau sourire." He was gorgeous and funny and under any other circumstances, she'd have enjoyed being with him.

"What does that mean?"

She shrugged nonchalantly and gave him her best flirty smile. "Maybe I'll tell you later."

As she filled a few drink orders, Cosette noticed the woman motioning her to come over. Was something wrong? She'd done exactly what she'd been told to do: strike up a conversation and flirt.

A quick glance revealed that the man was on his phone again, so she slipped to the back. "What is it?"

The woman smiled. "Looks like things are progressing nicely, so I'm heading over there now. When you bring him to the room, I want you to suggest taking a nice long bath together."

"But—"

"You must, and I repeat, must have him change his

clothes in the room first before you enter the bathroom. While you're in there, take your time. Have fun. I'll leave a bottle of bubble bath on the counter along with a radio, some lubrication and a six-pack of Fosters." Cosette wanted to throw up. "Then, when you're about to go back into the bedroom, I want you to go first. Tell him you want to get ready for him before he comes out. Then, sprinkle some of this around the room. But don't let him see you doing it."

She handed Cosette a small burlap pouch. It molded to her hand like a bag of salt. "What is this?"

"Scent-masking crystals that an old friend gave me. Guardians use it to absorb the lingering scent of sweetbloods, making it impossible for Darkbloods to follow. But it works both ways. It'll hide any trace that we were in the room."

"You mean he can smell you?" Almost reflexively, she sniffed the air and didn't pick up anything unusual.

"Guardians have a keen sense of smell. That's why I'm all the way back here. Do you think you can do it?"

That explained the latex gloves. The woman didn't want to leave her scent on Cosette for the man to detect. That also explained why she had to shower and change into fresh clothes right before she started her shift. Cosette stuffed the package into her messenger bag, which hung from a peg just around the corner. "Do I have a choice?"

The woman gave her a flat smile. "True."

"And when it's done—" God, now she was the one sounding clinical "—you'll bring my sister back?"

"You have my word."

Somehow, Cosette didn't find this reassuring, but what other choice did she have than to believe her?

The woman left through the back door and Cosette returned to the bar. A moment later she set the beer down in front of the man. "It's almost time for last call. Do you want me to bring you another one right away?"

"Sure, why not." He took a drink and licked the foam from his upper lip. Dropping his chin slightly, he looked at her pointedly. Unlike the woman, the whites of his eyes weren't gray, but they were intense. "I like living on the edge."

He was definitely baiting her, seeing how she'd respond.

Without blinking, she said, "I do, too."

Continued flirting combined with two more beers and he was eating out of the palm of her hand at closing time. She hadn't asked him his name yet—she didn't want to know. The less she knew about the real him, the better.

After waiting for the last customer to leave, she quickly cleaned up and said goodnight to Arnold. Something bad had happened to one of his employees last year, so now he always closed on Friday and Saturday nights. It made leaving with a customer easy.

"My place or yours?" the man asked as they stepped out into the chilly night air.

She pulled the door closed behind them. "I'm probably closer." She pointed through the alley to an old brick building on the next block over. It wasn't the apartment that she and her sister shared, but the predesignated place where she was to bring him. The woman would undoubtedly have things all set up by now. Cosette would do what she needed then get the hell out of there.

"Okay, then. Let's go." With a hand on the small of her back, he guided her down the alley.

CHAPTER TWELVE

THE OFFICE SANTIAGO kept in Seattle was smaller than the one at region headquarters, but it was masculine and tastefully decorated. A cluster of artfully arranged black-and-white animal photos covered one hunter-green wall. Bronze statues of eagles and rearing horses sat like sentries on the shelves but weren't overbearing. The window coverings were heavy and very Ralph Lauren. The front two corners of his desk featured majestic, hand-carved griffins and Roxy wondered if the other side was carved, as well.

She hoped he never had one of his tantrums here because the room and the contents were too stately and elegant to be destroyed so callously. "I like your office."

"Thanks, but I can't take any of the credit. The fiancée of our newest Council member has a design business and just finished decorating it. She had me fill out a five-page questionnaire, which felt like a personality test and then, based on that, she brought me sketches, photos and samples."

"I think she nailed it. The office is powerful, commanding and yet warm and comfortable. It feels like... like you."

The minute the words tumbled from her mouth, she

regretted saying them. He didn't need to know this was
how she felt about him, that she thought of him in any
way other than strictly business. She'd been a little too
personal, exposed herself emotionally and she didn't
want to go there. Just because they had sex didn't mean
they were on the road to Couplesville.

Or at least that's what she told herself. She couldn't
let herself slip and accidentally develop feelings for the
man just because he was amazing in bed and her body
ached for more.

And then, before she could shut it down, images of
last night bombarded her thoughts. His muscles were
hard and powerful, just as she knew they would be.
His chest and abdomen glistened with a slight sheen
of sweat as she caged him beneath her.

She was still surprised that he'd let her take the lead.
It wasn't what she'd been expecting given his bold,
brash personality. She'd held his arms above his head
and traced her lips along his tattoo, from his hairline
to his neck and shoulder, all the way down to where
it stopped at his groin. Then, as she cupped him and
pressed her palm to his chest to keep him down, she
slipped her mouth over his length.

Smiling to herself, she recalled how easily she'd
brought him to climax again. He groaned so loudly
as he came that a few items on the nightstand rattled.

He'd let her be the one in control last night—maybe
because he was weak from the lights or needed the
stress relief—but whatever the reason, she had the dis-

tinct impression that things wouldn't be the same the next time.

She hurriedly pulled out the list Santiago had given her earlier and looked for the few unchecked names. "Would the decorator be Charlotte Grant?"

"Yes, that's her."

"I haven't met her or her fiancé yet."

"Considering his position on the Council, they'll be at the awards gala," he said, sitting casually on the edge of the desk. "I'll introduce you to them then."

"Do you think that's wise? I mean, shouldn't I try to eliminate as many people as possible before that? What if whoever is behind all this plans to take advantage of so many of our VIPs being at the gala to strike again?"

"I just don't see how we can eliminate everyone before then. Those last remaining people on the list aren't scheduled to be in town until the event. But if you'd like, I can arrange a dinner date with Trace and Charlotte. Kill two birds with one stone."

Two at once? Hell, she'd eliminated half the people on her list while in the kitchen. The Seattle office wasn't very big.

She must've looked confused because he added, "Dinner with me. Checking names off your list. Those are two things. That should make the organized librarian in you happy."

She jerked her head up. "I'm not an organized librarian."

"Sure you are."

He really thought of her as a librarian? She didn't

think of herself that way at all. She wasn't rigid, stuck in her ways or overly organized. If you asked her, she was flexible and easy to get along with. "Why do you say that?" she asked, not sure she really wanted to know.

"Well, for one thing, I saw your suitcase. Your shoes were individually packed in their own little bags. Your herbs and candles labeled and cataloged."

"Okay, so I'm a good packer, that doesn't mean anything."

He raised his eyebrows in a maddening I'm Not Done With This Yet manner. "On the bathroom counter, you've got a little pill case labeled with all your vitamins."

"That...that proves nothing except that I'm committed to my health. Because you're completely the opposite of this, any sort of organization stands out to you. I'm normal and you're just jealous."

He laughed. "Is that so? Well, you've made playlists to match the various workouts you do for each day of the week. Monday is yoga day with earthy relaxation music. Tuesday is cardio with hip-hop. Wednesday is swimming, so there's no playlist. Thursday is—"

"You snooped through my music? That's like my private stuff. I can't believe you'd do that."

His guilty look quickly turned to a scowl. "It was sitting on the nightstand. What's wrong with that? Jesus. All I wanted was the name of the music you played when you gave me a massage. It's not like I read through your diary or went through your underwear drawer. Hell, I don't even know if you have a diary."

"Well, I don't, so don't go snooping around for it." She folded her arms and gave him her evilest stare.

He glared back. "I won't."

Why would he want to know the music she had played? "I thought you said all of this was a bunch of mumbo-jumbo?"

An impossible-to-read expression flashed across his face. He strode to a shelf and examined one of the bronze statues as if he'd never seen it before. "It was… I found it to be relaxing and I was feeling…stressed."

He was— Her music— Oh. She rubbed her onyx pendant and the wind in her sails sputtered out like a spent whoopee cushion. She wouldn't have guessed in a million years that he thought her methods had any merit. "Okay, I'm sorry. I shouldn't have jumped down your throat like that. You're welcome to look through my music anytime."

There was that little gleam again as he approached her. "Apology accepted. And…thanks. But admit it, Roxy, you're hopelessly organized."

She jutted her chin out. "I wouldn't call that a fault."

"I didn't say that it was."

"Saying that I'm hopeless sure makes it sound less than positive."

"You've never heard the terms *hopelessly romantic* or *hopelessly devoted?*" he asked. "Being romantic or devoted aren't negative character traits and neither is being organized. Besides, you didn't know that I'm an admirer of organized people. If it weren't for Jenella, my office up at region would be a chaotic mess."

That was a true statement if ever she heard one. "So what you're saying then is that organized people are your enablers?"

He reached out and snatched her hands so quickly that she didn't have a chance to move away. "Yes," he said, pulling her close and burying his nose in her hair. "I'd be hopelessly lost without…without the organized people in my life."

Her heart flip-flopped beneath her rib cage as her arms seemed to magically slip around his neck of their own accord. It sounded like he almost said he was hopelessly lost without her. But that was crazy. He wasn't the type to become dependent on a woman. His assistant, maybe. But her? She highly doubted it.

"I don't know about that," she said huskily. "I think you're overstating things."

She really needed to downplay what could be going on between them. If she wasn't careful, she could let herself get too attached to this man. Already she was being sucked into his world when she had her own issues to deal with. She'd been in Seattle for several days and yet she still hadn't looked into the lead she'd discovered about Ian's death.

She couldn't let go of the promise she'd made to Mary Alice. Having an all-or-nothing type personality, she had a hard time compartmentalizing everything and focusing on one task then moving to another. She tended to jump into something and let all the other commitments in her life suffer. If she let herself get involved with Santiago on a personal level, that would become her priority rather than the promise she made many years ago. And given what Mary Alice had done for her, she needed to make it her top priority again, which meant things needed to cool down between Santiago and her.

If she was able to let things cool down. God, he smelled so good.

"You're perceptive and you really listen to people, whereas I'm…" He ran his thumb over her jaw, making her inner thighs quiver. "I'm demanding and short-fused. They clam up around me, but with you, I'd imagine they'd talk all day." He pulled away from her slightly and cupped her face in his hands. His pupils expanded, crowding out all but just a ring of his irises. Seeing how emotionally stimulated he was really turned her on and a delicious heat pooled low in her belly.

He stared at her lips, making her desperately want him to kiss her.

"See?" he whispered, his voice rough like a callused hand. "Now you're doing it to me. You're an evil, wicked woman, Roxy. I'm not normally so open and talkative."

"I'm pretty sure you can't talk if I'm kissing you."

His mouth was hot against hers and she pushed her tongue inside. He smelled faintly of cigars and tasted like peppermint. A laugh rumbled in his chest, and before she knew it, she had one knee up on the desktop and was virtually straddling him.

"And normally I'm not this forward," she said against his lips.

"Believe me, I have no problems with you being forward when it comes to sex with me."

She hesitated, remembering how she'd taken charge with him in bed, as well. Had she gone completely mad? Yes, he was good-looking and an incredible lover, but she didn't need to lose her head either. "Well…I'm not used to it, that's all."

"Are you more comfortable with this?" And then, before she knew what was happening, he'd switched their positions.

Now it was her turn to sit on the edge of his desk. With her skirt bunched up around her waist, he was between her legs, unbuttoning his fly. When he freed that magnificent erection of his, a teardrop of liquid already glistened from its velvety tip. She bit her lip to keep from gasping and sounding like an idiot. He was the most beautiful male she'd ever seen. Proud, virile and commanding. It both frightened and thrilled her that his desire for her was so obvious.

Her breath came out all raggedy and uneven. She felt a tug, heard a rip and realized her thong was gone. He'd easily dispensed of it with a flip of his wrist. Nothing, not even a scrap of fabric, stood between them now.

He held the base of his shaft with one hand and reached for her hip with his other. She scooted to the very edge, expecting him to guide himself into her, but at the last moment, he plunged two fingers inside her instead.

"My hot little librarian is such a minx." He chuckled and the rumbling in his chest felt as if it were coming from hers. His voice was scratchy and rougher now. Like wet wool or a piece of sandpaper. "I wanted to make sure you were ready for me, but I'd say without a doubt that you're beyond that point and we haven't even gotten started yet."

She moved her hips as best she could on this hard desk, matching the rhythm of his fingers. "Should we even be doing this? I mean, what if someone walks in on us?" She glanced toward the door but couldn't see it behind him. His body was blocking it from view.

"Then they'll certainly get an eyeful." He didn't seem too concerned, but wasn't that the way of most males? Sexual activity, no matter what it entailed, took precedence over the need to keep up appearances. "If you're not a librarian, how about a professor?" he asked, his eyes sparkling with amusement.

Oh, God, he rubbed his fingers over a spot that sent electricity shooting down her spine. He seemed to enjoy watching her writhe in pleasure on top of his desk. Although her elbow scattered a neat stack of papers everywhere and her knee knocked over his pencil cup, he didn't seem to notice. Or if he had, he didn't care. His attention was one hundred percent fixed on her.

Despite never being brought to climax with just a man's hand before, she could tell she was getting menacingly close. The room seemed to be getting progressively smaller and every inch of her body was hair-trigger sensitive. Heat concentrated between her legs where he stroked her and his fingers seemed to be sliding in and out more easily. Even though his erection was quite large, if he guided the tip between her folds right now, she was certain her body was fully prepared to accept every inch.

"I'm not a professor," she said, grabbing his shoulders as if she were grabbing on to her last bit of sanity. She could feel his arm muscles flexing and contracting with every movement. Having seen them bulge and strain during his workouts, she imagined that they looked the same now as he pleasured her, which she found extremely erotic.

"Ah, but you do teach at the Academy," he whispered in her ear, pressing his thumb firmly against her center.

All of her nerves tingled at once, every last one, from her toes to her scalp and everything in between. Oh, God, she could feel it coming. It was almost here.

"Professors are…dull…boring…know-it-alls," she said, hardly able to speak, let alone think coherently.

"Not the gorgeous professor I know. She's far from dull and, believe me, she's never boring."

He gently twisted that little ball of flesh in such a way that she thought she might pass out from sheer pleasure, right then and there. She arched her back and pressed her hips into his hand. Normally, she'd be done with the foreplay and ready for intercourse, but she was so close now that if he stopped, even for a moment, she'd certainly die.

"And just to let you know, the next time I do this to you—" he pressed a little harder for emphasis "—I'm going to be doing it with my tongue."

Like shards of glass raining down from the sky, she

shattered into a million pieces around him. She probably threw her head back. Dug her nails into his shoulders. Maybe even cursed or called out his name.

But before she could catch her breath or remember her name for that matter, he pulled her to the edge of the table with a jerk.

"I'm incapable of being slow and gentle right now," he said, shoving her skirt even higher.

"Good. Because rough sounds good at the moment."

She gripped his shoulders and trembled with anticipation. This was going to be so damn amazing. Last time was incredible, but a small part of her felt as if she may have taken advantage of him in his weakened condition. Although he'd recently fed from a live host, he still wouldn't be one hundred percent back to normal yet, due to the UV damage he sustained.

His eyes blazed with hunger as he hastily positioned himself between her legs. It was only when she saw his fangs that she realized her own had elongated, as well. She turned away slightly, not wanting him to see her. She couldn't take his blood, he was still too weak for that. Besides, not every couple shared blood during sex. Many didn't. And when they did, chances were they were in a committed relationship. His acceptance of hers earlier had been purely out of necessity.

The velvety tip of his shaft slid into her opening, pressing heavily on her very sensitive core. Thanks to his skilled foreplay, she was more than ready for him, which was a good thing given his immense size. Then holding her bottom with both hands, he pushed himself all the way in with one commanding thrust.

"Santiago. Oh, my God." He filled her completely. She seriously was on the brink again though he'd hardly done anything. Just his body inside hers was enough to bring her to climax.

His only response was a growl then a few grunts as he began pistoning his hips, driving into her over and over. He was a relentless and eager lover, the ridge of his shaft having found a very sensitive area deep inside her. It was as if his body was designed to fit perfectly into hers because it pressed all the right buttons in all the right ways.

Her muscles clenched down tight around him in successively stronger waves.

"I'm…I'm almost there."

He grunted in response. His thrusts became focused, the friction between their bodies even more intense. "Take my blood, Roxy."

"Whaaat?" She could hardly speak. Had she heard him correctly?

"Drink from me. But hurry. I'm almost there."

There was no time to question him further. She was about ready to explode, as well. She didn't want to know if this was routine for him or not, because right now, it was just the two of them making love. Not their pasts or what had happened to them before this moment. And certainly not their futures.

His fingers fisted in her hair as she placed her lips on his neck.

"Yes, that's it. There you go." He was thick inside her, his movements short and focused. The friction was almost too much.

Her inner muscles tightened around him as she bit down. Instantly his coppery warmth filled her mouth, releasing a floodgate of pleasure more powerful than anything she'd ever felt before. It was so incredibly intense that she would've lost her hold on his vein and collapsed into a puddle on the desk if he hadn't held her to him.

He groaned and made one final thrust, releasing himself into her body.

And in that moment, the world froze, suspending time between before and after. Although she wished it could last forever, she knew it was as fleeting as a butterfly on the wind.

CHAPTER THIRTEEN

IT WAS ALMOST eight o'clock when Santiago and Roxy walked down Fifth Avenue and headed back to the field office, passing a coffee shop with the neon *S* and *P* burned out. Car tires spun loudly on the wet pavement, a reminder that although it wasn't raining now, it soon would be again. She'd hardly said more than two words since leaving the jewelry store a few minutes ago. He wondered why she was so distracted.

"'Coffee ho,'" he said, reading the sign and hoping for a reaction. When he didn't get one, he added, "I'll do you for a cup of Joe."

She didn't laugh. "No, thanks. I'm a tea drinker."

He gave her a sidelong glance. Was she messing with him or was she just not paying attention?

After the intimacies they'd been sharing lately—the laughing, the talking—he'd have thought a joke like that would've elicited some sort of response from her other than the bland one he got. One of her musical laughs. A punch in the arm. A snappy retort of her own. Anything.

At first he thought she'd been upset because it had taken a week until he'd had time to shop for the ring, but then she'd seemed fine at the jewelry store—silly, actually—as they'd looked through the various display cases.

"If I were Elizabeth Taylor, I'd totally pick that one," she'd said, pointing to a rock the size of a grape. "And if I were Audrey Hepburn, that one, the second one from the top—" a simple platinum band with three modestly sized diamonds "—would be the one for me."

"How about that one?" Santiago pointed to a skull ring with diamonds in the eye sockets.

"Angelina Jolie in her Billy Bob Thornton period."

"And that one?" A ring shaped like a butterfly.

"Mariah Carey."

It went on and on. "Jennifer Aniston." "Michelle Obama." "Queen Elisabeth." Even the salesperson pointed out a few of the more unusual pieces to see who Roxy would pick.

When the guy excused himself to help another customer while they continued to look, Santiago's curiosity suddenly got the best of him. "What about Roxy Reynolds? What ring is the perfect one for her?" He hadn't planned to ask her. He also hadn't meant for his tone to sound so serious, but the words tumbled out of his mouth. It was meant to be as lighthearted a question as the others, but it wasn't. And they both knew it.

She turned away from him, the silliness gone from the atmosphere as if it had never been there in the first place.

He hadn't wanted that game to end. He enjoyed seeing the way her eyes lit up mischievously just before she blurted out another celeb's name. Could he just scratch those last questions? She walked back to the first case they'd looked in and pointed to the simple Audrey Hepburn ring. "It's probably closest to that one."

So that was the one she wore on her finger now. They stepped off the sidewalk and crossed the intersection. "Aren't diamonds supposed to be a girl's best friend?"

"Huh?"

"I thought women loved diamonds."

"What? Oh, yes," she said absently. "They're nice."

What the— Diamonds are *nice?* Nice was a dog lying at your feet or the friend who brought you another beer without you having to ask or finding out it was double-shot day—two for the price of one—at your favorite espresso stand.

It was like she forgot they had just spent the past hour in the jewelry store and bought the ring—the Audrey Hepburn ring—that was now sitting on her formerly naked finger. Was she distracted with everything going on at the field office? Was that it? He wanted her to loosen up and laugh like she did at the jewelry store. He knew she took her work seriously. Was she suddenly remembering the events that led to this sham of theirs—that people had almost been killed? Maybe he was wrong to be having fun with this and should change his attitude to be more like hers. Treating it like the job that it was.

"You don't sound very excited." His first reaction was to be irritated by her disinterest, because he spent more on that thing than he did on his first car. He would've thought she'd at least pretend to be excited to wear it, but in the three blocks they walked since they left the jewelry store, she hadn't even once looked at how it sparkled in the moonlight.

For some reason he was more interested in the sudden turnabout in her mood. Normally, he didn't spend a lot of time analyzing why people acted the way they did. He dealt with them at face value and didn't care to know the minutia causing their actions. If their bad mood was caused by the stale cornflakes in their breakfast bowl, so be it. But she hadn't met his gaze once since they started walking back to the field office and it gnawed at his gut to know why.

"I'm sorry," she said flatly. "I'm excited. Really."

Yeah, about as excited as someone getting a root canal. He wasn't sure why he even cared about her reaction. He hadn't been hoping that she would enjoy wearing a ring he gave her, would he? If so, he was an idiot.

"Fine. Whatever." He lengthened his stride, making her almost have to jog to keep up. He headed a different direction from the way they came. Lined with a few strip clubs, unmarked doors covered in graffiti, and tiny convenience stores with bars on all the windows, this street was a showcase of the underbelly of what Seattle had to offer, which was why he avoided it coming in the first time. It bypassed all the glitzy shops, fancy restaurants and big department stores that they passed on the way to the jewelry store. But it was also a shortcut back to the office.

She looked confused. "I didn't mean to hurt your feelings. It's a beautiful ring."

"My feelings?" He made a big deal of laughing and rolling his eyes so as not to mistake things this time. Did she think he was a sensitive sonofabitch? "Please. My feelings are incapable of being hurt. You have to care about something in order for it to affect you."

His words came out harsh and to the point, but instead of backing away from him, she tucked her hand in the crook of his elbow as they walked. Did she not believe him? Then he recalled her skill at reading people. She must've sensed he was bullshitting her.

He kept his hands in his pockets, resisting the urge to put an arm around her shoulder where it naturally wanted to go. She was right, of course. There was no need to get all emotional about a stupid ring when it meant nothing, which was why he wasn't even the slightest bit hurt that she wasn't excited about it. "Why don't you—"

Her hand slid from his arm. He didn't realize she had stopped until he turned to find her staring incredulously across the street.

"They're open?"

What's open?

He followed her gaze to either the grungy-looking pawn shop or the strip club advertising naughty college coeds. "Are you wanting to make a buck?" he said jokingly.

She didn't laugh. "I've called that pawn shop so many times since we've been here in town, but I kept getting their answering machine. So I stopped by a few times only to see their 'back in an hour' sign posted on the door. I was starting to wonder if they were ever open."

That crappy pawn shop? The one with the bars on the windows and the partially burned-out neon sign? It didn't make sense. "You don't look like someone who normally frequents a place like that."

It wasn't quite the same thing as an antiques shop or an interesting secondhand store, he thought. Pawn shops were for people to make money off the shit they owned. Desperate people who were desperate for cash. Just then a skinny man wearing a stained sweatshirt came out and stopped on the sidewalk directly across from them to light a cigarette.

"It's probably nothing. Why don't you go on back to the office? I'll catch up with you later." She had a faraway look in her eyes that said she'd already dismissed him and was ready to tackle this on her own.

But he didn't want that. He wanted to remain a part of what she was doing and he had the sudden urge to understand what was going on. Did it have something to do with her attitude after leaving the jewelry store or was this something different? He may not be interested in the whys behind other people's behavior, but it occurred to him that he sure as hell cared about hers.

"You're planning to go inside? What the hell for?"

"Trust me. I'm not going to hock the ring you just bought."

For some strange reason, he noticed she didn't refer to it as *her* ring. "That's not what I meant."

"I can take care of myself, if that's what you're worried about."

"I...I wasn't implying that either." At least he didn't think he was.

Jesus, he hated how the words tumbled around his mouth like a bunch of pebbles when he was around her. But he really wasn't thrilled about her going into a place like that anyway, whether or not she could kick some serious ass. He knew for a fact she could, but that didn't make it easier for him to accept.

He got the distinct impression she didn't want him here, which made him want to stay all the more. "So tell me, what's going on?"

She turned her head and swept her gaze over him as if she were trying to determine whether he was worthy or not. He found himself standing taller and squaring his shoulders as a result of her scrutiny. On one hand, it made him mad that he cared so much about what she thought of him, but at the same time, he wanted to measure up to whatever it was she was looking for.

She sighed heavily. "Fine. I can tell you're not going to back down until I tell you the truth. Back when I was in Florida, I ran across a picture online of a sword this pawn shop was selling. Now that I'm here, I want to check it out, that's all."

"A sword? At that place?" He couldn't imagine them having anything of worth. Just a bunch of crappy used shit and what would she want with that?

"It looked a lot like Ian's blade," she added quietly,

the strain in her voice obvious. "I'm sure it's not the same one, but I wanted to check it out to see for myself."

So that was it. Even after all these years, she hadn't let go of him. She was still in love with the guy and she wanted to surround herself with things that reminded her of him. A deep, gnawing ache tunneled through his insides and took up residence in his gut. How could he compete with a dead man, he thought, but then he instantly chastised himself. He wasn't interested in Roxy that way. Sure, maybe a roll in the sack and some joking around, but that was it. Nothing long-term.

"A pawn shop with a Guardian weapon?" It didn't make sense. When a Guardian died, his commanding officer presented the family with his weapon in a quiet ceremony. It was a way for his service and sacrifice to be honored. Santiago had performed a few of them himself over the years. It was one of the hardest responsibilities of his position, but it was also very necessary. "Why would his family want to sell it?"

She recoiled as if he'd slapped her and her eyes instantly darkened. "They didn't. They never had the weapon to begin with. It wasn't recovered from the site where he was…killed."

"Then how…" The realization hit him like a piano dropping from an upper window. He recalled the blade retrieved from the DB up in Canada. Jenella was researching to figure out if it actually belonged to a Guardian. "You think the killer is trying to sell it."

If she could find his weapon and trace it back, maybe

it'd lead to who was responsible. Now he understood her motivation. Justice for a man she loved.

She shrugged. "Who knows if it's his actual killer trying to pawn it or if it's even the same weapon? Seems far-fetched, I know. But the photo posted to their website looked a lot like Grim, so I wanted to check it out while I was here."

"Grim?"

"Yeah, that's what Ian called his weapon. Short for the Grim Reaper. A blacksmith near Prague forged the weapon to his exact specifications."

"Petrov the Brave," he mumbled. A former Guardian who'd suffered a career-ending injury centuries ago, the man began forging weapons for his former comrades from newly discovered Mexican silver mines. His services were highly sought after and people waited for years for a chance to have a blade made by this master craftsman. Misery was one of his first blades.

"The one and only. Ian sketched out many possible designs—he was obsessive about it for a while—trying to come up with something that had meaning for him and his family and yet was functional. When Petrov was finished, it truly was something to behold."

"Well, let's go. I want to see it." It angered him to know that a weapon belonging to a Guardian could ever be sitting in a place like that. It was almost sacrilegious. He'd buy it, see if the thing needed to be restored, then he'd return it to the family.

"I'm not sure they still have it. Hell, I don't even know if it really was Grim to begin with. It's been so long since I've seen it in real life, I could be mistaken. A week after they posted the photo, it was gone."

Damn. "They probably sold it then."

"Yeah, but maybe they have a better picture so I can tell if it is the one I've been looking for. I honestly don't think it's the same one. How would Ian's blade have gotten clear up here from where he...died in Florida? But I couldn't *not* check out the lead."

"I'd have done the same thing. If it is his blade, maybe the owners can tell us who brought it in to the shop in the first place as well as who bought it."

She flashed him a quick smile before they jogged across the street to Mike's Pawn Shop. The buzzer on the door sounded like the noise a game show makes when you answer incorrectly. A man in a wife-beater—Mike?—sat behind the counter, watching one of those live courtroom reality shows. He barely glanced at them when they walked in then turned his attention back to the television.

The tiny space reeked of stale furniture, cigarettes and old Chinese food. Overhead lights cast everything in the dull haze of an old color photograph. Shelves crammed with used tools, video consoles and games, and camera equipment lined all of the dingy walls, while musical instruments and old computers filled the center aisle. A drum set sat near the door and Santiago and Roxy had to step around it just to get inside. The display case beneath the counter housed a variety of watches and rings and knives.

"You have a nice selection of blades here," she remarked. Santiago was looking over her shoulder into the same glass case, but all he saw were a few hunting knives, pocketknives and switchblades. All crap.

The man grunted a response without looking away from the television.

"Can I ask you a question?" The sound of Roxy's voice—lyrical and charming—contrasted sharply with their surroundings.

The clerk didn't turn around or even acknowledge her this time.

"The lady is talking to you." Santiago struggled to sound civil.

"Verdict's coming." The man held up his hand. "Hold on."

Roxy waited patiently, while Santiago wanted to jump to the other side of the counter and wring the guy's neck. The shrill ringing of a phone drowned out the screaming defendants.

"You gettin' that?" the man called to someone in the back. "I got customers." The ringing stopped just before the commercial break, and he turned to face them. "What do you need?"

Roxy smiled pleasantly at him, her face showing no signs of any frustration. Santiago didn't know how she did it, when he was itching to shove Mr. Court-TV against the wall and demand answers. "I'm looking for information on a large knife I saw on your website."

"A knife? We got lots of knives."

"No, I'm looking for a specific one. It's a sword actually." She stretched out her hands to show the size.

"It's got a hand-carved hilt with pearls and gemstones embedded in the handle."

"Don't sound familiar. Sorry."

"But I saw the sword on your website recently. Don't you remember?"

"Lady, we get a lot of things that go in and out of this place every day. I can't remember them all."

"But do you put all of this stuff up online?" Roxy swept her hand over the case and continued her pleasant, nonconfrontational manner, but he could hear the frustration creeping into her tone.

"Of course not. Just the high-end stuff and the stuff that we think would do well online."

Santiago had a hard time imagining a Neanderthal like him would even know how to use a computer, let alone put something up for sale online. The only buttons the guy would be familiar with were those on the TV remote control.

"It was on your site for a few days and then it was gone."

"Probably sold it then."

"Do you still have a picture?"

The clerk had a sour lemon face. "What for? It's not like I can sell it to you if it's already gone. Why don't you pick something else?"

"I think it may have belonged to a friend."

"Maybe you got the wrong website." He spoke slowly as if he were the one exercising extreme patience here.

"Come on," Santiago said to her. If he stayed any

longer, it wasn't going to be pretty. "This obviously is a dead end."

Roxy's shoulders slumped and she let him lead her toward the door. "Do you think he could've had his mind cleared?" she whispered as they stopped next to the drum set. "Maybe that's why he doesn't remember."

"Does he even have much upstairs to warrant clearing?" Santiago didn't bother to keep his voice down. "I seriously doubt it."

"Wait." An older man came out from the back room holding a stained rag and a bottle of solvent. Santiago hesitated, his hand on the door. "I might be able to help."

Roxy approached the display case again. "You remember the sword?"

"Yeah, I sure do. Never seen anything like it before in my life. I won't soon forget a blade that nice. It had a shine to it that you wouldn't believe."

"Do you have a photo?" she asked quickly. It was obvious she was trying to control her excitement, but she wasn't doing a very good job.

"It's probably around here somewhere."

The younger man looked irritated by all the talking. "Do you mind?"

"Yes, I do," the older man replied and he reached up and turned off the television.

"Hey, I was watching that."

"Yeah, and we have a customer."

Santiago didn't want to break the news that they weren't exactly customers. It wasn't like they planned on buying something here.

The man rooted around in various drawers, opening and closing each one, scattering junk everywhere, and just when they figured he'd come up empty-handed, he said, "Found it."

He unclipped a bent picture from a piece of paper and handed it to Roxy. "Is that it?"

She took it from him. "I'm…I'm not sure. Is this the only picture you have of it?"

The quality of the photo wasn't good, but even so, Santiago could see that it was a beautiful weapon. What he wouldn't give to swing the thing in his hand to feel the weight and the balance. In Petrov's foundry, he'd been instructed to strip to the waist while the man watched him wield weapon after weapon to observe how he moved. Apparently, it helped the man design the perfect blade for each individual. Had Ian done the same and that blade—Grim—was the result? While he'd have to examine it in person, from what he could tell, it very well could be a Guardian blade.

"Afraid this is the only one."

Roxy was trying to conceal her disappointment, but Santiago could see right through it. "I can't tell from this, but did it have black pearls embedded in the handle?"

"*Black* pearls?" The man examined the dirty rag in his hand, then grabbed a corner and tossed it onto his shoulder. "Yeah, I think maybe it did."

She turned to Santiago. "Ian insisted on the pearls even though they're not as durable as the gemstones.

Black pearls had been used in their family for generations."

"Do you know who bought it?" Santiago asked the man.

"No one. The seller came in and took it back. Said the money wasn't necessary anymore."

"What's his name? Do you remember what he looked like?" Santiago took the photo from Roxy and flipped it over but nothing was scribbled on the back. If the man wouldn't tell them, maybe Santiago could get his hands on the paper that the photo was clipped.

"Well, for one thing, it wasn't a he."

Santiago snapped his head up. "The owner of the knife is a woman?"

"I probably shouldn't say anything. Confidentiality and shit."

Santiago reached across the counter and handed him back the photo, letting his fingers brush the man's hand. "Tell us her name."

Blinking a few times, the man opened one of the drawers and pulled out the paper that had been attached to the picture. "Ann Black."

He narrowed his eyes. The name was entirely too convenient. Easy to remember…and forget. It sure didn't sound familiar and he knew a number of the local vampires. Could she be human? If so, how would she have gotten hold of such a weapon?

"What did she look like?"

The man scrunched his face in concentration, making his nose look even more bulbous. "Hard to say. I'd say she was about average height. A little shorter than you," he said to Roxy. "Not really fat or skinny. Brown hair, I think. Or maybe it was blond."

As if that narrowed it down.

"It was hard to tell what she looked like because she had on these huge-ass sunglasses. The ones that make you look bug-eyed. Movie stars and rappers wear them. You know what I'm talking about?"

Santiago nodded, a sourness taking root in his gut. Sounded like a DB.

"She didn't even take them off when she was inside. Funny thing was, it was dark when she came in. Wait. Is she a celebrity? Is that why you're looking for her? Are you guys like paparazzi or something? 'Cuz if you are, don't I get a finder's fee, for, you know, finding her for you?"

You haven't found her yet, asshole. "Do you have any contact information for her?" Santiago slipped him a couple of twenties.

The man's eyes lit up as he pocketed the bills and thrust the paper at Santiago. "She didn't leave a phone number, just her PO box. You could always send her a letter the old-fashioned way and see if she's interested in still selling it."

"Is that all you can tell us about her?" Roxy asked.

"Yeah, she didn't stay long either time."

"Thanks," Santiago said, ushering Roxy out the door. They could head to the post office and Roxy could try picking up her scent there.

"Hold on," the first clerk said. "She did take a liking to that ring there in the display case. I don't know if that makes a difference or not."

"A ring?" Roxy approached the counter again. "Which one?"

He pointed to an oversize sapphire ring next to a scratched Rolex. "She tried it on and I think she would've bought it but she didn't think it was the real deal. I showed her the certs and everything, but she didn't believe me."

"Can I see it?" Roxy shot a sidelong glance at Santiago. He could see the excitement in her eyes. Maybe she'd be able to pick up the woman's scent from an object she'd held recently.

Roxy made it appear as though she were examining it closely, but in reality, she brought it up to her face to sniff it. She gave an imperceptible nod. "Got it."

"I'll take it," Santiago said to the man. "How much do you want for it?"

"What?" Roxy's head shot up.

"I can tell you like it, darling," he said, pointedly. "It's just what you need." He pulled out his wallet and paid the guy his asking price, without bothering to dicker.

Out on the sidewalk, Roxy turned to him, looking a little confused. "You didn't need to do that."

He shrugged. "I know, but this way, you'll be able to track her more easily if you have the correct scent to use as a frame of reference. Let's head to the post office and see if you can match the scent there."

She stood on her tiptoes and kissed him quickly. "Thank you."

"What was that for?"

"I…I appreciate your support of what's important to me."

A half hour later when they got to the post office, they found no box with that number, and Roxy couldn't detect any Darkblood scent. They were at a dead end.

He opened the passenger door for her. "I'm sorry. I know it means a lot to you to find that blade."

Rather than climbing in, she pulled the collar of her coat up around her ears and walked to the back bumper of the Corvette. With her arms crossed over her chest, she stared absently at the railroad tracks on the other side of the parking lot.

He came up behind her and rubbed her back underneath the silky length of her hair. "I know it's disappointing, but it's bound to turn up. I can alert the Seattle field team to be on the lookout for a weapon matching Grim's description."

She kicked at a pebble. "I'm so mad at myself I can hardly think straight." Her breath fogged from the cold, mixing with his, and the tip of her nose had turned red.

"Why? You didn't know it was Grim. In fact, you still don't know for sure."

When she shoved her hands into her pockets, he made a mental note to swing by one of the ski shops and buy her a pair of warm gloves.

"But you don't understand. This is the closest I've come to finding Ian's weapon after years of searching.

And here I thought it was the flimsiest of leads, too. I should've jumped on a plane up here as soon as I found that photograph online. What was I thinking?"

"Why do you want it so badly?" Santiago really didn't want to ask the question because he was fairly certain he wouldn't like the answer.

"Let's just say I made a promise and I intend to keep it."

He turned back to the car. It was obvious that she was still in love with Ian and wanted this weapon of his to remind her of him.

They drove back to the field office in silence, the engine noise the only sound. He'd had fun with her tonight, but all he felt now was empty.

Clearly deep in thought, she twisted the engagement ring around and around her finger as if she was unscrewing it. "Why did you join the same military group that Ian did?"

Until he met Roxy, he hadn't thought of the Madrid Seven in years.

He shrugged. "Why do most young men join a group like that? For adventure. For the challenge. To get away from their fathers." And mothers.

A rain-and-snow mix began pelting the windshield so he turned on the wiper blades. The back and forth rhythmic sound reminded him of the even cadence of hoofbeats as he and the other warriors had galloped between villages in the dead of night.

"Your father?" She turned in her seat to face him. "Was he…abusive to you?"

"Physically? To me? No, it wasn't that."

"To your mother?"

"Only if you consider a broken heart to be abusive. Although my parents' union was deemed a good one—it produced my sister and me—my father was not satisfied and had many mistresses. It was a machismo thing. He told her that just as vampires cannot survive without human blood, the men in our family are not capable of being with only one woman. 'It's in our nature,' he used to say."

"Your poor mother. She must've been devastated."

"She dealt with it in her own way." He remembered the beatings, the verbal abuse that he and his sister had suffered at her hands. "But she was so duty-bound that the thought of leaving him never crossed her mind. She blamed herself—and us—for his actions. Said that if we were better, cleverer, more trustworthy, he'd stay with us."

"Did you ever talk to your father about it?"

Santiago laughed bitterly. "Yeah. He said his father was like this and his father's father was like this. And that when I grew up, I'd be like him, too."

"Is that why you never…you know…settled down?"

He shrugged. "I urged my mother to leave him, but she wouldn't. She continued to put up with his philandering ways, however, I couldn't put up with either of them, so I left home soon after my Time of Change and joined the Madrid Seven."

"And where are they now? Your parents."

"They died a long time ago."

CHAPTER FOURTEEN

ROXY SPENT THE next few weeks wandering around the
field office talking to various people, but so far, she
hadn't met anyone who triggered anything weird with
her intuition. Santiago had been working a lot, trying
to keep up with the demands of running both the region and field offices. Neither of them was any closer
to figuring out the traitor's identity. She was beginning
to wonder if there even *was* a traitor.

As she waited for one of the elevators to open in the
foyer, a Benny Goodman song played quietly over the
speakers and she tapped her foot to the beat. Ever since
learning swing from a navy guy she casually dated
years ago, she'd loved the big-band era. Too bad no one
danced like that anymore.

"Oh, good, you're heading out."

She turned to see Arianna coming around the corner. Brenna had first introduced the two of them up at
region HQ shortly before the explosion that changed everything. With a messenger bag slung across her shoulder, she twisted her chestnut hair and tucked it under
her scarf.

"Yeah, thought I'd better find something to wear to
the awards gala before it's too late."

"Can I ask you a big favor then? I need an escort out of the building."

Was this standard operating procedure in Seattle? "An escort?"

"Yeah. Santiago's orders. He's got the whole place on lockdown after what happened. Any humans in the field office must go out with an escort to make sure Darkbloods don't see or follow them."

"But it's cloaked." She'd been through the energy field a number of times since arriving here and it had never been down.

"The escort thing is an added precaution since humans can't scent Darkbloods like the rest of you can."

"In that case, of course."

She couldn't help but wonder if Arianna and Jackson had plans for her to become a changeling, thus solving that problem, but thought it'd be rude to ask. Besides being somewhat risky, turning one's mate into a vampire was a very personal decision and one that wasn't taken lightly. It'd be like asking a childless couple if they were going to have a baby.

Then she got an idea. "So, where are you headed?"

"I'm interviewing someone for my blog and after that, when rush hour's over, I'm heading back up to the safehouse."

The elevator dinged and the doors opened.

"Paranormalish, right?"

Arianna gave her a wary look as they stepped inside before pressing a button on the panel. "Santiago told you about my blog? What did he say?"

The big-band music was playing inside the elevator, too, and Roxy leaned against the railing. "He said it got Jackson into a lot of hot water but that he's impressed with what you've been able to uncover about Darkblood activity. Said it's been an instrumental tool in helping Guardians identify acts of violence by Darkbloods that previously would've gone unnoticed by the agency. He said you've got your finger on the pulse of the community and that you often hear about things before they do."

Arianna's mouth opened slightly as if she'd just run up a few flights of stairs and was trying to catch her breath. "Wow, he really does believe in what I'm doing. I knew he supported the sweetblood home, but I wasn't sure if his support of the blog was just lip service to Jackson. He's always storming around, cussing and swearing, that it's hard to know what he feels."

"Ha. Tell me about it."

Once they were past all the security checkpoints and Roxy hadn't picked up any Darkblood scent around the building, Arianna turned to her. "Where are you headed? Want to grab a bite to eat? Food, that is, not you-know-what." She laughed.

"What about your interview?"

Arianna checked the time on her cell phone. "It shouldn't last long."

Roxy wasn't expecting that, but she really liked Arianna's company. Only a handful of people knew why she was there, so it'd be nice to relax and drop her cover for a change. "Sure, and afterward, can you tell me where I should go to find something to wear to the awards ceremony? It's coming up soon and I haven't even thought about what I should wear."

"Better yet, after we eat, I'll take you to a few of my favorite shops. Vintage or new? Oh, wait, most of the vintage shops I like are only open during the day. It'll have to be new."

"Deal."

It was after six o'clock when they arrived at the coffee shop, a few minutes late for Arianna's meeting. While she interviewed the college guy, Roxy sat at a nearby table, sipping on a green tea. They weren't kidding when they said Seattle had a coffee shop on every corner. Try two or three on each block.

She couldn't help listening to part of the conversation. The guy told Arianna about a support group he belonged to that consisted of people who believed they'd been abducted by aliens. They met once a month at the same coffee shop. Arianna nodded, took notes, and asked a few questions. Apparently, she was going to feature the group on her website. Roxy looked around the room so as not to be too nosy.

A young couple wearing clip-in biking shoes were sitting on the same side of a table near the window. The man had one arm draped casually over the seat back and the other hand was resting on the woman's belly. If the woman was pregnant, she couldn't be very far along because her stomach still looked flat. Roxy wanted to look away, but no matter what she did—staring at the black painted ductwork on the ceiling or studying the retro-patterned upholstery on all the chairs—her gaze ended back on the couple. The man kissed the woman's cheek and she laughed.

Roxy grabbed a magazine from the coffee table and flipped aimlessly through pages of celebrity gossip. She used to dream of one day starting a family with Ian. Having grown up with only a brother, she wanted lots of children of her own. At first, Ian had said he wanted kids, too, and she really thought he meant it at the time—but then his addiction began and everything changed.

She was so engrossed in her thoughts that she didn't realize Arianna's interview was over and she was talking to someone else.

"So you've resorted to stalking me now, is that right, George?" Arianna's knuckles were white as she gripped the edge of the table.

The man—George—wore black slacks, a leather bomber jacket with a winged insignia on the back that said OSPRA, and a pair of Oakley sunglasses pushed up on his head. How could she have missed a guy like that walking in the door? He took the recently vacated chair, turned it around and sat down without waiting for an invitation. Arianna stiffened.

"I happened to see you here so I thought I'd come say hello."

"Bull."

"You don't have to believe me but it's the truth."

L...i...a...r...

The word whispered softly in the air, trailing off and

getting lost in the room while a faintly bitter taste hung on the back of her tongue. Roxy glanced behind her. A man with his service dog—a shepherd/husky mix, if she wasn't mistaken—was ordering at the counter. Near the fireplace, two women were knitting and carrying on a conversation without looking at each other. The couple expecting a baby had left.

She had to have imagined it. The sound was probably just her own breathing or that of the wind. The strange taste lingered until she took another sip of tea and it faded away.

"I had no idea you were here," George continued, "but when I saw you, I thought it'd be the polite thing to do to come say hello, especially after all we've been through."

L...i...a...r...

A little louder this time. And there was that strange aftertaste.

Her intuition hadn't been this strong in…well, forever. He was definitely lying to Arianna.

"We've been through nothing, asshole."

"Touchy, aren't we?" He started to say more, but a girl with stringy dark hair, who'd just come through the door, stopped next to him as if her feet had suddenly been glued there. Even her arms flailed as she tried to catch her balance.

"Oh, my God, you're that ghost expert guy! George… George…from the Olympic Society for Paranormal something, right?"

"The Olympic Society for Paranormal Research

Analysis. How gratifying to meet someone who follows me. Here, let me give you my card." George pulled one from an inside pocket, wrote something on it that looked suspiciously like an autograph, and gave it to the girl.

Who signs their business cards anyway?

"Can I have my picture taken with you? My boyfriend totally won't believe me." If the girl gushed anymore, she'd be hyperventilating.

"Of course," George said, his voice a little too loud. Roxy got the sense that he loved the attention. A few other people looked up.

Without asking Arianna, the girl shoved the phone at her. "Make sure you focus on us. Not past my shoulder or anything. Just touch the screen and—"

"Believe me. I know how to take pictures on a cell phone."

They posed and Arianna begrudgingly snapped a few pictures. The girl thanked George, not Arianna. Hunched over her phone, she walked away, probably uploading them to her social network sites.

George turned back to Arianna who stood up and was gathering her things into her messenger bag. "I think you're taking things too seriously. I was in the area because one of the local TV stations invited me to be a guest on one of their news shows. We recorded the piece and it'll be aired tonight."

Roxy waited for that inner voice and strange taste, but nothing happened. Maybe he was telling the truth about this part.

"Did Cult TV ask you to come talk about that two-headed horse again? What's it a symbol for again, I forget?" He opened his mouth to talk, but Arianna kept going. "Oh, yeah, the coming Armageddon. Wait. Was it the animal sacrifices they're doing up on Cougar Mountain? The TV viewing public loves stories about animals."

These guys seriously must have some history because Roxy doubted her friend would be this pissed off about the picture thing.

"No animals have ever been harmed in the making of my TV appearances."

Roxy almost laughed, but she checked herself just in time. This conversation—if you could call it that— was quickly devolving.

His face softened just a touch. "Listen, I know you don't like me, but I enjoyed the article you wrote last week and the video you posted was fascinating. I've been trying to get an appointment with old Mr. Simmons for ages, so it's nice to see that you were successful. What I wouldn't do to go on an investigation in that place."

He was telling the truth, but from the way Arianna held her arms crossed tightly over her chest and the frown on her face, it was clear that she thought he was feeding her shit.

"Why should I believe someone who's repeatedly tried to hack into my account? You're really on shaky ground in the whole 'I'm innocent' and 'you should believe me' department."

George exhaled heavily, the frustration apparent on

his face. "I've told you before but I'll say it again, I have not tried hacking into your site. Ever."

Arianna didn't look ready to back down. It was obviously time for Roxy to take on her role as a wingman. "Are you ready to go?"

George snapped his head in her direction, his watery gray gaze sweeping over her. Given his line of work, she hoped she gave off a human vibe. His smile made the corners of his eyes crinkle and he whipped out his hand in a borderline used-car-salesman fashion. "Well, hello there. Leaving before we can be properly introduced? I'm George Tanaka."

With such an abrasive personality, no wonder Arianna didn't like him, whether he was lying to her or not. "I'm Roxy, a friend of Arianna's." She wasn't going to shake his hand, but then her mean streak kicked in. Not bothering to put up her mental barriers to block the energy absorption, she held out her hand. Call it passive/aggressive or just being a bitch, but she wanted to make him a little tired.

His energy, which was nothing special, skimmed up her arm like she'd expected, but then she tasted a hint of sweetness on the back of her tongue. Weird. She let go and it was gone. Since smell and taste are closely related, she wondered if it was a scent of some sort that she'd detected instead.

He yawned then. A big one—the kind where your mouth stays open for a long time and your jaw pops. She could see his fillings and felt guilty that she'd made him so tired.

"That's my cue, ladies. I must be on my way. Don't forget to watch the news tonight. My segment goes on right after the second commercial. Nice meeting you, Roxy."

Arianna rolled her eyes as he left. Roxy bit the inside of her cheek to keep from smiling.

"What's so funny? He's an ass, isn't he?"

"It not that. I...ah..."

Arianna snorted with laughter when Roxy told her she'd taken his energy. "Oh, my God, I love you. Seriously. Will you be my BFF?"

"I'll definitely consider it," Roxy teased.

Arianna's phone rang once they got outside. While she was talking to someone at the safehouse, Roxy thought about what had just happened. Why was she suddenly having these powerful sensations about truth and lying? She mentally searched through her scent memories but it didn't compare to anything she'd ever experienced before.

"Everything okay up there?" she asked when Arianna hung up. Running a safehouse for sweetbloods had to be stressful.

"Yeah, we're just finishing up some minor odds and ends. Painting, tiling. That sort of thing."

"You know, I'd love to come visit sometime. That is, if I'm allowed." She knew the region kept the location on a strict need-to-know basis as it had the potential to be a vampire magnet, which would not be good when you're talking sweetbloods. Before Arianna could answer and tell her no, Roxy quickly changed the subject. "I was getting the strangest sensations back there in the coffee shop with George." As they walked, she told Arianna what had happened.

Arianna scowled. "You can't seriously think the guy is telling the truth, do you?"

"I'm saying I think that part of what he said was the truth. I've always been a good reader of people, but it's like my intuition has kicked into high gear lately."

"Then let's do an experiment." Arianna rubbed her hands together gleefully. "I'll tell you something and you have to tell me if it's a lie or not."

"Sounds like a slumber party trick," Roxy said.

Arianna pursed her lips and got a faraway look in her eye. "Okay, I've got one. Do we need to hold hands or something?"

Roxy reminded her that she only shook George's hand at the end.

"That's right. Okay, here we go." While they waited at a crosswalk, Arianna leaned against a streetlight and kept her expression blank. "Paranormalish isn't my first blog."

Roxy didn't feel anything different. "True."

"Very good." The light turned green and they crossed the street. "I ran a marathon last year."

L...i...a...r...

And there was that strange aftertaste. "False."

"Jackson loves sushi."

There it was again and Roxy laughed. "I take it he hates sushi?"

"Yeah, he hates anything raw. And seriously, before

I started cooking for him, he ate like a child. He'd eat the same two or three things over and over. He lived on peanut-butter-and-honey sandwiches—well, he still does, actually, but I try to mix it up now and then."

Roxy waited a moment. Nothing. "I can tell you're telling me the truth now."

Arianna brushed a strand of auburn hair from her face. "That's cool in a bizarre sort of way. Remind me never to lie to you."

"Speaking of food," Roxy said, "I'm starving."

"Regular food or the liquid variety?"

She laughed, marveling at how easy and fun it was to be around Arianna. Like so many of the people up here. "Both. But I'll wait till later to go find the other kind."

"It doesn't bother me like you might expect. I've seen Jackson do it a few times. Told him that I want to be a part of his life and that's an element of it."

Despite that admission, Roxy would never take blood in front of her human friend.

They found a little Italian place that seated them right away.

"Having said that about the feeding thing, if you order some fava beans to go with that Chianti, I probably will freak out a little bit."

"Don't worry. Beans aren't my thing." Roxy adjusted the napkin on her lap. "Vegetarian pasta? How do you feel about that?"

"A much better choice," Arianna said, examining the menu. "Yeah, Jackson worries about taking too much from me. I'll be glad when our changeling request goes through."

So that answered her earlier question. "How much longer do you have to wait?"

"At least a year from when we get married."

"And when is that?"

"I keep telling Jackson we should just elope. I've always wanted Elvis to marry us, but he wants a big wedding, so we'll see."

"Those Vegas weddings aren't all they're cracked up to be."

Arianna looked confused. "They're not?"

Roxy laughed and told her what happened in the hallway with Gibson. Then she flashed her ring.

"No way!" She grabbed Roxy's hand, twisting and turning it so the light caught on the facets. "That is seriously gorgeous. I cannot believe I didn't notice it. What was the look on Santiago's face when this all went down?"

"He was speechless."

Arianna shook her head, laughing. "Santiago? Speechless? I'd have paid money to see that. I'll bet it was hilarious."

Roxy recalled the horrified look on his face when she dropped that bomb. She got a strange sense of satisfaction knowing she'd shocked him, that she'd caught him totally off guard. "Yeah, it was priceless."

After dinner, the two women headed to the department stores to look for cocktail attire.

"Are you worried?" Roxy recalled the conversation

she'd had with Brenna, who was worried about putting Finn through the procedure. "You know, about the changeling process?" She held up a lavender dress and looked in the mirror. The hem hit just below the knee, but she decided she wanted something shorter. Sexier.

Arianna continued looking through the dresses hanging on a rounder, stopping at a green sequined top. "Not really. Lily is going to be my second sponsor and we're doing it up at the medical center. It's not without its risks, of course, but then, nothing worthwhile is."

It didn't take long for either of them to find dresses and shoes for the party. As they were walking back, the wind changed direction, and Roxy caught a whiff of something that made her hesitate.

"What's wrong?" Arianna asked.

"I'm detecting a strange mixture of scents. Darkblood, human and Guardian."

"You mean together? Not separate as if the three individuals were here at different times?"

"The energy signatures have virtually the same amount of deterioration. If they weren't all together at the same time, it was pretty close."

"Was there a capture done here recently? Maybe a DB had a human and one of the Guardians discovered them."

"I suppose it's possible, but Santiago told me it's been quiet lately. No captures or take downs. It is someone familiar. Although I haven't met everyone in the Seattle office yet, his scent has a few markers from there. And he's definitely a man."

"And the others…?"

Roxy sniffed the air again and stiffened. Not only were the human and Darkblood both female, but, if she wasn't mistaken, the DB's scent matched the ring.

Her thoughts turned to the pawnshop blade. What were the chances of this female being the same one? One thing she learned when she didn't fly up from Florida immediately when she saw that picture was that you needed to take advantage of every lead as soon as you had it because if you waited, the opportunity could be gone later. Could this really be the same individual?

"Can you track them?" Arianna asked.

The scent wasn't strong, but it was strong enough. "Yes."

"Well, then let's go."

"As in the two of us?" Roxy shook her head. "I don't think so."

Arianna moved the shopping bags to her other hand. "You sound just like Jackson. But believe me, you don't become a human comfortable living with a bunch of vampires without some decent self-defense training to bolster your confidence. Besides," she said, patting her coat pockets, "my knife skills aren't half bad. I've been working with Lily."

Roxy begrudgingly agreed. If she detected any active Darkblood scent, she'd call for backup and wait to go in.

The trail led to a dingy apartment building not far from the market. She eyed the narrow stairway up to what she assumed would be the residential area and didn't like the looks of it. This was no place for Arianna. "Listen, I'll handle it from here. Take my bags and go back to the field office."

"I'm not going anywhere. You can go in, but I'll wait outside. Consider me your backup."

Normally, Roxy would never have taken her up on it, but the only active scent was the human's. Both the Darkblood and Guardian scents were older. The human female must be somewhere inside.

"Take our bags and go over there." She pointed to a small coffee shop at the entrance where people were milling around. No telling if a Darkblood would be coming back soon or not.

Arianna took Roxy's shopping bag from her out-stretched hand. "Do you need me to call it in to the field office?

"Let me see what I'm dealing with first. It appears that only the human is here."

"Fine. If you need me, just call." Roxy liked the strength she saw in her friend's eyes. Given what Arianna had told her about how she met Jackson, she was no stranger to what vampires could do to humans. If anyone knew the plight a human faced in the hands of a Darkblood, Arianna did.

The stairs were narrow, littered with cigarette butts, and smelled of urine. Before Roxy got to the third floor, she could hear a woman's faint crying. It was coming from the same room as the target scent.

Roxy gently knocked on the door. "Are you okay in there?" she called. The crying stopped, but no one answered. "Please, I think I can help you."

She held her breath, listening, but still no answer.

Damn the Darkblood who fed from her, Roxy thought bitterly. She had a pretty good idea that they hadn't wiped this woman's memory after they'd taken her blood. Or if they had, it wasn't complete.

People with recollections involving vampires often ended up in mental institutions. Their stories so far-fetched and unbelievable, all because Darkbloods didn't bother to completely wipe their memories of the harrowing experience. That was one of the first edicts of vampire law—if they fed from a human they were to leave no trace. As a result, Guardians were tasked with cleaning up their mess in order to keep the existence of the vampires a secret from humans.

"I…I know what happened to you. Or at least, I have a pretty good idea of what happened."

"Who are you?" The voice came from just on the other side of the door. Roxy wouldn't have any trouble kicking it in, but she preferred to have the woman come to her on her own accord.

"A friend who can help."

The door opened a crack, but a chain prevented it from opening much wider. A young woman with tear-stained cheeks peered out at her. She brushed her hair from her face and that's when Roxy saw it. Two un-healed puncture marks on her wrist. She bristled. Just as she'd suspected.

"Who are you?"

"I'm Roxy. And before you think I won't believe what

happened to you, I wanted to let you know I know about the woman who did this to you."

The girl's eyes went wide. "You do?"

"Let's just say that I've been tasked to keep people like her, members of the Darkblood Alliance, under control."

"Are you…like them?"

Roxy thought about lying to her and then she remembered Arianna not far away. "Let me get my friend up here. You might be more comfortable with her here, too."

"I don't want anyone else here. You should leave." The young woman didn't close the door, however, which was encouraging. She hadn't mentally shut Roxy down yet.

"Please," Roxy pleaded, "my friend is…" She didn't want to admit that Arianna was human because that would draw attention to the fact that Roxy was not. "We can help you. We're not like that woman who… who did this to you."

"I'll…I'll think about it."

After sending Arianna a quick text, Roxy slid down against the wall until she was sitting on the floor just outside the door. An orange cat with mottled skin around its eyes and mouth came from around the corner and weaved around her bent legs. She opened her arms and he promptly climbed onto her lap and started purring.

She laughed. "Well, you're a friendly guy, aren't

you?" A rustle sounded from the door. The young woman was watching her. "Is he yours?" Roxy asked her.

"I don't know who he belongs to."

Roxy didn't look over at her, just kept scratching the cat's ears, which elicited even louder purring. "He's really sweet." A drop of saliva hung from one of his teeth and she chuckled. "Except for his drooling."

"I...I used to have a cat that drooled when you pet her."

Encouraged that she was talking, Roxy continued the conversation. "You did? So did I. Her name was Jezebel. I'm not sure if I'd rather have this or a cat who kneaded you with really sharp claws, although Jezzie did both. Now, I have a dog. Ginger. I really miss her."

The girl sniffed. "My cat's name was Buttons. He was black and white and all four paws were white, like mittens."

"Why didn't you name him Mittens?"

"We did, but my...my sister couldn't remember his name. Kept calling him Buttons."

The cat jumped from Roxy's lap and headed for the crack in the door. A few fingers stuck out low in the opening and he rubbed his back against the frame.

"You're one of them, aren't you?" the young woman asked cautiously.

Given that Roxy was sitting cross-legged on the ground, hopefully her intimidation factor had decreased. "Yes and no. I would never do to you what they did. Most of us have scruples. I'm here to make sure that—" She almost said *vampires,* but decided that word might be too frightening for the young woman to hear out loud. Verbalizing things gave them power. "—that it never happens to you or to anyone else." The cat came back and sat in her lap again.

"So are you a...a Guardian?"

Roxy cringed. How did she know that term? "No," she said, exhaling. Her breath ruffled the cat's fur enough that he shook his head, flinging saliva onto her jeans. "But I used to be one."

"What happened?"

Roxy sighed, remembering a moonless night almost a century ago. A humid summer night in the Keys, not cold, like it was here. Scents were more concentrated, more alive, in that kind of weather. Like a living petri dish where things grew whether you wanted them to or not. "My...partner and I were tracking several Darkbloods who had taken a human." Their victim was a sweetblood, but the girl didn't need to hear that whole explanation. "We split up and I managed to kill one of them, but the other one got away."

Ian had lied to Roxy, told her the Darkblood had escaped with the human, but that wasn't true. She didn't find out about it until the next night. The night that changed everything.

"He...uh...was killed by Darkbloods and I was blamed for not being there to back him up. No one listened to me. It got pretty ugly. So I quit."

A door slammed shut several stories below them and

footsteps bounded up the stairs. Arianna's green eyes were blazing when she got to the top. "Where is she?"

Pointing to the door, Roxy stood slowly, the cat still in her arms, and shook off the ghosts of her past.

Ignoring the fact that it was chained, Arianna thrust her hand through the small opening and touched the young woman's shoulder. "What did those bastards do to you?"

"You're...you're not one of them?"

"No, I'm not," Arianna answered. "I'm just as human as you are. Can we come in?"

"She's not...human," the young woman said, looking at Roxy.

"True," Arianna admitted, "but she's one of the good guys and we're both here to help."

The young woman narrowed her eyes. "How do I know you're not just saying that? How can I trust either of you?"

"Do you think we humans can fight these guys ourselves?" Arianna asked. "Believe me. I've tried. We need the help of people like Roxy."

"You've fought them before?" the young woman asked skeptically.

The elevator at the far end of the hallway opened with a shuddering groan and a human male stepped out. His keys jingled as he unlocked his door and slipped inside.

"We can't talk out here," Arianna said. "Can we come in? I promise I'll tell you all about it."

"You...you will?"

"Yeah, I even killed one of them." Arianna made a face. "God, it was disgusting."

"You did?" the girl said, echoing Roxy's thoughts. She didn't know Arianna had killed a Darkblood either.

"Yeah, but that's nothing. Those in her line of work—" she jerked her head in Roxy's direction "—kill these bastards all the time. Right, Roxy?"

She nodded. "I've charcoaled my fair share."

"In fact," Arianna said, "she killed two of them several weeks ago and she wasn't even armed."

Roxy rolled her eyes. Brenna must've told her.

The girl unfastened the chain and opened the door. She wore jeans, a T-shirt with a pub insignia, and was barefoot. Once they were inside, she closed the door and turned to face them, a hopeful yet wary expression on her face. Roxy backed away slowly to make sure she wasn't encroaching on the young woman's personal space.

The dingy room was sparsely furnished with just a bed, a table and two chairs, and a small kitchenette. Devoid of virtually all personal items, this couldn't be where she lived, could it? It was more like a rent-by-the-hour motel room.

Roxy continued. "It's my job to find those who did this to you and make sure they never do it again. What's your name?"

"Cosette."

Arianna was looking at the unhealed marks on the young woman's wrist. "Did you see this?" she asked Roxy.

"She fed from you, didn't she, Cosette?"

She nodded and one thick tear tracked down her cheek. "Me and my sister."

"Your sister?" Roxy hadn't picked up the scent of another human. In fact, she couldn't detect any other scent, human or vampire.

Cosette explained how she and her sister had been taken captive by Darkbloods who said if she didn't agree to help, her sister would be killed. "She called Yvonne a sweetblood and said her...her blood was really valuable. Told me I needed to seduce a guy she pointed out at a bar—she called him a Guardian—if I wanted to see Yvonne again."

"And did you?" Roxy asked quietly.

"I—I'm not sure." She held her arms tightly around her middle, looking like she might get sick. "I think I...must have, but I can't remember anything about... it...or him."

A partial memory wipe.

"Where did it happen?" She couldn't smell that any vampires had been in here recently. Guardians or Darkbloods.

Cosette frowned. "I...I don't remember the name of the bar, but she had me bring the man here."

No way. Why hadn't she smelled his scent inside the tiny room? She dropped to her hands and knees and felt around the threadbare carpet. And there it was. A few tiny crystals, no bigger than coarse salt, stuck to her palms. Scent-masking crystals. That explained why she didn't detect anything.

"Can you remember anything…anything at all about him? A name? An impression?" Roxy stood and continued inspecting the room. She was fairly certain that no one had died here so at least that was comforting.

"No. Nothing." Cosette rubbed her forehead. "It's like there's a hole in my memory."

Why was she instructed to bring a Guardian back here and seduce him? Roxy wondered. Darkbloods wouldn't hesitate to kill a Guardian they found in a vulnerable situation.

Could they have stolen something from him? Planted something on him?

Roxy's hands went cold.

Of course.

She couldn't believe she hadn't thought of it before. This could explain why she hadn't detected a traitor within the field office. It was entirely possible that the person didn't know they were being used.

You had to know you were a traitor in order to lie about it.

She needed to get ahold of Santiago.

Cosette waved her hand in front of her face as if all of this was unimportant, like she was wiping these questions out of her thoughts. "She promised she'd bring my sister back, but so far, she hasn't. I'm beginning to think that she was planning to keep her all along. Maybe—" Cosette's voice faltered "—maybe Yvonne is already…gone."

"You don't know that for sure," Arianna said, putting her arms around the young woman while casting a doubtful glance at Roxy. "We can help. And so can my fiancé, Jackson."

CHAPTER FIFTEEN

THE OPENING BAND at the blues club had just finished playing so everyone poured outside for a smoke before the headliner took the stage. When Roxy had called Santiago, he told her to get to the nearest populated place and wait for him. Crowds were good—they were relatively safe with all these people around, but Roxy fingered her blade anyway.

She picked up the scent of a few vampires nearby, which she wasn't sure were peaceful members of their society. One hadn't fed recently but the other smelled fully blooded. What she couldn't tell was if he'd completely drained the human or just had a healthy sip. Another couple—a youthling male and female—were making out on a nearby park bench. One of her legs was across his thigh and his hand was up her shirt.

A group of college-age guys walked by the amorous couple.

"Jesus. Get a room," someone yelled.

"Ten bucks if you go down on her," said another.

She could see a potential altercation brewing so she moved in that direction to stave it off. That was the problem with a vampire's higher libido. If you weren't careful around humans, you stuck out like a freak, which was why most establishments that catered to their people had private rooms for this sort of thing. She didn't know if there were any around here or not.

The male youthling lifted his head. His pupils were fully dilated. "Fuck off, you little shit. You're just jealous."

Roxy didn't say anything, just sat down on the edge of their bench and gave the couple a closed-mouth smile.

The male youthing's eyes narrowed as he recognized she was a vampire. "Who are you?"

"A friend who doesn't want there to be any trouble. Isn't there somewhere less public than this? I'm sure you don't mean to draw such attention to yourselves, do you? After all, you won't be able to take it as far as you'd like out here anyway. Am I right?"

"Calder, let's go," the young woman murmured, pulling him to his feet. "She's right. We can finish this over at the Pink Salon. Besides, I'm thirsty and they make the best Bellinis over there." She stood on her tiptoes and whispered something into his ear. He smiled and let her lead him away. "Thanks," she mouthed to Roxy.

"Ah, Roxy?"

She turned to see Arianna and Cosette talking to a bouncer not much taller than they were, but he had biceps as thick as a horse's neck.

"You coming in or not?" he said to them. "I don't have all night."

"Are we, Roxy?" Arianna asked. "Your call."

She didn't want to go in if they didn't have to. A few dark patches down the street looked to be more than empty shadows. It could be Santiago and Jackson, and in that case, they'd be leaving soon. But on the off chance they were Darkbloods... She recalled hearing that this was a popular part of town for Darkbloods to sell their wares to their customers. "Hold on."

"Listen, lady—"

In an instant, she closed the distance between them and passed a hand over the bouncer's temple. "There's a fight in the back and they need you inside. And while you're at it, we'll take a table near the front and a round of drinks," she said, careful to keep her voice low. "I'll have a...a peach Bellini and my friends will have..."

White wine and a glass of ice water were their answers.

"Now, go," she said with a flick of her fingers, shooing him away. He'd probably wonder later why the hell he was ordering drinks for these customers.

"Yes, ma'am," he said and disappeared inside.

Great. She didn't look old enough to be a ma'am, did she? Even though some of her students referred to her that way, she would never get used to it. That term should be used for people Mary Alice's age, not hers.

Slightly irritated, she turned back around and that's when a movement caught her eye. Two shadows pulled away from the darkness at the end of an alley. She shot a warning glance over to Arianna and Cosette only to find that they had gone inside.

The shadows continued to move, hugging the side of a brick building, then flowing across a side street like liquid darkness on the pavement. Since she was upwind, she couldn't tell if they were Santiago and Jackson or Darkbloods. When she'd talked to Santiago, she assumed he was bringing a medic team, which would mean more than two shadows. Then it occurred to her, what if the line was bugged? Could Darkbloods have learned she had Cosette and that they were here? If only she could've brought the young woman to the field office but human visitors were strictly forbidden unless they had prior clearance. She tried to remember what she'd said on the phone. Had she used the young woman's name? She didn't think so and yet—

The two shadows morphed into men just outside the ring of light from a streetlamp. Her heartbeat quickened and she palmed her blade. Darkbloods traveled in pairs. These were big men and she was—

Although their faces were hidden, she recognized the broad-shouldered silhouette of the first one. With a confident air about him, Santiago strode past the wrought-iron post and headed toward her on the cobblestone sidewalk, Jackson right on his heel. She sheathed her weapon and let herself relax for the first time since finding the woman in that dingy motel.

"What are you guys doing sneaking around like that?" she said. "I thought you were a couple of Darkbloods."

Santiago shrugged. "Easier this way. Parking down here at this time of night is a bitch."

"Where are they?" Jackson asked, looking straight past her. She started to tell him that they were at a table near the front, but he interrupted. "Never mind. I see them." He brushed past her without waiting for her to finish and headed inside.

Santiago scanned the people milling around in the area outside the clubs. "I want you to accompany Arianna and the young woman up to the safe house. Jackson and I will take over from here and search for the Darkbloods who did this."

"No." She did not drag them to this club and wait only to be told she wasn't necessary.

He raised one eyebrow, giving her a look that said he wasn't accustomed to having people defy him. Well, he could just kiss her ass. She was going with them whether he liked it or not.

"I will not allow two humans, one of whom appears to be a Darkblood target with valuable information about the enemy, to drive two hours alone at night. With Alfonso gone, the safe house isn't staffed with one of our kind."

"Then have Jackson go with them."

"He's a Guardian, Roxy. I need him with me. This person may be responsible for what happened to Dom. This is an ongoing investigation and you are not part of it."

She was getting nowhere with him. "And who is going to track the scent?"

"He and I will—"

"I can do it much faster than either of you. This is what I do." She bit her lip, wondering whether to tell him about the Darkblood female's scent matching the one on the ring.

He had that unbendable look on his face. "You will do as I tell you."

"There you go, being a jerk again." She paused to get his reaction, but he seemed unfazed, so she had no other choice. "It makes sense that Jackson accompany Arianna and Cosette since no other Guardians are up there. What if Darkbloods come after her when they discover she's no longer in that dingy motel room?"

"But—"

"Besides, I'm almost positive that the Darkblood behind this is the same one who tried to sell Ian's sword."

Santiago's head snapped up. "The woman? Are you sure?"

"Yes," Roxy answered. "I recognized the faint scent from the ring back at the motel."

He ran a hand over his short hair. "Jesus, Mary and Joseph."

"My sentiments exactly."

"Listen, Roxy." She had a feeling she wasn't going to like what he had to say. "This woman could be the Seattle area sector mistress, a woman named Ventra Capelli. We've been trying to find her for months, but she's proven to be very elusive."

"So let me track her. If we get a lock on her location, you can call in your team."

"My point is—"

"That I'm just a teacher, right?" She knew exactly what he was implying. She glared at him and damned if he didn't look sheepish. "So don't go trying to tell me that I'm not coming, because I am. I intend to find this woman and figure out what she knows about Ian's death. And if you don't *approve*—" she made finger quote marks "—then I'll go by myself. Fortunately for me, I'm not a Guardian, which means I am not technically under your authority here or in the field office."

He grumbled something, but frankly, she was tired of listening to his lame excuses. For the first time in decades, she finally had a bonafide lead regarding what had happened to Ian and she wasn't about to run along because Santiago thought she couldn't handle it. She'd been handling things herself for as long as she could remember. She didn't need him telling her what she could and couldn't do.

"I'll let you come with me on one condition."

She put her hands on her hips. *This had better be good.* "And what would that be?"

"This is my deal, my assignment. I realize you don't work for me, but when we're out in the field, you take orders from me. I don't care if you agree with me or not. This isn't only about you. I have other people to consider, people who do work for me and I can't have you undermining my decisions or endangering the lives of others because you decide to go off on your own. Is that understood?"

She thought about her choices. Go it alone or go it with one of the finest Guardians working for the Agency. In the end, it was an easy decision.

SANTIAGO WHITE-KNUCKLED the steering wheel. She was still in love with Ian. There was no doubt about it.

Frustration heated up his insides as it looked for a place to fester and grow. He wanted to throw something, yell every curse word he knew, but instead he managed to drive along in silence as the cold night air whipped around from the rolled-down window.

He recalled seeing a female duck whose mate had been hit and killed by a car. She'd called to him over and over, wandering around the parking lot aimlessly for hours, waiting for him to answer. Not knowing where to go or what to do, she'd fly away for a while only to return a short time later.

Without warning, a chasm opened in his gut and it felt as if something had been plucked out. There was no room in her heart for anyone else but Ian, and Santiago had been a fool to think otherwise.

They drove around in silence as the rain became slush then snow. Roxy's hair whipped across her face, her eyes closed as she took in all the scents.

It was for the best anyway, he thought. He had no business falling for someone. Not now, not later. He needed to consider it a blessing in disguise that she wasn't available emotionally. He wasn't relationship material anyway. Who was he fooling?

His mother's shrill voice rang in his ear like an echo, claiming he'd grow up to be just like his father, that he was untrustworthy. He gripped the steering wheel tighter and felt his foot pressing down on the accelerator.

With Cosette's blessing, Roxy had insisted they stop by the girls' apartment in order for her to pick up something she could use as a scent marker for Yvonne. The Darkblood female's scent was too faint to track from around the motel, so she'd hoped the sister's scent would lead straight to both of them. They followed it across one of the Lake Washington bridges and east into the mountains.

"It's gotten a little stronger since we got off the freeway," Roxy said, her eyes still closed. "But careful. Not too fast. We're getting closer."

"How can you tell?" Wasn't a scent a scent? You followed it until it didn't go any farther? Given the higher elevation, the snow was starting to stick to the road, so he downshifted rather than using the brakes.

"Imagine dipping a spoon into a bowl of honey and drizzling it onto a piece of bread. If you move the spoon quickly, the trail of honey is stretched thin, but if you slow it down, the line becomes thicker as more honey is deposited onto a smaller area. Same thing happens with a scent. It became more concentrated once we took the exit and slowed down. There's more of the scent to smell. And when it gets even stronger, I know they must've been slowing down. It gets thicker, you know?"

It occurred to him that if he and Jackson had done this without Roxy's help, they'd still be in downtown Seattle. Jesus H, this woman was good. He wanted to stay pissed off at her but he was too busy being impressed.

"There." She pointed to an overgrown road leading up into the trees. She wanted him to drive his car through that mess? "Yvonne—if she's still alive—is somewhere up there."

He glanced at the lightening sky. Sunrise was less than an hour away. They didn't have a lot of time.

"You'd better not be thinking about waiting till sunset tonight," Roxy said.

"The thought had crossed my mind."

"The girl could be dead by then."

He slowed down. "She could be dead now."

"Yes, but the longer we wait, the more likely that possibility."

"It's just you and me, Roxy. If we wait till tomorrow, a few other agents could join us."

"Like I said, Yvonne could be dead by then." Then she added, "Let's hide the car here and continue the rest of the way on foot."

He didn't know what it was, but she had a manner about her that made you automatically do what she wanted before you questioned it much. Like a teacher. Or a damn hypnotist.

Ten minutes later, they were shadow moving through the trees and arrived at a small clearing at the top of the mountain. Out of necessity, he let her go first but it afforded him the chance to watch her from behind. She effortlessly melded with the darkness as if they were one and the same, dancing past the tree trunks and through the bushes. But as the sky lightened to a pale gray, it made shadow moving more difficult, so by the time the forest opened up, they weren't able to move with the darkness at all.

He had a bad feeling about this. One mistake could cost them and they'd be stuck out in daylight.

She stopped near a downed tree and he moved in right behind her. In the center of a clearing stood an old gothic monstrosity, complete with gargoyles guarding the front entrance, crumbling stone steps, and a sagging front porch. Morning glory vines snaked up the sides of the mansion and twisted under the eaves like a spreading disease, choking and covering everything in its path. A few of the windows had been broken out at one time and from what he could tell, the vines had found their way inside, as well. Given the condition of the outside, he'd hate to see what the inside looked like. It couldn't be much better. He had a hard time imagining that anyone would want to live in such a place.

But then he remembered the coffins. He'd destroyed many dens where Darkbloods had been sleeping in them and this place was probably no different. In fact, he'd be surprised if he *didn't* find any coffins here. Sick, if you asked him. And twisted. He enjoyed beds with sheets and mattresses along with a nice roof over his head.

Darkbloods relished living in the same conditions as their violent ancestors before they began grouping into any sort of organized societies. Old decrepit structures abandoned by humans. Cemetery crypts. Caves carved into the sides of mountains. As he looked around, it certainly felt like the perfect Darkblood lair. It wouldn't surprise him to learn that they were using dirt from their homeland to line the bottoms of their coffins, an old wives tale from long ago that said the soil from your homeland would bring you great power and prosperity. It was a way to never forget where you came from.

And Darkbloods, looking to return to their violent roots, took this to heart.

"Can you smell that?"

He smelled nothing but the damp forest air. "No."

Roxy leaned against a tree trunk and closed her eyes. He started to say something but she held up her pointer finger, a gesture that told him to keep quiet for a minute because she was concentrating. He wanted to know if there were Darkbloods inside and whether or not the sweetblood girl was still alive. As he waited for Roxy, he brushed a damp fern from his boot, clasped his hands behind his head then got antsy and folded them across his chest.

"Shush," she whispered without opening her eyes.

"What? I didn't say anything."

"I can hear you moving."

"I'm not moving."

"Yes, you are. You're fidgeting."

He made a sound of protest. "What are you talking about? I'm just standing here."

"Well then stand there more quietly," she said. "I'm trying to concentrate."

And then there it was. The beginning of a smile. Oh, she tried covering it up right away by chewing on her lip, but it was too late. He'd seen it. Clearly, she was enjoying hassling him.

It occurred to him that despite all she'd seen—his outbursts, his tantrums, his attempts to torture himself—she wasn't scared or intimidated by him. She didn't hesitate in telling him what to do. Or in this case, what not to do.

No one nitpicked him. Ever. Or treated him like he needed to be managed.

So the fact that she did and felt comfortable enough doing so made him feel…special, different. And he realized he…liked it.

Her eyes flew open and she grabbed his arm.

Busted. He instantly felt guilty that he'd been staring at her.

"Yvonne is inside and still alive. But barely. Someone fed from her recently and came close to draining her. Two, no three, Darkbloods are on the premises. One of them might be outside, but I can't tell for sure. It could be the state of disrepair—the broken windows and dilapidated roof—that makes the scents read as if they're outside when they're not."

"And the Darkblood female—is she there?"

Roxy's shoulder's slumped with disappointment and she shook her head. "No, she's not."

He sent a quick text to the capture team waiting on standby, before the two of them sprinted toward the back of the structure where they crawled through a broken window into what was probably a butler's pantry at one time. Santiago slipped Misery silently from its leather sheath. The wood floor creaked beneath their feet as they crept into the dining room.

Torn wallpaper hung from the two-story walls, exposing the lathe and plaster underneath. Either someone had tried to remove it and abandoned the project or moisture had deteriorated the paper to the point where it was coming off in sheets. Some of the doors of the built-in cabinets lining parallel sides of the room were gone, making the small room look like a gaping smile with a few missing teeth. In the center, under a candle chandelier that had recently been lit, was a long table covered in plastic with a dozen high-backed chairs tucked in around it.

"Smell it now?" she whispered.

He nodded. The sweetblood scent was strong. Bloodletting or a feeding must've happened here recently.

"Yvonne?"

She nodded somberly.

With a curious expression that he couldn't quite read, she turned her attention to a chair that wasn't pushed in all the way and ran her hand over the ornately carved back.

"There's something familiar…" Her voice trailed off.

It didn't take a rocket scientist or an expert tracker to figure out that many humans had died in this room. The blood scent was thick in the air. She had to be as sickened by that knowledge as he was. But unlike him, she hadn't been out in the field to see this sort of thing on an almost daily basis as he had. Having run across his fair share of debauchery over the years, he'd gotten used to it, his heart numbed to the inhumanity of it all, whereas she'd been stuck in a classroom. This sort of thing had to be disturbing for her.

Roxy touched him, her fingers resting lightly on the back of his hand, right above Misery's handle.

"Yvonne's down this way," she whispered, using the tip of her blade to point through an arched doorway to the left. Her breath skittered over his earlobe, reminding him of last night when she'd exhaled softly after she'd climaxed and collapsed on top of him. Since that first time, they'd made love every day. She'd become his beautiful habit. "And DBs—" she jerked her chin the other direction "—are over there."

When she removed her hand, his skin continued to tingle with her residual energy.

"I'll take care of them," he mouthed. "You go find the girl."

She moved catlike to the other side of the room, despite her less than delicate combat boots. The black fatigues were loose fitting and rode low on her hips and yet somehow they clung to every curve. He recalled how she'd changed in the car into the clothes he'd brought for her. Without any preamble or warning as they flew over the I-90 bridge, she'd peeled off her skinny jeans in the passenger seat of the Corvette and wriggled into her combat gear. It took all the concentration in the world to keep his eyes on the road. A few times he'd caught himself drifting, and a van behind him honked for him to stay in his own lane. But he couldn't help himself. Her tiny black-and-red thong, not the road in front of him, had been a magnet for his eyeballs.

All of this darted through his mind as she crept from the room. The instant she was gone, he felt colder, motivating him to get this thing done as quickly as possible so they could be together again.

Was she as attracted to him as he was to her? Would her adrenaline be as pumped up after a mission as his was where she'd want sex as much as he did? He wanted nothing more than for her to be in his bed again, writhing with pleasure underneath him. Gripping Misery in his left hand, he slipped through the other doorway and crept down the hall, staying as close to the edge as he could in order to eliminate any squeaks in the floorboards.

The flickering light of many candles illuminated the long hallway casting grotesque shadows on the wall. Either the place didn't have electricity or they chose not to use it. The air felt damp and he wouldn't have been surprised to learn that moss was growing inside.

A low murmur of voices came from a room on the far side of a grand foyer. Two males. The third one had to be nearby.

"Hey, I wouldn't do that if I were you," one of them was saying. "She loves that thing. It's her pride and joy."

"It's an amazing piece, isn't it?"

Santiago heard the sound of a blade being whipped through the air.

"Yes, so put it back," the first one said.

"I'm not hurting anything, so chill. It's balanced like nothing I've ever held before."

Santiago was dying to see what he was holding. It had to be a Guardian blade.

"Yeah, and she'll cut your balls off with it if she finds out. Maybe you like taking risks and don't have an attachment to them. I, for one, wouldn't want to chance that they'd regenerate correctly."

"You're such a pussy. She'll never know. Not unless you tell her."

"I wouldn't be so sure. I swear, she's got a third eye. Did you hear what she did to Tomas?" They both groaned.

"Yeah, but that was different. He fucked up. I'm not going to. Do you think it's true what they say about *Santa Muerte* silver? That it can sap the strength right out of you with just a touch on your skin?"

A flash of white-hot anger surged through his body. They fucking did have a Guardian blade. Was it Grim? If so, Roxy was going to be thrilled to get it back. If not, well, he would see to it that it was returned to the family it belonged to. Misery felt lighter and more agile in his hand as if encouraging him to take action. He still hadn't detected the third Darkblood, which Roxy had insisted was somewhere nearby.

"That's what I've heard," the first one said. "I think it was made by Petrov the Brave, that smithie in Prague who makes a lot of Guardian blades."

Santiago exhaled silently. It most likely was Grim then. He knew what it meant to Roxy to get it back and he would be the one to give it to her. Readjusting his grip on Misery, he stood poised, ready to spring.

"Where did the Mistress get it, do you know?"

"Nope, but I heard the guy gave it up 'cuz he was addicted to Sweet."

What the fuck? Santiago hesitated, his blood running cold.

Why would a Guardian—Ian?—give his weapon to a Darkblood? That made no sense at all. This asshole had to have the story wrong because a Darkblood had charcoaled Ian with his own blade.

He inadvertently leaned against the wall causing a floorboard to squeak under his foot. The two DBs stopped talking. He cursed himself for being so careless, having been counting on the element of surprise. Two, possibly three against one, when both sides possessed superior Guardian blades, wasn't what he'd call good odds. He could go in now or wait for them to come to him. Something told him to hold off charging into the room—an unusual decision for him as he normally preferred to be on the defensive.

Holding perfectly still, both hands on Misery's hilt, he waited, ready to swing the sword if they came out of the doorway.

"You sure the girl's locked up?" the first one said, his voice low.

"Even if she wasn't, she's not going anywhere. Didn't you see the condition they left her in? I'm surprised she lived through it. I think it's just the old house creaking."

Neither said anything for a moment as they were apparently listening for more sounds. Santiago sent out a silent plea to Roxy to be quiet.

"If that's the case, maybe we should visit the girl ourselves."

"You can't be serious."

"Well, if she was almost dead, who's to say she wouldn't have died later anyway. We could both have a few sips and finish the job."

"God, you're an idiot. You think the Mistress wouldn't figure out that we killed her?"

"We could get rid of the body. You know, tell her the girl died while she was away, so we buried her." Santiago heard a slap and the guy yelped. "Ouch. What'd you go and do that for?"

"Look around you. She's collecting the bones, stupid. She'd either kill us for disposing of the body or she'd dig it up for the bones, find out we lied, then kill us. And duh, the girl's a sweetblood, you don't think we'd reek of her if we drank from her?"

"Hmph. It was just a thought." The metallic sound of the blade going into or out of its sheath effectively ended that part of their conversation. "I still can't believe this belonged to a Guardian who was addicted to Sweet." It was as if the second one was reading Santiago's thoughts.

"Hypocrites, huh? They can get hooked just like the rest of us and be desperate enough to do anything—include giving away their prized weapons—for more."

He hoped to God they *weren't* talking about Ian now. Part of him wished for closure for Roxy and Ian's family, but this kind of news, if it were true, would devastate them and ruin their reputation. From what he knew about the O'Gradys, they were staunch supporters when the Council was formed centuries ago. To learn that the last male heir, the one who would've carried on the family name had he lived, was a Sweet addict would be heartbreaking—not just to them but to Roxy, who had loved him.

He'd known a few people who'd had this happen to them. They lost everything. Their reputation, their standing within the close-knit vampire community, their family and friends. They were ostracized and sent to a rehab facility where they often were never heard from again. But Guardians were often executed for the very reason he was hearing now. They couldn't be trusted to do the job they were assigned to do.

Getting a handle on a blood addiction was difficult if not impossible to overcome. You couldn't stop once the urge was ignited. You could dress it in pretty clothes, trying to hide it and pretend that everything was fine—and it may be fine for a while. But the yearning continually swam below the surface, waiting for the opportunity to strike.

If the sword really was Ian's, could this be true? And if it was, did Roxy know? He thought about how devoted she was to his memory and decided that she couldn't have known. They'd been together before she'd become a tracker, so his addiction would've been easier for him to cover up.

If a Guardian killed a human, they were executed. The Council rules were very clear on this. And an addict was one step away from becoming a Darkblood sympathizer, if they weren't one already. He recalled the lengths Jackson had gone to when he'd thought he was succumbing to the pull of his dark nature. He'd been willing to give up everything, including the love of his life and a job he cherished, because he hadn't been able to control himself. If Ian had been an addict, he'd have done everything in his power to hide it from Roxy. She'd be devastated to learn this news.

A strange concoction of emotions stirred in his gut. Part of him felt terrible for her, but another part, the selfish part, was pissed off that she was wasting her time pining for a man who was not only dead, but who was a secret Sweet addict and willing to compromise his integrity.

One of the Darkbloods laughed. Fuck being sneaky. He was tired of this bullshit.

He palmed a few *chaken* throwing stars, flipped their tiny switches and jumped into the room. With a flick of a wrist, he sent the blades flying. They landed with a *thunk* square in the chest of the shorter one and the guy went down. As Santiago swung to his right, he heard the low vibration as the blades burrowed deeper.

"Get these things out of me." The guy's voice was higher pitched than it had been earlier and he clawed at his chest. "Motherfu—" An innocuous little pop sounded, like a pin piercing a water balloon. One of the silver blades had hit its mark and the DB began to charcoal. His knees buckled and he sank to the floor, his limbs folding in on himself. Soon, he'd be a pile of ash. Santiago made a mental note to retrieve his little blades when this was over.

One down, one to go.

Santiago spun around, swinging Misery in an arc toward the second guy. Something flashed in his peripheral vision. The DB was on the other side of the room now. He'd moved faster than Santiago had expected. Santiago ducked to the left and rolled into a half somersault, knocking over a table as a knife whistled past his ear. An urn and a large black candelabra with six or seven lit candles crashed to the floor, igniting the heavy drapes covering one of the windows.

"What have you done?" The tall man with thin, white-blond hair lunged forward and grabbed the long blade his friend had been holding a moment earlier. The high-pitched sound it made as it slid from its sheath confirmed that it was indeed a Guardian's weapon. It flashed like a mirror, reflecting the flames.

Santiago couldn't afford to make another error. Even one nick could incapacitate him enough to make him unable to defend himself. But Misery would inflict the same damage on the Darkblood, as well.

"Are you referring to your friend or the house?" Although Santiago had a pretty good guess.

The man stammered before answering, his eyes were black orbs in a too-white face. "Both."

Ha. He couldn't hide the hesitation in his voice. He'd meant the house, not his friend—it didn't take a shrink to figure that one out. Darkbloods weren't usually paired up with their buddies. It was more of a trainer/student relationship. Then, when you were trained, you did the same for others wanting to join the movement.

"Fortunately, I don't share the same affinity for this place as you do."

Their swords clanged together over and over, the DB matching every thrust and parry. Sweat covered Santiago's brow as the temperature of the room skyrocketed as more of it was being consumed by flames. Unlike most DBs, this one must've had some formal fight training. This. Was. Ridiculous.

He switched Misery to his left hand—being ambidextrous came in handy sometimes—and leveled a glancing uppercut blow to the DB's midsection. The guy went flying and his own blade clamored to the floor. Santiago had never fought with the finesse that some of the other Guardians did and he wasn't above fighting dirty. The DB landed on the sofa. It skidded along the floor and tipped onto its back, bringing the flaming drapes with it. In a moment, the whole side of the room was ablaze and flames were licking across the ceiling.

Santiago leaped over to his now unarmed enemy. He'd finish the guy off and then he'd find Roxy. This old place was a tinderbox and would burn quickly. Where the hell was she anyway? She should've located the girl by now.

Groaning in pain, the DB rolled to his side and threw something into the fire. It landed with a faint *clink*. "You think you're going to rescue the sweetblood?" The look in his eye said to Santiago that he'd try anything if it meant he'd live. A dangerous Darkblood is a desperate one, especially when he thinks his days are numbered. "If that's what you came for, I'm afraid you're out of luck."

"Is that so?" Santiago was not impressed by the rant-

ings of an almost dead guy. Imminent death had a way
of bringing out the best…and the worst in people.

"That—" the man indicated the fire "—was the key.
You'll never get her now."

Santiago laughed. "You think not having a key will
stop me?" He'd just kick the door in, if Roxy hadn't
done it already, and free the human prisoner.

Even as blood leaked through the guy's fingers and
had spread down his sleeve, the DB smiled. "She's…
locked up, my friend…with silver alloy chains…around
her wrists and ankles. That's what…the Mistress does…
with all her toys."

Santiago hesitated. Silver chains? He wouldn't be
able to touch them in order to pull them from the wall
without suffering a significant energy loss. He scanned
the flames and rubble in the fireplace. If he could even
find the tiny metal key, it could be partially melted by
now and useless. A tiny voice sounding suspiciously
like Kip's reminded him that it was protocol to carry a
set of latex gloves when out on patrol.

A crack then a crash sounded behind him. He spun
around just in time to see a portion of the roof fall in.
Sparks and embers shot everywhere, including onto
his leather coat.

The DB coughed out a humorless laugh. "Good luck.
Looks like you're going to need it."

CHAPTER SIXTEEN

THE TUNNEL, which had to be almost two hundred feet long, started at the bottom of a narrow wooden staircase at the back of the house. Although torches lit up a small circle of space every fifteen or twenty feet, darkness was plentiful enough that Roxy was able to easily shadow move. Coming back the same direction, assuming she was successful in freeing Yvonne, would be a different story. From what Roxy could discern from the scent, the young woman had lost a lot of blood, so her ability to walk out under her own power may be a problem. Maybe there was a way out at the other end.

She morphed out of the darkness and took shape in a small, dungeonlike room without windows and thick with the scent of Sweet. Her gums throbbed a little, but because she'd been expecting to encounter a sweetblood, that was the extent of her physical reaction. Candlelight from a lone candle flickered silently on the stone walls and the absolute stillness of the air was a thick buffer around her, muting out all sound. Against the far wall on a low cement table was a gleaming mahogany coffin with the front third of the lid propped open. Stone steps led up to it and a small red-and-white cooler sat near the head along with a water bottle.

Was the young woman in that thing? Roxy started to approach the crimson-lined coffin, but before she could peer inside, a small noise from a dark corner of the room drew her attention. Carved into the stone wall was a cutout, a narrow niche no bigger than the twin mattress it held. A young woman huddled in the center, shackles around her wrists and ankles, the chains affixed to the wall. Only one thin blanket covered her as she shivered.

"Yvonne? Is that you?" Roxy knew from her scent that it was, but she asked anyway to soften the shock of her sudden presence. "I'm a friend."

The young woman's lids flew open, her gaze darting around the room in terror. Her deathly white complexion and pale blue lips made it look as if a slight breeze could blow straight through her and make her bones rattle. Roxy's heart went out to her. She was a petite thing and those chains were much too heavy to tolerate for long. She had to be miserable.

"Who's there?"

Even though Roxy wasn't part of the shadows, it was clear Yvonne hadn't seen her yet.

"Shh. It's okay," she said in her calmest voice. "Your sister sent me." She stepped a little closer and handed the young woman a small stuffed animal. When Roxy had spotted it on Yvonne's bed in the sisters' apartment, she knew it'd make the perfect scent marker. "Cosette gave this to me to give to you. Said this little hedgehog is your favorite."

"Cosette sent you?" The young woman looked warily

at the toy that wasn't much larger than the palm of her hand. A mixture of relief and disbelief flitted behind her eyes as if she were wondering whether this could be some kind of trick.

"Yes. She told me what happened to the two of you. All of it—the woman in your apartment, the blood-letting, the promise Cosette made to secure your release."

"How did you find me? Are you…the police?" She asked it hesitantly, as if she didn't really expect the answer to be yes.

"You could say that. What was done to you and your sister was horrible. My…my associate and I were able to track you here and we will see that justice is served against those who did this to you."

"They're monsters, you know. Vampires. And they—"

"Yes, I know," Roxy said, interrupting her. There'd be time enough for that later. But now, first things first.

"Where is Cosette? Is she okay? Is she here with you?" Chains clanking, Yvonne struggled to roll to her side. She clutched the hedgehog to her chest as if the exertion from the movement was a little too much. And it probably was.

"Yes, she's with a colleague of mine and is sick with worry about you." Roxy eyed the chains but stopped herself from yanking them from the wall. "May I?" She reached slowly for the shackles around Yvonne's ankle, so as not to startle her.

"They're locked and I think that...that woman has the key."

The instant Roxy's fingers closed around the chain, fire shot through her hands. Cursing in pain, she let go. Welts in the shape of links tracked across her palms and she could feel the energy pouring from her system.

Silver. The damn chains were made of silver.

The girl's eyes widened and she scrambled as far away into the corner as she could. "You're...you're one of them."

Roxy staggered backward and hit the low-lying table, sending the coffin crashing to the ground. "Yvonne, I—"

"Vampires can't touch silver. She...she told me that."

"You're right." She grabbed the plastic bottle from the ground and poured water onto her hands. It cooled the burns a little, but the weakness remained. "And, yes, I am a vampire. But I'm nothing like the woman who is holding you here."

"Don't...don't hurt me." She drew her knees to her chest, tucking her hands under her bare toes, to make herself as small as possible.

"I'm not going to—"

A thin wisp of smoke wafted into the room from the tunnel.

"What the hell?" Was the mansion on fire? Where was Santiago? "Come on. We've got to get you out of here. Is there an extra key around here?"

"Stay away." The young woman's voice had that high-pitched, you're-a-monster tone.

"You've got to believe me, Yvonne. I'm here to help. Your sister wouldn't have sent me if she didn't trust me." The smoke was thickening. They seriously needed to get out of here.

"How do I know that she's even alive? That you're not just saying that to get to me?"

Roxy's patience was wearing thin. "Well, for one thing, if I was like the woman who took you, I wouldn't give a shit what you thought. I'd probably rip your throat out right now and replenish the energy I just lost from that silver. And second of all, it's my job to keep people like you safe from people like her. So whether you cooperate or not, I'm taking you with me."

Yvonne didn't move, but she didn't argue either. "The only key I've seen is the one she keeps in her pocket." She shuddered as if recalling an unpleasant memory.

"Then I'll have to break them somehow."

A quick glance around revealed no tools stacked anywhere or objects she could use as one. Except for the coffin, the tiny room was bare. She'd have to do it with her hands either by breaking the links or pulling them from the wall. Normally, something like this wouldn't be much of a problem, but she wasn't at a hundred percent given the energy drain, and the fact that the links were silver made it tricky.

Removing her jacket, she turned it around, and slipped her hands into the sleeves. She'd use them as makeshift gloves to cover each hand. With her hands protected, she grabbed the chain, braced her feet on the wall for leverage and pulled. Nothing.

The smell of smoke was getting stronger. She hoped to God Santiago was all right. He'd need to manage things on his own until she could get Yvonne out of here.

She pulled again, harder this time. Sweat rolled down her temple as she ground her teeth together and her fangs pricked her lower lip. Feeling a slight give, she leaned more of her weight into it. Finally, one of the links broke, sending her backward against the overturned coffin.

"You did it!" Yvonne held up an almost-two-foot length of chain still attached to her ankle, but not the wall.

"One down, three to go." Roxy pushed herself up and reached for the next one.

The second chain was even harder than the first. No matter how hard she tried, none of the links would give way, so she concentrated on where it was affixed to the wall. Changing her grip, she pulled and strained. Finally, after what felt like forever, the bolt moved slightly. Roxy changed the angle and pulled again. This time, it loosened further and she was able to slide it out of its crumbled hole.

Ten minutes later, though Roxy was sweaty and exhausted, Yvonne was finally freed. She leaned against the wall, feeling much weaker than when she'd started, almost nauseous. This wasn't the beginning of another panic attack, was it? If it was, she didn't have the luxury of waiting till the sensation passed this time. The smell of smoke was so strong now that she could almost taste the acrid flavor of burning wood on her tongue. Soon they'd be coughing, struggling to find oxygen.

With the broken chains dangling, Yvonne swayed and steadied herself on the coffin. "I feel sick."

Ha. That makes two of us.

"Blood loss will do that to you." She looped the young woman's arm over her shoulder to support as much of her weight as she could and they shuffled toward the doorway.

Okay, they weren't going to be able to move very fast like this. Not only would she need to support Yvonne's weight for two hundred or more feet, but she had to make sure the chains didn't inadvertently touch her skin. If only the tunnel wasn't so damn narrow, she thought. If she could muster up the energy, she could carry Yvonne and probably move faster than if the young woman had to travel all the way on foot.

She poked her head into the tunnel where the smell of smoke was even stronger. "Maybe you should wait here while I go for help." She'd find Santiago and between the two of them, they should be able to get Yvonne out of here.

Yvonne's eyes widened. "Don't…don't leave me."

Roxy wasn't sure whether the young woman actually trusted her now or not. "Are you strong enough for a piggy back ride?"

"I…I can try."

After zipping her jacket all the way up to her neck, she squatted down for Yvonne to climb onto her back, but something on the floor drew her attention. Next to the coffin was a small antique clock and a copy of *Gothic Homes* magazine. Regular-looking items that you'd keep on your nightstand.

"Don't tell me she sleeps inside that thing every day?" Roxy asked with disgust. She could only guess that when the woman woke, she'd take the few steps over to where Yvonne was chained. Her own private sweetblood supply, available whenever she wanted it.

"You mean you don't...sleep in coffins?"

"I prefer a bed with sheets and blankets. Preferably an electric blanket, actually."

"Oh. That's...good. I'm sure her friend sleeps in coffins."

"Her friend?" Was Yvonne referring to other Darkbloods, she wondered?

She told Roxy about what had happened shortly after she arrived. The well-dressed man had seemed so distinguished at first and yet had turned out to be no less a monster than the woman.

An edible centerpiece? That was seriously messed up. Poor thing. So that explained the plastic on the dining room table. But who was he? A lover? A guest? She'd mention it to the capture team so they could find out as much as they could about him from Yvonne before wiping her memory.

"Okay, climb on, but don't let any of the chains touch me. I can't afford to lose any more energy." Things would be hard enough as it was.

The chains snaked around Roxy's legs as if they were trying to trip her up. The young woman was frailer than she thought—hell, without the extra weight of the silver, she'd be as light and inconsequential as a down feather in a windstorm. But given Roxy's reduced energy level, it wasn't all bad. She would've had a lot harder time carrying a healthy girl Cosette's size.

Her foot caught the edge of the magazine, exposing a white sticklike object underneath.

It was a bone. A human radius.

The bitch slept with the bones of her victims? *God, she's twisted.* Roxy wanted nothing more than to get the hell away from this place as quickly as possible.

"What's wrong?" Yvonne asked.

"Nothing. I'm… It's fine."

Then she remembered all of the torch holders in the tunnel. There had to be dozens of the strange criss-crossed sconces. She hadn't bothered to examine them very closely at the time because she'd been hell-bent on following Yvonne's scent, but she'd be willing to bet they were made of bone.

Looks like we got here just in time.

They'd only advanced about twenty feet into the corridor when the smoke got substantially thicker. It swirled like little eddies of water around the bone torch-lights and made visibility difficult. Roxy crouched as low as she could. Her human passenger wouldn't last much longer in this. Yvonne coughed and raised her hand reflexively. The silver chain flicked against Roxy's cheek, burning it.

Roxy stumbled and fell to her knees, unable to catch herself. Something in her wrist popped as it hit the stone floor, the same wrist injured all those years ago in that alley with Ian.

"Sorry," Yvonne said, choking. Her coughing was getting worse.

"That's okay." Roxy tried to stand again but the ligaments in her legs felt like liquid. She might be able to survive smoke inhalation, but Yvonne sure as hell wouldn't. And neither of them would survive a fire.

"Hang on." Ignoring the pain in her wrist, she pushed herself up and started forward again. Whatever injury she'd sustained, the tissue would regenerate in a few days. She kept that in mind with each painful movement. They had to be about halfway by now.

A loud crack sounded ahead of them and a shower of sparks filled the corridor as one of the wooden support beams fell, completely blocking their path. There was no way around it.

"I think we might need a plan B."

"What's plan B?"

"I don't know. Ask me when I figure it out. But it looks like plan A isn't happening." She did a little hitch to keep Yvonne from slipping, then turned and headed back to the tiny room.

After setting Yvonne down, she grabbed the phone from her pocket to call Santiago. Maybe he could—

Three missed calls from him. She quickly hit redial. He answered on the first ring.

"Where the hell are you? Are you all right? Do you have the girl?" He sounded more worried than pissed.

"Yes, and we're okay, but not for long. It's really

smoky in here and we're trapped." She told him about the long tunnel. "I'm going to need your help."

THICK BLACK SMOKE filled the hallway and flames had reached one of the walls by the time Santiago pushed open the door to the library at the far end. This place was a goddamn tinderbox. It couldn't have been more than five minutes since the candle had ignited the drapes.

With his hands out in front of him, he headed to the far right corner. If the bookshelf was still open, he should see a narrow stairway. If not, there was a lever somewhere. She had said it was on the third or fourth shelf, but frankly, he'd just rip the whole thing from the wall rather than risk precious time feeling around for a hidey-hole handle. Not only was this place going up in flames but dawn was right around the corner.

His leg hit the edge of a table and a few objects clattered to the ground. "What the hell?" He stumbled, shot a hand out to catch himself, and touched a few hard, cylindrical objects on the surface. Wood dowels? Not quite. They were connected at weird angles and too irregular. Bones? His fingers skimmed over the knobby end of one of them. Maybe. He'd be willing to bet they were human, too.

He found the bookcase Roxy had described, but when he felt around for an opening, there was only the wall. It must've closed behind her. Well, he sure as hell wasn't going to fumble around for the handle. Gripping the sides, he gave it a good jerk. Except for some books falling from the shelves, nothing happened. He put more muscle into it, but the shelf still didn't give way. What was it made of anyway? He took a step backward, poised to give it a good kick, when his phone vibrated. It was Roxy.

He'd told her he was on his way. Had they gotten out? Had something happened? "What's wrong? Where are you?"

"Are you almost here? The smoke is getting really bad." She sounded calmer than he'd have expected for someone trapped in a fire.

"I'm in the library, trying to get through the bookshelf. I'll be there in a minute."

He could hear coughing in the background, then the sound changed as if she'd cupped her hand over the receiver. "She's not doing well. I'm afraid if we don't get her out of here soon, she's not going to make it. She wasn't in good shape to begin with. Please, you've got to hurry."

"Okay, I will."

"Did you find the lever?"

"Not yet," he said, feeling a little guilty for not even trying.

"Goddamn it, Santiago, I can tell you're lying. The bookcase is heavy, as in lead-panel heavy, and it's reinforced with steel. You might be able to muscle it away from the wall but that'll take time. And time is something we don't have."

"How do I get it open?"

"Use the damn handle to unlock the slide bolts."

She walked him through it with the calmness of a 911 dispatcher and his fingers soon found a tiny lever on the back of the third shelf. The bookcase slid easily, as if mocking his efforts to strong-arm it. *Ask nice and I'll open. If not, screw you.*

"Got it. Be there in a minute."

"Okay. Be careful. We'll be waiting."

Hanging up, he shoved the desk into the opening to keep the bookshelf from sliding closed. There wasn't much time until it caught fire as well, so he'd have to move fast.

He glanced over his shoulder. Flames had reached the room now and were advancing across the wall, curling the wallpaper and giving the place an eerie golden glow amidst the hazy smoke. The air crackled and hissed like the inside of a popcorn popper.

He vaulted over the desk and through the opening in the wall. A steep, narrow staircase led downward and curved out of sight. A series of torches lit up the stone walls and a few dusty cobwebs hung from the ceiling. But what most surprised him was a chute running parallel to the stairs, reminding him of a slide at a water park or a luge track. He didn't have time to contemplate its purpose. All he knew was that it would get him to the bottom faster than if he went on foot. Given all the smoke, shadow moving would be difficult. He jumped onto the chute, crossed his arms over his chest, and as he made his body rigid he shot downward, picking up speed around the curve.

Jesus, Mary and Joseph. If he wasn't trying to save

someone from a burning building and get out alive himself, this might actually be fun. Had Roxy done this, too, when she came down? He'd have to remember to ask her.

When he got to the bottom, the chute was angled perfectly that he landed right on his feet. The smoke was thinner, making it easier to meld with the shadows, and he raced down the corridor.

He soon arrived at the collapsed area that Roxy had told him about. Wooden support beams, bricks and debris filled the tunnel, making passage impossible. With his bare hands, he began removing the rubble, throwing the crap haphazardly behind him like a dog digging in the yard.

He hadn't gotten far when Roxy called again, but when he answered, all he heard was static. It didn't surprise him that he had shitty coverage down here. He was about to pocket the phone when he saw the message indicator. She'd left him a voice mail?

He clicked his earpiece.

"I smell a Darkblood nearby," she whispered. "I can't figure out where it's coming from though. Hurry."

A surge of adrenaline shot through his veins. He'd run out of time. But as fast as he removed bricks and debris, more came down from the sides to fill the void. His skin heated up almost unbearably even though the fire was still a good distance behind him.

How often had he told his people that some human deaths could not be avoided? Sure, they could try to help them, but at some point, there wasn't much they could do. They were collateral damage in this war. A strong offense against Darkbloods was the best way to prevent humans from dying, but Guardians couldn't prevent them all.

He grabbed a wooden beam and pulled it from the rubble, sending sparks flying everywhere. Why would Roxy sacrifice herself like this? Surely she could've made it out of the tunnel if she hadn't been bringing the human female with her.

She was different from him in so many ways, her mind wired on a separate frequency, and yet it was as if he couldn't get enough of her. He wanted to know how she ticked and what made her that way. She affected him unlike other women, getting him to think about things in a whole different light. Yes, many things about her were maddening and yet—

The sound of crackling wood echoed through the passageway. Then with a loud rumble, more debris fell from above, filling the tunnel and sending sparks everywhere. He jumped backward, narrowly avoiding being hit by a brick. Darkbloods were near and the house was coming down around them, yet he wasn't any closer to Roxy.

Nothing is going to stop me from getting to her. Nothing.

No sooner had that thought crossed his mind when something strange began to happen.

The tips of his fingers tingled and the little hairs all over his body stood on end as if there was an electrical storm brewing in the atmosphere or he was stand-

ing near a power line. Then, without warning, a surge
of energy seemed to pulse outward—the exact opposite sensation of what he experienced when absorbing
it from a human.

Bricks he didn't touch went flying. Boards and rubble scattered.

He staggered backward. What the hell was going on?

Incredulous, he examined his hands as if he'd never
seen them before, like they belonged to an alien. But
they looked the same. They were large, his left hand
slightly calloused at the base of his forefinger from
where he held Misery, the right pinkie finger not quite
straight from an old injury that hadn't regenerated correctly. Nothing had changed, and yet a strange energy
buzzed just below the surface of his skin.

He flicked his fingers and the rubble around him
sounded as if it had been hit by hundreds of pebbles.
He merely thought about moving the rocks and they
scattered out of the way. Soon, a path had been cleared
and he was on the other side. He didn't have time to
figure out why this was happening or what had caused
it—he'd do that later. For now, he cared only about getting Roxy and the girl out of this place and away from
Darkbloods.

He sprinted through the tunnel, the smoke too thick
now, making it difficult to shadow move. By the time
he got to the end, that strange electrical sensation was
gone.

On the floor of the small room, Roxy was supporting
the young woman's head on her lap. She'd been staring

at the ceiling and turned her head when he entered. The tension in her expression melted into a calm, unhurried smile that said she knew he'd come. Seeing her confidence stirred something deep inside and made him feel as though he was capable of anything simply because this woman had never doubted him.

He opened his mouth to speak but she held a finger to her lips.

"A Darkblood," she whispered. "Up there somewhere. There must be an opening that I don't know about."

He pulled out the key discarded by the Darkblood and hoped it wasn't so badly damaged that it wouldn't work. Fortunately, it still fit perfectly. He quickly unlocked the shackles from the female's wrists and ankles and scooped her up.

"Let's go," he said, pulling Roxy to her feet, taking care not to touch her silver burns. "I'll take care of our Darkblood friend when we get outside and then you will feed from me."

CHAPTER SEVENTEEN

A THIN LAYER of ash covered the fresh snow. Ventra's hands shook with rage as she stooped to grab a handful of the charcoaled remains of her house. The still-warm embers fell from her fingers, leaving an inklike sticky residue on her skin.

Her bone collections—gone. Clothes, electronics, the sweetblood female—gone.

Even the sapphires she'd purchased after becoming the Seattle area sector mistress were somewhere in this rubble. Everything she owned or cared about had been reduced to an insignificant pile of ash. Not since her Time of Change as an orphan on the streets of New Orleans had she felt so empty. Having risen through the ranks of the Alliance, she'd sworn to never, ever be in that situation again. And yet, here she was.

Using a long stick from the rubble, she sifted through the ashes. It had taken her months to collect all those human bones. Maybe some of them hadn't burned.

When she arrived on the scene at sunset after having spent the day in one of her dens, she was shocked and sickened to find her beautiful mansion almost completely destroyed. She'd assumed the condition of the house's electrical system had caused the fire, because the knob-and-tube wiring was old with pigtailed wires scattered everywhere behind the plaster walls.

"A death trap," an electrician had told her shortly after buying the place. "To bring it up to code, the whole place needs to be rewired."

She couldn't care less about bringing it up to some arbitrary human standard. All she wanted was for the simple twenty-first-century conveniences to work— lights, hot water, furnace.

When she contacted him later to schedule the work, he refused. He was too scared to come back out, which was entirely her fault. She'd let herself drink from the man without wiping his mind completely. Fear, especially chronic fear, made the blood taste that much better, but it was a habit that sometimes backfired. When she didn't kill her victims, she prided herself on her ability to make a perfectly sane person go crazy.

Visiting asylums around the turn of the century had been Oskar's idea. She and her on-again-off-again boyfriend would fine-tune their craft on victims no one would believe anyway, slipping in to feed from the same people night after night. The two youthlings had gotten lots of practice. She should've known better than to do that to a human she still needed.

Thank the Dark Maker that Loric Rayne, the Alliance representative, was gone. She mourned how perfect the mansion had looked for his visit.

What would've been his opinion of her had this happened while he was here? She shuddered. An electrical fire that could've been prevented would have served to demonstrate how lazy and stupid she was. At the very least, he'd have questioned her ability to manage things and make decisions even more than the Alliance already was. As it turned out, she had every expectation that he'd be giving her a favorable report. He seemed to have been impressed with what she'd been doing here and her plans for the future—having that sweetblood girl on hand had been perfect. She tried to look on the bright side that this fire hadn't happened a few days ago.

And at least the mausoleum, barely visible on the far side of a stand of leafless maple trees, was still standing. That was one of the reasons she'd bought the place. It reminded her of Lafayette Cemetery from her childhood and how far she'd come since then. But now look at her. Right back where she'd started. Homeless with nothing to her name. She kicked at a charred piece of wood and a fountain of tiny sparks shot out. A flame licked up and over the surface as if it had been waiting for her to free it.

Although she doubted the frail human sweetblood had lasted more than a few minutes in the smoke, she sent Alistair over to check, leaving Ventra alone with her frustrations. She grabbed the charred remains of a sofa, sending the thing flying through the air where it landed on the other side of the still-standing, yet teetering chimney. A metal rod from something structural caught her eye. It would make the perfect baseball bat, she thought as she picked it up. She swung it at the chimney over and over, cursing when it didn't topple.

"Ma'am, I found something."

She jerked her head up. Alistair was tentatively picking his way through the snow with something in his hand. He moved stiffly, like someone who spent most of his time behind a desk programming computers, not functioning in the real world.

Since the demise of Xtark Software, she had him doing all sorts of tasks to keep him busy. The vampire was too talented for her to lose him to one of the other sectors.

Besides, the hidden phone app that allowed her to listen in on Guardian conversations had been his idea, so she needed him around to manage the data and troubleshoot any issues that arose. Once the program remotely activated the microphone, she'd been able to listen in on all sorts of conversations. In a short time, she'd learned a lot about the Agency's operations here in the Northwest. Information she couldn't wait to use.

She'd never have known about the planned raid on the Darkblood holding facility as well as other smaller ones. This new source of intel was going to be the key to fully restoring her reputation with the Alliance.

Alistair stumbled awkwardly over a charred piece of furniture, catching himself just in time. She turned away in disgust and picked up a broken piece of her favorite china, stamped U.S.S.R. on the bottom.

Why were all the smart ones lacking when it came to physical prowess? Everyone, that is, except Oskar. Not only was he physically amazing with his jet-black hair and long, lean body, but he was ruthless and utterly brilliant.

"Look at this," Alistair said.

"What is it?" she snapped. Thinking about her long-ago life always set her on edge.

"A stuffed animal."

"You mean a human child's toy?" She pinched her lips together in disgust.

Procreation. Why would anyone want that? She'd never been interested in being a broodmare. A weak, vulnerable vessel while a life developed inside her. No, thank you. If she wanted youthlings of her own, she preferred to create them from fully grown humans—beautiful changelings that she could control. Teaching an adult how to use and manage their new blood urges was much more preferable than raising one from scratch. She thought about a few of her favorites among those she'd made over the centuries—most of them dead now.

The sweetblood girl would've made a fine changeling. That silky copper hair. Those wide, dewy eyes.

Hell, who was she fooling? Ventra hadn't successfully turned a sweetblood in years. Bringing one to the edge of death and not draining them completely was next to impossible. And even if she was able to stop, the second vampire whose blood was needed for the change process was likely to finish the job. That had happened once or twice.

However, the sister, who was not a sweetblood, was still very much alive. Ventra smiled to herself. Maybe making a changeling would help take her mind off this mess.

Alistair cleared his throat and turned the toy over in his hands. The thing was soggy and covered with dirt. She couldn't imagine why he'd bother to come show her. Unless...

"Where did you find it?"

He pointed toward the hill behind him. "Over there near the old cemetery."

"Kids were poking around here?" Had they broken in and started the fire? A cold lick of fury trickled down her spine. If insignificant human children were responsible for this, she'd track them to their beds, slip into their windows at midnight, and give them a nightmare they'd never forget.

"I don't think so, ma'am. I didn't pick up any other human scent."

No humans? She scanned the darkness. Maybe he was right. Not only was the place too remote, but a few of her men had died in the fire. Unless they were complete morons, they'd have heard if a group of marauding human adolescents had broken into the house and stopped them before the damage could escalate.

She grabbed the toy and sniffed it. It smelled like— No. It couldn't be.

She held it to her nose again just to be sure, but the scent was unmistakable. It wreaked of her sweetblood from the crypt. Problem was, Ventra knew for a fact that the girl didn't have such a thing in her possession.

She stormed through the tall weeds and the stone sculptures that had once graced a manicured yard. The mausoleum stood on the hillside, its heavy cement door cracked open.

"Did you leave it in that condition?" she accused Alistair. She rarely used this entrance and when she did, she was careful to secure the door upon leaving.

"I...I didn't go in." He pointed to one of the headstones. "I found the toy lying about fifteen feet away."

She pushed the door open and stepped inside the tight space. A stone angel stood against the far wall, its hands spread wide, its pious face looking down on her as if she were a child of the heavens.

She cursed.

The cement slab had been shoved aside and a thin line of gray smoke was wafting out of the hole. She peered into the hazy air of the underground crypt. Her coffin was overturned and the girl was gone.

She hadn't died in the fire after all. Someone had taken her.

The fury in her veins was now ready to explode. Had one of her people done this? It wouldn't have been the first time a Darkblood had a serious lapse in judgment when it came to a sweetblood.

But burn down my house?

Did her authority not mean anything to them? Were they not afraid of her? She'd tear the guilty parties apart piece by piece until they were screaming for her to stake them. Limb regeneration, which started right away, could be very painful, especially when the bones weren't quite in alignment.

Could this really be one of her own? Of course, the

possibility existed that it was the work of Guardians. First they destroyed Xtark Software but would they go after her home? She'd kept close tabs on them via the listening app but hadn't heard that they knew about this place. In fact, their superstar tracker, a woman that Ventra had once tried to kidnap, wasn't even in the country right now.

Footsteps crunched behind her in the snow then Alastair cleared his throat. Her patience was worn down to a sharp little nub. He wore a sweatshirt with a ridiculous green robot character, high-top sneakers with the laces untied, and his longish hair was pulled back in a ponytail because he probably was too lazy to go get it cut. How could anyone ever expect to be taken seriously dressed like that? He was a hundred-year-old vampire and should be well past that immature youthling stage by now. She wanted to tell him to grow the fuck up, dress like he wanted to be treated.

But the guy had talent. And because of that, she needed him. If only that human who'd worked for Xtark were still alive. He was a computer genius, too. It made her uncomfortable to rely too heavily on one individual, which was what she was doing with Alastair. She rubbed the exasperated sting from her eyes then gave him a "what now?" stare.

He stuttered a moment before the words came out clearly. "Franz found…a place a few miles away."

"And?" She did not have time for the poor communication skills of a guy who'd rather be talking source code and operating systems.

"He…he said a car was parked in the underbrush recently and there are tracks in the snow leading here."

She looked over his shoulder into the snowy forest. "Where?"

"Back on the main road."

Without addressing him further, she morphed into shadow, slipped through the forest and soon met up with Franz out on the main road.

"Where is it?"

He adjusted his eye-patch and simply pointed to a spot about twenty feet away. In a flash she was over there, scanning the snowy terrain. Two sets of tracks led toward her house and three sets of tracks came back.

"Guardians were here. I can smell them." Franz was behind her. A former Agency tracker who had changed his allegiance for reasons she didn't know or care about, he had a sense of smell that was better than most Darkbloods.

Her enemy had done this. Stolen her sweetblood and destroyed everything.

Her beautiful, gothic home with its stunning Bone Room, Extraction Chamber and old crypt.

How could she not have known about this Guardian operation? Why had they not heard anything?

Snow crunched under her feet as she thought about the Agency personnel with the app on their phones: a capture agent, an admin assistant and the best one of all—the Seattle field team Guardian that Cosette had seduced.

If none of those people were privy to this mission, what did it mean?

She turned her attention to Alistair and his stupid robot T-shirt. "Are you not recording everything from those apps?"

He took a half step backward. "N-no. I mean… Yes. Everything is recorded."

"Why did we not hear about this?" she demanded.

"I…I…"

Franz interrupted, "Given there was no discussion about this raid, maybe it was someone outside the field. Guardians, yes, but maybe not Seattle-area Guardians. You did almost kill their field team leader. Maybe they brought in a big dog."

Several Guardians injured, including their local leader. Yes, it made sense that they'd bring in someone else. Tristan Santiago, their region commander, she thought with disdain. It had to be.

After the explosion, he'd be desperate to find out who caused it. By burning down her house was he sending her a message? Was this his way of marking his territory, telling her to beware because he had a bigger dick and wasn't afraid to use it? A calling card that said I'm-More-Powerful-Than-You? The more she thought about it, the more she was convinced that he was the one responsible.

Ventra laughed to herself.

We'll see about that.

If she could take care of the region commander, no one in the Alliance would ever question her abilities again. Her reputation would be restored tenfold and she'd have a lot of capital with the Alliance that she could use to her advantage.

She stooped to examine a footprint, placing a hand on the indentation as if she could tell who made it and cursing her diminished capacity to smell. How long would it take, if ever, to get it back?

What if... An idea began to take shape in her head.

What if she didn't feed from humans and instead ate actual food for a while, would her sense of smell get better? Maybe it wouldn't be as good as a Guardian's, and certainly not up to a tracker's standards, but anything had to be better than this. But could she even stomach eating food?

She thought about what this Guardian hotshot had done. Had he walked through her house before he torched the place? Gone through her things defiling her beautiful bone sculptures? Just the thought of an Agency pig stepping foot inside her home and destroying her prized possessions was enough to bring on some serious blood lust. Fangs elongating, she morphed into shadow and headed toward the nearest human establishment.

He wanted to make this personal? Fine. Two could play that piano. She could make this very personal. And, fortunately for her, she knew just where to start.

Before she did though, she'd stop off in town and kill

a human or two. But then she remembered her newly formed plan and hesitated.

"Damn." She'd have to settle for a bloody rare steak instead.

CHAPTER EIGHTEEN

ROXY TURNED GRIM over and watched how the blade glinted in the light like a razor-thin sheet of ice. All of the black pearls were still embedded in the hilt. It was gorgeous, just as she remembered. She almost couldn't believe it was real.

"Santiago, I can't tell you what this means to me to have this. Thank you." Tears stung her eyes but she didn't care.

Mary Alice had done so much for her and to finally give this back to her was almost incomprehensible. She'd dreamed of what it would be like. How she'd hand it to the woman and know that this closed a dark chapter in both their lives. It wasn't often that you got a chance to repay someone who'd done so much for you.

Maybe they could both move on now. Hell, who was she kidding? Mary Alice was much more pragmatic than Roxy and had moved on years ago, whereas Roxy still needed answers. It was a debt that needed to be repaid.

He shrugged. "No big deal. When I saw the Darkbloods with it, I wondered if it could be the same blade, so I grabbed it."

"No big deal?" she repeated. "Santiago, you went out of your way to rescue it from the fire."

She recalled how they'd encountered the one remaining Darkblood as they were spiriting Yvonne away. The whole place was ablaze when they climbed over the desk into the library. Santiago had kicked out a window and they clambered outside, but just as they passed a spindly maple tree doubled over by the weight of the snow on its limbs, they caught wind of the Darkblood. Santiago sprinted across the snow and quickly took care of the guy. Instead of coming straight back as she'd expected, he ran into the burning building. She had no idea why until he came out a few moments later, sweaty, covered in soot and holding Grim.

"Nothing, not even this blade, is worth your life." A knot in her throat made it hard to say anything more.

He didn't look at her. Didn't he believe her? Didn't he realize how incredibly happy she was that he not only rescued her and Yvonne, but that he retrieved this blade for her? Sure, he might be doing it out of loyalty for a fellow Guardian, but it meant the world to her.

She set the knife down on the credenza then turned back around to face him. He'd shifted his weight as if he was going to move away but she grabbed his hand instead. His dark gaze met hers, but she couldn't quite read his expression.

Was he sad? Disappointed for some reason? She knew he was still concerned about Dom, but according to Mackenzie he was doing much better, and the prognosis from Dr. DeGraff was that he would be making a full recovery. They were well on their way to discovering the source of the leaks. With her heightened abilities, she was confident she could ferret out who wasn't being truthful, although from what Cosette was able to remember, the so-called traitor may actually have no idea he was being used.

She ran her hands up his arms, over the tattoos on his neck and cupped his face. His light stubble made a raspy sound as she rubbed her thumbs over his jaw. Maybe he couldn't understand why she hadn't left the young woman when the situation seemed hopeless—she'd heard enough of his motivational speeches to his people about how Guardians couldn't be expected to save every human. But she couldn't just walk away and he knew it. So despite this difference in philosophy, he supported her. Didn't make her feel as if she were wrong or foolish or that she had to abide by his way of doing things. Even though he was the CO, he let her be herself and didn't try to force her into his way of thinking. It took a pretty amazing man to do something like that. His appearance in the doorway of that tiny smoke-filled room was the first time she realized how hard she was falling for him.

Standing on her tiptoes, she slowly kissed him. She wanted to draw out the seconds to breathe in and sear to her memory everything about him.

He smelled faintly of pine and citrus from the body wash in his shower. She'd forever associate those scents with him. She ran her fingers through his short, slightly damp hair then down over his shoulders and back. His muscles flexed with power under her hands. And his chin, with its stubble, chafed against hers. Like roughing up the surface of your nails so the polish adheres better, a small amount of pain was good. It made the pleasure of the kiss more pronounced.

He tasted like mint, probably from one of those toothpicks he liked to chew on, and she slipped her tongue past his lips. His mouth moved against hers, kissing her back, and she suddenly needed more. As if sensing this from her, his demeanor changed. He went from letting her be in charge to taking control himself.

He kissed her deeper as if it was his turn to drink her in. His arms wrapped around her, pulling her close with a jerk and she gave a little gasp. The steel-like hardness of his erection rubbed against her hip, and she realized just how desperately she needed to feel him inside her. To emphasize this fact, a delicious warmth curled low in her belly as her body was readying itself for him. There'd be no need for foreplay.

She fumbled with his fly as he shoved her against the wall, but she had no trouble finding his erection. Her fingers barely fit around it.

He groaned as she moved her hand up and down his length. "Keep that up and I won't last long."

"But I want to put my mouth here."

"No, we do this together."

Somehow he'd managed to remove just one of her legs from her jeans and shoved his knee between her thighs, forcing them wider. Grabbing her bottom, he lifted her up and her legs went automatically around his waist. The warm head of his shaft skimmed her inner thigh as he settled her lower.

Until.

There.

He found her.

And in one thrust, he was inside.

She was pretty sure she either cried out or moaned. Or maybe that was him.

"You feel…so amazing, Roxy. I'm not…going to last long."

She loved hearing that. "I do?"

"You're hot and—oh, God—very silky."

Her inner muscles tightened around him immediately and every nerve ending tingled as if it were on fire. At this angle, the base of his shaft rubbed perfectly against her sensitive bud.

"And you're incredible, Santiago. Perfect." And as she said those words against his lips, she knew she wasn't only referring to the sex.

In this position, big, sweeping motions were impossible, but the lack of friction didn't matter. They fit together perfectly, moved together perfectly. She could feel it coming. And she was pretty sure she couldn't wait for him.

"You're close, aren't you?" His breath rasped in her ear.

"How…how can you tell?"

"You're tightening around me. In little waves that seem to be getting stronger and stronger."

"You…you can feel that?"

"I'm acutely aware of everything you do."

She had a feeling he meant more than just lovemaking, but right now that was all she could think of.

He brushed the hair from her neck and she knew instantly that he was searching out her vein. Her heart did a little somersault as if it were calling out for him to take what it was offering.

"Are you...close, too?" She could hardly think clearly enough to form the words.

"Extremely" was his husky reply.

His breath was hot against her skin as a powerful surge of pleasure radiated from her core. She wanted to scream and shout from all the rooftops, but instead she gripped his shoulders and hung on. Her toes curled and every part of her body went a little numb except for where they were joined.

"There. That's it, my love," she thought she heard him say. "Let yourself go."

She was still climaxing when two sharp points struck her flesh. Although he'd taken her blood before, it still surprised her. She should've been ready just in case, but she sucked in a sharp breath anyway. Immediately, his thumb began stroking her jaw as if to soothe her. And it worked. The searing pain lasted just a moment before morphing into an even deeper pleasure.

"Yes, Santiago," she heard herself say. "Oh, my God, yes."

He groaned and his shaft pulsed impossibly thicker. Two quick thrusts were all it took for his seed to be pumped deep into her body.

HE AWOKE TO find Roxy sprawled over him, her silky blond hair covering his chest. Besides doing it against the wall, they'd made love several more times in bed like a couple of first-time youthlings who didn't know when they'd have a chance to do this again. He rubbed his hand along the channel of her spine. She was trim and athletic, but not overly skinny. She had curves and he loved that about her. One of her hands was between his legs and he became aware that he was growing hard again.

Not only was he physically attracted to her, but he was falling for this woman who had such a unique combination of strength and vulnerability that he found so incredibly attractive.

He'd taken her blood again. Normally, he refrained during sex, but with Roxy it was a natural part of the process, like foreplay or climaxing. If they continued this charade of a relationship and continued making love, would he always feel this way? Recalling how her blood made him feel—strong, powerful—he had a feeling he would never tire of it. She was an addiction and he didn't want to be rehabbed.

But a relationship with her made no sense. Not only did they live on opposite sides of the country, but it was clear when she got Grim back that she wasn't ready to move on from Ian. A part of her still loved him, and Santiago was selfish enough that it bothered him. Besides, she deserved a better future than the one that would be inevitable with him anyway.

If his parents were right, that the males in his family were not meant to be monogamous and couldn't be trusted, then he definitely wasn't the right man for Roxy. She'd been through too much in the past. She deserved a better man than he was, someone who was capable of loving only her. Someone trustworthy and honorable.

He started to move away from her, but Roxy stirred and her hand brushed his balls.

What he wouldn't give to be the right man for her, he thought as he grew harder. He'd slay demons and dragons for her, cherish her, support her hopes and dreams. He'd make love to her every day, and if she and the good Lord were willing, the union *would* be a good one and there would be children.

But this wasn't a fairy tale—this was real life, and in real life things rarely worked out the way you wanted them to. He didn't want a family who would only be hurt when he fucked up.

Careful not to wake her, he got up and grabbed his robe from a peg in the closet. He planned to head to the kitchen for something to eat or see if anyone was in the game room, but there, in the corner next to his favorite pair of boots, sat the UV light. He couldn't remember the last time he'd used it. Weeks ago maybe, right after he and Roxy had arrived. The thing had been his crutch for so long that he felt almost awkward looking at it now.

Glancing toward the bed, he noticed Roxy was awake, staring at the ceiling with a far off, melancholy expression.

He came to her and sat down. "Did I wake you?"

"No, I've been awake for a while. Thinking."

He climbed in next to her, forgetting about his plans to raid the kitchen. "About what?" He twisted a strand of her hair around his finger and marveled at how many different shades of blond there were.

She pushed herself up on one elbow and leaned over him. He couldn't help but notice how natural it felt to have her leg crooked over his and her breast resting on his chest. Although he wanted to make love to her again, he was sated for now, content to just be in bed with her, talking.

"I'm thinking about Ian's mother, Mary Alice, and how she'll react when she knows we found Grim."

He remembered what the two Darkbloods said about the owner of the blade and shoved it out of his head. It couldn't be true. "You two are close." Was that what happened to mothers and almost daughters-in-law?

"She became like a mother to me when Ian and I first met. My own mother passed away a few years before and although she didn't replace Mom, she filled that void in my heart, you know? And when everything happened with Ian… Well, she was my most ardent supporter."

"What exactly did she do for you, Roxy? You've never told me why the two of you are so close." It did seem unusual that a mother of a slain Guardian would support someone suspected of having been involved with his death.

"If it hadn't been for her and her family's influence,

I probably would've been brought up on charges even though the evidence they had against me was nil."

He blood heated and his fingers gripped the sheet beneath him. It was that goddamn Dax Sturgeon, out to prove himself as a hotshot new region commander. "He used you, Roxy. Saw you as a way to up his political capital. Some people need to knock others down in order to climb up and make themselves look taller."

"Ha. Mary Alice said something similar." Roxy flopped back on the pillow and stared at the ceiling. "She always hated that guy. But you know, I was almost ready to quit the Agency all together. I was tired of the bullshit, but she convinced me to stay, to apply to the newly established Tracker academy. Said I shouldn't let one asshole cause me to give up what I loved to do. I'm not sure what I would've done had I quit, so I'm glad I listened to her."

He twirled his finger around a strand of her hair again. Hearing her say this was bittersweet. A tiny part of him wanted her to say that she hated her job and would move out here to be closer to him. But he supposed it was just as well that she didn't.

"Are you going to notify the Council that we've located Ian's blade?" he asked. "I'm sure they'd want to present Mary Alice with it during a formal presentation."

Roxy sighed. "It's a nice thought, but Sturgeon is still the CO down there. He'd be the one doing the presenting and I know she'd never want that. She hates the guy even more than I do. I'll just bring it back to her myself."

"What if I did it?"

Her head snapped up. "What are you talking about?"

"It doesn't need to be the Guardian's actual CO who makes the presentation. I'd be honored to present it to her."

"You'd do that?" She pushed up on one elbow again and stared at him, the specks in her golden eyes sparkling more than normal.

"Like I said, I'd be honored, but only if you think she'd be up for it."

"Oh, God, she'd love it." Roxy planted a quick peck on his cheek. "She lives for tradition and formalities. She celebrates all the old holidays and finds an excuse to throw an elegant party for any occasion. This would mean so much to her."

"We could make the presentation at the awards ceremony gala. Many of the West Coast VIPs will be here and it will be quite the affair."

"Do you think there's time? It's just a few days away."

"If you can get her up here, we'll make it happen. You've met Jenella. She's capable of organizing anything. After you confirm with Mary Alice, we'll get the ball rolling."

"Thank you," she said against his lips. "This will be wonderful. It means the world to me. I...uh... Thanks."

He thought she was about to say something else, but with a sigh, she got up and padded across the room. Naked. Despite the fact that he should be thoroughly sated, all the available blood in his body rushed to his groin again.

He adjusted his growing erection. "Where are you going? Are you coming back?"

In the doorway to the bathroom, she turned. The light from inside silhouetted her breasts, stomach and hips. "I'm going to take a quick shower then head into the field office."

He didn't want her to leave just yet. "The bed's warm, but only when you're in it."

She smiled at him but didn't budge. "I want to hang out in some of the common areas, make sure I've talked to everyone here. Cosette has no memory of who she slept with, but at least I know now that I'm trying to find a male."

Before he could convince her to climb back to bed just for a few minutes, a knock sounded at the door.

Roxy cocked her head and sniffed. "That's weird. It's Arianna…and she has food. I'll be right there," she called. Grabbing her T-shirt and yoga pants from the back of a chair, she cast him a glance as she quickly got dressed. "Wasn't she up at the safehouse with Cosette?"

Santiago pulled up the sheets, making sure he was covered. "I thought so."

When Roxy opened the door, Arianna was standing there with a tray of food. "Rise and shine. Sorry to bother you guys, but I heard voices so I knew you were awake."

"Oh, my God. You brought pastries."

Santiago sat up. Pastries? As in cinnamon rolls?

"How did you know I was famished?" Roxy took the tray from her and brought it over to the bed.

A gooey cinnamon roll stared him right in the face. Yes!

"Thank you—both of you—for finding Cosette's sister," Arianna said from the open door. "She's still being checked out by the medical staff, but she's going to be all right. These goodies are courtesy of Cosette. Their mother owns a French bakery back home and the sisters can make just about any kind of pastry there is. She's been so worried about her sister that she's been baking up a storm ever since she got up there. It's been like therapy for her as she waited. Of course, Jackson's in heaven. We left so quickly last night that I didn't grab my things. When Cosette heard I was driving back, she insisted I bring you some goodies."

Santiago laughed. Jackson's eating habits were legendary.

"Tell her thank you," Roxy said, breaking off a piece of the cinnamon roll and popping it into her mouth. "Oh, my God, this is amazing. You don't know how starving I've been lately. She should seriously open up a bakery herself."

"Well, don't eat it all," Santiago teased. "Save some for me."

"That's such important work you're doing with the sweetblood safehouse," Roxy said, licking her thumb. She still had frosting on her cheek, but he didn't reach over to wipe it off. He found it charming that she was a messy eater sometimes.

"Thanks," Arianna said quietly. "It's not much but it's my way of contributing." Having lost her mother to Darkbloods when she was a child, she was motivated to help other families impacted by the same thing.

"Are you crazy?" Roxy said. "I'd say that's a lot. I'll bet if you talk to Cosette or Yvonne, they'd say it's huge what you're doing."

With her hand on the door, Arianna turned to leave, but she hesitated and looked straight at Santiago. "I know this little—" she made a stirring motion with her fingers "—whatever this is, started out as fake, but if you let her go, I'm going to be pissed."

THE NEXT FEW days leading up to the awards ceremony were a whirlwind. Mary Alice was flying in, which meant Roxy needed to order flowers, get a card. She wanted to fill the woman's room with bouquets of her favorite flowers upon her arrival—irises, tiny pink roses, white tulips—and didn't know if they were in season or not. At Jenella's recommendation, she visited a popular florist downtown who was able to handle everything. Seeing a well-stocked drugstore on her way back to the field office, Roxy realized she needed a few things for the gala. Lotions, hair care products, clear nail polish.

But an hour later, as she stood in the bathroom adjoining Santiago's bedroom, she tried to keep her hands from shaking. The blue plus sign on the pregnancy test was as bold and easy to read as a billboard.

That explained some of the nausea she'd been having. The increased appetite. Because she assumed it was related to those old panicky feelings she occasionally suffered from, she'd been meditating even more lately, thinking she needed to get a better handle on her body.

If it hadn't been for a strange heaviness in her lower abdomen that she'd noticed at the floral shop, she wouldn't have even thought to pick up a test when she walked down that aisle in the drug store.

She slumped to the floor and covered her face in her hands.

At one time in her life she'd have loved knowing she was expecting a baby, even though the chances were slim. Most pre-Change youthlings dreamed of being one of the few capable of producing children. But now? Why did the fertility gods suddenly decide to visit her? It had never dawned on her to use protection. None of their people did, so she wasn't about to blame Santiago either. This was crazy. This…this *fling* wasn't even real.

What was she going to do now? Santiago didn't want children or a family. He didn't want a wife.

Their society dictated that if a couple produced children, they should have more. People would pressure them to get married. And Santiago, being an honorable man, would probably step up because he thought it was the right thing to do. He would be thrust into the same situation as his parents, who married only because his mother got pregnant. Their society had enough unhappy marriages brought about in an effort to produce more offspring.

Although her father had died when she was very

young, she still remembered her parents laughing and loving each other. She wanted what they had and wasn't about to compromise simply because of a plus sign on a pregnancy test.

The facets on the wedding ring cast cheery rainbows of color on the bathroom walls, reminding her what a joke this all was.

She wallowed in self-pity for a while, letting her negative attitude run amok as she used the whole box of tissues. When she crumpled up the last one, she decided she'd had enough.

She pulled herself off the floor and stared at her reflection in the mirror. These were the eyes of a fighter looking back at her. Having overcome adversity in the Guardian ranks to succeed as a tracker, she'd have to buck the system and reinvent herself. She'd done it before and she could do it again.

She'd tell Santiago about the baby, but she wouldn't let him talk her into anything. She'd make it clear that she was perfectly capable of doing this on her own. He'd be welcome to come visit anytime and when the child was older, he or she could visit Santiago.

She tossed the pregnancy test into the trash and turned on the shower. This had to be a sign, pushing her to stop this charade. This fake romance of theirs had produced results that were entirely too real and it was time for it to end.

ROXY SLIPPED THE turquoise sequined dress over her head. Because it fit her curves like a glove, she had to shimmy it down over her hips.

He tried not to stare—they needed to be in the field office foyer in fifteen minutes—but he couldn't help himself. It was like having his own private peep show.

She contorted around, arching her spine in an effort to reach the long zipper. The gown dipped dangerously low in the back, molded around her bottom and stopped midthigh. He quickly adjusted his growing erection as he grabbed the car keys from his desk.

One thing was sure. When they got back to his quarters tonight, he was going to exercise his faux husbandly rights again.

She held the front of the dress to her chest and stepped into a pair of beige high heels. He wasn't going to be able to take much more of this.

"Can you zip me up? I can't quite reach it."

Santiago folded his arms and took a step back. "Isn't there someone else who can do it?"

For a moment, she looked as if he'd just slapped her. God, he could be such an idiot sometimes.

"What I meant to say was…" His heart felt as if it had swelled in his chest. He was pretty sure that if he took a deep breath right now, it'd have nowhere to go. Why did he have such a difficult time expressing himself around her? He wasn't normally at a loss for words but she'd made him tongue-tied and now she was hurt. Maybe he was trying too hard. "It's just because you look so gorgeous. Too gorgeous. If I help you, I might accidentally get confused and take it off instead. You plus that dress equals trouble for me. I'm just recognizing my weakness, that's all."

The pain in her eyes was gone. Good. He couldn't stand having her mad at him. But now it was replaced with a sly little smile. "Weakness? As in just one?"

"Oh, I have others. Good scotch. Cinnamon rolls. Salt-and-vinegar chips." His real weakness, the one that ran in his family, wasn't one he wanted to mention, however.

His mood started to dampen and he turned away from her. This playful banter was fun, but at some point, their little game would be over. She'd go back to Florida and he'd go back to the region offices.

"Well, then I'm honored to be included on such a delicious list." She came around and adjusted his bow tie even though he was fairly certain it was straight, then she slowly looked him up and down. "God, I could say the same thing about you."

Before he realized what she was doing, she pushed him against the wall of the bedroom, and caged him between her arms. "Roxy… We can't…" People were waiting for them.

Her lashes were thick and long, and she'd done that little cat-eye thing to make her eyes even more dramatic. She gave him a no-nonsense, don't-disagree-with-me, this-means-business kiss. The kind that said she was in charge and wasn't going to put up with his shit. He had to admit, he rather liked being manhandled.

Then she reached for his belt.

"Hey, hold on." He grabbed her hands. "What are you doing? We don't have time for this." He wanted to have time for it and the now-heavy weight between his legs wanted it, but they were due at the Edgemont Hotel in less than thirty minutes. If she wanted to fool around, she'd have to wait till later.

She pushed his hands away and unzipped his fly anyway, as if he hadn't registered a protest. She was on a mission and wasn't about to let him stop her.

Cool fingers slipped into his boxer briefs and wrapped around his erection. If he wasn't already leaning against the wall, he'd have been staggering backward already.

"Oh, wow, what do we have here?" Her kitten-soft tone was beguiling.

He pressed his palms on the wall behind him, trying to keep his thoughts straight but having a hard time. He hadn't expected this. At all. "We really shouldn't be doing this now."

She kept stroking him.

"We don't have time," he choked. "People are waiting for us."

"Don't worry. This won't take long."

A sleeve had slipped down her shoulder and from this angle he could see the tops of her creamy breasts. She wasn't wearing a bra—God, the advantages of that slinky dress were increasing by the minute—and one dusky pink nipple was almost visible. What he wouldn't give to have it in his mouth right now.

She scooched her gown up a little and—

Oh, God, she kneeled down in front of him with her heels pointing out crazily behind her.

She was going to do *that?* His heart was beating

so hard he was positive she could hear it. Although he wanted to tangle his fingers in her hair, he had the wherewithal—barely—to know he couldn't mess it up.

He pinched his eyes shut. Ground his molars together.

He felt her hot breath on him first and then—oh, God—her mouth.

Suddenly, there was nothing more important than the next few minutes. Everything else would have to wait.

CHAPTER NINETEEN

WITH MORE RESPECT, dignity and honor than Roxy had ever dreamed, Santiago presented the sword to Mary Alice in front of dozens of VIPs at the old Edgemont Hotel. He looked amazingly handsome up on the stage, his muscular body dressed in an Italian tuxedo.

"Years ago, well before the formation of the Council and the Agency, Ian and I served together as brothers in arms. And although we lost touch with each other, we both went on to become Guardians. I'm honored to have worked with him and call him a friend."

Santiago presented the newly polished and restored blade to Mary Alice.

"I can't thank you enough," the older woman said later, dabbing her eyes. "You don't know what this means to me."

"If it hadn't been for Roxy, the weapon may have never been recovered."

Mary Alice patted Roxy's knee. "She's a good egg, this one."

After Santiago left to talk to a few West Coast Council members, Mary Alice turned to Roxy. With her white hair piled high atop her head and secured with an antique comb, she wore a pearl-gray dress with a

Cameo broach at the neckline. Two bright spots of color spotted on her cheeks.

"Tell me about that young man."

Young man? Oh, she must mean Santiago. Maybe when you got to be Mary Alice's age, everyone looked as if they'd just passed their Time of Change. "What would you like to know?"

"He's very dynamic."

Roxy stifled a smile. That was the understatement of the century. "He is. Very."

"And he can't seem to take his eyes off of you."

"Well, I don't know about that."

"He likes you, Roxy," Mary Alice said, giving her wineglass to a waiter who was refilling glasses. "Actually, it's more than just *like*."

"That's a relative term." She grabbed her water glass to give her hands something to do. "None for me, thanks," she told the waiter who then left.

Mary Alice took the tiniest sip of wine, barely enough to wet her lips. "You know, a woman doesn't get to be my age without being able to recognize when a man is in love."

Roxy glanced around and lowered her voice. "Santiago is not in love with me. He's just very convincing." She'd already explained to Mary Alice about their faux relationship and why.

The older woman smiled. "I think you need to open your eyes, Roxy. It's as plain as the nose on your face."

Her face heated and she suddenly felt a little lightheaded. This had happened several times in the past few days. Morning sickness or nerves? "I'm not sure if I'm ready to be in a relationship."

"And why not? You're a vibrant young woman with your whole life ahead of you."

"Are you saying I should pursue a relationship with him? You'd be okay with that?"

Mary Alice frowned as if that was the dumbest thing she'd ever heard. "Honey, I want you to be happy. You do not need to keep living your life in an attempt to keep *me* happy. You've done more for me than you'll ever know. I'm fine. It's time for you to move on, live life for yourself rather than lamenting a past that was never meant to be your destiny."

SANTIAGO GRABBED A stuffed mushroom and a napkin when a waiter walked by with a tray of them. The night was a success, as far as he was concerned, he thought as he glanced around the room. The presentations had gone well and Mary Alice had seemed truly grateful. Agents from Seattle, Portland and Vancouver were stationed at their posts in various locations around the room and more were outside. He hadn't wanted to take any chances with a potential security breach, and so far, things had been going smoothly.

"She's really quite amazing, isn't she?" Santiago turned to see Rand St. James staring in Roxy's direction.

The new field team leader in San Diego was Hollywood handsome with piercing green eyes, a square jawline, and perfect white teeth that looked like a cosmetic dentist's wet dream.

"Who are you talking about?" Santiago knew damned well who St. James was talking about, but he had to act like he didn't. "There must be over a hundred people here." He fought to keep his voice monotone and semidisinterested.

"I'm referring to Roxanne."

Santiago gripped his glass of scotch so hard it was a wonder it didn't snap. He didn't like the sound of her name on the guy's lips.

"I heard that—"

"Yeah, we got married." *So back the fuck away from her.* Until they sorted things out, confirming there was no traitor, St. James didn't need to know the truth.

Mr. Perfect raised one eyebrow. "Interesting." He took a sip of his drink. Santiago started to excuse himself, but the guy started talking again. "Did I tell you that one of the tasks the Council has assigned to me is setting up a West Coast campus of Tracker Academy? I had no idea she was going to be attending this event. I had planned to talk to her in the next few weeks to see if she's interested in transferring over."

Santiago had heard that the Council was toying with opening another branch of the Academy, but he hadn't heard that they'd actually decided on the location. He spotted one of the Seattle area's Council members, on the other side of the room. Why hadn't Trace told Santiago this had been decided yet?

He wanted to reiterate to St. James that they were

married, that they'd have to talk things over together whether she'd accept the position or not, but he kept his mouth shut. It would come out soon enough that it was all a sham anyway.

VENTRA FORCED HERSELF to eat another hors d'oeuvre. About the only thing she could stomach was the steak tartare and sashimi. Anything cooked, especially vegetables, made her want to gag. She subtly adjusted her wig then spritzed on a little more perfume.

Once this was over, she was going to suck half of Seattle dry just to get the taste of human food out of her mouth. But her experiment had worked. She was at a Council event and no one seemed wise to the fact that she was a Darkblood. Having eaten only human food, no blood whatsoever for what felt like forever, she'd begun to smell less like an all-blood drinker and more like a weak-ass Council supporter.

She found their machinations very entertaining. The rules, the procedures. It was mundane and boring. But when they presented that old woman with the sword—Ventra's sword—she had a hard time restraining herself. Not only was that weapon rightfully hers—she'd killed the Guardian who gave it to her—but Santiago announced that he had destroyed her house and all the things that were important to her. Because of him and the efforts of his people, her standing within the Alliance was in jeopardy.

Tossing the cherry from her drink over her shoulder, she drained the glass. She'd eaten enough solid food. The alcohol burned as it went down, but she rather enjoyed it. Perhaps when this was all over, she'd add some of it to her all-blood diet. Or maybe have a blood cocktail.

She watched as he talked to that old woman, while he had his hand on the back of the blond in the turquoise dress. Another male came up to them and she noticed how he subtly put his body between them, like he was protecting the woman, keeping her away from other males. It was clear she was his possession. Someone he cared about.

She smiled to herself, careful not to flash fang, for she knew a woman who was about to make his life much much worse.

CHAPTER TWENTY

MITCH HELD THE phone away from his ear. "I've got Dom on the line. He wants to know how the evening's going. Do you have a minute?"

Santiago had been keeping an eye on two youthlings who looked like they might be up to no good. One whispered into the other's ear and they soon left the foyer where Santiago and a few of his men were standing. "Uh…"

"Want me to tell him you'll call him later?"

"No, I can talk now." He took the phone from Mitch, but before he put it to his ear, he motioned to Kip. "Can you check on those two? It might be nothing, but I don't want to take any chances."

"Yeah, sure." Kip left after the youthlings.

Santiago held the phone up. "Hey, buddy, how are you?"

No answer.

"Hello?" Still no answer. He gave the phone back to Mitch. "The call must've dropped."

Mitch cursed. "I've been having so much trouble with my reception lately, I'm tempted to flush the phone down the toilet."

"Me, too," Jackson said. "But Cordell got me fixed up, right Cordy?"

Cordell finished taking a swig from his beer and wiped his mouth with the back of his hand. "Whatcha got?" Mitch handed the phone over. "Maybe your memory is jacked up. Have you powered it down lately?"

"Yeah, just yesterday."

"Okay, that's good." Cordell swiped his finger over the screen. "Do you have a lot of pictures or videos? Sometimes that will bog things down. Or too many apps."

"You can check, but I don't think so."

"Nope, you don't have half the pictures that some people have. You should see Arianna's phone. It's a mess." He and Jackson exchanged a knowing glance.

As Cordell played with Mitch's phone, Santiago scanned the small crowd. With the official part of the evening over, people had begun to leave already. There was Trace and his fiancée, Charlotte, talking to St. James and another man as they headed toward the main exit doors. He could just see Roxy from here, still near the stage with Mary Alice and a few other women. Another woman in a blue dress was approaching her, so it didn't appear Roxy was anxious to leave yet. Santiago and his agents would wait until everyone was gone before they left as well, although maybe it wouldn't hurt to send a few of them home now.

He turned to say something to them when he noticed that Cordell's face went from chocolate-brown to ash and his mouth was ajar.

Mitch and Jackson started to ask him what was wrong, when he held a finger to his lips. "Nope, everything looks fine. Must be happening because we're inside a building."

He looked at them pointedly then mouthed, "Say something. Normal."

Jackson and Mitch hesitated.

"Okay, that's what I thought," said Santiago, making up a reply.

A waiter carrying a water pitcher walked past them. Cordell grabbed it and promptly dropped the phone into the water.

"What the—"

Mitch lunged for the pitcher but Cordell held it out of his reach and mouthed, "Shut up." Then pointing to Jackson and Santiago, he snapped his fingers and mouthed, "Let me see yours."

"Not if you're going to do that," Jackson said in a loud whisper.

Santiago had no idea what was going on, but it had to be serious. Cordell was not the jokester Jackson was. The two men reluctantly gave him their phones and he started thumbing through the screens.

"Do you know which horse won the Mile?" Cordell asked. "I heard you had money on it again."

Santiago knew this was just small talk. "Yeah, Slew Me Again won by two lengths. You should've seen him come from behind. I won $50 thanks to a tip from Kato. The guy knows his horses."

"Okay, you're both good." Cordell handed their phones back. "Mitch's was the only one affected."

"What the hell's going on?" Santiago shoved his phone into his inside suit pocket.

Mitch's face went blank. "How? Why?"

"He had a hidden app installed on his phone," Cordell explained. "Someone must've gotten access to it somehow."

"That doesn't make sense," Mitch said, almost to himself. "This phone is never off my person."

"Well, someone got it off of you without your knowledge then. From what I could tell, it gave someone the ability to activate the microphone from a remote location."

"You mean, someone could have been listening in on his phone conversations?"

"Not only that but—"

"How…how could I miss a strange icon being displayed?" Mitch ran a hand through his hair and shook his head, clearly still not believing what Cordell was saying. "I'm on that thing all the time."

"That's the problem," Cordell said. "There was no icon. Just the program installed in the phone's operating system."

Santiago glanced around the room. "A listening device? A bug? But we have security measures in place to detect them."

"Yes, sort of, but it used the phone's hardware, so it's not actually a bug that would turn up in routine checks. Much like the applications that use the phone's built-in camera flash to work as a flashlight, this one used the microphone already there. The only thing hidden is the icon because someone didn't want him to know it was there. Not only could Mitch's phone conversations be heard remotely, but I'm imagining other conversations could be heard, as well. Anyplace he's got his phone with him, the individual on the other end could activate the microphone and listen. Have you noticed that it needed to be recharged more often?"

Mitch had a faraway look in his eyes as he stared into space. "That's how they knew." His voice was hoarse, strained. "They knew where we were going to be and what our plans were because of me."

"It would appear so," Santiago said, feeling suddenly like a sitting duck. All of them.

Mitch continued. "If it weren't for me, they wouldn't have known about the warehouse raid. Dom and the others were almost killed because of me."

"Wouldn't be surprised if it utilized GPS coordinates, too, and could track your whereabouts." Cordell held the pitcher of water up to look at the phone. "I can't wait to analyze this further although I don't know how much I'll learn since it's probably ruined, but it's worth a try."

Jackson thumped him on the back. "Look on the bright side, Mitchie. We found that traitor."

Mitch looked like he might throw up.

Santiago's gaze darted around the room. "I've got a bad feeling about this."

"How so?" Jackson asked.

"Darkbloods have been too quiet since we torched the sector mistress's home."

"And?"

"And, no doubt she's been planning to retaliate. Wouldn't you if your home were destroyed and your sweetblood pet taken? This woman is ruthless, bold and relentless. What better way to get back at us than at an event like this with Guardians, Council members and members of the vampire community here? If she's been listening in on Mitch the whole time, she knows every detail about our security plans."

Jackson looked around nervously. "I see what you're saying. So what do we do?"

"We've got to get everyone out of here," Santiago said. "This place is a prime target."

"An evac?" Jackson asked.

"Yes, mobilize all the agents," he said, calling over his shoulder on the way to the podium. "I'll make the announcement, then we get everyone out of here as quickly as possible."

The Guardians scattered.

"What's going on?" Roxy asked, just as Santiago was getting to the stage. "You look worried and—"

"Take Mary Alice and get out of the building. Now. Head back to the field office and wait for me there."

"Why? What's wrong? What about you?"

"I'll be there soon. Just go." He grabbed the microphone, not at all sure what he was going to say. "Ladies and gentlemen, can I have your attention please?"

Ten minutes later, after checking in with all the other

Guardians and finding that everyone, including Roxy and Mary Alice were safely outside the building, he made one last pass through the ballroom to make sure everyone was out.

Good. The place was empty. Maybe Darkbloods, or whoever bugged Mitch's phone, hadn't planned to do anything tonight in the first place. But it was better to be safe than sorry. He heard the sound of silverware and glassware through a small door at the back of the ballroom. Must be the staging area for the wait staff, but he jogged over there to be sure.

When he got back to the field office, he'd put the whole place on lockdown and have Cordell check—

"Well, what do we have here?" a woman's voice crooned.

Before he could spin around, handcuffs snapped around his wrists and ankles and he was forced to the ground. Silver. He felt the energy drain at the same time that he smelled Darkblood stink. With a knee in the center of his back, he struggled as someone duct-taped his mouth and another forced a hood over his head.

"Don't fight the inevitable." Her voice was close to his ear, as if she'd gotten down on her hands and knees. "You're mine now."

Ventra. The Alliance's sector mistress. It had to be.

Her voice reminded him of someone who was trying to calm a chicken right before its head was cut off.

The sleeves of his tuxedo were shoved up and something cold pinched the skin of his forearms. He heard what sounded like a hole punch right before he felt the burn.

Aw, Jesus.

She was spiking his skin with silver—two in each arm—and energy poured out of his system.

He went as limp as a rag doll there on the floor behind the ballroom—he would not be able to move under his own power. Was this what Cordell had felt when he'd been paralyzed in that car crash as a human, unable to move his legs until he'd been transformed during the changeling process?

His thoughts were interrupted when two sets of hands hoisted him up and dragged him down what felt like a narrow corridor. They smelled like Darkbloods, so why didn't Ventra? She smelled only of hair spray and perfume.

When they stopped, the bottom of the hood gaped open for a moment and he could see they were near the service elevators.

He was thirsty—man-in-the-desert thirsty, needing blood so badly that he could almost smell it. Through that small opening, he saw feet, then legs, then blood. They'd killed a human. But he was so weak right now, so desperate, that if he had even an ounce of strength left, he'd have dropped to his knees and lapped it up like a dog.

As Roxy waited at the field office for Santiago and the rest of the Guardians to return, an uneasy feeling began brewing in her gut that she couldn't seem to shake.

After changing into jeans and a T-shirt, she was going to escort Mary Alice back to her room, but her stomach twisted again. She barely made it to the restroom in time. Anxious to get Mary Alice settled so she could go down and wait for everyone, she splashed her face and quickly brushed her teeth. All she knew was that there was a possible security breach at the hotel, but she had no idea what had happened.

"Morning sickness or something else?"

Roxy looked up to see Mary Alice staring at her as she exited the bathroom. "Excuse me?"

"Or maybe a little of both."

She was going to deny it, just like she tried to do with Arianna, who'd guessed the truth as well, but she'd never been good at lying. Seemed she was better at detecting liars than being one. "How'd you know?"

Mary Alice wrapped her arms around her, the hug so strong it forced all the air from her lungs. "Well, for one thing, I could hear you getting sick in there. I'm not deaf, you know. Besides, I just *knew* the two of you were a good match and this proves it." Roxy cringed. "Congratulations, honey. I'm so thrilled for you. And what does Santiago have to say about it?"

Feeling guilty, Roxy wriggled out of the woman's bear-hug grip and slumped into a nearby chair. "Actually, I haven't said anything to him yet. I…I haven't quite come to terms with it myself. But I will."

She quickly told her about Santiago's views on settling down.

Mary Alice looked indignant. "Well, if he's not interested in being a father and—"

"It's not that. I think he's afraid of doing the same thing his father did. He knows what it did to his sister and him. So I want him to know I'm okay doing this myself. He can visit us and the baby and I can visit him."

Mary Alice *tsked* and rolled her eyes. "Then I might have to have a little talk with him."

"No," she said quickly. "Please…just…no. People do it all the time nowadays anyway. I don't want to force him into doing anything. I want a relationship like my parents had and if I can't have that, well…then I don't want one at all."

"If he doesn't want you and this baby, then I want you to move in with me. Ginger's already going to be upset not having a huge estate to roam and explore anymore. And she's getting along so well with Barnabus, even though he still hisses at her once in a while."

"But—" Her phone rang. She grabbed it quickly thinking it was Santiago, but it was Jackson.

"Roxy, is Santiago there with you by any chance?"

"He's still over at the hotel."

There was a pause on the other end of the line. "No, he's not. We're still here and uh…I think something happened."

She jumped to her feet. "What's going on?"

"We found a dead body near the freight elevators. Although I'm no tracker, Santiago's scent is back there along with one or two Darkbloods."

The world stopped rotating on its axis for a moment.

She was instantly transported back to that night in Key West when she couldn't find Ian. "Were there any—" She couldn't even say the word.

"No ashes," Jackson said as if reading her mind. "But we think he was kidnapped."

"I'll be right there." She hung up the phone, shoved her feet into a pair of boots and grabbed her jacket. "Darkbloods have Santiago," she told Mary Alice, "and I'm going to track him." Realizing she had no weapon of her own, she eyed Grim. "Do you mind if I borrow this?"

"Yes, yes, of course."

Twenty minutes later, she was back at the hotel, and Jackson was waiting for her in the ballroom.

"The freight elevator," she barked. "Where is it?"

The moment she got there, she knew. Ignoring the human body, she definitely picked up Santiago's scent and that of two Darkbloods. But there was someone else, too, and this smell was much subtler than the others. Not nearly as pungent. And there was something about it…

As they rode the elevator down, she inhaled deeply, filtering the scents again in an attempt to categorize them better. Two Darkblood males—yes, but then there was the female. Fully blooded from the dead human. Was she a Darkblood? Roxy wasn't quite sure. Maybe. Maybe not. And the scent—except for the gorged-on-blood smell—was somewhat familiar.

Could the Alliance have a sympathizer somewhere in the Council ranks? Someone who wasn't officially a Darkblood, but who subscribed to their beliefs? Such individuals did exist—people who lived the Council lifestyle but who secretly supported Alliance efforts when they could.

Hair spray and…cheap perfume.

Instantly, she recalled a woman at the party wearing a blue dress and coke-bottle glasses. Roxy had been at the buffet table when the woman walked by. All Roxy could think about was how strong her perfume was because it almost made her sick to her stomach. At the time, she had blamed the pregnancy for making her so sensitive, but it must've been the woman. What a horrible mistake she'd made not following her instincts.

"Jackson, are the teams ready to head out? Because Darkbloods definitely have him."

"Yep. We're ready."

The elevator doors opened onto the service entrance and they sprinted down the alley to where the rest of the Guardians were waiting.

"There were two, possibly three others," she said.

"Three? I thought you said there were only two Darkbloods."

"Yes, but there's someone else with them."

"Did they take another prisoner?" Jackson asked. "I could've sworn all the guests have been accounted for."

She told them about the woman.

"A sympathizer," he said through clenched teeth.

"Or the sector mistress."

The Guardians were gathered around several black-panel vans when Jackson and Roxy emerged from the alley.

Gibson stared at her, lines of confusion on his forehead. "What are you doing?"

Before Roxy could say anything, Jackson piped up. "She's tracking them so we can get to Santiago."

"But...you're just his wife."

Yeah, and I'm pregnant so you'd better not mess with me.

"Your point is?"

"You've got to be kidding. Come on, honey, leave the tracking to the experts. Go back to the field office where you belong and wait for us to do our jobs."

Fangs elongating, internal temperature ratcheting up, she was going to rip his throat out and enjoy doing it. "Sorry you didn't get the memo, but I'm coming whether you like it or not."

Suddenly Jackson was between them.

He grabbed Gibson by the collar, shoved him against the side of the building, flashing his own set of fangs. "She's not 'just' anything. She might be the only one who can save him."

CHAPTER TWENTY-ONE

THE LIGHT BURNED. It was everywhere. Though he kept his eyelids pinched shut, the sunlight seared straight through to his eyeballs. No matter which way he turned his head, he couldn't seem to get away from it. His wrists and ankles were shackled with silver, and he was spread-eagle on some hard surface.

"One piece of advice," the woman's voice crooned. "The more you struggle, the faster you expend what little energy you have left. Although I suppose if you want your death to happen faster, please be my guest."

His lips were so cracked he wasn't sure he'd be able to talk. How long had he been here? Judging from experience, he had to have been out in the sun at least five hours now. While he hoped he'd have built up a tolerance to those damning rays from the previous punishments he'd inflicted on himself, he'd never done it with silver spikes in his skin. Each tiny metal piece felt as if it were conducting the UV rays directly into his body. He didn't think he had the strength left to lift his pinkie let alone his whole body.

"If you want to kill me, do it and be done with it."

Ventra laughed. "Ah, he speaks at last."

"Where am I? What is this place?"

"Just one of the dens I have scattered throughout the area."

"Your place?"

"Oh, you thought you'd burn down my house and that would be the last of me? Sorry to ruin your day, but I'm not stupid enough to keep all my eggs in one basket. I didn't get this far up in the Alliance without keeping a few hideouts around that no one knows about."

He heard a rustle of fabric. Was she in a daysuit? Was that why she was able to be out in the sunlight?

"Speaking of my house that you burned down, I know you must've noticed all the bone sculptures."

"They were grotesque…and demonstrate…your in-humanity."

She laughed. "Well, actually, the bones were both human and vampire, so you're only partially correct."

Vampires? His people charcoaled when they were killed by silver. What was she talking about? He heard the sound of fine metal being pulled from a scabbard. Misery? He tried squinting his eyes but it was too bright.

"Why do you think I'm wasting my time killing you slowly like this? I want to preserve your bones. I have a lot of sculptures to replace. Based on my experience and the amount of UV light today, you'll last maybe a few more hours."

Something pierced his thigh. He felt the pressure first, then searing pain. It was Misery.

"You know, I could press right here—" she wiggled the blade and he screamed as white-hot pain shot everywhere "—give it a little whack—I love your weapon, by the way—and sever your femur." She twisted it again and he could feel Misery's point scrape along the bone. "But I need it intact." She withdrew the blade, but the burning sensation remained. "However, I have no need to keep the flesh undamaged."

"They'll find you, you know." His voice was a hoarse whisper.

"How will they do that without a tracker?"

"A tracker?"

"You think I don't know? Your tracker, Lily, is out of the country. By the time your people bring in someone from another area, it will be too late for you, I'm afraid. I'll close up this den and move to another. I'll be long gone with your bones before they find it."

She didn't know about Roxy, then. Thank God they'd kept the reason for her being in Seattle a secret from almost everyone.

"Why are you doing this?"

"Other than to add to my collection? Let me tell you." Another rustle of fabric and a chair squeaked as she sat down. "You and your people are done making me look bad. I've worked many years to get into the position I'm in now and I'm not going to let you take that away from me. I earned this."

"Earned this?"

"It's time that I made *you* look like a fool to your superiors. Why do you think I was so bold back there, snatching you right under everyone's noses? Take the leader out and the group will falter. Do it boldly, and their faith in the system will be shattered."

"You don't know my people then. Taking me out will make little difference. If anything, they'll come after you with a vengeance."

"Will they, or will they simply say good riddance to an ineffectual manager? That sword presentation you did tonight—" Shit. She was there? How did they miss that a Darkblood was in their midst? "—won't be done for you when you're gone, you know. You're too much of a disgrace. Mission after mission foiled, some of your agents almost killed, now you, their leader, taken and killed. No, Santiago, even if they had this fine weapon of yours, they would not be doing that presentation for you."

That wasn't true. He had support from the Council. "The weapon is just a formality. The ceremony can be done just as easily without it."

"It can be, but will they choose to do so in your case? I know a few people on the inside who told me a track record of poor performance would make such a post-humous honor questionable."

It felt as if he'd been punched. "What people on the inside?"

She laughed. "I've been sworn to secrecy and that means I won't even tell a dying man." He heard the rattle of ice in a glass. Oh, God, he was so parched. What he wouldn't give for just one sip.

"You know, I'm surprised you did a presentation for that particular sword—what did you call it? Grim?

Because the Guardian I took it from wasn't exactly a model citizen. He was a Sweet addict."

"And where did you hear that? From the person you bought the blade from?"

"I didn't buy it. He gave it to me in payment for some Sweet right before I killed him."

Despite the evidence, he still didn't want to believe it. "Ian was killed down in Key West. He wasn't addicted to Sweet."

She spat out a bitter laugh. "Don't believe me? I got my start with the Alliance down there. Ian used to buy from me. Quite regularly, in fact. Addicts have a way of lying and bending the truth in order to keep their problem a secret." Using the tip of Misery's blade, she picked at a silver spike embedded in his calf, causing him to shout. "You Guardians think you're so high and mighty, that you're able to resist temptation. But when it comes down to it, you're just as weak as the rest of us. Ian simply decided to stop fighting it."

He was glad Roxy would never know the truth. She had loved Ian once with all her heart. Her memories were all she had of him now and this knowledge would destroy even those.

"I watched his mother all night. Laughed my ass off at the proceedings. If only everyone knew that the man you were honoring was an addict. God, I came so close to yelling it out. I'd have loved seeing the expressions on everyone's faces."

How had she slipped in without anyone knowing a Darkblood was present? Their odor was unmistakable and neither he, nor any of his people had noticed it. Not even Roxy. "How did you avoid detection?"

She groaned and rolled her eyes. "I ate nothing but human food for the past several weeks and didn't once drink human blood. It was awful. After we got what we came for, I drained the first human I saw."

That guy near the elevator.

"Why you do that is beyond me," she continued. "Vampires were meant to feed from humans. It's in our DNA. Why fight it?"

It wasn't the first time he'd heard that argument, he thought as he lost consciousness.

ROXY LOOKED OUT over the ravine, the Tolt River over two hundred feet below them. "He's on the other side."

They'd followed the scent trail all night, but it was clear that Darkbloods had known they would be doing this as there were many dead ends, switchbacks and circular trails. She'd gotten them as far as she could before they had to stop at a safehouse for the day. As soon as the sun dipped below the treetops, they headed out again. It was the longest damn day of her life.

"Holy shit, that's way the hell down there. How did they get across?" Jackson asked, coming up behind her. "Is there a bridge I'm missing?"

She pointed to a small gondola nestled in the trees on the other side of the divide. "They took that."

Gibson stood with his hands on his hips, shaking his head. "We're so fucked." He turned around, a defeatist expression plastered to his face as if he was ready to give up and go home. God, she hated negative people.

"Let's see if there's a control panel or a rope to pull it back across," Tambra said. "Maybe it's as simple as pressing a return button."

"And you're sure he's…still alive?" Mitch asked, worry reflected in his eyes. Roxy knew he felt responsible because the hidden app that fed information to Darkbloods was on his phone. As they were mobilizing the teams at the hotel to track Santiago, he'd asked if he should go.

Jackson had insisted Mitch was part of the team, that the incident hadn't changed anything. "You had no way of knowing that the young woman in the bar was a Darkblood pawn," he'd told his friend. "Besides, what available guy with a johnson wouldn't have taken her up on an offer like that?"

"Yes, I'm certain." Roxy hoped the confidence in her tone would help settle Mitch's guilty conscience. "I tracked the latent scent to get here, but we're close enough to where he's being held and the wind is with us. The scent I'm picking up is a live one."

Hang on, baby. We're almost there.

Something jolted her. A sudden awareness. As if she'd been sleeping and suddenly heard a strange noise at the window or the front door creak open. Her heart cranked from zero to sixty like a horse out of the starting gate.

"Shh," she told herself. *Calm. Relax.*

Using her meditation techniques, she concentrated

inward, shutting out other stimuli for a moment. A warm, content sensation rushed through her body, similar to the one she felt after making love to Santiago when she rested her head on his chest and listened to his heart beating. They completed each other, settled into each other's cracks and crevices, making the other better and stronger than they'd been on their own. She realized now just how much she loved him. He was close and he was alive. She was sure of it.

But before she could rejoice in that fact, she knew he wasn't okay. She could almost picture him, prone on a hard surface, unable to move.

Was he restrained? Was he sleeping? She reached further inside. He was tired. Bone-tired. And in terrible pain. His lips were dry and cracked, his skin red. Good trackers could pick up emotions in the scents they were following, but to get an actual vision of the subject was something she'd never experienced before.

However, she couldn't be sure that this was an accurate assessment or just her overactive imagination at work because she was so worried about him. She'd never been emotionally attached to someone she had tracked before. The scent, his scent, had virtually no energy signature as if it had been sucked right out of him, reminding her of when she'd found him under the UV lights, only worse. Much worse. She was glad she'd thought to bring a few vials of blood along just in case.

Tambra jogged back up the path, a smudge of dirt on her cheek. "No go. It's attached to the other side."

"Shit," Jackson said. "We'll have to find another way around."

"That could be miles away before we can get across," Gibson said.

"I did find these, however." Tambra held up two harnesses, some length of rope and several heavy-duty carabineer clips.

"You don't mean…" Jackson stared wide-eyed as if she were holding a couple of cobras.

"Yep. If someone can get over to the gondola and release it, we'll be in business. Anyone game for a little adrenaline rush?"

Roxy grabbed one and slipped her arms through the straps before Jackson pulled her aside.

"Are you crazy?" he hissed. "What about…you know what?"

Her blood pressure cranked up as she glanced around to make sure no one had heard him. Figured Arianna had told him about the baby. Roxy had confided in her friend, who'd been thrilled, telling her not to say anything until she'd had a chance to tell Santiago.

"Can I at least mention it to Jackson?" Arianna had said.

"Only if he can keep a secret," Roxy told her.

"Listen," she whispered to him now, "I don't plan on dying. And just because I'm pregnant doesn't mean I'm an invalid. If this is the only way to get to Santiago, I'm doing it."

"What's going on?" Sadie said, emerging from the forest as if she'd just jogged up a flight of stairs, not run three miles through the woods. As a changeling, she couldn't shadow move through the darkness like the rest of them could, so she was just getting here. Tambra explained what was going on. "Sweet. I'll go." Sadie grabbed the other harness and put it on as if she'd done it a thousand times.

Roxy didn't know much about the woman, but she'd seen her a few times in the field-office gym. A petite thing who stood no more than five foot four, she took her workouts as seriously as a military bootcamp, logging hours on stair machines and lifting barbells the size of her head. Roxy rarely saw her just hanging out with the other agents. Maybe being a changeling made her feel as if she had something to prove, that she had to fight to demonstrate she was just as capable as the rest of the team.

"You?" Gibson asked, looking the woman up and down.

"Jesus. Do you ever get tired of being a pig?" Tambra asked.

"There's nothing to it." Sadie examined the clips she'd gotten from Tambra then put on a pair of gloves she'd pulled from somewhere. The woman was like a female MacGyver. Or a boy scout—always prepared. "I'll zip line it over to the other side and either send or bring the gondola back for the rest of you. From the looks of it, only two at a time will fit, so you'll need to pair up."

"There," Jackson whispered. "She can go. Not you."

But it would take time to get the whole crew to the

other side and who knew how much time Santiago had left.

"Do I have this on right?" Roxy asked Sadie.

The young woman brightened. "You're game, too?"

Game as in this was fun? An adventure? More like this was an obstacle on the way to her goal and nothing was going to get in her way. "You can deal with the gondola and I'll get a jump start on Santiago's location."

Jackson started to argue again, but Roxy held up a hand, silencing him as Sadie checked everything. She didn't need to hear his "voice of reason," his millions of excuses why she shouldn't go.

"Yep," Sadie said, stepping back and tucking her hair behind an ear. "I'd say you've got it."

Within minutes the two women were at the edge of the ravine. Sadie made sure Roxy was clipped in properly to the overhead cable before she fearlessly climbed to the edge.

"Watch what I do then do the same thing. Wait till I get to the middle, then you can go." She pushed off and zipped along the line.

Although her heart was in her throat, making it hard to swallow, Roxy concentrated on her end goal—getting to Santiago—not the river far below.

"It's not too late to wait," Jackson said, but when Roxy gave him a death stare, he stepped back and said, "Ready?"

"Ready as I'll ever be." She shoved off instantly and was hanging on a thin wire, soaring hundreds of feet above the raging river. The wind, laced with icy rain, whipped her hair around and hit her face like tiny needles. At the center of the line where it dipped the lowest, she came to a halt, the momentum unable to carry her upward to the other side. Panic shot through her and her mind froze for a moment.

"Hand over hand," Sadie called from the other side. "That's what I had to do." Roxy must've been so focused on getting herself in gear that she hadn't paid attention to what Sadie was doing.

Don't look down. Don't look down.

A warm feeling came over her then, as if Santiago had wrapped his arms around her, showing how much he believed in her. *Okay,* she thought, huffing out a steamy breath of air. *I can do this thing.* Thank God someone had given her a set of gloves to wear because she advanced hand over hand all the way to the far side and didn't look down once. No use freaking herself out more. Sometimes the truth, no matter how real it was, didn't need to be acknowledged.

"Great job," Sadie said, pulling her up, a huge grin plastered to her face. "What a freaking trip that was, huh? I haven't done that in ages."

"Yeah," she said mindlessly, high-fiving Sadie's raised hand. All she wanted to think about now that she was back on solid ground was getting to Santiago, not how her life had flashed before her eyes while being suspended zillions of feet above a river. She fumbled with the harness and double-checked Grim.

You with me, buddy? You're charcoaling Darkblood tonight.

She eyed the contraption Sadie was messing with. The term *gondola* was somewhat of a misnomer. It was basically just a metal cage with moss growing on the top, held to the cables by a few rusty pulleys. It didn't look promising. "Is that going to work?"

"We had something similar on our property growing up, so I'm familiar with them. Besides, it's been used recently. Someone oiled a few of the moving parts."

She peered back over the chasm. Jackson paced back and forth. Tambra and Mitch watched with their arms crossed. Gibson was busy tossing sticks over the side. "Think you can handle it from here?"

"Go on ahead," Sadie said, her fingers covered with grease from the pulley. "I'll send this thing over for the rest of them and the gang will be right behind you."

"You're a good egg, Sadie." The moment she said it, she laughed at herself. Jesus, was she getting old or what? That was something Mary Alice had said about her not long ago. She cast a grateful look over her shoulder before she melded with the shadows and moved through the forest.

Santiago's scent was strong now—she could almost feel his energy thrumming in her veins. Blood bonds, while not common, could happen when compatible couples shared blood and sometimes one's latent abilities became heightened. Or at least, that was what she'd taught her beginning tracker classes. Vampire physiology and history was a required course. Although Lily was the only individual she knew who'd actually experienced this. Before her friend had confided in her, Roxy didn't know that such a thing was really possible, that it was real and not just the stuff of legends. Not only did Lily and Alfonso share their thoughts, but Lily had told her how her tracker senses had intensified since sharing that bond with him.

Roxy recalled what had happened at the coffee shop with Arianna and George. Being able to detect a lie wasn't something she'd been expecting. Maybe her intuitive abilities had increased because Santiago's blood awakened something inside of her. They certainly had shared a lot of blood. More than she had with Ian or anyone since. Maybe that explained the ease with which she got pregnant.

"I've been blessed with a good union," she'd heard her father say to her mother when they celebrated the last wedding anniversary before he died. "I'm a lucky man."

"Even with only two youthlings?" Roxy's mother had dreamed of having a large family and had been disappointed when no more children came.

With an exasperated sigh, her father set down his glass and pulled her mother in close. "Having one for each hand is about as perfect as it gets. A man should want no more children than he can look after."

Roxy and her brother, Noah, had been hiding under the dining room table and giggled when their parents kissed. Her father's laugh sounded somewhat like a sonic boom as he reached down and pulled the kids onto his lap. He let them each have a bite of the dessert their mother had made for the occasion. Even though the memory was almost a century old, it was still so vivid that Roxy could almost taste the berries and sugared pastry now as she shadow moved through the trees.

Her mother and father had an incredible love for each other and their union was definitely a good one, but could a union still be considered good if the love was one-sided? Their society said it was, but she didn't think that was enough for her. She wanted more. She wanted what her parents had and she didn't want to settle for less.

No doubt everyone would think hers and Santiago's would be a good and fruitful pairing. Too bad he didn't feel the same way.

Even though it didn't make sense—Santiago was brash, hot-tempered and swore like a multi-lingual sailor—she loved him. Apart, they seemed so different, but together... Well, they just worked. Or at least, that's how she felt. He'd made it clear he wasn't interested in getting married or starting a family. Ever. And because she wanted what her parents had, she wasn't about to force him.

At least times had changed and society's rules had loosened. She could raise a child on her own. Human women had been doing that for several decades now and she'd always considered herself to be pretty damn capable. When Lily had found herself pregnant that was exactly what she'd done, even though she'd received a lot of pressure from her parents. She didn't want to enter into a loveless relationship, so she fought their society's conventions. It hadn't been easy, but then what worthwhile things in life *were* easy? If Lily could do it with a family who disagreed with her, then surely Roxy could do it with no family telling her what to do. It wasn't like Noah was going to turn up after all these years. Last she heard, he was in Eastern Europe somewhere.

Fifty feet in front of her the forest thinned out. She slowed her pace and stopped at the edge of a large clearing. Evergreen trees that came no higher than her chin grew in neat little rows stretching as far as she could see. Was this a Christmas tree farm or land reforestation after a clearcut? They'd passed a few places like this along the side of the mountain road and that was what Jackson had told her.

Staying within the cover of the forest, she moved along the perimeter. The scent was getting stronger but she couldn't see a structure of any kind. Either he'd been taken underground or the place was cloaked. She sent a quick text to Jackson with her location.

As an owl hooted in the distance and crickets chirped in the bushes, she debated her options. If the place was cloaked, someone could be watching from inside the force field and she'd never know it. They'd spot her as she ran through the clearing and take her out before she knew what had hit her. And if that didn't happen and she was able to make it, breaking through shouldn't be a problem—even if it was set to maximum. But who knew what awaited her on the other side? A Darkblood could be standing there, ready to take her out with one chop of a blade. If they were holding Santiago underground, then there may be only one entrance, making an intruder like her easy to detect. God, these options sucked.

She inhaled the cold air slowly, filtering each of the scents and going over what she knew. The night smelled of Darkblood, but something about it had been bothering her the whole time she'd been tracking it.

Roxy reached into one of her pockets. *Please let it be there.* But she felt nothing. Shit. Of course it wouldn't be there. She'd left the pawn shop ring in another coat pocket back at the field office. But she couldn't shake the feeling that she was tracking the same woman.

As she waited for the team to arrive, she pulled Grim from beneath her jacket, careful not to make a sound, and she took a deep whiff. Just solvents and clean cotton and *Santa Muerte* silver. No Darkbloods.

She debated from which angle they should approach the cloaked area and her phone vibrated with a text from Jackson.

Gondola broke. Trying to fix. Don't go in without us.

Shit. Her heart hammered in her chest and it had nothing to do with her recent run through the trees. They were still back at the ravine? She'd figured they'd almost be here by now. She debated asking which side of the river they were on, but she decided it wasn't important. She couldn't wait a minute longer to go in for Santiago.

Hurry. I'm going in now.

Jackson would be pissed, but that was his problem.

She'd have to take the direct approach and hope that no one spotted her. Pulling out one of the smaller blades she'd armed herself with from the panel van, she took one step into the tree farm when she heard a rustle in the bushes to her left. Holding herself perfectly still, she tried not to stir anything around her. A twig cracked and the crickets quieted. Shit. Who was there?

It was as if the entire forest was holding its breath as well, waiting.

One heartbeat. Two.

And then a young buck took a few steps into the clearing. She'd been so focused on tracking Santiago and sifting through Darkblood scent that she hadn't been paying attention to the various animal scents around her. The buck raised his head and looked straight at her, chewing on a few pieces of grass hanging from his mouth. His golden coat shimmered in the moonlight as he took a few more graceful steps into the tree farm. She caught a glimpse of a doe and fawn in the thick forest behind him. Even amidst all this chaos, life could be simple and beautiful if you just knew where to look.

A shot rang out, piercing the calm like a pin to an overinflated balloon. The sound shocked her back into action. Roxy flattened herself against a tree before the echo had faded. They'd seen her. The element of surprise was gone. Bushes and branches snapped around her as the deer evidently ran off.

Now what? If she waited for the others, Santiago's captors could execute him. Her only hope was to keep going. It would take them a moment to figure out she was by herself. Maybe she could—

Movement to her right caught her attention. The buck. He took one step and fell.

Whooping laughter erupted from somewhere straight ahead, then, as she watched, the force field cracked and disappeared. There, not fifty feet away, sat a beat-up mobile home, the no-frills kind that contractors used. And on top of it, sitting in two metal lawn chairs, were two Darkbloods, both armed with shotguns.

"I got him."

"That was a fucking nice shot."

"Yeah, it was, wasn't it?"

The door jerked open and Roxy could see someone's head. A woman. Oh, Jesus. It was the same one from the gala with the hair spray and perfume. Was this Ventra?

"What the hell are you two idiots doing?" She sounded nothing like Roxy had expected. At the gala, she could've sworn she'd heard the woman speak with a British accent, but this was pure American trailer park. It was as if she were a chameleon, able to blend in to various situations.

"We shot a buck. A three point."

"Yeah and you probably alerted any Guardians in the area that someone's here. Did you even think about that?"

As they argued, Roxy knew she didn't have much time. If she waited to cross the clearing when the cloaking field went back up, she'd be a sitting duck, just like that deer. Her only chance to get inside was if she acted now, while they were distracted and arguing. There'd definitely be no waiting for the rest of the group now.

.Following the shadows at the base of the nearest row of trees, she moved like the wind toward the back of the trailer. When she got within ten feet, a snap of electricity charged the air. She dived inside as the cloaking perimeter became active again.

She crouched near a trash can that smelled like blood. Santiago's blood. Clothes or towels maybe, soaked in it. She ground her teeth. *Don't focus on the negative,* she told herself. Only the positive. This meant he was close. She could feel his presence as clearly as if she were looking upon his face. He'd been tortured, yes, but the nature of his scent was a live one and it was coming from inside the trailer. If only there was a back window or some way to sneak in, but there was nothing, just an unbroken expanse of dirty yellow siding. She concentrated on him now and could feel his pain in tiny pinpricks all over her skin, as if it were coming from her own body.

When she got her hands on that woman, justice would be swift. Grim would be getting a workout tonight.

Roxy? Is...is that you?

Santiago? She could hear him as if he'd just spoken aloud but the words had gone straight into her head.

Where are you? Who is with you?

I'm here. At the trailer. Jackson and the rest of the team will be here soon.

Stay away, Roxy. The place is...

The front door banged shut with a metallic clank and the whole trailer shivered as the woman went back inside. Santiago's voice faded from her mind despite her best efforts to renew the connection.

"Bitch," one of the guys on the roof whispered. The lawn chair squeaked as he sat down again.

"Shut the hell up. She'll hear you."

The first one made a sound of disgust. "That's one fine-looking buck over there. Couldn't just let it walk around without taking the shot. I couldn't help myself."

As the two continued to whisper/argue, Roxy noticed a shadow from the tall trees lying across the side of the trailer. Fighting while in shadow form was difficult, but not impossible. She melded with the darkness again and slipped up the side of the trailer.

She was on the roof now. In one movement, she stepped forward and swung Grim hard. It flashed in the moonlight right before the tip penetrated through flesh and bone. Instantly, the first guy started to charcoal.

"Whaat…"

The second one didn't have time aim his rifle before Grim struck him in the chest. He was able to get off a shot right before the heart muscle was pierced, but it went above her head and into the trees. His body fell off the roof and began to charcoal just outside the front door.

"You idiots. I told you to—"

Roxy swung off the roof, feetfirst into the trailer, hitting Ventra in the chest with her boots. They came down on the floor together. The woman rolled to her right and something flashed silver. A blade.

Roxy dipped as a blade sailed past her ear.

"Well, what have we here?" Ventra crouched like a cat ready to spring and stared at Grim as Roxy held the blade out in front. "Ah, I see you brought my weapon back to me."

It made her sick to her stomach that Ventra ever considered Ian's blade as her own. "You may have had it in your possession once, but it does not belong to you. Whoever you bought it from was not the rightful owner."

She slashed it in an arc, which was difficult in this cramped space, but the woman sidestepped away.

"How do you know *I'm* not the rightful owner?"

"Because it belonged to Ian O'Grady and I was with him when he commissioned it to be made."

The woman tilted her head, her white-blond hair framing her face like a frizzy halo. "Ian O'Grady," she repeated. "Up until last night at the gala, I hadn't thought about Ian in years."

Roxy was stunned. Ventra actually knew Ian?

"Oh, you didn't know the two of us were acquainted?"

"Impossible. He was my fiancé. That is, unless he tried to kill you once and you got away."

The woman threw her head back and laughed. "Ah, he didn't tell me he was engaged. Funny thing is, when men are fucking women they shouldn't, they fail to mention little details like that."

It felt as if someone had reached inside her belly, rearranged everything, then pulled it all out. Even though she physically ached, her mind wouldn't accept Ventra's confession. Ian would never have cheated on her, and especially not with a Darkblood. "You're lying."

"Am I? People are willing to do all sorts of nasty things to feed their own addiction. Lie. Cheat. Steal. Fuck."

Roxy's eyes blurred with rage. She shook her head to clear her vision then lunged. Ventra sidestepped her again and swung her blade. Roxy heard the rip of fabric before she felt the sting. Shit. It was silver. Energy leaked out of her, but at a rate that told her it wasn't *Santa Muerte* silver. That would buy her a little more time.

"He would never have done something like that."

The woman's laugh was harsh. "Then you didn't know him like I knew him. He was desperate for some Sweet so he gave me his prize possession—that knife you're holding. Grim. Such a fitting name for a weapon that delivers the bleakest possible outcome for its opponent. Remember that long scar down the inside of his thigh?"

Roxy almost choked. Ian had been gone for weeks on Agency business shortly before his death and when he returned, he had that long silvery scar. "A nasty fight with a vicious Darkblood," he'd told her when she'd asked him about it. If only her senses were as acute then as they were now...

"I gave it to him," Ventra whispered. "Things used to get a little rough when we were in bed. I liked to feed from him that way."

She wanted to call Ventra a liar but the bitter taste on

her tongue never materialized. That little voice in her head that whispered *liar* was silent. So Ian hadn't been faithful either. But with…with this horrible woman? The enemy? Thank God the man was dead. If he wasn't, Roxy would've killed him herself.

Ventra continued. "That's why it's one of my favorites."

Roxy darted her gaze to the right. Santiago had to be behind one of the doors in the short hallway. She needed to keep the woman talking until the others got here. She had no illusion that she could take the woman down herself without the element of surprise. "Your favorite? Then you sure have a strange way of showing it. Why the hell would you have it at a pawn shop?"

Discomfort flashed in the woman's eyes before they narrowed to slits. "You…ah…saw it there?"

Busted. Roxy was so done with this. The woman. Ian's lies. Everything.

She lurched forward and thrust the blade. Ventra arched her back into a C-shape, narrowly avoiding Grim's point again. Damn.

Roxy's energy still hadn't recovered and desperation threatened to unravel her. Where was her team? Shouldn't they be here by now? She wasn't sure how much longer she could last. "Where is he? What have you done with him?"

"Santiago? Oh, he's here. He hasn't told me what I need to know yet, but he will. Especially now that his *wife* has arrived." She said it like a dirty word. "I'd say that's the ultimate leverage."

What specific information was Ventra trying to get from him or did it even matter? As the region commander, he had knowledge his enemies would kill for. "He'll never cave."

The woman's smile was one of the evilest Roxy had ever seen. "He'll bend all right. Just like Ian did. Let's see. Were you the girlfriend in London, Key West or Milan? He spoke highly of all three of you."

A bitter taste instantly filled her mouth. The woman was lying. She was attempting to shake Roxy up but Roxy wasn't biting. The knowledge that she could see through this woman's lies bolstered her confidence.

"You're sadly mistaken about so many things. Namely, Santiago and I were never married. It was just a sham in order to find the source of the leak and we did. What have you done with him?"

Insecurity appeared momentarily across the woman's face then, just as quickly, it was gone. "Let's just say that I was really pissed off at him and took out some of my frustrations. I'm feeling much better now. Does it bother you that I've got another one of your men right where I want him?"

Roxy lunged again. Grim was heavier now as she swung it. Something flashed, clanked against her blade. Grim flew out of her hand, hit the floor and spun away.

The woman jumped at her. Roxy tried to move, but her foot caught on the edge of something and she tripped. Like a vulture, the woman fell on her chest and pressed her blade to Roxy's throat. Just the feel of the silver on her skin weakened her further.

"How many are with you?"

"What?" Roxy croaked.

"How many of your little Guardian friends will be knocking at my door?" She let the tip of the blade dig into Roxy's flesh. More energy poured out and her hands dropped from the woman's shoulders.

"A dozen or more are coming." A slight exaggeration maybe. But would they get here in time?

Roxy? What's going on?

Thank God, Santiago was still alive. Had he been unconscious? Was that why she hadn't heard him again till now?

I'm sorry, Santiago. I'm not a trained fighter anymore. I'm just a teacher. She's more skilled than me.

She felt a pulling deep inside her body and her fingers flexed. A faint *snick* sounded off to her right. Ventra didn't seem to notice it because she raised her weapon over her head, ready to land a death blow.

Something touched Roxy's hand.

It was Grim. She didn't ponder how that had happened. With the last of her strength, she grabbed it and swung hard, just as the woman's arm came down. A sizzle and dull thud sounded as the blade made contact.

Ventra screamed. "Fucking bitch." She fell backward, holding her arm at a strange angle as blood poured from the wound.

Had the limb been severed? Roxy pulled herself up using the edge of the counter.

The woman's gaze darted around the room. With an awkward, shuffling gate, Ventra retrieved a dirty towel near the sink and held it to her arm. Roxy saw a flash of white. Bone?

She needed to get the woman to leave. If she attacked, Roxy wasn't sure she had the strength to lift the heavy sword again. "I'll bet you're tired, your energy seeping out quickly. Much more quickly than me since Grim is made from *Santa Muerte* silver. Frankly, I'm surprised you're still standing. Guardians will be here any moment and if you're still here, justice will be swift and merciless."

"Justice? What is justice?" The woman spat the words like chewing tobacco. "Is it upholding laws… that not all of us believe in? Is it…penalizing those… who chose to live our lives honestly, as we were meant to live? I don't call that justice. I call that tyranny."

Roxy couldn't hide her disgust. "Tell that to the man you killed at the hotel or to the sisters you just abused, because what they experienced was about as far from justice as you can get."

"I'm not…talking about humans." The woman peeked at her injury under the rag and hissed. "What's a few of their lives anyway? They're able…to reproduce and repopulate…more quickly than we are. They're like…goddamn rabbits. And just as expendable."

"There's the difference between me and you. I don't consider humans to be animals."

Reaching one-handed for her weapon, the woman stumbled again and the blade skidded under the banquette seat.

"It's getting worse, isn't it? You know, I've experienced acute silver poisoning before myself." When she'd been a Guardian in training many years ago, it was a requirement for all rookies. "First there's intense pain that radiates outward from the injury. Then it's followed by severe muscle weakness and lethargy. Am I right?"

"Fuck you."

"Then confusion sets in, and paranoia. You don't know what's real and what's fake. Sometimes there are hallucinations. Soon, you're not going to be able to walk, or maybe you're past that stage now."

Roxy's phone vibrated in her pocket. Jackson? She started to reach for it but winced.

The woman froze, her eyes as wide as dinner plates.

"Yeah, you guessed it. My backup has arrived." Roxy had no idea if this were true or not. For all she knew it could be Jackson texting to tell her they were still having problems getting across the ravine.

With a defeated hunch to her shoulders, the woman stumbled to the open door, blood soaking her sleeve and dripping on the vinyl floor.

She paused, looking out beyond the dim light from the trailer. "This isn't over," she said without turning around. "I didn't get…where I'm at…without knowing when to retreat." Then she disappeared into the night.

If only Roxy had the strength to go after her, but at least she knew the woman probably wouldn't get far. When the Guardians did arrive, she'd be easy to track with all that blood.

The air inside the tiny trailer was cold. Almost dead. Her head throbbed as she tried to walk.

Santiago? Where are you? How had he moved Grim to her hand like that?

Maybe her blood had given him heightened abilities, as well.

But she heard nothing from him.

"Santiago?" she called aloud this time.

Still nothing.

Oh, God, was he gone? She reached inside herself but no longer felt his energy stirring in her veins. Tears poured down her cheeks as she hobbled through the tiny kitchen, following his scent. He must have used the last of his strength to help her.

An acrid smell filled the air and an orange light glowed outside the grimy window. In what was undoubtedly her own brand of justice, the woman had set the place on fire.

CHAPTER TWENTY-TWO

SANTIAGO PULLED AT his restraints, but they didn't give. He tried to summon the last of his energy to direct Roxy to him, but there was nothing left to draw from.

He wanted to find her, throw his body over hers and protect her, but he couldn't move. Never had he felt so helpless. It was one thing when it was just your own life at stake. You could fuck up all you want. But it was a completely different scenario when it involved the life of the woman you loved.

Another crash sounded, but this time the whole trailer shook. Ventra had set charges all around the place. He'd tried to warn Roxy, but either she hadn't listened to him or didn't hear. He didn't feel the heat yet, but then maybe it was because he was so numb that he couldn't feel anything anymore.

"Jesus H, Santiago."

Jackson? Either that or the gates to hell were staffed by someone who could be his twin.

"I'm here, buddy. Let's get these things off you and get you out of this place."

Something touched his arms, then the chains binding his wrists and ankles clanked to the ground.

"Roxy." His voice was hardly more than a whisper. "Is she…?"

"Don't worry," Jackson said. "We have her."

As strong arms hoisted Santiago up off the hard floor, a million mallets pounded inside his skull. The silver spikes Ventra had painstakingly embedded into his skin dug in anew as Jackson carried him out of the trailer, every footstep jostling a fresh round of agony. It was his last sensation before everything went black.

"IS HE GOING TO BE OKAY?"

Soft lips touched his forehead and he smelled eucalyptus oil. Roxy either had it on her skin or she'd burned a candle. The rhythmic sound of a monitor beeped to his left, while her relaxation music played somewhere near his right. He inhaled deeply and the knots in his muscles loosened.

"Yes, he's going to be fine." He didn't need to open his eyes to know that was Dr. DeGraff. He must be up at the region medical center. "He's lost a lot of blood and energy and we removed dozens of silver spikes, but he'll be back to his old self in no time."

Roxy's warm breath flitted across his cheek. She was close. He turned his head slightly toward her and instantly felt her lips against his.

"See?" Dr. DeGraff said. "He's doing better already."

"Is there anything I can do to help him? Ease some of the pain?"

"It's clear that you have a calming effect on him and

I'd imagine your blood would as well, but I know you've given him a lot already."

She had? He licked his parched lips and tasted the familiar tang.

"Do you think it will be okay to give him more, considering—"

How much had he taken? She'd been injured as well and he didn't want to jeopardize her own recovery.

"Just limit him to a few sips and you should be fine. Are you eating well and getting plenty of rest? I don't want you to overdo things."

"I'm feeling much better, but I can't believe how famished I've been."

Thank God, he thought. If being hungry was the extent of her problems, then she must be fine.

"That doesn't surprise me." The doctor gently patted his foot. "Thanks for literally going out on a wire to save him. Despite his tirades and hotheadedness, we love him around here. He's the glue that holds this place together. I don't know what we'd do without him."

After Dr. DeGraff said goodbye and left, he could've sworn Roxy exhaled and said, "Me, too."

His eyelids and hands were leaden. Although he desperately wanted to see her, hold her, his muscles wouldn't listen to his brain, but he must've made a noise.

"Shh. I'm here, Santiago," Roxy's voice purred in his ear. "I'm not going anywhere."

Lips brushed his forehead again and then her wrist was at his mouth. He didn't make a conscious effort to feed from her, but instinct took over, knowing his body needed this. His fangs elongated, and when they sank into her fragrant skin, she let out a little breath that fluttered across his face. In one heartbeat, her blood was filling his mouth.

"That's it. There you go," she said soothingly, running her fingertips along his scalp as he swallowed.

For the briefest moment, the thought occurred to him that her blood tasted slightly different than it had before, but he promptly forgot as he swallowed again.

CHAPTER TWENTY-THREE

SANTIAGO STOOD AT the window of region headquarters, staring at the dark wilds of British Columbia spread out below him. Tiny beacons of light winking in the darkness drew his attention away from the turmoil in his gut. A marine vessel moved steadily across the inky black of Horseshoe Bay. Everything looked so quiet and peaceful from up here, as if its purpose lay in its very existence at this precise moment in time. Not yesterday, not tomorrow, but right now. Even the flashing lights of a fire truck heading into town on the far side of the bay seemed orderly, defined and grounded in the present. All that serenity stood in stark contrast to the dilemma raging inside him.

"You've got to tell her," Dom said from the couch behind him.

In the window's reflection, he saw Dom rub his shoulder and wince. The regeneration process could be long and painful, especially when it involved joints or whole limbs. Dom was lucky in that he didn't lose the arm in the explosion, but his shoulder and elbow had been shattered.

"If you respect her." Alfonso was rubbing some sort of furniture oil on the bookshelf, trying to repair the damage from Santiago's last tirade, which seemed like eons ago now. Even though he and Lily had just returned from their trip, Alfonso never hesitated to fix or adjust something, no matter how menial, when he saw that it needed to be done.

Jackson propped his boots on the coffee table, grabbed a sandwich from his pocket, and took a bite. Good to know the guy was making himself at home. "Yeah, it's only fair."

Santiago spun around to face his three closest friends. Why didn't they understand his position? Did they not know what he was going through? "Fair. What is fair? Telling someone that the love of her life was a loser and an addict? Why should I do that? It will only tarnish her memory of him. What good does that do?"

"She deserves to know the truth," Jackson said, chewing.

"How she processes the information should be her decision, not yours." Dom took a swig from his beer, a direct violation of Dr. DeGraff's no alcohol orders during his recovery process.

The old familiar rush of anger filled him from top to bottom. At first, he wanted to punch something, hear something break.

But then he took a deep calming breath and recalled the soothing, almost hypnotic sound of Roxy's voice, the feel of her fingers as she massaged him.

Imagine you're on a beach, your toes in the sand. The water comes in, laps at your feet, then goes back out again. Millions of little air bubbles fizzle and pop on the sand around you. A tiny crab scurries for shelter under a smooth stone. The next wave barely reaches your toes. And the next one doesn't even touch you. Gradually, slowly, just like the tide, these knots of tension, frustration and anger loosen inside you. Release them into the water to be taken out to sea. And as the tide goes out, all that's left on the beach is a calm, relaxed you.

Only then did he realize how much he had changed. Even though many things still pissed him off, he seemed better able to handle his reaction. Roxy's methods had been working. He'd even been listening to that music of hers while in his office and he kept a scented candle on his desk.

Santiago drained his glass in one swallow, the scotch giving him a nice burn all the way down. "You didn't see her or Mrs. O'Grady at the awards ceremony, Alfonso. They were so proud of Ian and his accomplishments. His mother is going to put Ian's Guardian blade in a place of honor at her house. She'll call her friends. Have a private get-together where she brags about his accomplishments all those years ago. They'll drink tea, wine, talk about the good old days. Time has softened the pain of losing her son so now all she has are her memories. It would devastate both of them to know that Ian was a Sweet addict who sold his sword to a Darkblood for a hit."

"They should still be proud of him," Alfonso said. "As a Guardian, I'm sure he had many accomplishments."

Santiago couldn't expect Alfonso to understand. He'd once been addicted to Sweet himself.

"Well, you do what you have to do." Jackson licked the remnants of his peanut-butter-and-honey sandwich from his fingers. "But I think you should be honest with her. She's a big girl. Wouldn't you want to know if the tables were turned?"

If the situation were reversed, it wouldn't matter what he'd want. He was trying his damnedest to put himself in her shoes, and this news would devastate her. "Consider this. Don't you think a tiny part of her would always wonder if I made it up to get her to stop loving him?"

So that she'd love me instead.

Dom set down his beer bottle with a *clunk* and eased back on the couch. "So you love her then."

"Yes. No." Santiago grabbed for the bottle of scotch but it was empty. *Shit.*

"What are you really afraid of?" Alfonso didn't look up. Instead, he continued rubbing a cloth over the wood as if he could wipe away all of Santiago's wrongs with a little elbow grease.

"I'm not afraid of anything." Santiago slammed the glass down, splashing what was left of its contents on the table. "It's an age-old strategy. Disparage your opponent in order to make yourself look better. Well, I'm not doing it. I don't know how or why he got addicted. All it takes is one taste and suddenly that's all you can think about. You give up everything you once held dear just for another hit and that's what happened to him. It isn't pretty. You, of all people, should know that, Alfonso."

Alfonso turned to face him, his expression flat, his eyes dark. "Don't make this about me, my friend. You're dancing around the issue and you know it."

"I don't know what you're talking about."

"Your opponent?" Alfonso asked. "That's an interesting way to describe Ian. What are you competing with him for? Some kind of posthumous prize?"

"The dude is dead," Jackson said.

"Exactly." Santiago strode back to the window and watched another boat cross the bay. "A relationship between Roxy and me will never work in the long run. We're like oil and water. She and I are completely different."

"I wouldn't be so sure." Jackson scratched his belly.

"If I didn't know better," Alfonso said quietly, "I'd say you're in love with a woman for the first time in your life, and that scares the hell out of you."

"Let me tell you," Dom said. "Love can be scary, but so. Damn. Worth it."

"I'm…I'm…"

He pressed his forehead against the cool windowpane and closed his eyes. He wanted to deny it, but he couldn't. The truth was he did love her. More than he ever thought possible. His heart ached when she wasn't near him. He was a better man because of her and he wasn't sure how he'd manage without her.

"Tell her," Alfonso said gently. "She needs to know how you feel about her."

After the men left, Santiago got drunk as he watched boat after boat cross the bay.

MITCH THREW THE last of his things into a duffel and walked down the halls of the Seattle field office for the final time. God, he hoped he didn't run into anyone because he hated goodbyes. He didn't want to explain himself. He'd been doing that a lot lately and didn't have the stomach for it any longer. Everyone meant well, or at least most of them did.

"It wasn't your fault, Mitchie."

Then whose fault was it that one of the best field team leaders was almost killed?

"It could've happened to any of us."

But it didn't.

"Cordell found the app on a few other phones. It wasn't just you."

Yeah, but I'm the only Guardian. I should've known better. I'm trained to notice when something's not right. They're not.

For the billionth time he replayed the scenario in his head. The bar. The waitress. Her seduction. That shitty motel room.

He should've known something was wrong. What the hell happened to his instincts? His good sense? Looking back, he could see now how nervous the young woman—Cosette—had been. She'd been awkward and shy in the tub as if it were a new experience for her. She hadn't been a virgin, but it was clear she wasn't well versed either. Her lack of confidence should've been a red flag. He should've seen it as an act, that it wasn't natural for her to come on to a perfect stranger like she had. But no, all he'd cared about was that she was hot and she wanted to have sex with him. He'd been blind to all the rest.

To think that Darkbloods—correction, Ventra—were in the next room, screwing with his phone the whole time practically made him sick. It still did.

Jesus! How could he have missed that?

A better man, a better Guardian would've noticed.

Well, no more.

His footsteps echoed in the passageway, solemnly marking his departure. Things had been pretty dead around here lately and that suited him just fine. He'd just as soon not run into anyone right now. Chances were, no one would even notice he was gone anyway.

Santiago had needed medical treatment after they rescued him from the trailer, so Jackson and Roxy had taken him up to region headquarters. Dom was still recovering but should be back to the field office soon. That is, if there was a field office after this. He'd heard rumors that given this latest breach in security, the Council was considering shutting the office down completely.

His part in that potential outcome had been the last straw. There was no place for him at the field office any longer. Or as a Guardian, for that matter. He'd proved himself to be incompetent and ineffective and it was time to move on. To where, though, he had no idea. It wasn't as if he could go home.

Stepping into the elevator, he pushed *Lobby* and leaned against the back wall, grateful that he hadn't run into anyone. He didn't want to hear someone's opinion why he wasn't a loser and how he shouldn't be leaving. That he was indeed a valuable member of the team and very talented. Bullshit. He knew the truth.

A clean break without any drama was what he needed. He'd find his own place in the world.

But just as the elevator doors started to close, a hand shot out and they opened again.

Wearing black cargo pants, boots and some sort of bizarre harness over an Army Ranger sweatshirt, Sadie walked in.

He groaned internally.

"There you are," she said. "Cordell's been looking for you."

"Why?"

"He's replacing all of our cell phones with new ones. Installed another layer of security or something to prevent what happened to you from happening again."

"Good."

She tucked her short hair behind an ear. "Where are you going?"

"Nowhere."

"Then what's that?" She indicated his duffel.

"Some of my stuff."

Folding her arms over her chest, she stared at him. He averted his gaze and watched the elevator panel instead.

"You're leaving, aren't you?"

He shrugged. "Maybe. Maybe not."

She hesitated a moment as if she were trying to figure out what else to say. "Listen, you're not still pissed off that Ventra got away from us, are you?"

He huffed out a breath but didn't reply. While the others were helping with Santiago and Roxy, he and Sadie had tracked Ventra to the highway. She was bleeding a lot, but it evidently hadn't slowed her down enough and she'd escaped anyway.

"You're fast. Much faster than me." He noted a faint tinge of regret in her tone. It always bothered her that as a changeling, her abilities didn't match up to a born vampire's. "But even you can't outrun a Ferrari."

Another reason he was a dismal failure as a Guardian. Gravely injured, their enemy should've been easy to catch. He'd have gladly staked her himself, given what she'd done to humiliate him.

"I'm leaving the Agency," he said flatly.

Sadie exhaled and didn't say anything for a few moments. When she spoke, her voice was soft. "How can I get in touch with you?" The two of them had hooked up in the past, but neither of them had romantic inclinations toward the other.

"You can't."

"But—"

"It's time I moved on, Sadie. It was good while it lasted. There's no room for me any longer. Especially if things are in a state of upheaval. I don't want them to manufacture a job for me just because."

She fastened and unfastened one of the harness closures, the repetitive clicking noise the only sound inside the elevator for a moment. "Where are you going to go?"

"I'm not sure yet."

She pulled out a scrap of paper and scribbled a phone number. "I'd very much like to stay in touch. I know of some... Well, when you're ready, give me a call. Okay? I'll be around."

The elevator doors opened silently and they walked through security together, not saying another word. He nodded at the two security guys, neither of whom he recognized. Things were changing already. Out with the old guard and in with the new.

With one hand on the door, he turned to look at Sadie. If he wasn't mistaken, he saw a glimmer of moisture in the corner of her eye. "Take care of yourself." He hooked a finger under the harness strap at her shoulder and gave it a little tug. "Don't do anything I wouldn't do."

Then he stepped into the night and disappeared into the shadows.

ROXY COULD TELL Santiago had been drinking the moment she entered his office. Not only could she smell it, but several empty bottles sat on his desk next to a glass. Maybe she should come back later when he'd sobered up. Hearing that you were going to be a father was the sort of news that should come when you were cognitively able to handle it. Then again, it was also the kind of news that could drive you to drink. At least maybe this way, he wouldn't notice how nervous she was.

He was staring into a computer monitor and barely looked up when she entered.

"Hard day?" she asked.

"Nothing I can't handle."

At least he hadn't resorted to another tantrum or self-torture. Or she didn't think he had. She glanced around the room but didn't see anything broken or out of place. But then alcohol was a more accepted crutch. At least it had been for Ian.

"Leave me alone," Ian had said to her the last time they'd been in their house together. "I'm not hurting anything. Everybody gets drunk now and again."

It wouldn't have been a big deal, but he'd been attempting to cover up the fact that he was addicted to Sweet. Maybe he thought he could cover up the real problem. Or maybe he was just guilty and drinking was his way of coping.

But either way, his lying had gotten out of hand and had affected every aspect of their lives. He'd forgotten about plans they'd made together, leaving her to eat by herself at restaurants when he'd fail to show up.

When he no-showed his mother on her birthday, Roxy had broken down and told the woman what had been happening. Mary Alice could be sweet and charming, but that day Roxy saw a side of her she'd never seen. The woman had a come-to-Jesus meeting with her son, told him that if he didn't shape up, he was going to mess up his life, sully his family's good name and lose the woman he loved. He promised he'd change, said it'd never happen again, but then it all started up soon enough.

He never did admit he had a problem. When Roxy had first confronted him about it, he said he'd been around a sweetblood whom he'd helped get away from a Guardian and that was why he smelled like Sweet. But these excuses started getting more and more difficult to believe. Sitting next to a sweetblood on the train. Staking a DB who'd just drained and killed a sweetblood. The worst lie was when he was gone for a few days and said Darkbloods who forced him to take Sweet had imprisoned him. He said they were trying to convert Guardians over to the Darkblood side. Believable enough—it had happened before to other Guardians—but it was the second time he'd used that excuse and he didn't want to tell their superiors. He'd made up a story about being sick when he hadn't shown up for work. When she told him he should seek out help, he refused. He said he didn't have a problem but that if he did, he'd be able to kick it on his own.

She recalled what Ventra had told her about having an affair with him. God, what an asshole. There were probably other lies he told that she didn't know about.

She thought now about coming around the desk and massaging Santiago's shoulders. He looked stressed out and tired. Clearly the events of the past two months had caught up with him and now that the gala was over, he was letting that stress show. Her fingers itched to help him, but given what she had to discuss, maybe it would be best if she kept things more formal.

She perched herself on the chair in front of his desk. Santiago swiveled away from her but not before she saw the worry lines around his eyes. Ever since he'd been released from the clinic, it was as if he'd been avoiding her. And now that Lily was back, Roxy wasn't needed up here any longer.

"What's wrong?"

"Nothing."

L...i...a...r...

Okay, even if her intuition hadn't been more heightened lately, she could've figured that out.

"If now's a bad time, I can talk about this later."

"Talk about what?" he said gruffly with just a slight slur of words. He shuffled through some papers on his desk and she got the distinct impression he didn't want to make eye contact with her.

She didn't really want to get into a deep conversation when he was angry and drunk about the fact that she was going to make him a father.

"That's okay. It's nothing. I can see you're busy." She pushed herself to her feet and headed toward the door. "I'm packing my things to head back home, so I can just talk to you about it later before I go."

"You're leaving? You mean…"

"Yes, with Lily back, the situation in Seattle resolved, and…now that I have answers about Ian's death, I think it's time I get back to my regular life. Mary Alice has been dog-sitting Ginger for long enough."

What that "regular life" would look like now that she was going to be a mother, she didn't know. She stood at the door, waiting for him to say something. To protest her going back to Florida. To tell her he loved her. But he didn't.

He clutched the glass, probably wishing it wasn't empty. "When…when are you leaving?"

"I thought about taking a red-eye tomorrow night, but we'll see." She really didn't want to tell him the news over the phone when she got home. Better to do it in person.

A war of emotion crossed his face. It looked like he wanted to say something but just didn't know how to say it.

Santiago, tell me. Please.

He put his hands to his head and pinched his eyes shut. "The blade. Grim. It was…"

No, no, I can't. His thoughts echoed in her mind like they had back in the trailer. Then it was as if a steel door closed and she didn't hear anything more.

She didn't understand. What couldn't he tell her?

Perplexed, Roxy looked at him, waiting for him to continue out loud, but he didn't. "What about Grim?" she prompted. "Are you getting flack for having made that presentation?" She wouldn't doubt that Sturgeon had a fit when he found out. He loved the limelight and would be pissed to discover that someone had stolen his thunder.

Santiago's hands were balled into fists and for a split second she thought he was going to send all the items on the top of his desk flying. "Nothing. I'm… It's nothing."

L…i…a…r…

Her breath caught in her throat. Why would he lie about Grim? Was he covering up something?

She walked around to his side of the desk and started rubbing his shoulders. Instantly, a bitter taste filled her mouth, the same as when George from OSPRA had lied, only this was ten times stronger. She pulled away from him. He definitely was lying about something. And it was a big one.

"Santiago, you need to tell me what's going on."

"Don't you have some packing you need to do?" he said gruffly. Then he stood, swayed a little. In an effort to steady himself, he knocked over the bottle and sent it crashing to the floor.

He was much more inebriated than she thought. He was drunk and lying to her. Just like Ian.

She headed toward the door. Forget about telling him this information in person. She'd gone down a similar path with Ian. A man had ruined her life once with his lies and drinking and addiction. She wasn't about to let it happen again. She'd try to talk to him again in the morning, but if that didn't work, she'd do it over the phone. From Florida.

She left his office without saying goodbye.

CHAPTER TWENTY-FOUR

How COULD HE be such a fool? He put his head in his hands and listened to the sound of Roxy's footsteps as they faded down the hall.

When he made his way back to his quarters—an hour later, ten hours later—her things were gone.

The first thing he noticed was a small black box sitting on his desk among the books and papers. He didn't want to open it up but he forced himself. Inside was the ring he had bought her when they were fake married. Although it sparkled against the black contrast, it had looked prettier sitting on her finger.

He set it down and trudged past the bed, the table, the closet. The space felt hollow, empty without her. *He* felt empty without her.

She'd come to tell him something and he blew her off, afraid to confront the truth with her, and now she was gone.

The water in the shower sprayed his skin like tiny needles, exhilarating and painful at the same time. He'd get cleaned up then go apologize, try to talk her out of flying back to Florida tonight. Tell her—no, ask her—to stay around just a little while longer.

But when he got to the room she'd been staying in

when she first arrived at region headquarters a lifetime ago, she wasn't there. He went to the next room, but it was empty, too. He grabbed his cell and called her.

No answer.

He waited a minute and called again.

Nothing.

It wouldn't surprise him to learn she was avoiding him again. He checked the sanctuary to see if she was lighting candles. She wasn't in her classroom either.

Numbly, he made his way back to his rooms and he dialed Jenella's extension. "Where's Roxy? I can't find her anywhere and she's not answering her phone."

"Uh…I thought you knew."

"Knew what?"

"She left for Florida right before dawn, sir."

Gone? Roxy was gone? He fell to his knees, every bone in his body feeling as if it had shattered. "But she said she wasn't leaving until tomorrow night."

"Yes, but one of the VIPs who attended the awards gala offered to fly her home on his private jet, so they were able to leave earlier. The plane was scheduled to leave around ten o'clock." There was a slight pause. "That would be right about now."

Rand St. James. He should've guessed as much. That sly, backstabbing sonofabitch.

He threw the phone and it hit the wall with a crack. The back of his neck prickled, his ears heated and a dull roar reached out from his subconscious until it was all he could hear. Before he knew it, items on his nearby nightstand began to rattle. A few books fell from the shelves. While earthquakes weren't uncommon for the Northwest, he knew this was entirely man-made. By him.

He stormed into the bathroom and splashed cool water on his face, feeling it trickle down his neck and dampening his shirt. But it didn't make a difference. He still felt the same. Lost. Dead. Alone. He slumped down onto the closed toilet seat lid and put his head in his hands.

Why was he always fucking things up? Why couldn't he be like others, calmly and rationally maintaining relationships with people—human and vampire? In the time she'd been here, Roxy had made friends with almost everyone, whereas people scattered when they saw him coming. She'd been here a few short weeks and he'd been here for years.

He imagined her in the plane on the tarmac calmly drinking a cup of roasted green tea before speeding down the runway and taking off, heading far away from him, while some other man was trying to engage her in small talk. Was she even thinking about Santiago right now or had she mentally sloughed him off? Was St. Dicko making the moves on her already?

Alfonso's words kept ringing in his head. What was he afraid of?

He stood and stared at his reflection in the mirror. The dark, bloodshot eyes. The military-short hair. The menacing black tattoos.

This was not the face of a fearful man. He lived life by his own set of rules and people either did what he told them or they got out of the way. These were not the eyes of someone who was afraid of anything.

Except for one thing.

He was afraid of losing Roxy and how lost he'd be without her.

ROXY PAID THE taxi driver, grabbed her bags and walked through the wrought-iron entry gates of the compound. She could've asked him to drive her all the way in, but given the way he stammered and gripped the steering wheel when they pulled up to the entrance, his apprehension was obvious. Like many humans in close proximity to a group of vampires, he instinctively knew he'd be surrounded by potential danger if he continued past the twin gargoyles at the bottom of the driveway.

Even though it was after midnight, little light streamed from the first pod-complex she passed, and the lawns out front were empty. She'd never noticed before how much the people here kept to themselves. They didn't socialize like they did at the Horseshoe Bay Region. In the enclosed walkway leading to her town house, she passed a man who taught at the Academy with her, but for the life of her, she couldn't remember his name.

"Hey, how's it going?" she said, smiling.

He didn't look up from his tablet device, just nodded his acknowledgment and continued walking.

After spending so much time at a place where everyone was friendly and welcoming, she wasn't looking forward to her old routine were people stuck to themselves. At one time, she'd relished her privacy, didn't want people nosing around in her business, but now, it just felt…lonely.

When she got to her town house, she planned to quickly unpack, throw in a load of laundry then drive over to Mary Alice's estate to pick up Ginger. At least her dog would be excited to see her and keep her company.

How long should she wait before she came up with an excuse to go back to Seattle? She touched her still-flat belly. At least now she'd have reason to visit regularly…as long as Santiago wanted to see them. Maybe she would consider Mary Alice's invitation to move in with her. The woman would be ecstatic. And so would Ginger.

On the plane, Rand had told her that the plans to open another branch of Tracker Academy on the West Coast were a go. He'd fished around to find out whether or not she was interested. Maybe she'd look into that further. Being a mother would mean a new life for her anyway.

She put her key in the lock and immediately heard barking. That was strange. Mary Alice didn't tell her she was bringing Ginger home. Maybe she hadn't gotten Roxy's message that Rand had needed to make an overnight layover in Denver. If she'd flown commercial, she'd have been home before now.

When Roxy opened the door, fifty pounds of shaggy, black excitement greeted her, and she laughed. "I missed you, too. How did you get in here?" She dropped her bags and wrapped her arms around her dog, scratching her belly and behind her ears. "I was worried you'd forgotten about me."

"Impossible. You're the most unforgettable woman on the planet."

Roxy's head jerked up and there, not ten feet away, Santiago stood in the door to her kitchen. With his hands tucked casually into the pockets of his jeans, he leaned against the doorjamb, one foot crossed over the other. He appeared to be completely at home in her house.

Her heart cranked into overdrive, beating like an uneven load of laundry and just as loud. She had a million questions for him, but when she tried to say something coherent, her tongue was as thick and rubbery as one of Ginger's chew toys. "Whaaat?" was all she could manage.

Amusement simmered behind his eyes and a corner of his mouth quirked. Was he laughing at her, her dog's antics or the whole situation?

"I wanted to talk to you," he said in that gravelly voice that rubbed her in all the right places.

Collecting her thoughts, she stood and brushed the dog hair from her shirt. She tried to curb her excitement at seeing him again. As much as she wanted to wrap her arms around him and fall back into their easy routine, they had unresolved issues that needed to be dealt with. His sudden presence had to mean—

"What are you doing here? How did you get inside?"

"Mary Alice let me in."

Her eyes narrowed. So Mary Alice was in on this?

"But…why did you come?" There was that rubbery tongue again. "Why didn't you just call?"

He took a step toward her, but she backed away from him. Whenever he touched her, her brain went on hiatus and her body took over. He obviously had something important to tell her and she wanted all her wits about her when he did.

"Because I wanted to see you."

"Ever heard of Skype before?"

He was undeterred by her sarcasm. "I wanted to *see you* see you. You know, face-to-face." He snatched her hand before she could pull it away and led her into the living room, where they sat on the leather sofa. She was still holding her keys, so he took them from her and set them on the coffee table, then he angled to face her. "First, I need to apologize to you. I wasn't completely honest with you about something."

Her heart stuttered. A girlfriend he hadn't told her about? A deadly disease? A secret identity? The ridiculous and the probable played out in her mind in the span of a breath or two.

"What do you mean you weren't honest?"

"You specifically asked me something the other day in my office and I lied to you. It's been bothering me and I tried to find you, but you'd left. I wanted to tell you the truth in person."

Sweat formed on the back of her neck and she peeled off her lightweight sweater. Now it was her turn to feel guilty. Here she was, planning to tell him via a phone call that he was going to be a father. She suddenly wanted to delay talking about what he came here for, even for just a moment, because if it was confession time, she had a doozie. "How did you make it down before I did?"

"Let's just say I had a little help."

Help? Was he saying… Then it dawned on her. Of course. "That overnight layover in Denver was because of you." She poked his thigh with her finger and left it there a little longer than necessary before she pulled it away. What she wanted to do was push him back on the couch and kiss him silly, but that was her body talking, not her brain.

"What can I say? I have friends in high places." He stood and paced to the window overlooking the darkened lawn below. When he turned, he almost tripped over Ginger.

"Ginger, come." Roxy snapped her fingers but the dog didn't listen.

Santiago reached down and scratched behind her ears. "You'd better listen or you'll get in trouble. Trust me, you don't want her mad at you. It's torture."

She laughed. Even though she was nervous about what he had to tell her, she couldn't help it. She loved the crazy way he talked to Ginger. In fact, from that very first day when he'd paused to calm the barking dog in the Search and Rescue vehicle to the time she saw him feeding that squirrel, he'd surprised her with how he acted around animals. She'd always known you could tell a lot about a person that way.

He cleared his throat. "I learned something that you should know, but I withheld the information from you."

"Go on."

"When I found Grim at the mansion with those two Darkbloods, I overheard them talking about the original owner. I thought about telling you, but I had no way of knowing if it was true or not. And then I heard the same thing from Ventra."

She shivered. "What did they say?"

"First of all—"

"They said something bad about Ian, didn't they?"

"Roxy, they…they…" He exhaled loudly. "Yes. They said he was a Sweet addict." If his shoulders were any stiffer, they'd be brushing his ears.

"And that's what you lied about."

"I should've told you up front and let you draw your own conclusions." Santiago kept his gaze firmly plastered on the ground between the toes of his boots. "I'm sorry, but I knew how much you loved him and I was concerned that the knowledge would devastate both you and Mary Alice. I just didn't see the sense in telling you something that didn't matter any longer."

"So you were protecting my memories of Ian?"

"Yes… I…I didn't think you'd believe me and that you'd just assume I was trying to make you fall out of love with this great guy so that you'd fall in love with me." He was talking faster now as if he wanted to get it all out. "I'm not telling you this to make myself look better in your eyes, to get you to stop loving Ian and… and love me instead."

Her heart puffed up impossibly large in her rib cage until she was sure she would burst, and tears stung the back of her eyes. He was in love with her? Even with his cynical views on love and relationships, he...he loved her? The lump in her throat made it hard to swallow. "That's impossible, Santiago."

Disappointment darkened his expression and he started to turn away, but she immediately reached for his warm, strong hands.

"Because I already love you."

His head snapped up and he searched her face as if trying to read whether he'd heard her correctly.

"I started falling in love with you from the very beginning."

His eyes went wide. "You did?"

"You may be bold and brash, but I love you. Even when you found out about my history with the Agency, you believed in me, supported me. That meant...means the world to me, Santiago."

He stroked his thumb along her jawline, sending trickles of pleasure down her spine.

"Then come back, Roxy," he whispered, his breath stirring a few strands of her hair. "I'm not the same when you're away. I don't like myself without you. I know I'm hardheaded, difficult to get along with and I can be a complete and utter ass, but you're the best thing that's ever happened to me."

His erection pressed against her hip, a sure indication that this deep conversation would soon be over unless she put a stop to it. She should tell him her news now, not later after they'd made love. He needed to understand exactly why she left in the first place. Given what he'd told her earlier about his thoughts on marriage and family, would he change his mind about wanting her back? At the very least, he should have all the facts in order to make an informed decision. But her hands, which were flattened against the warm plane of his chest, refused to push him away. Instead, they wrapped around his neck.

"I love you," he said against her lips, "and, if you'll have me, I want to spend the rest of my life with you."

That was all her brain needed to hear before it shut down and her body took over. He swept her into his arms and carried her to bed.

CHAPTER TWENTY-FIVE

THEIR CLOTHES LAY in heaps on her bedroom floor, her ceiling fan blowing cool air onto their naked bodies.

He slipped one finger, then two inside her. She was hot and slick already.

"We...we need to talk," she said against his lips as she arched her hips upward, rocking against the rhythm of his hand.

"We've been talking. Now it's time for this."

Her legs fell open, her sex glistening and ready for him. He needed this, needed her, beyond anything he could've imagined. Covering her body with his, he prodded her inner thigh and easily found her center. As he buried his nose in her hair, he thrust into her hard and she gasped. Or was that him? She rose to meet him and he slid all the way to the hilt.

Oh, my God.

This is... Yesss.

His voice? Her voice? It didn't matter. Like this, they were one anyway.

They moved together, ebbing and flowing. Higher and higher.

How could he ever think he'd be capable of straying as his father had? Roxy was his everything. He needed nothing more out of life than what this woman could give him.

Trust. Honor. Love.

She deserved to have those from a man.

For the first time, he knew in his heart he could give them to her. He was that man. It didn't matter what his father had said or what he'd predicted. Santiago was a strong man and in control of his actions and his future. And his future was this woman under him.

She pulsed around him, squeezing him tighter. Stronger. Milking him.

Until...

The pressure in his balls intensified until she was all there was in his world. Her taste. Her sound. Her smell. Her feel. He fisted his hands in her hair and held on for dear life as—

Oh, God, oh...

Picture frames on her dresser rattled on the far side of the room. A book on her nightstand shimmied to the edge. The lampshade on her desk rocked back and forth.

Until...until...

Oh, God, yes...yes...

The pressure exploded in a blinding fury. Molten heat shot into him. Over and over he spasmed, filling her body until there was nothing left. Until he'd given her everything.

Neither of them said anything for a long while. With their sweaty bodies still joined, their rapid heartbeats slowed down together and the in and out of his breathing blended with hers.

He was still inside her when she said again, "Santiago, we need to talk."

ROXY RETURNED FROM the kitchen with two glasses of ice water, a box of crackers, a jar of peanut butter and a butter knife.

"Sorry. No other food in the house."

"That's okay." He straightened the sheets, making room for her on the bed. "I'm not really hungry. We can go out later for something to eat."

"I'm hungry now." She set down the tray and sat cross-legged on the bed.

"Don't worry. I won't kick you out of bed for eating crackers."

She handed him his water, not knowing quite how to start. Spreading some peanut butter on a cracker, she hoped it'd calm her upset stomach. Morning sickness and nervousness about how he'd handle the news that he was going to be a father made for an upset tummy.

"First of all, thanks for telling me about Ian. I appreciate that you have so much respect for my and Mary Alice's feelings that you weren't sure how to handle the news."

"Well, I—"

"Except we already knew."

He sat up in bed, the sheets puddled around his waist. "What?"

"I knew about his addiction," she continued. "In fact,

I made excuses for him at the Agency because I knew they'd execute him if they found out. That's what caused all my problems. At first, I bought into his lies that he was serious about kicking it and would never touch the stuff again. But he lied so many times about quitting that I lost track."

"Oh, God, Roxy, I had no idea."

"Now that my intuition is stronger, I wonder if he'd still be able to fool me. I knew right away back at your office that you were bullshitting me about something."

"I'd say he would still be able to deceive you because the person would have to know they're lying for you to detect the deception. Addicts often believe their own lies until, *bam,* they're using again." Santiago grabbed a peanut butter cracker and stuffed it in his mouth.

"Shortly before he died, I decided I'd had enough and broke up with him."

Santiago dropped his hands and stared at her, shock plastered across his face. "You and Ian weren't together when he died? But I thought…I thought you loved him."

"I did at one time. Or at least I thought I did. But when he seemed to care more about his addiction than he did about me, my feelings for him faded away."

Santiago stroked the back of her hand with a finger. "And here, this whole time, I thought you were still in love with him. That I was competing with a dead man."

"There was no one important, Santiago," she said, kissing him on the cheek. "That is, until you stormed into my life."

"Yeah, I have a tendency to do that sometimes."

She grabbed the knife from him and spread another cracker. "A short time later, he comes to me all panicky, needing my help. He'd been assigned to rescue a sweetblood but almost killed the guy instead."

She recalled how the streets in Key West were quiet that night, the humidity so thick you could cut it with a blade. Although weather forecasting wasn't nearly as accurate as it was now, people were saying a huge hurricane would be making landfall the next day. Many of the residents had evacuated. The cantina was deserted as Ian led her around back to where the man lay on the cobblestones. His heartbeat was faint, but at least he was alive.

"I told Ian to turn himself in while I rushed the guy to our medical center. Maybe with his family's influence, Ian could get the help he needed. He broke down and told me that his mother would be devastated if she found out he was still addicted. Little did he know, but she'd already suspected he hadn't kicked it. Better than finding out her son had killed a human, I told him. He kept saying how he couldn't do it. I assumed he meant that he couldn't kill the man, but now I'm not so sure." She realized she'd been spreading the peanut butter for an inordinately long time, so she set down the knife. "And that was the last time I saw him alive."

"I'm...I'm so sorry, Roxy," he whispered. "What about Mary Alice?"

"She and I remained close even after Ian's ashes were discovered. In fact, it was at her urging that I left him in the first place. She said if he couldn't get his act together, that I deserved to find someone better. He needed to hit rock bottom before he'd come to terms with his addiction."

"But afterward, after he died, you almost took the fall for him."

"Because I'd covered up so much for Ian, basically enabling his habit, they thought I had done something to get him killed. That I, as his partner, wasn't where I was supposed to be when he was attacked by Darkbloods."

"That is such bullshit." Santiago tossed the knife down with a clatter. "He was a Guardian, for godsake. He was plenty capable of looking out for himself. They should never have accused you of anything."

She smiled at him gratefully. "I was all set to quit the Agency, but Mary Alice talked me out of it. She reminded me how much I loved helping people and fighting for our cause and that I couldn't quit altogether. I decided to focus my efforts on being a tracker, rather than being an agent, so I wasn't reporting to the same people. Turns out it was a good move."

"Yeah, I'd say so," he said, lying back against the pillows. The *thwap, thwap, thwap* of the ceiling fan was the only noise for a moment. "You're amazing, Roxy."

"Huh?" She sure as hell didn't feel amazing. Especially with this morning sickness.

"It's a great example of how you turned adversity into a positive. I've got tremendous admiration for people who reinvent themselves." He reached over and brushed something from her cheek.

"You do?"

"Yes, I've got several people working for me who did the same thing. It takes a lot of courage."

She just hoped his positive feelings wouldn't be dimmed by what she was about to tell him.

SANTIAGO COULD TELL something wasn't quite right. Roxy nibbled on her crackers as if she were a bird. Normally, she didn't fuss over her food so much.

He set down his glass of water and turned to face her. "I wanted to tell you that I talked to Trace Westfalen. You remember him. One of our local Council members. There's been talk of opening a Tracker Academy branch on the West Coast."

"Yes, Rand told me."

He bristled at the familiar way she said his name even though the guy had helped Santiago out by making that layover. Since she knew about the new branch already, did this mean she wasn't interested? Okay, if that was the case, maybe it was a good thing he did fly down here. Maybe he'd visit a few of the field offices and see if they needed someone like him. Sturgeon was a jerk, but he wouldn't have to work for him. It wouldn't be easy leaving his position in the Northwest, but he didn't want to be apart from her either.

"They've been talking about it for years. In fact, it was at my insistence. I even volunteered to head it up."

"You did? You're willing to move out to the West Coast?" He jumped to his feet and would've spun her around the room, but she held her hands out, preventing him from doing so, and shook her head. Confused, he sat down again. "Well, that's fantastic, isn't it?"

She kept staring at her hands. She definitely didn't look happy. Maybe she didn't want to move to the West Coast after all. Jesus. Was that a tear in her eye? Could she be upset with him? Could it be that she wanted a commitment from him before she moved across the country?

He grabbed her hands and knelt at her feet. "Roxy, I love you more than I ever thought possible. Will you make me the happiest man in the world and be my wife?"

"And if it's a good union…"

"I don't care about those old-fashioned conventions. Your work is an important part of who you are and it doesn't matter to me what people consider a good union or not. A coupling doesn't need children to be a valid one."

She angrily brushed a tear away. "You don't get it, do you?"

He was even more confused. Here he went again, not understanding what in the world was going on.

"It's too late. The union is already a good one."

A warm flush spread throughout his body. Did she— Was this— "It…it is? How do you know?" He was barely able to get the words out.

"Because I took a pregnancy test back in Seattle and Dr. DeGraff confirmed it. I'm pregnant."

He was going to be a father? His hands shook as he sat back on his heels. She was talking but her words didn't register in his brain for at least a full minute. A father? Him?

"I was going to tell you before I left, but then there was that business about you lying and I decided I didn't want to be with another man who couldn't be honest."

"God, I'm sorry, Roxy."

"Yes, I know."

"So why are you so upset? Do you...not want a child?"

"Of course I do. But it's been my dream to have a marriage like my parents. To raise a family with the man I love."

"I...I don't get it. You seem upset that our union is a fruitful one." He stood and walked to the window, those old feelings of helplessness stirring inside. "If you'd rather not get married, to hell with our societal conventions. I'd never force you into a marriage you don't want. My parents had a marriage like that and it was a disaster. If you don't love me enough to be my real wife, just a fake one, I still hope we can raise this child together."

She choked. "You do? But I thought..."

"You thought what?"

"You told me you didn't ever want to be a father or a husband. I love you, but I thought—"

"Oh, my God, Roxy. Are you completely crazy?" He strode over to the bed, pulled her to her feet and spun her around. Ginger started barking.

She put her hand to her stomach. "Santiago, I'm going to be sick."

HE PUT HER down and she rushed to the bathroom. As she wretched into the toilet, he rubbed her back calmly and patiently, then gave her a damp washcloth when she was done.

"I'm sorry you had to see that," she said after it was over.

"Don't ever be sorry for anything you do. You're carrying my baby. Our child. We do this thing together."

"You… We do?"

"I love you and want to spend the rest of my life with you."

"So you're…okay with this?" She caught a glimpse of herself in the mirror. She looked like death warmed over.

"Other than the fact that the most beautiful woman in the world loves me, it's the most amazing news I've ever heard."

"I thought you never wanted to be a father. That your parents got married and stayed together only because their mating produced children."

"I was jaded, hard-hearted, but you opened my eyes that there is so much more to this crazy world when you have someone by your side who loves you. The difference between my parents and us is that they had no love for each other. They were forced into a marriage that neither of them wanted." He kissed her cheeks, her hair, her hands. "I'm ecstatic, Roxy. The only other thing that makes me happier than knowing I'm going to be the father of your child—that something of me is growing in you—" he choked and brushed away a tear "—is that you love me."

She let him lift her gently up onto the counter and she wrapped her arms around his neck. He smelled like peanut butter, sweat and the sweet scent of sex. And she loved him more than she ever thought possible.

"When is the baby due?" he asked, nuzzling her neck. His hand slid up her shirt and fondled her breast."

"Dr. DeGraff says that I'm about eight weeks along."

"Eight weeks?" He pulled back, his eyes wide. "That means…"

She smiled and cupped his face in her hands. She couldn't wait to tell him the rest of the news. "Yes, that means the first time we made love I got pregnant."

He threw his head back and laughed. "Well, that doesn't surprise me."

"It doesn't?"

"Maybe my father was partially right. He told me that the men in our family are very virile and because of that, it's our duty to spread our seed."

She grabbed his face, pulling him close so that their noses touched. "I will have none of that. Your seed stays with me," she said playfully.

"You know what that means, don't you?" He brushed her nipple with his thumb, sending shivers of delight down her arms.

"What?"

"If you got pregnant so quickly, then this probably won't be our only child. That is, if you want more."

She laughed, happier than she ever imagined was possible. "I already know that."

He pulled away from her, held her at arm's length, his dark eyes glistening. "And just *how* do you know that?"

"Because I'm… We're having twins."

* * * * *

From *New York Times* bestselling author

HEATHER GRAHAM

**A tantalizing trilogy
from the Krewe of Hunters series**

Available now!　　Available now!　　Coming August 28.

Pick up your copy wherever books are sold!

www.Harlequin.com

MHGTRI12R

A long-lost sword

A willing heroine

**A quest to prevent humanity's sacred secrets
from falling into the wrong hands**

Share the daring adventures of archaeologist Annja Creed
as she travels the world in search of forgotten treasures and
hidden truths. Will her journey end in triumph…or tragedy?

Available Now   Available September 2012

Read Annja's adventures six times a year!

Look out for Rogue Angel™,
available wherever books are sold.

www.readgoldeagle.blogspot.com

RA62157R

REQUEST YOUR FREE BOOKS!

2 FREE NOVELS FROM THE PARANORMAL ROMANCE COLLECTION PLUS 2 FREE GIFTS!

YES! Please send me 2 FREE novels from the Paranormal Romance Collection and my 2 FREE gifts (gifts are worth about $10). After receiving them, if I don't wish to receive any more books, I can return the shipping statement marked "cancel." If I don't cancel, I will receive 4 brand-new novels every month and be billed just $21.42 in the U.S. or $23.46 in Canada. That's a saving of at least 21% off the cover price of all 4 books. It's quite a bargain! Shipping and handling is just 50¢ per book in the U.S. and 75¢ per book in Canada.* I understand that accepting the 2 free books and gifts places me under no obligation to buy anything. I can always return a shipment and cancel at any time. Even if I never buy another book, the two free books and gifts are mine to keep forever.

237/337 HDN FEL2

Name	(PLEASE PRINT)	
Address		Apt. #
City	State/Prov.	Zip/Postal Code

Signature (if under 18, a parent or guardian must sign)

Mail to the Reader Service:
IN U.S.A.: P.O. Box 1867, Buffalo, NY 14240-1867
IN CANADA: P.O. Box 609, Fort Erie, Ontario L2A 5X3

Not valid for current subscribers to the Paranormal Romance Collection or Harlequin® Nocturne™ books.

Want to try two free books from another line?
Call 1-800-873-8635 or visit www.ReaderService.com.

* Terms and prices subject to change without notice. Prices do not include applicable taxes. Sales tax applicable in N.Y. Canadian residents will be charged applicable taxes. Offer not valid in Quebec. This offer is limited to one order per household. All orders subject to credit approval. Credit or debit balances in a customer's account(s) may be offset by any other outstanding balance owed by or to the customer. Please allow 4 to 6 weeks for delivery. Offer available while quantities last.

Your Privacy—The Reader Service is committed to protecting your privacy. Our Privacy Policy is available online at www.ReaderService.com or upon request from the Reader Service.

We make a portion of our mailing list available to reputable third parties that offer products we believe may interest you. If you prefer that we not exchange your name with third parties, or if you wish to clarify or modify your communication preferences, please visit us at www.ReaderService.com/consumerchoice or write to us at Reader Service Preference Service, P.O. Box 9062, Buffalo, NY 14269. Include your complete name and address.

PARA11

Two different classes, one common desire.

A lush new historical romance from

DELILAH MARVELLE

His fortune stolen, young Matthew Milton is finished playing the respectable gentleman. In the slums of New York, only ruffians thrive. But from the moment he arrives in London and encounters the voluptuous Lady Bernadette Marie Burton, he can't help but wonder about the pleasures he's missing. Or just how much he's willing to risk—not only to bed her, but to prove his worth…

Available now!

™ www.Harlequin.com

PHDM646

LAURIE LONDON

77645	TEMPTED BY BLOOD	___ $7.99 U.S.	___ $9.99 CAN.
77586	EMBRACED BY BLOOD	___ $7.99 U.S.	___ $9.99 CAN.
77544	BONDED BY BLOOD	___ $7.99 U.S.	___ $9.99 CAN.

(limited quantities available)

TOTAL AMOUNT	$ _____
POSTAGE & HANDLING	$ _____
($1.00 FOR 1 BOOK, 50¢ for each additional)	
APPLICABLE TAXES*	$ _____
TOTAL PAYABLE	$ _____

(check or money order—please do not send cash)

To order, complete this form and send it, along with a check or money order for the total above, payable to Harlequin HQN, to: **In the U.S.:** 3010 Walden Avenue, P.O. Box 9077, Buffalo, NY 14269-9077; **In Canada:** P.O. Box 636, Fort Erie, Ontario, L2A 5X3.

Name: _____

Address: _____ City: _____

State/Prov.: _____ Zip/Postal Code: _____

Account Number (if applicable): _____

075 CSAS

*New York residents remit applicable sales taxes.
*Canadian residents remit applicable GST and provincial taxes.

HARLEQUIN® HQN™
www.Harlequin.com

PHLL0812BL